Praise for
FLAWLESS

"High-energy . . . Spanogle has an undeniable gift for creating tension and movement. For page-turning fun, this gory medical thriller has all the elements." —*Publishers Weekly*

"A very clever novel . . . well-drawn characters, a smart story, plenty of suspense . . . [Spanogle] could give Michael Crichton a run for his money. Skilled storytelling." —*Booklist*

"Gripping." —*Mystery Lovers Bookshop News*

"Witty . . . Exciting reading." —*Mystery News*

"Before beginning, clear your calendar for a couple of days. Once you start you won't be doing much else."
—*Times Record News* (Texas)

"Combines cutting-edge medical research with a taut, psychological portrait of a young doctor on the edge . . . Spanogle's first novel elicited comparisons to Michael Crichton's early medical thrillers. The similarity is even more pronounced in the young author's second novel."
—*Watsonville Register-Pajaronian*

Praise for Joshua Spanogle's Bestselling Debut
ISOLATION WARD

"Combines a wonderfully flawed yet stereotypically smart-ass hero with a plot that moves as rapidly as a lethal virus."
—*Entertainment Weekly*

"An unusually strong first novel...[with] **all the ingredients for a fun read**...Like Michael Crichton before him, Spanogle may find himself having to make some interesting career choices soon. For what it's worth, there are already plenty of doctors in the world."—*San Francisco Chronicle*

"**Spanogle has applied the paddles and delivered a real jolt of excitement with this debut novel.** A funny, smart and skilled writer at the beginning of what readers will hope is a long and prolific career."—*Publishers Weekly*

"Readers of this **engrossing and intellectually wrought** first novel will happily await Spanogle's next."
—*Kirkus Reviews* (starred review)

"It's been a lot of years since a young medical student named Michael Crichton created a brand-new genre with *The Andromeda Strain,* and since then not too many people have managed to join him in the ranks of medical-thriller writers. Well, make some room. Josh Spanogle—another young medical student—has written a **topical, compelling, and terrific first novel.** *Isolation Ward* **is smart, it's surprising, it's challenging, and it's destined to be the foundation for a long career.**"
—Stephen White, *New York Times* bestselling author of *Kill Me*

"The well-trained insider meets the natural-born storyteller in Josh Spanogle. *Isolation Ward* is that genuine rarity: a page-turner. **Its high-flying science is as clear as its action scenes are exciting, and its vivid characters top both. Pick it up and you won't put it down.**"
—S. J. Rozan, Edgar Award–winning author of *Absent Friends*

"A medical student at Stanford, Spanogle knows his subject, and the result is a **chillingly realistic medical thriller with real urgency**.... Readers will have a time putting down this incredibly fast-paced novel.... *Isolation Ward* is **definitely a medical thriller worth reading.**"—*BookPage*

"A fast-moving and enjoyable read."
—*Mystery Lovers Bookshop News*

"Impressive... Spanogle expertly weaves in a good deal of science but keeps his main focus on his smart-aleck, very likable hero and a well-developed, engrossing plot.... **Spanogle propels** *Isolation Ward* **on a fast track that doesn't slow down.** The author handles each twist like a pro.... As *Isolation Ward* illustrates, Spanogle should be able to have a dual career—doctor and author."
—*South Florida Sun-Sentinel*

"A furiously fast-paced debut."—*Fort Myers News Review*

"A fun read."—*Charleston (SC) Post and Courier*

"Spanogle might become a medical John Grisham."
—*Yale Alumni Magazine*

"Spanogle grips us as much by the escapades of a bad boy in a China shop as by his virtuosity with a well-obscured mystery. He writes deep and detailed."—*Mystery Scene*

ALSO BY JOSHUA SPANOGLE

Isolation Ward

FLAWLESS

JOSHUA SPANOGLE

BANTAM BOOKS

FLAWLESS
A Bantam Book

PUBLISHING HISTORY
Delacorte Press hardcover edition published September 2007
Bantam mass market edition / April 2008

Published by Bantam Dell
A Division of Random House, Inc.
New York, New York

This is a work of fiction. Names, characters, places, and incidents either are the product of the author's imagination or are used fictitiously. Any resemblance to actual persons, living or dead, events, or locales is entirely coincidental.

Cover design by Jae Song
Cover photograph © Jason Homa/Getty Images

Library of Congress Catalog Card Number: 2007010618

ISBN 978-0-440-24229-1

Printed in the United States of America
Published simultaneously in Canada

www.bantamdell.com

OPM 10 9 8 7 6 5 4 3 2 1

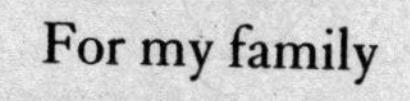
For my family

ACKNOWLEDGMENTS

I am deeply indebted to:

Those who sifted through *Flawless* and gave me pointers on everything from databases to the intricacies of Chinese names: Chantal Forfota, Michelle Hlubinka, Danielle Bethke, Mark Holtzen, Robert Cook, John Spanogle, Daniel Sullivan, Yohko Murakami, and Alberto Molina. I'd especially like to thank Eli Cooper, Austin Bunn, and Jennifer Sim, who read through multiple drafts and engaged in endless conversation to inch this book closer to completion. Every writer should be so lucky to have such skilled and energetic friends.

Dr. Julie Parsonnet, Dr. Pennan Barry, and Dr. Vik Udani for their expertise and advice regarding medicine and public health. I would also like to mention my debt to Stanford Medical School for fostering an environment conducive to all forms of intellectual inquiry and expression.

Jim Granucci of the San Mateo County Sheriff's Office, and Inspectors Jameson Pon and Henry Sito of the San Francisco Police Department. For someone who has spent much more time in medical school than at the police academy, their input was invaluable.

Alice Martell of the Martell Agency. A writer could not ask for more in terms of advocacy and support. Every day I trudge to the computer for another round, I'm thankful I have Alice in my corner.

Kate Miciak at Bantam Dell. I hope Kate knows how lucky I am to have an editor as brilliant as she is. It is through no fault of hers that this book is anything but, er, flawless.

My family and friends. Though the phrase "there for me" may sound trite, it is appropriate here. I am truly humbled that these people have always been there for me, through all the ups and downs that characterize the lives medical and literary.

FLAWLESS

1

THE HEAT WOKE ME.

I became aware of perspiration through my scalp, of a rusty orange glow behind my closed lids. I opened my eyes and saw crisp light dance through a palm tree outside, saw it play across the living room floor. There was an immediate sense of disorientation: Palm tree? Living room?

Why was I on the couch?

Right. Brooke. Nasty fight.

I raised my head off the chenille pillow, felt as though someone were grinding my brain beneath their boot. Unwisely, I tried to remember events of the night before. First, dinner and a bottle of that high-alcohol zin California vintners seem to be addicted to these days. Then the party with Brooke's friends. The glass after glass of good Scotch pushed into my hand.

It was all coming back.

The friend of Brooke's friend—the lawyer in jeans and French cuffs who thought he knew how to fix health care in the country. He'd droned on about the free market and incentives and how forty-seven million uninsured "isn't really *that* many." Eventually, I couldn't take it anymore. I'd bellied up to the conversational bar, armed with a killer buzz and a self-righteous 'tude. I saw Brooke's face fall when I opened my mouth, but I couldn't stop myself. "Idiot" was mentioned somewhere along the way, then "do your homework," then "moron." The next thing I knew, Brooke's hand was tugging mine and we were at the door, saying our good-byes.

Oh, and after beating a retreat from the party—Brooke whispering to our host, "I'm so sorry, he's been under a lot of stress," me shooting back, "It's stressful teaching a rock to think"—we got into the car and I still couldn't quit. "What a dickhead," I said. "What a complete dickhead." Little did I know that the hostess of the party was trying to make the gent in the French cuffs.

Terrific work, McCormick.

I closed my eyes and tried to sleep again, but there was the sunshine and, now, some shuffling. The bedroom door opened, then the bathroom door opened and closed. Didn't even catch a glimpse of Brooke.

In my defense, my hard-drinking days were long gone, the guy *was* an idiot, and I actually had been under a lot of stress. I had just effected a cross-country transfer in life, from Atlanta to San Francisco. Not only was this a big red-state-to-blue-state shift, the move also marked a kind of a break point in my career. I'd been finishing up a two-year stint as an officer in the Epidemic Intelligence Service at the Centers for Disease Control and Prevention and would have been happy to work with the organization for a few more years. Initially, they said they'd love to have me stay at headquarters in Atlanta, that they wanted to groom me for more administrative duties. Not only did I not want to touch anything like an administrative duty, I certainly didn't want to be in Atlanta. The humidity makes me break out.

Despite the offer of further employment at CDC, my ride there had been somewhat rocky. Granted, the year before, I got a few feathers in my cap for solving a case that extended from Baltimore to San Jose, but those feathers had been plucked from ruffled institutional poultry. Not to mention that I decided to blow off a meeting with my superiors—a meeting in Atlanta at which I was to be honored—following the whole tragic fiasco. Technically, I was AWOL at that time, since the CDC and U.S. Public Health Service still had some vestiges of the Navy from which they were born. That storm blew over when my boss got in touch with me at my rented vacation house and convinced me to be on the next plane back East if I ever wanted to have a career to gripe about. I returned to Atlanta for one day, then flew back to California to finish the vacation.

After that, the rest of my tenure as an EIS officer was a hodgepodge of the mundane and the exciting: work in the office, three weeks in Angola to help deal with the Marburg virus mess there. Crunching through databases one week, spraying bodies with bleach in 110-degree heat the next. Another day in the life, right? By the end of my two years, things actually seemed to be on the up-and-up. Negotiations about where I would find myself seemed to be going well; there were a couple of non-Atlanta positions in which I was interested, a couple of people who were interested in me filling those positions. At that time, though, CDC was under assault by an ideological executive branch filled with fanatics who had little use for the truth. Reports were being edited, science was being politicized, all that crap.

Scientists and epidemiologists don't generally cotton to lying and manipulation, so CDC had been slowly bleeding good people. When a friend of mine quit in protest after crucial data in a report she wrote had been dropped—she'd shown that condom education had no effect on promiscuity—I followed her out the door. I can't abide idiocy, which can make for problems in a government employee.

On the personal front, my life was just about as complicated. Not that it was bad—it was actually quite good for a guy whose batting average with women hung in the low double digits. After an idyllic month seaside with Brooke, I went back to Atlanta. She stayed in California, grinding away at the Santa Clara Department of Public Health. Somehow, we managed to keep the bicoastal relationship alive for almost a year. A paycheck decimated by transcontinental plane tickets was proof of my feelings for the woman. When I finished with the EIS, I tried to get Brooke to move. Anywhere but Northern California, I begged her. The last place on the planet I wanted to be was the Bay Area; even Baghdad looked attractive by comparison. If push came to shove, I would have stayed in the Southeast, pimples be damned. San Francisco was a place so filled with personal baggage I got a backache just thinking about it. But Brooke was pretty well ensconced, so I moved West a month before that tête-à-tête with the moron lawyer. No job, no place of my own. I made the move for love.

It was, perhaps, another mistake.

"You going to look at apartments today?" Brooke asked.

She stood in the archway to the living room, arms crossed in front of that athletic body, blond hair pulled back in a ponytail. Tight white T-shirt. Cotton panties, no pants. She looked very sexy and very pissed.

"Subtle, Brooke."

"I just don't know if this is working," she said. "You living here."

I rolled my head on the pillow, toward the boxes and duffels piled against the wall of Brooke's living room. All my life, contained therein. "At least it will be cheap to get these back East."

"I don't mean here, California. I mean living here, here. My house. You know what I mean."

"I'm not living here, sweetie. Unless you consider my toothbrush in your bathroom living here."

"Nate . . ."

"Brooke . . ."

She sat on the chair at one end of the couch, affording me a generous glimpse of the panties. She caught me looking and crossed her legs.

"Okay," I said, "I may be having a little difficulty with the transition—"

"A little difficulty? You've already alienated half my social circle."

"Be a circle-half-full person, Brooke, not circle-half-empty."

"Can you stop joking for once? Jesus."

"I need a glass of water." With superhuman effort, I pulled myself off the couch and shuffled into the kitchen. I was worried my head might explode, which would mean quite a cleanup for Brooke and which would undoubtedly annoy her more. Brooke's cat, Buddy, skittered from the kitchen when he saw me, freaked maybe about the exploding head. I found water and Tylenol and shambled back to the sofa.

"I already apologized for last night," I said. "About two billion times. I'm not apologizing again."

"I'm not asking for another apology, Nathaniel." *Nathaniel.*

I took a big gulp of the water. "So what are you asking for?"

"I don't know." She looked around the house. It was a two-bedroom on the outskirts of Palo Alto, a town halfway between San Jose and San Francisco. The digs were nicer than my apartment in Atlanta, which looked like it had just rolled off a conveyor belt in Shanghai. No, Brooke's place was all hardwood floors, white walls, and good light. She'd done a decent amount of nesting, and the house had all the girl-touches: MoMA and Ansel Adams prints, high-maintenance plants, and, despite the cat's best efforts, not a speck of dust or hair to be found. Brooke was a public health doctor, after all. Oh, and then there were the bikes, the backpacks, the ice axe and climbing rope. Those things were, thank God, in the shed, so I wasn't constantly reminded that she had one-upped me in the masculinity department as well. I could still beat her at arm wrestling, though.

So, in terms of basic comfort, her place was ideal. Unfortunately, it was also near the university where I'd spent the glory days of my medical career before getting kicked out.

"I got this place because it was bigger," she said, "so, you know, if things worked out . . ."

My emotional antennae, numb as they are, sensed danger. "Things aren't working out?"

"No, it's not that. Or maybe it is that. I got it because I thought maybe you could stay . . . for a while. So there'd be enough room."

"I thought you got it because it was closer to San Francisco, where I was going to find an apartment."

"That, too."

"Well, which is it?"

"It's both, Nate. It can be both, can't it?"

"Sure, but maybe it would be better if we'd communicate these things."

"Would that have changed anything?"

"No, I guess not . . ." I geared up for some relationship-speak. "Look, we're just getting used to this. A year apart, Brooke, of course we're going to rub each other the wrong way sometimes. And yes, I had too much to drink last night, and yes, I was stupid enough to engage in a conversation about health care with an uninformed, know-it-all bonehead. I'm in a part of the country that has eons of painful history for me, I don't have a job, I'm trying to make it work with someone I know best from telephone calls. And all my crap fits into that Corolla outside. Of course there's going to be bumps."

"So this is about you? Your crap, your Corolla, your job? Why take it out on me and my friends? Why let it infect my life?"

Unwise for me to engage in emotional jujitsu with a master. Also, she was probably right.

"Okay, I'll try not to let the virus of my insecurity infect your life."

Brooke shook her head.

I said, "To answer your original question: I do have appointments to see places up in the city. Two of them. You want to come?"

"I'd love to, but I have to run the dishwasher." She smiled, the first real smile I'd seen from her in fifteen hours. "I'll come if you stop being so dramatic. 'Virus of my insecurity.' Please."

I rolled off the couch onto the floor and crawled to her, grunting like Igor. "Whatever you wish, Master. No drama. No insecurity virus, Master." Brooke giggled and kicked at me. "Yes, yes. Beat me, Master." I grabbed a leg and snaked my hand under the T-shirt, hooked my finger in the panties.

Then the goddamned cell phone went off.

"Must get phone, Master. Might be landlord calling about apartment."

I crawled to my jeans and fished out the phone.

"Is this Nate McCormick?"

I didn't recognize the number that popped up on the cell's caller ID. I didn't recognize the voice, but I didn't think it was a landlord; people trying to sell or lease me things usually buttered me up by calling me "Doctor."

I told him it was.

"Nate—it's Paul Murphy."

At that, my head cleared and my guts pulled tight, cinching down like a hangman's knot at the instant the trapdoor opens.

2

PAUL MURPHY. NOT A NAME I'd heard in a long time. Not a name without its—how should I say?—its *complexities.*

"Paul," I said. "Murph. Long time."

"Ten years, by my count."

"God. Ten years."

"Ten years, yeah." He cleared his throat. "Uh, so how're you doing?"

"Fine," I said, looking at Brooke. "You?"

"I'm pretty good. Pretty good." But he didn't sound too convinced of it. When I knew him, back in med school, back in the dark days, Murph was one of those gregarious, hail-fellow-well-met guys. He could keep a conversation rolling with an autistic.

"So what's up?" I asked.

"Oh, not much. Still working on the answer to cancer."

"You figure it out yet?"

"Yeah. Forty-two. That's the answer."

Both of us forced a laugh, and the conversation once again lost momentum.

"So, Murph, what's going on?"

"Oh, sorry. Yeah. I work for a biotech in South San Francisco. Two kids. A monster of a mortgage. The works. You still in Atlanta?"

"No. I'm out here now. Just moved."

"Oh, wow. Great. They said you left CDC, said you might be out here."

"Who said?"

"The CDC. That's how I got this number."

"They're not supposed to give it out."

"I know a guy who works there. Vik Patel. You know him?"

"No."

"Good guy. He was at school . . . He came a little after— Anyway, hope it's not a problem I called. I told him it was real important we talk . . ."

Again, that lull. If the conversation kept stalling like this it *would* be a problem. I was fighting a mother of a hangover, and was having trouble navigating a stilted exchange with a guy I hadn't seen in a decade, with a guy who, back then, I would have loved to see dangling from the rafters. On the other hand, what did I have to do? See a couple apartments? Real vital stuff.

Plus, whatever had transpired between Paul Murphy and me in the past, he had once been a friend. And something was obviously bugging the guy.

"So, Murph, what's up?" I asked for the third time.

"I got some questions, Nate. You have time?"

"Sure. Shoot."

"I was hoping we could get together. Not over the phone."

"No problem. I have a wide open schedule next week—"

"I was hoping to see you today. It's kind of important."

"Uh, okay. I have some things later this morning—"

"Perfect. How's three o'clock?"

"I have a couple appointments in San Francisco—"

"Great. I have to drop my son off at a soccer game in the city. Sorry to push, Nate, really, but you know . . . You deal with this stuff all the time."

"I don't really know since I don't know, you know?" I said. Red flags were springing up all over the place—the odd nature of the conversation, Murph's edginess, the fact that he'd called me, despite our history.

"Three o'clock, right?" He gave me the address of a coffee shop in San Francisco's Haight district.

"Sure. Three o'clock." I was about to hang up, when something struck me. "Hey, Murph, how'd you know I was at CDC?"

"That Chimeragen thing last year, Nate. It was all over the papers here. Man, you sure had your fifteen minutes."

3

THAT CHIMERAGEN THING.

It was, as Murph said, all over the papers a year before. Fifteen minutes of fame and fanfare, a lot longer than that in physical therapy. My scars are still there. So are Brooke's.

After I hung up the phone, I opened and closed my left hand, still somewhat stiff, still crisscrossed with glossy scar tissue.

"Another apartment?" Brooke asked. She stood in the doorway, hair wet, a towel wrapped around her. I smelled moisturizing lotion. Normally, this would unleash a tsunami of desire, but Murph's call had unsettled me and I wasn't feeling particularly Lothario at the moment.

"Old friend from med school," I said. "We're having coffee later today."

"Good," she said, too enthusiastically. "See, things might not be so bad here after all."

"Maybe not," I said. But I didn't believe it.

So, perhaps I should explain why I hate the Bay Area—a place that every other person on the goddamned planet seems to love so much. First, I went to med school here for an MD-PhD and got kicked out. Second, my heart was broken here. Third, everyone constantly says how idyllic the place is and I must be nuts not to be gaga over it. Fourth, the price of real estate. Fifth, the traffic. Sixth, the lack of seasons. Seventh, the fact that Brooke wouldn't let us go elsewhere to start anew and every day reminded me she had some deep-core selfishness in that athletic body of hers. Eighth, *that Chimeragen thing.*

But I made the choice to be here. A big boy has to live with his decisions.

Anyway, I can bitch about the Bay Area, but the place was easy on the eyes, especially in September. Brooke and I were driving up the 280 toward SF in her red convertible BMW, top down. The morning fog had burned off to the top of the Santa Cruz mountains—a blanket of white drawn back over the dark green hills. I swung the car to the left lane and settled in at about eighty, looked over to Brooke. She wore sunglasses and a scarf around her hair. It wasn't hard to picture her as a fifties movie star. Lauren Bacall, maybe. My hand went to her knee; her hand went on top of mine. We drove in blissful coupledom. Well, almost.

"You should call Ann," Brooke said. "Apologize for treating the lawyer that way, if you want."

I loved that: *if you want.* There was no *if you want* about it.

"I did her a service." Ann—hostess of last night's infamous party, good friend of Brooke's—was a lawyer herself and could probably have held her own. But she had been drinking, and I'm kind of a knight-in-shining-armor type, always ready to rescue the damsel in social distress, whether or not she wants it. I can also bench-press a thousand pounds and shoot lasers out of my eyes.

"A service? How do you get that?" Brooke asked.

"I demonstrated what a dumbass he was. She should thank me."

Brooke shook her head as if to say, *You just don't get it.* Then she actually said it.

"Don't get what?" I asked.

"You think she doesn't know what he's about?"

"No. If she did, she'd have clobbered him with a wine bottle."

"Okay, Nate. First of all, you don't know the guy. Second, you met him when he was sloshed and spouting off."

"In vino veritas," I said.

"Honey, he called you a self-righteous, arrogant asshole who can't see the forest for the trees."

"Never trust a drunk."

"Third, Ann just turned thirty-six."

"So?"

Brooke looked at me, then through the windshield,

then shook her head again. "Ann's going through a tough time."

"Sorry to hear that." And I was, actually, sorry to hear it. *Welcome to the club, Ann.* "Rough birthday, huh?"

"Yes. Rough birthday." Brooke kept her eyes on the road, then said, "Society is utterly screwed up."

"Whoa. Where did that come from?"

Brooke began fiddling with the iPod, rummaging through the tracks without settling on anything. "She's a good-looking woman, right? At least, that's what I think. *I* think she's beautiful. But she's got it in her head that she's still single because she's got wrinkles and bags under her eyes."

She settled on a song I hadn't heard before. Something low and droning.

"That's what they make Botox for," I said.

Brooke rolled her eyes. "You know what Ann's birthday present to herself was?"

I shook my head.

"Botox and Restylane. There you go, Nate. You're a genius. You pegged her."

"Well, she looked good." I smiled. Brooke didn't. I tried again to lighten the mood. "She'll be married before her next birthday present."

"Stop it," Brooke said.

I glanced at her, tried to read what was going on. Because of the conversation, I found myself focusing on the fine lines of her brow, around the mouth. They gave her skin a texture I liked, a lived-in mien that I found serious and beautiful. "Let the Botox needle never touch the creases in Brooke Michaels's face," I said, then immediately wished I'd kept my mouth shut.

"God! How is it that you always manage to say the wrong thing even when you're trying to say the right thing?"

Years of practice, I thought.

Brooke began stabbing her finger into the iPod again. She found an old Cat Power song. Angry and raw. "You know what it's like watching a friend go through this? Watching her put on a new face, parade herself around like something's actually changed? Seeing her throw herself at some jerk?"

I desperately wanted to be done with this conversation. I reached my hand over to Brooke's knee and said, "So, we're in complete agreement here: Ann could do better than that fuckwit."

"And she probably will. But that's not the point anymore. The point is you're making Botox cracks and you don't even know how not funny that is." She slid her knee from under my hand. "And if you can't see that, then *you're* the fuckwit."

I had a zinger on the tip of my tongue, something about an army of fuckwits, but kept it to myself. Brooke was, obviously, unsettled. Perhaps it was concern for her friend or a true distaste for society. Perhaps it was more than that, and she was, in some oblique way, talking about us. Perhaps she was getting a little restless herself, a little frustrated with having wasted a good year with her current beau, the fuckwit.

4

WE SAW TWO PLACES IN the city. Neither fit the bill for the future Maison de McCormick. For someone used to Atlanta rents and real estate, the experience was sobering and shocking and depressing. Fourteen hundred for a one-bedroom that was billed "artist-chic," which evidently meant that the landlord hadn't done maintenance since Jackson Pollock and his cronies slapped paint onto canvas. Then there was the twelve-hundred-dollar walk-up studio with the bathroom smaller than a casket.

"It's one of the hottest new neighborhoods," the landlord said. She was a gaunt middle-aged woman with hair pulled into a bun so tight it gave her a virtual face-lift.

I took Brooke's hand and we descended to the street.

"Maybe I'll just buy," I said. "The yield on my trust fund isn't what it should be and I'm looking for a place to park a couple million."

Brooke smiled. "Why don't we pool our trust funds and buy a city block?"

"Or just buy the city. I always wanted to own a city."

"I'll have Daddy call the mayor."

Truth be known, Brooke's daddy was a retired high school teacher in Virginia. And though I always wanted to be landed gentry, I trace much of my lineage through a long line of yeoman farmers and deadbeat dads in

Pennsylvania whose investment capital never made it to the next generation. I knew somebody who had a trust fund, though, but I hadn't talked to the guy since college and thought it unlikely he'd gift me a couple mil.

I looked at my watch. Just before two o'clock. I turned to Brooke. "Coffee?" I asked her.

5

ON THE WAY OVER TO the Haight, I brought Brooke up to speed on Paul "Murph" Murphy. Twelve years before, when I was grinding away in the lab in hot pursuit of my PhD, Murph rolled into the Dunner Building, a brand-new doctoral student in cancer biology. His lab was next to mine, and we shared a microtome—a machine for cutting thin slices of frozen tissue. Back then, Murph sported a Grizzly Adams beard and the laid-back attitude of someone who'd always been big man on campus. Murph had played football at Iowa and then went pro for a season with the Colts before a knee injury sidelined him for life. Wasn't a big deal, he said, he was second-string anyway. But one night he and I were drinking after a couple of his experiments failed and we got to talking. And suddenly, there was none of the "aw shucks" bonhomie anymore. "You know that old phrase? An athlete dies twice?" he asked. I hadn't known that old phrase, but it stuck with me ever since: *An athlete dies twice.* There was tragedy and poetry in there somewhere.

Anyway, we became friends. Maybe it was the shared misery of the lab, the nightly bitch sessions about the life scientific, or that I had drifted away from classmates who had not decided to pursue a PhD. But for a while, at least, Murph became my closest friend in school.

Things went sour between us when I had my troubles in the lab, that whole "massaged data" fiasco. Murph, I assumed, would be on my side through the process, despite my side being relatively indefensible. I hadn't expected him to be quite so goddamned Boy Scout about things. I'd hoped for a letter from him to the disciplinary committee, talking up my character, how I'd been a stand-up guy except for one teeny-tiny transgression. What I got was an e-mail, back in the days when e-mail was just a bunch of ASCII text. It went something like this: "Nate, you're a liar and a fraud and a discredit to the science that goes on here. I can no longer associate with you, you morally corrupt hack." Okay, those weren't Murph's exact words, but that was the gist.

And so that's how Paul Murphy became a symbol to me of moral inflexibility, of self-righteous hooey, of holier-than-thou Science with a capital "S." I was done with it and done with him.

After they threw me out of school, I never spoke to him again—I made it a point never to speak with him again. My friend, my buddy, my pal. The fucking Boy Scout.

When I finished regaling her with the tale of Murph's betrayal, Brooke was quiet for a while. "You never told me this before."

I could say I kept the story tucked away because I didn't

think it was important anymore, but that would be a lie. I didn't talk about it because I hated that part of myself. The weak parts, the lying parts. I'd spent ten years trying to erase what I'd done and who I'd been. But as Cain knew, some marks are impossible to scrub clean.

"But I had to tell you sometime," I said. "I had to come clean."

We were in the coffee shop, and Brooke sipped at a big cup of green tea. "I'm glad you did," she said, ever the budding shrink. Her face was softer now, kinder.

I softened my look, too, though I couldn't be sure if I had done a brave thing by airing my dirty laundry, or had just manipulated my girlfriend with a little Nate-shows-some-vulnerability gambit. Honesty is not always honest.

"Anyway," I said, "we'll see what good ol' Murph has to say about things. If he brings a rope or handcuffs, flash some leg, distract him so I can escape."

I leaned back in the creaky wooden chair, took in a *mise-en-scène* that was one hundred percent San Francisco—the pierced and inked couple sitting near the window, the graybeard in a rock concert T-shirt reading Sartre, the four people in opposite corners batting away on laptops, working on business plans or the next Great American Novel. And the place had about a billion different types of tea and coffee, from Gunpowder to Panyong Needle to Sumatra Mendheling.

"Why is he calling you now?" Brooke asked suddenly.

"CDC-type question, I think."

"Ah. And you're a famous disease hunter."

"Yeah, the one who drives an '88 Corolla."

Brooke purred. "What more could I want than a man

who whines constantly about his car but who wears it like a badge?"

"It anchors me in a world of rampant materialism. It's my way of subverting the paradigm."

"Oooh. You are so Marxist. I love it."

"Workers of the world unite, you have nothing to lose but your cable subscription."

"Don't stop. Revolutionary zeal gets me hot."

"Reality TV is the opium of the masses. The gears of capitalism are greased with the hand cream of high-tech workers . . ."

"My God, Nate. You should write these down."

"My agent's peddling the manifesto to Hollywood as we speak."

Brooke laughed and ran her hand up my leg.

I liked where this was going, and I thought about inviting Brooke into the bathroom to sublimate her politics into some quickie sex. As it turned out, I didn't even get a shot at foreplay under the table. In the doorway to the coffee shop stood seventy-five inches of scientist. No beard this time, no faded flannel. Paul Murphy had come a long way, baby. He wore a polo shirt under a butter-colored suede jacket, jeans, his feet shod in those expensive "dress sneakers" that everyone seemed to be wearing that year. Murph had clearly arrived, in more ways than one.

He didn't recognize me, so I held up two fingers in a little wave. He saw the gesture, smiled, then saw Brooke. The smile faded as he walked over to us.

"Nate," he said, and clasped a huge paw around my hand. Even now, even though I could see the beginnings of a paunch splaying the sides of the jacket, I sure as hell wouldn't want to be on the other side of a line of scrimmage from the guy.

"This is Brooke Michaels," I said. Murph reached across the table; Brooke's hand disappeared into his. "Also late of CDC. Dr. Michaels works with the Santa Clara Department of Health."

Murph sat and we did the requisite catching up: kids, house, career. Murph, though, didn't seem to have much patience for the small talk. He picked at his fingernails, he bounced his knee. He barely looked at Brooke.

Abruptly, she said, "I'm going to do some shopping, guys. Let you catch up." She stood. "Need a new navel ring."

Brooke didn't have an old navel ring.

She didn't look back as she punched through the door. *Uh-oh,* I thought.

"Sorry, man," Murph said.

I watched the door swing shut behind Brooke, turned back to the giant in front of me. Paul Murphy was screwing up my life for a second time.

"It's sensitive," he said.

"What is?"

Murph huffed in a breath, held it, then blew through pursed lips. "You deal with stuff all the time, right?"

"What kind of stuff?"

"Sensitive things." He looked like he'd just robbed a bank. "You get what I'm saying?"

"Not really. You're in trouble?"

"No, no. Nothing like that. But there are some things going on . . ." His head jerked back and forth, then he got up and sat in Brooke's seat, which, I noticed, afforded him a clear look at the café door.

"I might be in a little bit of a . . . tough situation," he said.

"Okay . . ."

He reached across the table and gripped my wrist. "I figured the public health people were where I should go to first."

"I'm not public health people anymore. Not for the time being, anyway."

"Oh," he said, taken aback. "Where are you working?"

"I'm sort of between jobs." As Murph loosened his grip on my wrist and receded into his chair, I had this burning feeling of being judged by him again. This time for not having a job. "You knew I didn't work for CDC anymore. You think I just popped out here and picked up another gig in some county department?"

"I assumed . . ."

Yeah, I thought, *you assumed. And you were so self-absorbed you didn't ask me about it on the phone. Could have saved me a trip, asshole.*

Murph looked down at the table; his knee bobbed like a sewing machine needle. Some internal battle was being waged to which I was definitely not privy. It was like watching an opera with the sound turned down.

I gave him a few more minutes, stirred my Ethiopian Harrar with a spoon, first this way, then that.

"How are your parents?" I asked. Maybe some more small talk would break the logjam.

"Doing better than they've been in a long time."

"Still in Iowa?"

"Still there."

This was going nowhere. I glanced at my watch. "Look, I should go find Brooke. Do some relationship maintenance." I scanned his face to see if maybe that would get Murph off his butt. It didn't. "Give me a call when you're ready to talk. Or not to talk. Whatever. We'll grab a beer, shoot the breeze about old times."

He looked up at me, face straining a smile. "I don't know how to approach this yet. I thought I did, but . . . I'm under a lot of stress."

"Sure. No problem. Gimme a call." I pulled out a pen, then remembered. "You have the number."

"Yeah."

He took out a card and handed it to me. It was a thick white rectangle, embossed with the words *Tetra Biologics,* and a logo that involved a blue semicircle fading to a spray of tiny blue dots. Underneath was *Paul Murphy, Principal Scientist, Research,* along with his contact information.

"See ya, Murph," I said.

"Nate, I got to say something." His eyes darted away, then settled on me, drilled me. "I'm sorry about that situation way back when."

"Don't sweat it—"

"No." He gripped my wrist again, painfully. "I am sorry. I've been sorry about it for ten years. I had a stick up my ass back then, but . . . but people change, right?"

"People change, Murph."

"So, why'd you shut me out, then?"

I didn't want to tell him I shut him out because I couldn't stomach what I thought was a glaring lapse in loyalty. I didn't want to resurrect that Nate McCormick from the grave. I gave him an answer to his question without really giving him an answer. "I'm sorry for that."

"Okay. Good. I'm sorry, you're sorry. Can we call it even?"

I wanted to get out of there. Murph's almost desperate attempts to make amends, his clutching my wrist, his pleading, knocked me off balance. This ain't really how the menfolk act with each other.

"I wish we'd had the chance to reconnect," he said.

"We're reconnecting now."

"Yeah, I guess we are."

Still, I could see, plain as day, that something much greater than making good with an old friend raged hotly behind the blue eyes. That *tough situation.*

On the way out of the café I looked back. Murph was staring after me: 220 pounds slouched in a chair, surrounded by a motley crew of San Franciscans, every inch of him—every pound—fracturing.

6

BECAUSE HE WAS A FRIEND, because he had come up with some sort of apology to me, Murph and his worries occupied some mental space. But that only lasted for a few minutes. The pressing concerns of hearth and home reared their ugly heads.

"I think the second place was cute," Brooke remarked as we made our way south on 280.

"You're kidding me."

"It was kind of cozy."

"My mother's womb was cozy. That place was molecular."

I pushed the Bimmer to ninety, getting more and more annoyed at Brooke's subtext. Annoyed at being jacked back and forth over the past few hours between intimacy and distance. Wind whipped and I almost had to shout. "So you went out shopping and had a chance to think and . . . ?"

"I just don't think you've been trying very hard to find a place."

"I wasn't sure how hard you wanted me to try and find a place."

"Now you know."

"Jesus, Brooke. Because I yelled at Ann's guy at the party? That's what started all this?"

"That and a hundred other things. Your friend obviously didn't want me around—"

"He was preoccupied—"

"—And he's not the only one. You're miserable, Nate. You mope around all—"

"Oh, God. I've sent out résumés."

"How many?"

"Four, I think. Three . . . Look," I said, "I'm not going to justify myself to you."

"This is what I'm talking about!" she shouted. She stabbed at the damned iPod, which started to take on a lot more significance than its role as a music player.

"What?"

"It's not *justifying,*" she barked. "We're living together, Nate. Supposedly, we're a couple. Supposedly, we're in love. Couples talk about things, couples support each other. It's not *justification.* You were the one talking about communication. Well, freaking *communicate.* You're so half-assed about being here. All your shit in boxes. It's like you're waiting for things *not* to work out so you can just pack up and leave. Get back to your *real* life."

"That's bullshit, Brooke," I said. But, of course, it wasn't.

We blew past those spectacular mountains, those golden hills. The two feet between us could have been a thousand miles. Brooke said, "I love you, Nathaniel McCormick." It sounded like a good-bye.

7

AFTER WE GOT HOME THAT night, Brooke and I made love. I use that term deliberately; I'm not a vulgarian when it comes to sex, but neither do I usually go for mawkish euphemisms. Anyway, love was made, and it was pretty damned sad. I couldn't shake the feeling we were shuffling toward some denouement. Or maybe we were already there. In any case, to figure it out—or to avoid figuring it out—I took off the next day, a Sunday. I drove south to Big Sur, along Route 1, that ribbon of asphalt grafted to the edge of the continent. I S-curved from stunning vista to stunning vista, the Toyota taking well to the road. So what if it wasn't a BMW? I loved the Corolla. Screw Bavarian Motor Works. Screw Brooke Michaels. Screw our relationship, which was turning out to be more high maintenance than her car.

I spent the day hiking around the hills by my lonesome. Each time my thoughts drifted to Brooke, I reoriented, tried to focus on myself. I came West to be with her. No other reason. And I'd done nothing but be with her for the previous month. I mean, what else should I have done? She was the reason I came, and I had her.

And having her was not enough. So, why stay in the Bay Area? Why be there even later that afternoon? Part of it was that I had no other place to go. Part of it—a significant part, if I was being honest with myself—was that something had been poisoned, so insidiously that I hadn't noticed it was happening. But I wasn't sure the doctor had pronounced just yet.

After the hike, I got a room in a rambling motel composed of little log cabins. Someplace called "The Pines." I bought a six-pack of a random microbrew and polished off four before I drifted to sleep.

Monday, I drove back to Palo Alto. Brooke was, thank God, at work. From the laptop, I sent out four more résumés. I made appointments to see three apartments. Then, since I was feeling lonely, since I had nothing better to do than sit around and pet the cat, I dialed the guy who several lifetimes ago had been my best friend.

8

CHITCHAT, CHITCHAT. IT TOOK ME five minutes to pop the question, to open myself to some rejection. I mean, come on, I didn't want to seem desperate, right? Finally, I went for it: "So, Murph, you up for grabbing that beer?"

"Uh, sure. Hey, listen, let me call you back in five minutes."

He hung up. Three minutes later, my phone rang.

"That's better," Murph said. "Just wanted to step out of the office. Walls with ears and all that." I could hear wind hitting the receiver of his cell phone. "So, yeah, it would be great to get together."

"Okay. You name the time. I got nothing but it, lately."

"What?"

"Time."

"Right. Unfortunately, I don't. Deadline at work. PTA meeting for my son's school tonight—"

"Like I said, my schedule's free."

"We do need to talk, man. Really. Okay with you if I kill two birds with one stone? I got something being delivered, and I was wondering if you want to meet me there. A place in South San Francisco."

"We're not talking meth shipments or anything?"

Murph laughed. "More fun than that. When's the last time you blew a hole in something?"

When I stepped through the glass doors into the Mid-Peninsula Regional Gun Club two hours later, I wasn't sure exactly what to expect—twitchy, nervous guys dressed in camo, pictures of Osama with Ka-Bar knives stuck into the forehead, some of those "Kill 'em All Let God Sort 'em Out" T-shirts. But this place seemed pretty tame: racks of hunting jackets, pants, and gloves. Eye protection. Silhouette targets. Except for all the firepower in the locked glass cases, I could have been at a shoe store . . . well, that and the periodic explosions from somewhere in the back.

Murph was standing to my left, staring at something on top of one of the glass cases. The guy across from him looked like a shoe salesman, actually, except for a cocksure smile on his face. He nodded to me when I entered. Murph looked up.

"Hey, Nate. Come here."

I did. And I saw what was occupying Murph's attention.

"This, my friend, is a Smith & Wesson 686, Distinguished Combat Magnum." He held the lump of gleaming metal lightly in his hands. The revolver was brushed steel—no bluing—and looked like it could kill even without firing a shot.

"Pretty handgun," the shoe salesman said.

Dale nodded. "Nate, this is Dale Connolly. Dale, Dr. Nate McCormick."

Two can play at the nonverbal, my-dick-is-bigger game: I nodded back.

"Dale helped me choose this monster," Murph said. "Double-action. Takes .357 or .38 Special."

"Your friend was leaning toward a Glock 18. Nine millimeter. Big guy like him, though, you need a big gun. Glock'd be like a peashooter."

"Glock was automatic, though," Murph said.

"Automatics, they're for . . ."

You could tell what Dale Connolly thought of automatics.

From the banter, I guessed neither Dale nor Murph sensed that I didn't know jack shit about Glocks or 686s or double-action.

Murph popped open the cylinder, spun it; it moved silently. "Want to hold?"

"Sure," I said. Not that I really wanted to, but one has to keep up appearances.

The gun was surprisingly heavy. Two and a half to three pounds, probably. I turned it over in my hands. Very solid. Very deadly.

In the range, it became obvious that I didn't know the action from the cylinder from my elbow. Now that Dale was out of the picture, I didn't have to worry about keeping up the façade. And I was worried now that I might kill myself or kill Murph.

I said to Murph—shouted to him, since we both had on ear protection—"I don't know what I'm doing!"

Murph heard it. So, it seemed, did the folks in the lane next to us. Some Latino guy and his white girlfriend. They watched me out of the corners of their eyes.

"I thought you knew how to shoot," Murph said.

"There was an article in the paper about that thing last year—"

"That doesn't mean I know how to use a gun. Besides, I didn't have to load the bullets."

The Latino guy and his lady were definitely spooked now. They ran the target back and began to pack up.

A cannon at the end of the range went off a few times.

Murph showed me how to load the Smith & Wesson, how to squeeze the trigger slowly on exhalation. He showed me how to put the big silhouette target in the target retriever and run it to five, ten, fifteen yards. He took the loaded gun in his hand. "Watch me."

The cannon downrange went off again. "Jesus," I said. "What's that guy shooting?"

"Probably the same thing we are. Watch."

Murph ran the target to ten yards, took his shooter's stance, and blasted the black silhouette figure. I could feel the concussion in my chest each time the gun went off. After six shots, Murph hit a switch next to him and the retriever slid toward us. He pulled off the target.

Three shots in the center field, two just outside, one at the right shoulder. "Need to get used to this," he said, then looked at me. "Knock 'em dead, McCormick."

He handed me the gun.

In the parking lot, after an hour of pumping hot lead through cold paper, I was still a little jazzed. As I said, I was never comfortable with guns. That changed, though, after forty-some rounds and eight mutilated targets. Both of us had loosened up with each other. Nothing like firepower to fertilize a little male bonding.

"Not bad for a fem-bot," Murph said. "You keep the targets."

"You're damn right I'm keeping them. I'm papering my bathroom with these babies."

My hands still tingled. I opened and closed the left—my bad hand—which was stiff from gripping the living daylights out of the Smith & Wesson.

" 'Dead-Eye,' " I said. "What do you think of 'Dead-Eye'?"

"Christ, McCormick. I've created a monster."

"Now, if I could just put the little holes in the middle of the paper more often . . ."

We arrived at Murph's Mercedes SUV. He put the gun case on the backseat and slammed the door. Murph hadn't kept his targets.

"Now, as a public health doctor, I have to warn you about guns and children . . ." I was half kidding. Half.

"Lockbox in my bedroom, under the nightstand. Kids never go in the bedroom."

"Kids always go in the bedroom. Kids find keys."

"These kids are less than four feet tall, Dr. Public Safety. Key's on top of the wardrobe, seven feet up."

"Smart." I looked around the parking lot, which was sandwiched between a road that fronted the highway and the long, low building that housed the gun club. Other tenants included an auto glass shop and a rug importer. I guess it made some business sense: if there was ever a serious run on Persians, at least they would be well defended.

"So," I said, gearing up to ask the question I'd wanted to ask for the past hour, "why the gun?"

"Man's got to defend himself in this day and age."

"Right. Where do you live again?"

"Woodside."

"Right."

"We get trespassers in the area, they hunt for mushrooms. Chanterelles." He was smiling, but the smile faded. "I'm serious about defending myself, Nate."

The jocularity was gone now, replaced by the edginess I'd seen in the café. Murph scanned the parking lot, the glass shop, the rug importer. "There's some bad stuff going on, man. Really bad stuff. I don't know how I got into it."

"Got into—?"

"I mean, of course I know. But I never thought it would go this far."

"What are you talking about, Paul?"

"I need your help. I really, really do."

"Okay, buddy. You have my help, but you need to tell me—" I stopped myself when I saw an awful look cross Murph's face. "What?"

"Shit. *Shit.*" He was staring over my left shoulder.

I began to turn my head. Murph hissed, "Don't *look,* for Chrissake." He opened the back door of the SUV again. "I can't believe they're here. It's going too fast, Nate. It's going way too fast."

"Who's here?" I was shooting looks all over the lot now, Murph be damned. I saw nothing out of the ordinary.

Murph opened the gun case, took the Smith & Wesson in his hand, slammed the back door.

"What the hell are you doing?" I asked. Murph didn't answer, just opened the driver's door and climbed inside. He dropped the gun into his lap.

"The white Cadillac at the end of the lot," he said. I looked and, sure enough, there was a white Caddy idling in front of the rug importers. I hadn't noticed it before. "They want me to know they know. Shit."

"Murph, you have to tell me—"

"Stop by my house. Late tonight, eleven or so. I'll show you what I have. Make sure no one's following you." He smiled, a big forced thing obviously aimed at whoever sat in the white car.

"Don't call me, okay?" Murph said, grinning at me. "Just show up at the house. Google the address."

He told me the address in Woodside—a small horse-obsessed town for rich cowboy-wannabes—located on the Peninsula not far from where Brooke lived.

"I need help here, Nate. I really need help." He racked the transmission into reverse, then backed out of the parking space. Surprisingly, Murph pointed the nose of the Mercedes toward the end of the lot where the Cadillac idled. The Mercedes crawled across the asphalt and I saw Murph shift in his seat. I saw him lift his right hand to the window. There was something in it—the gun, I assumed—darkly silhouetted through the glass. He wasn't aiming, he was just holding. The Mercedes's left blinker went on, and he rolled through the stop sign at the end of the lot, motored up the road.

The Caddy arced a wide turn, and I caught a glimpse of two figures inside. Left blinker flashed, and it disappeared along the frontage road in the same direction as Murph's SUV.

Nerves now. Feelings I hadn't experienced in a year and never wanted to experience again. I scanned the parking lot: just a bunch of middle-aged, middle-tier cars and trucks.

It's nothing, I told myself. Murph's just freaking out.

Maybe the white Caddy was skippered by a geezer who had a thing for rugs. A geezer and his wife who were now so scared by Murph waving a gun at them they were taking themselves to the cardiologist's office for a quick checkup on the tickers.

But no. Murph knew that car. He knew who was driving it. And its presence scared him out of his mind.

9

AS I PARKED IN FRONT of Brooke's place, I tried to figure out what Murph had gotten sucked into and why he'd gotten sucked into it.

The "why," actually, was easy: if Murph couldn't let a little data-fudging slide, he certainly hadn't crossed any lines. But neither could he let "really bad stuff" go unaddressed. Because Murphy was a fucking Boy Scout.

But sometimes being a Boy Scout can be dangerous. Ask any whistle-blower.

By the time I settled into Brooke's couch, I'd managed to quash my paranoia. How could I be paranoid with a neurotic cat assaulting a dust bunny on the carpet? Besides, lightning doesn't strike twice. I'd already paid my dues when it came to lightning.

So, I spent the rest of the afternoon squarely in the banal: tooling around the Internet, looking for more housing and job opportunities. In a moment of weakness, I nearly called Brooke and asked her to sniff around the local health departments to find out if there were any openings. But I didn't. I still had something of an ego left.

Late in the day, I did end up calling Brooke to let her know I was back from Big Sur and to tell her I wouldn't be around for dinner, that I was going to be eating with Paul Murphy. She acted nonplussed, but there was satisfaction hidden there. The subtext—that she was happy I was making friends—seemed patronizing to me.

I would not, of course, be dining with Paul Murphy. Dinner ended up being a solo affair at a burger joint close to campus. I took four hours to eat a Canadian-bacon burger at the bar, down a couple of beers, and watch the Giants go to extra innings with the Colorado Rockies. I chatted with a couple other womanless guys—a grad student from the university, an aging hippie who was really into biodiesel. As the tenth inning rolled into the eleventh, my mind drifted back to Brooke. I stabbed a fry into the salt-dusted cardboard tray. To think I could have been downing a salad with a beautiful woman.

I cut my losses while the game was still tied and started the fifteen-minute drive to Woodside. Apartment complexes and streetlamps quickly gave way to a moonless night that obscured horse country, gentleman vineyards, and monstrous Italian-villa knockoffs. I followed the Google directions through back channels shrouded by oaks and redwoods and arrived at a drive marked by two mailboxes. Fifty yards in, the drive split. Two wooden signs with numbers on them were nailed to a tree. Murph's place was to the left. *Not doing too badly for yourself, are you, buddy?*

In another two hundred feet, I could make out the

house. It was a low building, with dark wood siding that fit in well with the enormous pines surrounding it. A big picture window was brightly lit, scrimmed by a curtain; the porch lights were on. Very Norman Rockwell in a California sort of way.

I pulled my car in front of the house and got out. I shut the door, the sound popping through the silence. There was the same musty organic odor that I'd smelled that morning down in Big Sur. All of it—the sights, the smells—was very pleasant.

I walked to the front door and stopped. It was open.

10

I REMINDED MYSELF I WAS standing in what was probably one of the lowest crime areas in America. I'd be surprised if they ever locked the doors here. Still, it didn't feel right; it was suddenly so damned *quiet.*

I knocked twice on the door. "Murph?" I said.

Nothing. I punched my finger on the doorbell, heard it ring in the house. Silence closed in again.

I stepped back to the drive and walked over to the carport. A blue Lexus sedan and the Mercedes SUV filled the spaces. Everyone, it seemed, was home. I went back to the front door, scuffed around the porch a little. I decided not to ring the bell again. Didn't want to interrupt *Goodnight*

Moon or whatever it was parents were reading to their offspring these days.

I gave it a couple more minutes, my ass parked on the hood of my car. Then I dialed Murph's cell phone and walked back toward the home.

From inside, I could hear a phone ring, then stop. In the earpiece of my phone, Murph's voice started: *"You've reached the voicemail of Paul Murphy . . ."*

"Murph," I said through the crack in the door. Then, louder: "Hey, *Paul.*"

No one responded. I pushed open the door and stepped into the house. "Paul!"

To my right was a living room, clad in wood paneling, one wall dominated by the big picture window. I could now see why the window shone so bright from the outside: a stylish halogen floor lamp lay toppled on a thick Oriental rug, blazing up at the curtain like a floorlight on a stage. Somehow the bulb hadn't broken; somehow it hadn't started a fire on the rug. I picked up the lamp and set it upright.

Against the wall, a wooden entertainment center spit wires from its empty maw, from where a TV and stereo had once been. A book lay open on the floor. Kid drawings and teacher evaluations were strewn across a leather chair and its ottoman and cascaded to the rug—gold stars and red pen marks with "Good!" all over the pages. Toys and children's books were scattered around one end of the room. But no children, no parents.

"Hello?" I said. I listened to my voice die out.

The hallway looked straight back to the kitchen. From there, I could see a marble countertop, could hear very faint classical music wafting. I walked forward. The kitchen was decked out with the finest appliances bourgeois culture had to offer: Wolf range, Viking refrigerator, things too big to cart away quickly. Drawers hung open, a few odds and ends of silverware were scattered across the floor. The music—now no longer music, but the soft baritone of some guy talking about Mahler—came from an old, cheap radio on the countertop.

Near the sink, the floor was covered in trampled cookies, a cracked glass jar lying amongst them. "Oh man, oh man," I said, heart pumping now.

I jogged back to the hallway. "Hello?"

Off to my right ran another hallway. Dirt streaked the hardwood floor; it looked as if a couple of kids had tear-assed through the place with muddy shoes. At least I hoped that's what happened: crazy kids with mud all over them, hot pursuit through the house, giggling, lamps knocked over, cookies crushed underfoot. *Please let it be that,* I thought, even though all evidence argued against it.

I eased open the first door I came to, fighting a mounting panic. It was a child's room. I could make out a crib in the corner, a mobile with fish dangling above it. There was something in the crib. I flipped on the overhead light and saw it was just a crumple of blankets.

There was a bathroom across the hall, another room on the left, which I entered. Another kid's room. From the decor, a boy's, a little older. Blue walls with posters from Pixar movies. A blowup of Barry Bonds. An airplane hanging from the ceiling.

There was a mattress on the floor, shadowed from the light in the hallway. Sitting on it, leaning against the wall, was a child. The boy, I thought. Another child was curled across his legs. The boy's arm was across his sibling. His head was slumped; he was sleeping. Cute. It was all very innocent and I felt myself relax a little.

"Hey, guys—" I said, voice hushed, and turned on the light. "Sorry—"

But they didn't hear me.

Somewhere—somewhere in that moment between the images flooding into my brain and my realization of what they meant—I felt something in me break down. My gears just froze. All those years of training, all those codes called in the hospital, where you're sprinting down corridors to the room of someone whose heart just stopped, all those times where you know exactly what you're supposed to do—get the epinephrine, grab the defibrillator, push the atropine—all that distant experience abruptly failed me. Maybe if I'd been better trained, if I'd been an emergency medicine doc, if I'd been a trauma surgeon, maybe then I would have moved faster. But I was not and I did not.

I stepped across the room and looked down at a tow-headed boy and his blond sister. The little girl, eighteen months at most, clutched a stuffed rabbit. Her head was pulled back and her throat sliced open, blood blackening the white fur and pink ears and floppy pink bow of the rabbit. The boy's eyes were fixed on his sister. A great bib of crimson stained his pajamas, discoloring the footballs, soccer balls, and baseballs that decorated them.

Kneeling, I reached for the little girl's wrist, hoping for a pulse. Nothing. The wound through her neck was deep enough to have severed most of her windpipe; it was open, gaping at me. I rolled her on her back and pulled down her pants, stuck a hand under her diaper and pushed into her groin, hoping to feel a butterfly beat from the femoral arteries. For thirty seconds I fumbled, first with the left side, then with the right. My fingers felt only cooling, doughy flesh.

Pulling back my hand, sticky now, I reached for the boy's wrist. No radial pulse. I laid him next to his sister, felt for femorals underneath the gluey red pajamas. Nothing and nothing. I put my ear to the gash in his neck, willing some sort of breath sound, but all I could hear were the faint calls of the tree frogs outside.

So, I gave up and, slumped on my knees, tried to figure what to do next. My brain wouldn't work. After breathing deeply a few times, after touching my fingers to my thumb and feeling the tack from the blood between them, I stood, sick to my stomach.

"Murph!" I screamed.

I ran from the room. I tore down the hall, realizing too late that what I'd thought was mud on the floor was nothing of the sort. I ran toward a door at the end of the hall.

This room was lit softly by a single bedside lamp. It was a big room, with a bed opposite me, under a long row of windows. A figure sat in a chair at the foot of the bed, facing away from me. Another figure lay on the bed. Neither moved.

Drawers had been ripped from their dressers. A jewelry box lay broken on the hardwood floor.

The figure on the bed was a woman: blond, dressed only in a nightie, lying faceup, each hand bound to a bedpost. Her throat, like her children's, had been cut. Blood glossed the small breasts and rib cage. Her legs were twisted in front of her, kicked to the side, pulling her body away from her right arm. The bindings on her wrists—nylon cord, it looked like—cut deep into the flesh.

I forced my eyes to the figure at the foot of the bed. His

wrists were handcuffed together behind the chair, a big leather and oak thing that looked solid and antique. Another set of cuffs bound the first to a thick crosspiece between the chair's legs. He was slouched, the weight of his body pulling hard at the upper limbs. Both shoulders—it didn't take a medical degree to figure this out—were dislocated. And it didn't take his best friend to realize that the figure in the chair was Paul Murphy. I rushed to him.

"Paul?"

I have seen horrible things in my life. I have seen disease dissolve tissues. I have seen people drown in their own blood as tiny capillaries in their lungs fragmented and burst. I have seen a human head split apart from a gunshot. But this . . .

Both of Murph's ears had been sliced off. Both his eyes were gouged out, leaving black, caked holes. Blood seeped from his mouth, down the clean-shaven chin. Like the others, his throat had been cut. Between his feet—also cuffed to the chair—lay the two ears. Next to the ears lay his tongue.

Then there was the blood. There was so much goddamned blood.

"Oh, no . . ." I said.

And then I heard it, a faint rush of air popping through liquid. I yelled Murph's name, and there was a change in the sound, a kind of clutch. An acknowledgment. A sign of life.

A dry-cleaned shirt hung on a clothes tree next to a dresser. I tore off the plastic bag surrounding it, took it over to Murph. His tongue—what was left of it—was swollen and occluded his airway; air bubbled through the bloody wound in his throat.

As I was about to press the shirt to his neck, I forced myself to calm down. I went through my ABCs: Airway, Breathing, Circulation . . .

Airway.

I dropped the shirt and ran to the kitchen, to the sink. It had one of those removable nozzles attached to its water supply by a flexible hose. I yanked the nozzle out as far as it could go, grabbed a butcher's knife from a slotted block holder and cut the hose. I sliced off the nozzle. Not perfect, but nothing at all was perfect about this night.

In the bedroom, I cut the tubing to about a foot long, threw the remainder and the knife onto the bed. I pulled Murph's head back as far as I could to open the wound in his neck. The trachea opened like a jet-black eye, air sucking through it. I swallowed and eased the hose six inches into his trachea. Murph struggled, then coughed. I pulled back an inch or so. Breath rushed in and out.

Airway, check. Breathing, check. Now circulation.

Blood oozed from the torn jugulars. The carotids were, thank God, still intact, or he'd have been dead. I circled behind him and wrapped the shirt around the back of his neck, pressing the fabric to either side of the trachea stiffened by the flexible hose. I held the fabric tight, felt the cotton sink into cartilage, to muscles, to vessels and other things it should not have been touching.

"Come on," I urged. I said it like we were going somewhere, like there was some end point to this. But stanching his bleeding was no end point; at best, it would give me a few minutes. I needed help. I needed real help, not the bullshit efforts of someone who dealt in microbes and who is a moron when it comes to trauma.

I looked at his wife—I assumed it was his wife—on the bed, looking for any sign she was alive. "Damn it," I said.

And then I saw her chest move. It rose and fell slightly, a tiny up-and-down traced by one of her breasts.

Letting go of the shirt, I rushed over to her, put my ear close to her mouth, close to the opening in her throat. The faintest sound.

I looked over at Murph; I could almost see the last of his blood running from his neck.

"Damn it. God*damn* it!"

Back to the foot of the bed, to the remainder of the hose. It went into her trachea, down to the carina, back about an inch. I ripped off a pillowcase and tied it around the wife's neck. It was a sloppy job, not tight enough to be effective. But it was her *neck,* for Chrissake. I couldn't tourniquet her goddamned neck.

Mrs. Murphy lay there, twisting weakly against her bonds, an eighteen-inch piece of kitchen plastic jutting from underneath her chin.

I might as well have been the gardener for all the good I was doing. So I did what the gardener would do, which was probably the most effective thing I'd done all evening. I dialed 911. My hands were slick with blood and trembled and it took me three attempts to get it.

Finally, the dispatcher picked up. I screeched, pathetically, "I need help!" I tried to cradle the phone on my shoulder so I could continue to push the pillowcase to Mrs. Murphy's neck. The cell dropped to the bed, then to the floor.

I picked it up.

"There are dying people here!"

"Sir, what's your address?" The voice was businesslike.

"I don't know. There's someone alive here. Two people. Two dead kids. I'm a doctor. I'm trying to keep them alive."

"What's your address?"

"I don't know! Laurel Road, I think." I tried to remember the number, and failed. I got the phone between ear and shoulder and pressed down on the pillowcase into Mrs. Murphy. She struggled weakly. "3299, I think. I don't *know*! Get someone here now! Get them *now*!" And the phone dropped to the floor.

The tinny voice of the dispatcher squawked. I let her chatter away.

Murph stirred.

"I can't believe this. I can*not* believe this!"

I looked down at the woman on the bed, at my hands compressing her neck. As pathetic as my efforts were, they might keep her alive until EMS arrived.

While Murph died.

I screamed, loud, unintelligible.

How do we make these decisions? To decide who will die? I felt rage, rage at the impossible choice, rage at my own impotence, rage at being so alone. Rage at both of *them,* if you can believe it, for being so barely alive and making me choose. I screamed again. Under my fingers, Mrs. Murphy stirred.

I chose. Whether it was because we had some history, whether it was because I thought Murph might be able to better tell me who did this, I don't know. What I do know is that removing my hands from his wife's neck was harder than anything I'd done in my life. What I do know is, in that moment, I killed her.

I circled behind Murph and put my hands to his neck

again. He tensed and thrashed against his restraints, against me. I could feel the muscles in his neck tighten, could almost feel the blood pumping harder. "Murph, it's me. It's Nate. Just . . ." My voice broke apart. ". . . Just hold on, okay? Just calm down, buddy, okay?"

And he did.

I looked at the woman on the bed. "Mrs. Murphy, do *not* die. You will not die, you hear me? Do *not* die."

Everything was still except for the sound of the tree frogs drifting in through the open window, the tiny sucks of air from Murph and his wife, my sporadic yelling.

"You will not die."

But, of course, she did. There was a shudder through her body, then the chest stopped moving. My hands were locked down on Murph's neck. I did nothing to help her, except spew out useless words.

"You *breathe* goddamn it!"

My head dropped between my arms, and that's when I realized I was crying. "Please breathe," I said quietly.

To get my mind off my own ineptitude, I began to talk to Murph. I told him we were going to find whoever had done this. And I said to him over and over again, "I'm sorry. I'm not made for this. I'm not trained for this." By the time I heard the sirens, all I was saying was: "I'm sorry, I'm sorry."

Murph was dead. He'd been dead for five minutes, I guessed. His life slipped away quietly, without fanfare: no shudder, no death rattle, just something, then . . . nothing. No breath moving through the gash in the trachea. I didn't even bother to find a pulse, since I didn't want to take the shirt away. I didn't want to give that up.

Light—blue, red, white—skated across the trees outside. Moments later, footsteps, shouting.

"Police!"

I called out. More shouting. I heard, "Two children!" Then, from down the hall: "This is the police!"

"I believe you!" I screamed. "Get in here!" I was losing it. Hell, I'd been losing it since I stepped into this house, but things were really falling apart now. "Sorry. Sorry. Sorry."

"Is there anyone else in the house?"

"I don't know!"

In the hallway, a cop was shouting, securing the scene, I supposed, for the crime lab folks who would descend like locusts. I felt the house filling up with people.

"In here!" I yelled.

Feet shuffled along hardwood floors. "The sides!" someone yelled. "Keep off the footprints."

Suddenly, I heard someone breathe, "Oh my God . . ." There was a lull in the action; I pictured the scene through their eyes: two blood-drenched bodies, drooping plastic hoses sticking out of their necks, like freaks from a sci-fi film.

Someone said, "Sir? Are you okay?"

I nodded.

The police—three or four of them by the sound—fanned into the room. A voice: "Jesus Christ." Another: "Don't touch anything." Then, "Sir, is there anyone else in the house?"

"I don't know," I said. "I don't think so."

"Get the paramedics in here!"

"They're dead," I said.

Some shifting and rustling.

"They're *dead*!" I barked.

One of the policemen stepped toward me. He was a beefy Asian guy in police tans. He looked down at Murph, then up at me. Voice even, he said, "We'll get the paramedics—"

"They're dead, all right? I'm a fucking doctor and they're dead."

I heard commotion and two people—the paramedics—burst into the room like a couple of overeager schoolchildren. There was a lot of shouting as they dropped their medical kits and a female paramedic set to work manhandling Mrs. Murphy's body. The male half of the team came over to me. Shock flashed across his face when he saw the earless, eyeless man, the hose jutting from his neck; then he got down to business. "Keep that pressure there," he told me.

I wanted to punch him.

The paramedic—red hair, skinny, too young, sunglasses propped on top of his head even though it was deep into the night—began to flutter around the corpse, assessing Murph's status.

"He's dead," I said.

The kid glanced up at me. "Thanks." And he kept feeling around.

"I'm a doctor, you idiot. He's dead."

So now the kid wanted to punch me. Great. But at least he stopped the shenanigans. The other paramedic straightened up over Mrs. Murphy. She shook her head.

Slowly, the Asian cop reached a hand to my arm. I stiffened and he took the hand away.

"Doctor—?"

"Yes, I am a goddamned doctor. My name is Nathaniel McCormick. I'm a public health physician. *I am not trained for this kind of thing.*"

"It's all right," the cop said softly. "You . . . ah . . . you did the best . . ." He turned to someone behind me, nodded. "We can take it from here."

"No," I said.

The policeman took a moment, then nodded again. There was some quiet shuffling, and I felt a large hand on my shoulder. "Come with me, please, Doctor," a voice said. The big hand gently pulled me.

Every instinct I had wanted to fight, to swing my fists, kick, thrash, to keep these bastards from making me give up. But it was in that instant that I knew Murph was dead—knew not just intellectually, but *knew*—and that my fingers pressing cotton to flesh wouldn't do a damned thing, that they didn't do a damned thing.

I gently released pressure from the shirt. It was a final concession.

Dull pain flowed into my hands; I looked down at them, clawed, curled, caked in blood. My left, the damaged one, ached. I hadn't felt the pain until that moment, and I wished the pain were greater.

I turned from Murph's body, saw the policeman whose hand had been on my shoulder. He was a big white guy, blond hair. He looked something like Paul Murphy. Or, at least, how Paul Murphy used to look. Another guy, Hispanic, stood at the doorway, gun drawn but held down. He was there, I assumed, to shoot me, if it came to that.

The big white guy led me to the door. "Careful," he

warned, pointing to the blood-streaked floor. "Try to walk along the sides of the hallway. Evidence."

And I left the room with my dead friend, his dead wife, and San Mateo County's multicultural finest inside, that word—sorry, sorry, sorry—circling through my brain.

11

ON THE COUCH IN MURPH'S living room.

Some life had come back into my hands, enough so that I could hold a coffee cup. The house buzzed like a hive by that time: floodlights had been brought in, police tape, measuring tape, cameras, brushes, evidence bags. The paramedics had gone, to be replaced, I assumed, by a coroner. There were crime scene guys, more police. There were reporters, too, I overheard, but they had been stopped at the main road. And there was Detective Bonita Sanchez, who had brought me the coffee.

"You ready to talk?" she asked. She was fiftyish, a little overweight, hair pulled back tight against her head. Tough. "As hard as woodpecker lips," as a friend of mine used to say. But she was nice to me, and I was thankful for that.

"No," I said.

She nodded and walked toward the humans circulating in the other part of the house.

I felt the heat of the coffee cup bleed into my hands. I leaned my forehead against it, felt its warmth.

There was a time, in medical school, when one of us would cut a class and we would joke, "Uh-oh, someone's going to die." Same thing when it was one a.m. and someone left the group study room. We might have been kidding, but the gist hit home: that little void in your knowledge, that tiny gap opened by cutting class, would end up killing someone.

All of us—medical students, residents, attending physicians, chiefs of surgery—are haunted by this, by ignorance. Supposedly, it gets better with age and experience. But, still, there are the Morbidity and Mortality conferences. Still, there are the malpractice suits.

So you worry. You worry that the lecture you slept through in residency contained some scrap of information that would have saved a life. You worry that if you'd just studied a little harder, if you'd just spent a little more time in the hospital, if you'd just taken that extra rotation in trauma surgery, you wouldn't have been holding your hands around the neck of a dead man, doing nothing more than prolonging his pain for a few more useless minutes. You wonder if you'd been someone else, Paul Murphy and his wife would still be alive.

At the same time, you tell yourself that nothing could have been done, you wrap yourself up in that comfort blanket. You lie.

"Dr. McCormick?" Detective Sanchez sat on the ottoman opposite me. I guessed she was ready to talk whether or not I was. "I know this must be very hard, but we have to move quickly."

I took a sip of the coffee and nodded.

Detective Sanchez produced a small pad and a pen. She looked at me. Then she said, "You're lucky, you know. You could have stumbled in on whoever did this."

"And maybe that wouldn't have been such a bad thing."

"Dr. McCormick . . ." she said. But I guess my face told her any look-on-the-bright-side chitchat was a nonstarter. She got back to business. "How do you know the family?"

I told her. I told her about Murph and me years ago, about coming back to the West Coast. Detective Sanchez said she knew my name somehow and we finally got around to *that Chimeragen thing*. Then she switched back to fun things, like who might have slaughtered Paul Murphy.

I told the detective about Murph being worried about "really bad stuff." I told her about the white Cadillac. I told her he was going to show me something tonight, to explain it all. I told her about the gun. Everything I said went into the little book. She asked me five different ways about Murph's big secret, to tease something out if I'd been hiding it. I may be an incompetent physician, but I'm not an idiot.

"I do not know, Detective Sanchez. He never told me. And if you ask me again, I will leave, and you can arrest me, get Abu Ghraib with me, and still I will not know."

The detective's face tightened. "Okay, Dr. McCormick. Let's go over it one more time. Just to make sure."

Somehow, going over it one more time seemed easier than protesting.

12

THREE HOURS AFTER IT BEGAN raining cops, I was allowed to leave. The Corolla was parked near the house, so I spent twenty minutes waiting for drivers—of police cruisers, of the coroner's van, of the blue, funny-shaped forensic lab van—to move their vehicles and let me out. Bonita Sanchez was helpful here, snapping at various municipal functionaries. Without her, I'd have probably been at Murph's place until Christmas.

I drove down the long driveway, through a phalanx of reporters and TV station vans clustered on Laurel Road. There was a lot of hubbub in the ranks as I made my way out, and I kept it slow to avoid crunching anybody with a boom mike, camera, or tape recorder. What a saint I am.

For the first time in a while, I was glad to see Brooke's place. I fumbled with my keys, slouched inside. The only thing I could think of was Murph's eyeless, tongueless face, the bloodied kids, the dead wife. So I tried to think of nothing.

Brooke woke when I bumped into the nightstand. She looked at the clock, groaned. "I guess you don't have to be anywhere tomorrow," she said. I stood in the dark, contemplated going to the couch. "Nate."

She turned on the light. I guess the blood all over my clothes had some effect. She bolted upright in the bed.

"Oh, my God." She didn't ask if I was all right. She knew, I assumed, that I wasn't. "Oh God, Nate."

I walked to the bed and lay flat on the covers. Brooke's arms enveloped me, her legs curled behind mine. She just held me, arms tight around me like she feared I'd slip away.

And I, knees pulled to my chest like a fetus, watched the images play before my eyes: Murph, his wife, the kids. They would not leave me, just kept flashing through my brain over and over and over.

13

I ROSE AT FIRST LIGHT, feeling cored out. Too much to hope, I guess, that I would sleep well. No one could sleep carrying so many bodies around in their heads.

My clothes went into the washing machine and I stood by, naked, watching the water fill the basin. After the fill, I cut the cycle and let them soak. You have to do such things to get blood out. Then I took a shower.

After all my botched and frenzied efforts, after all the police and sirens and reporters, this is what it all comes to, doesn't it? As I scrubbed in the shower, I wondered when I would finally get the blood from under my fingernails, from inside my pores. Out, out damned spot and all that.

I toweled off and looked at the ghost of myself in the fogged mirror. Then I turned on the shower and got back in. Under the lukewarm stream, I opened my mouth to the water, tried to wash everything, every part of me, even the insides.

The door to the bathroom opened and shut, then the door to the shower. "You're going to turn into a prune," Brooke said, taking a bar of soap in her hands. As she glided the bar over me, I spun the story of what had happened.

"What are you doing?" Brooke asked. She'd decided to take the day off to be with me. A small gesture, but I appreciated it. I appreciated not being alone.

"Checking the paper," I said, logging into her computer.

"You sure you want to?"

"Of course not, but I sort of have to."

"Why?"

"Because I want to relive it again, Brooke."

She scowled, but cut me some slack. I was in some sort of psychological shock, right?

I brought up the site for the *San Jose Mercury News*. Brooke stood behind me, brought her arms around my neck, and laid her head on my shoulder.

In the "Latest from the Newsroom" section, I found what I was looking for. " 'Family of Four Slain in Woodside Home,' " I read aloud.

"Why are you doing this to yourself?" Brooke asked.

" 'Paul Murphy, thirty-five, his wife, Diane, thirty-two, and their children Drew, five, and Stephanie, two, were found murdered in their Woodside home at approximately twelve a.m. this morning. San Mateo Sheriff's Department officers arrived on the scene after the bodies were discovered by a friend of the family.' At least they didn't—oh, shit, they did. 'According to an official close to the investigation, Paul and Diane Murphy were alive at discovery and died shortly before police arrived. A spokesman for the coroner's office said the cause of death for all four victims was "severe trauma to the head and neck."' "

I continued, "Incompetent physician Nathaniel McCormick, despite his pathetic efforts, was unable to help either Dr. or Mrs. Murphy."

"It doesn't say that," Brooke said.

"Subtext." I scanned the rest of the short article, found nothing I didn't know, and logged out of the website.

We had breakfast at a place in Menlo Park. Tables were spread out on a large patio. It was all very airy, light, and normal.

While waiting for the omelets to arrive, Brooke reached over and took my left hand. She held it lightly in hers, tracing with a finger the scars that crisscrossed the palm, the carpals and metacarpals, the wrist. Because of the scar tissue, my grip was stiff. But—forgive the pun—I have to hand it to the surgeons and physical therapists: I can still type, I can still tie a tie, I can still, evidently, fire a gun. I might have to defer those dreams of playing Carnegie Hall, though.

"I can't believe this happened," she said. "Who has things like this happen to them twice? In two years?"

"A sinner in the hands of an angry God," I said.

"Got religion, Dr. McCormick?"

"Just dragging up references from an American Studies class I took in college."

The waiter, a lanky kid in an emo punk T-shirt that

had some Laundromat logo on it, dropped the food on our table.

I said, "Be careful, Brooke. You should break up with me now. Being a friend of mine seems to have serious consequences for health and life."

She smiled. Then the smile faded, and she looked down at her plate. Guess the warning struck a little too close to home.

"You okay?" she asked.

"Sure." I looked at her. "No."

She took my hands again.

"I don't know what to do," I said.

"There's nothing to do."

"There's always something to do." I dropped her hand, stood up, and walked away, fishing my cell phone from my pocket.

"I saw the paper today," I told Bonita Sanchez. "Any progress on who did this?"

After a pause, the detective drawled, "I can't comment on that."

"Sure you can," I said. Sanchez said nothing. "Have you spoken to the Murphys' friends?"

"Stay out of it, Doctor."

"Come on, Detective. It's not like I'm some joe off the street—"

"But you are some joe off the street, Dr. McCormick. You were witness to a crime, nothing more. At least that's what we hope, right?"

"What does that mean?"

"I'll let the ambiguity stand, Doctor." So the ambiguity stood, not so ambiguously signaling me to back off.

"He was my friend," I said.

"Look, I can only imagine how upset you must be. And I'm sorry—I truly am—for what you must be going through. I'm sorry for the family, I'm sorry most of all for those two kids. But I am up to my ta-tas in this investigation. I don't have time to not answer your questions." She sighed into the phone. "If it's any consolation, I'm taking this very personally."

"Why should that be a consolation?"

"Because people go to San Quentin when I take things personally. People get the needle."

"All those people from Atherton who get the needle?"

She laughed. "Where'd you learn your manners, *mijo*? I was twenty years in Oakland before coming here. Now, I realize you saw some pretty dark things last year—"

Last year? Why did everybody always have to dig up the past?

"—but you haven't seen anything. Trust me on that. And trust me that we'll do everything we can. And, finally, trust me that you do not want to get on my bad side."

"I trust you, Detective. Did you find anything out about that white Cadillac?"

"There are a lot of white Cadillacs in the world, Doctor." I cursed myself for the thousandth time for not noting the license plate number of the car.

"I'm hanging up the phone now," Sanchez said.

"I know—you're up to your ta-tas." I hit End on the phone.

14

BROOKE WAS TOOLING ABOUT THE house, cleaning up the kitchen or something. From my station on the couch, I caught a glimpse of her as I flipped Murph's business card between my fingers.

"Tetra Biologics?" I asked.

"I don't know anything about them, Nate. I told you. Google them."

So I did.

"The answer to cancer," I said to myself. Then to Brooke, who was not in sight, "Transcription factor inhibition. I guess this is what Murph was working on. Get this: 'Tetra Biologics has programs in cancer research, diabetes treatment, tissue regeneration, and novel antivirals.' Don't you love that? 'Novel antivirals,' like anything that anyone does these days isn't called 'novel.' "

"Fascinating." Brooke sounded decidedly un-fascinated.

"They've been around for five years," I said. "They're not public," I said. Brooke gave no response, other than the *clink-clink* of dishes being returned to their places. I went to PubMed, the governmental listing of nearly every scientific paper published in the last thirty years. Forty-one articles came up under Murph's name. The most recent ones concerned transcription factors and cancer. I pulled up the abstracts and found out what institution Murph was working at when he did the research. "Looks like he was pretty productive at Tetra."

"Great."

"He probably had friends there."

"Probably," Brooke shouted. I thought I heard tension creeping into her voice.

"I wonder how long he was there?"

Silence.

"I should probably pay them a visit," I said.

Brooke appeared in the kitchen doorway, tea towel in hand. "Why?"

"Because I need to find out what's going on."

"You told the police everything?"

"Of course."

"And you don't think they're looking into this?"

"I don't know. I forgot to ask the detective whether they were looking at his workplace."

"Yes, better call them and tell them to look there. I'm sure they haven't thought of it." Sarcasm dripped from her lips.

"More hands can't hurt," I said.

She huffed, turned, and went back into the kitchen. "Why are you *doing* this?"

"Because I promised Murph I'd find out who—"

"And then what, Nate? Then what?" She was back in the doorway, the towel balled in her hand. "What exactly are you going to do that the police can't? And what are you going to do if you do actually find out who did this horrible thing? Grab a posse and go string 'em up at the old oak tree? Cuff 'em and throw away the key?"

I didn't have an answer for her.

She stepped over to the couch, knelt in front of me, took my hands in hers. The towel was wet against my skin.

"Nate, I'm scared, really scared. What these people did terrifies me. It terrifies me that you'd probably be dead if you'd shown up ten minutes earlier. It terrifies me that you want to find these people, to let them into your life. You did that last year. You can't do it again."

"I'm scared, too."

"Then *stop* this."

"I can't."

"Why?" Her eyes glistened. "Is this all about giving yourself some purpose? A quick fix because the rest of your life is in flux?"

"His kids and wife, Brooke . . . I promised."

"He's *dead.* He doesn't give a damn about your promise." The tears welled. "I took off work to be with you today, to curl up, watch movies, go to the beach maybe, or just sit around and hold your hand or have sex with you or whatever you need. But you don't want any comfort, do you, Nate?"

"He used to be my best friend."

"Since when? Ten years? Two days ago you couldn't stand the thought of the guy."

"Okay, well, we might have had some unresolved issues."

"So they're going to stay unresolved, aren't they? He's *dead,* Nate. I'm not. I'm slipping away from you. I'm trying not to, but I am. And you're not reaching out at all. I don't want to play any more games, I don't want to give you any more hints. Because I know you see them and you just don't seem to care."

"I am reaching out."

"Please don't say that. Oh, Nate, please don't say that when you know you're not." Brooke's head was now buried between my knees, her tears dampening the denim of my jeans. She looked up. "Just get a job. It doesn't have to be forever, just so we can get back on our feet. But please stay away from Tetra Biologics. Please don't call that detective anymore. Stay out of it. Please."

I sat there, listening to her cry. She was right. Murph's family's death did give me a reason for being on the planet at that moment. It gave me an answer to the question I'd been avoiding for months: Why am I here? Simple: To find out what happened to these people, to snatch a little justice for them.

But I wondered, too, how much I was running toward something, how much I was running away. The trajectory of us—of Brooke and Nate—had been so clear a month before. Get life back on track, get job, move to own apartment, then move back in with Brooke. Get married. Kids. Mortgage. All that grown-up stuff. Now, the view of us was so hazy, I couldn't even see through to the next day.

So is that what this was, some juvenile commitment phobia? That the train was moving too fast and this was my pathetic attempt to slow it down?

I stroked the hair of the woman I loved—there was no doubt that I loved her—and said, simply, "I'll stay out of it. I promise."

15

WE SPENT THE REST OF the day together, Brooke and I, doing our best to get the relationship off life support. It was pretty good, all in all, if you don't count the moments where Murph and his family intruded. And they intruded—with their sliced-up necks and desperate final breaths—quite a bit.

Sex, lunch, a trip to the beach. We rounded out the day with a flick: some Jennifer Aniston vehicle Brooke wanted to see and which I was reasonably sure contained no violence. A late dinner. Some kissing. Bed.

I could be cynical and say the day was just another iteration of what became our collective m.o.—heavy discussion or fight, make up, things get good for a day, then it's same old same old. But this was not really the same old. I carried four bodies with me now, to every conversation, every meal, every kiss.

The next day I cracked a little. Brooke was at work and I found myself with nothing to do. Idle hands and such. My deficient doctoring the night of Murph and family's murder had been getting to me and the only way I could think to alleviate the guilt was to beat myself up a little more about it. I called a guy I knew from residency, now a trauma surgeon in North Carolina.

Ted Black returned my page after two minutes. Gotta

love the efficiency of a surgeon. In addition to having the fastest hands in his class, Ted was actually a nice guy. So after the requisite catching up, after I gave him the grisly details, all he said was, "They were goners, Nate. Nothing else you could have done."

"There's got to be something."

"Through both external jugulars, probably deep enough to nick the carotids? No way, bud. You get an airway and apply direct pressure and say your prayers. Hope to God they get to the OR in time. You say your prayers?"

"I think so."

"That's it, then. You did all you can. Don't think any more on it."

Easy for Dr. Black, whose job toughened him for defeats like that. Not so easy for a medicine doc like me.

I thanked Ted, and we made vague plans to get together when we were next in each other's orbits.

So, that's it, then. Guilt moderately assuaged, emphasis on *moderately*.

I called some of my job leads; they hadn't yet reviewed my CV or my application. Calls to landlords were more fruitful, and I set up appointments to see two places in the city.

Here I was: not keeping my promise to Murph by keeping my promise to Brooke. What a mess.

With the rest of the day open to me, and with Brooke MIA somewhere at the S.C. Dept. of Public Health, I took a little trip over to my former university, to the med school library. If Brooke called, I could always say it was just a little trip down Memory Lane. Shitty memories, sure, but still . . .

What I wanted was some access to databases to which

the university subscribed. Those would be the best places to find anything out about Tetra Biologics. I wasn't paying the company a visit, right? Just a little recon.

I also didn't want Brooke stumbling through the history files on her computer.

It had been just over a year since I'd visited the medical school. Since returning to the Bay Area, I made a point to avoid the place. Bad memories grafted onto bad memories transplanted into more bad memories. Still, being there wasn't entirely unpleasant. Some people get a sense of the sublime from mountains; I get it from big academic medical centers. In addition to the buildings I knew well—one that housed my first lab, one where Murph and I had done the bulk of our work—there rose a relatively new clothespin-shaped building high to one side of the parking lot, wine-colored banisters running around the top two floors. The inside face of the clothespin was all glass and labs and looked out to a granite courtyard. The outside looked like it had been lifted from a 1960s motel.

I walked into the low-slung medical school building—which everyone wanted to see torn down but which never would be, owing to its landmark status. This was the oldest part of the complex, designed by a famous architect who had a thing for poured concrete, inner courtyards, the color beige, and, bizarrely, a vague swastika design that found its way onto all the exterior walls and columns of the place.

The library encircled one of the courtyards, this one with a large tree that kept the cleaning staff busy by raining sticky detritus over the cushy outdoor chairs and tables beneath it.

In the computer alcove, I started with Google, then

went to LexisNexis. There was a reason I never contemplated an analyst job on Wall Street: the work was so tedious it made working in a lab seem like the most exciting thing on the planet by comparison. After forty minutes, I had managed to dig up some information that wasn't very interesting to me but might have been to the Wall Street folks. To wit: Tetra Biologics was formed five years before by a former professor of Biochemistry and Molecular Biology from the University of Illinois at Chicago and a business guy who'd formerly headed a small medical devices company. The professor's name was Tom Bukowski and the money man was Dustin Alberts. No public filings, so the company was in private hands, held by a few venture capital firms, some investment from Big Pharma, a small investment firm called Gold Coast Capital. They had exactly one drug on the market: an interferon used to treat multiple sclerosis. The rest of their drugs were in some lower stage of development. Two of those were in the FDA approval process, very close, it seemed, to getting to market. One was the transcription factor inhibitor that Murph had been working on. The other was some tissue regeneration project for wound healing and "other soft tissue defects." Well, good for Tetra and its investors. Yawn.

As I was about to slip into a REM cycle, I came across something interesting, not just to the Wall Street guys, but to salacious news outlets and, frankly, to me. Tom Bukowski, one of Tetra's two founders, was dead.

I expanded my search to older articles. It seemed that August two years before had been not so good for Tetra, and decidedly bad for the company's Chief Science Officer. On August 23, Bukowski was on a deep-sea fishing trip out of Monterey, California, when an explosion tore through the boat. Bukowski was killed, along with a man named Peter Yee. The captain and the first mate were also goners. Neither Peter Yee's nor the first mate's bodies was discovered. Bukowski's corpse—part of it, anyway—was found by students from a local diving class.

The articles revealed there was some question of foul play, but the investigators concluded that mechanical error caused the explosion. The "mechanical error," it was thought, stemmed from a faulty fuel line and accumulated diesel fumes belowdecks. Lawsuits from Bukowski's family against the boat's owners and against the manufacturer of the engine were settled out of court.

I searched a little longer. I found nothing about Paul Murphy's good friends at Tetra. Nothing about his buds with whom he might have discussed "really bad things."

In the courtyard, I betrayed Brooke for the second time that afternoon. I called Bonita Sanchez. The detective wasn't ecstatic to hear from me, but, as I reminded her, I hadn't pestered her for a full day. That seemed to work, and she opened up a little. By "a little," I mean she informed me they continued to give 110 percent to the investigation. I asked her if she'd spoken with Murph's friends and relatives. Of course, she said. I asked her if she'd spoken with his colleagues at Tetra. Of course, of course.

In the end, she finally did soften enough to come clean with me. "It's starting to look like a home invasion gone bad," she said. "I'm sorry." Then she swore and told me she'd kill me if I talked to the press. Since I was feeling pretty kindly toward her for the candor, I said I wouldn't.

Still, after the call, I couldn't stop poking at it. Murph was dead—Drew and Stephanie and Diane were dead—

and those deaths threatened to go unexplained. Worse, those deaths threatened to be meaningless. Tragedy compounding tragedy.

So, perhaps I should explain some of the "unresolved issues" between Murph and me ten years ago. I wasn't, actually, booted from school following the whole massaged-data fiasco. They had asked me to take a leave of absence, and I did, finally settling into a brainless job at the coffee shop on campus. As I said, Murph had been pretty self-righteous about my problems in the lab and with my PhD. What I didn't say is that the guy bent over backward to make amends.

For more than two weeks, with barista Nate McCormick slinging his lattes and cappuccinos, Paul Murphy would stop by for a daily cup of coffee. Each day he tried to engage me in conversation. At first, his overtures seemed pathetic to me—the efforts of someone who couldn't see I had no intention of keeping him as a friend. As week one bled into week two, his persistence became annoying.

Eventually, Murph worked himself up to a big apology for being so strident about my problems in the lab. By then, though, self-righteousness had become mine.

"Great," I told him, flipping my little towel over my shoulder and motioning him down to the end of the bar. "All water under the bridge, right?"

"I was kind of hoping so," Murph said.

"You want it both ways, buddy? Look like a Boy Scout for the department, then get me back on your side because you feel *bad*?"

"I'm just saying that I'm sorry—"

"Well, don't say it, man. Too late." I turned from him,

headed back to the cash register. The line was getting long, and Becca, the other barista, kept shooting me desperate glances.

"Good luck with your fabulous career," I said loudly. "Or whatever." Two words like stakes in the heart of what had been my best friendship in medical school. My last image of Paul Murphy was this: the big man looking at me as though he'd been slapped in the face. He stood for a moment, sighed like a wounded animal, then slumped out the door.

Less than a month later, I assaulted some idiot while on duty at the coffee shop. A week after that, the school sent me packing.

Ten years passed and Murph offered another apology in another coffee shop. This time I accepted, taking my first baby-steps toward patching things up with him. I think I had every intention of making him a friend again, but some sadist with a knife had deprived me of the opportunity. And now I was left with unresolved, unrelieved guilt. Guilt at having shut the man out, guilt at not having been able to help him or his family.

So, had guilt placed me in the library? Probably. Anger? A need for vengeance? Those, too. But beyond such venalities was a sense that the world had been knocked off-kilter by his murder and balance needed to be restored. I wanted to inject a little justice into an unjust world.

I couldn't really go hoofing around Murph's social circle, since I didn't know where that social circle was, and I was now sure the police wouldn't help me get started. Another thing I was sure of, though: the circle intersected Tetra Biologics somewhere.

To assuage my conscience for talking to Bonita Sanchez when I'd promised not to, and for even considering a trip to Tetra, I put in a call to Brooke. "What are you wearing?" I asked.

"Crotchless panties. I have a meeting with my boss later."

Brooke's boss came in at about five-eight, two-fifty. A heart attack waiting to happen.

Just as I was telling her I was at home repacking boxes, a stream of medical students hemorrhaged out of a classroom somewhere and flowed into the courtyard.

"What's that noise?" she asked.

"Squirrels," I said, then told her I needed to grab a golf club and deal with them. I don't think she believed me. Neither of us played golf.

"How's the job search going?" she asked.

"Super. They just offered me a position as the Commandant of Health for the State of California."

"Wow. I didn't even know there was such a position."

"There wasn't. They're creating it especially for me."

"Couldn't happen to a more stable guy. Hey, I need to go," she said. "I really do have a meeting with my boss."

I made it a point to thank her boss someday for his impeccable timing.

Back in the library, trying to make good on the job-search fib, I started trolling through the listings on the computer. Made researching Tetra look awesome by comparison.

Besides, I wasn't really thinking about jobs. I was thinking about how to get inside Tetra. Security is a bitch these days, especially in a field like biotech where people were very freaked about corporate espionage. So, how to sleuth it out? I suppose I could camp outside in Tetra's parking lot, collar people as they left work. No, too creepy, especially after what just happened to one of their colleagues. I could always find an employee list and visit them at home. *Really* creepy. I could get a job with the cleaning service, rummage through files. Interesting. I wondered what they'd pay.

Since I was on the job-hunting tip anyway, I cruised over to the Tetra Biologics site, to their "Careers" section, which was given top-bar real estate on the home page. A word to kids everywhere—college students, teens, and tweens—study your science, boys and girls. Science is where it's *at,* jobwise. But if those nitwits in Washington and Wichita get their way, we'll all be debating the finer points of what day, exactly, God gave the sloth his three toes, rather than working on anything useful.

Okay, time to dismount from my high horse, which, I believe, was created on Day 4, sometime in the afternoon, right after the creation of sparrows, and right before . . . There I go again.

Jobs, ladies and gentlemen. And what a job it was: Tetra's Assistant Medical Director—Antivirals. It was situated in a category called "Drug Development, Medical/ Clinical Affairs." The ideal career move for a guy who'd spent the last few years hunting down those infectious buggers.

Oh, boy, wouldn't Brooke be proud? Truth is, she'd probably castrate me, but what the hell? I needed the work.

I pulled out my jump drive, uploaded my CV through their website. Done. Simple as that.

Well, maybe not that simple: Brooke's tear-streaked face came into view. Definitely not simple.

I walked through the scuffed gray hallway, past the lawn where, in med school, we tossed the football between classes, past the modernist bench where Gary Bortner chipped his tooth doing a handstand to impress Melissa Patch. I smiled. Those were the easy days, before I'd slipped off the rungs of my ladder and landed in a career- and social-isolation ward. As if on cue, darker places slid into the scene: the Dunner Building, where I'd tinkered with the research that got me kicked out of school. The Heilmann Building, where my old mentor had her lab.

It was difficult to believe I was back in this place. Not just back here, but stuck here, for a little while, anyway. What kept me pinned and wriggling on the wall were the images of those two dead kids, of a dead man and his murdered wife, of plastic kitchen tubes sticking out of their throats as their last breaths hissed and faded to nothing.

And I, in some weird paradox, hadn't felt so alive in months.

16

"GOD, THOSE KIDS," BROOKE MURMURED as we wove our way between granite headstones back to the car. We'd just sat through the eulogies, watched four caskets being lowered into four holes. Big ones for Murph and his wife; depressingly small ones for the two kids.

The kids, I thought.

In my life, I have had the misfortune of seeing children die; you don't do two years in the backcountry of a nearly failed sub-Saharan state and not see that. AIDS, malaria, sleeping sickness. I spent years railing and screaming at disease; it is my life's work. I am far too familiar with the Third Horseman of the Apocalypse. Ultimately, he is a frustrating opponent. He is an abstraction. Raging against him is like raging against poverty or war or the moon: it's futile. Best to put your nose to the grindstone, pick your battle—HIV, flu, TB—and win the ones you can. Still, though, I rage.

It should not have been a shock to me how furious I became when listening to the eulogies for this family, but it was. What killed these two kids was not abstract. What killed them had a face. It was someone who could be blamed and who should be punished. Someone who could bleed.

When we reached the car, Brooke hugged me and murmured: "Grieve for them. This is the time for that."

She should have known me better by now.

The next few days came and went, creeping by, as time does for those who are out of work, friendless, depressed, who mark the hours by watching the sun crawl across the sky. I checked my e-mail. I checked voicemail. I was concerned only about one communication, really. A little missive from some generic HR functionary at Tetra Biologics. I didn't care to be contacted by anyone else. I didn't want Tetra to be scooped.

As it was, Tetra was scooped, by a bunch of landlords and a policy center at Berkeley, the California Emerging Infections Program. The co-director of the program tried to set up an interview with me for later that week. I put her off with some malarkey about a conference in Florida. I should have thought twice about that—she was an infectious disease doc, after all, and knew about all the conferences. I said it had something to do with hedge funds.

A day later, I finally got what I was waiting for: the call from Tetra. The HR woman said that my résumé looked very interesting and they'd like to bring me in to talk. Would tomorrow be all right? Sure, I said. You move fast, I said. We sure do, she said.

After the call, I walked a few blocks to a florist, picked up a bouquet of flowers for Brooke. Irises, her favorite. I hoped they would somehow say what I had such a difficult time articulating. Come to think of it, I probably had a hard time articulating things because I didn't know exactly what I wanted to articulate.

Back at her apartment, I put the flowers in water and decided to take a run. Though the rest of my life was falling into disrepair, I'd somehow managed to keep up my workout schedule. Brooke had forgotten her iPod at home; I strapped the thing on and left the house.

Left or right? Life's big questions. I glanced up and down the block. About fifty yards away, on my right, a black SUV was parked. Someone was behind the wheel. Had I seen the vehicle on the trip to the florist? Maybe, but my nerves jangled a little. I turned to the right and ran toward the SUV.

I didn't get a good look inside. As I started to run, the SUV—a big Lincoln Navigator—rolled into the road and roared past me. Inside, a man was talking on a cell phone. I slowed and looked back, not able to see the plates. The Navigator braked at the stop sign at the end of the block, and eased a right turn.

Probably just a real estate agent on a house call, I thought. Probably just that.

17

"GODDAMN IT, NATE!"

I played around with the salad—some arugula-walnut creation of Brooke's—and kept my eyes on the plate. The irises sat in a vase between us. "It's a job," I said.

"It's not a job," said the salad's creator. "You think I'm an idiot?"

"I didn't have to tell you."

Truth is, I didn't really mind keeping it from her. But I let slip that I had two interviews over the next week. Brooke pressed, of course, about where they were. I didn't want to give her a bald-faced lie, so I'd blurted it out. Moron.

"They probably need people now more than ever," I said. "Seems like their employees just keep dropping like flies."

"Stop the damned joking, okay? For once, just stop the damned jokes."

"Fucking language, Dr. Michaels."

Now, that wasn't really a joke—not one of my better ones, anyway—but Brooke sure as hell didn't like it. She tossed her fork onto her plate—"I really can't take this anymore"—and violently ripped off a piece of bread. "Don't you have any respect—any respect at all—for me? For us? I'm at work and I'm worrying about you and I'm thinking there's no way in hell you're staying away from that detective and from fucking Tetra Biologics. But then I say: 'Brooke, stop being so *suspicious*. Nate loves you. He wouldn't—' "

"I do love you."

She leveled a stare at me that could flatten a city. "—Nate loves you. He wouldn't disrespect you like that."

There was a long silence. I said, "I guess you know me pretty well, don't you?"

"I guess I do," she snapped. "You're such a little boy, Nathaniel. 'Oh my life is confusing now. I really can't figure out what I want.' " She was mocking me. " 'But look! My ex–best friend in the world got himself murdered. Why don't I run around and try to figure out what happened? Why don't I shut Brooke out? She was just a tiny part of my life anyway.' " She shot a very unkind look at me. "Try to make an adult decision for once, Nate. Act your age and think about what really matters just this one time."

Okay, I admit that last sentence, the one about acting my age, changed things. It pissed me off.

I took one last bite of the salad, set down my fork with what I hoped was a strong-silent-type deliberation, and stood up.

"You don't really care too much about people, do you?" she spat. "The sick ones, sure, the dead ones. But people—living, breathing people you actually have to negotiate with—how much do you care for them? Tell me, how much did you really give a damn about Paul Murphy before he got himself murdered?"

From the living room, I grabbed the bag with my toiletries, the duffel with wardrobe basics, the garment bag—

I did have an interview, after all—and my laptop bag. With all that crap, I must have looked like a tinker going to market. Wished that I could have exited with just my attitude and a razor.

Brooke never moved from the table; she had a good enough view from where she was.

"Mature, Nate. Just take off. Just leave."

And so I did.

All the stuff went into the back of the Corolla. Trunk slammed. Door opened violently. Don't know who I was performing for. The block was quiet. No people, no movement. A few cars parked along the side of the road, but no one in them. The only sound was the swishing of vehicles on the Central Expressway a hundred yards away.

Brooke might have been overreacting—and that little boy shtick was unfair—but I understood where she was coming from. Truly. But a man's got to do what a man's got to do, right? Paul Murphy was my friend, right?

I made a big deal of walking wide circles around the car, so anyone at all interested would know I was making my exit. One last look into the little house with good light, one last long look down the block.

And that's when I saw it, far up the street, in a shadow between the pools of light cast by the streetlights. Black SUV.

I walked toward it a few steps, couldn't tell if anyone was inside. Then I raised my arms, extended the middle finger on each hand.

Come and get me, you pricks.

18

THOUGH OTHER PARTS OF THE country boast about their biotech—Boston, Philly, the DC–Baltimore corridor—none of them came close to the Bay Area in terms of sheer density and number. There are nearly 1,500 biotechs in the U.S. The Bay Area has over 800 of them.

The region was blessed with a collection of world-class universities—UCSF, Berkeley, my old haunt—an aggressive venture-capital culture, and great weather. Many of the industry's graybeards were conceived and birthed here, given names that sounded like they came out of some awkward sci-fi–Greek mythology hybrid: Genentech, Chiron, Affymetrix, Scios. And though the companies had spread through the region like bacterial colonies on an agar plate, South San Francisco was the heart of it all.

Tetra Biologics had managed to score choice real estate in South San Francisco, a mile or so from Genentech, the great patriarch of the lot. Genentech periodically had very good years. When it did, investors took the cue; the money spigots tended to open from the big institutional funds and from the VCs down in the Valley. When it had a bad year—well, no one ever said biotech was an easy business.

Tetra's building turned out to be a shock of white girders and aquamarine glass. Its shape was like the bow of an ocean liner, chopped off somewhere around the shuffleboard courts, the rest of the ship, I assumed, having sunk to the bottom of the San Francisco Bay. Consistent with the maritime vibe, steam poured from two large vents at the top of its six floors and refugee seagulls clustered in a corner of the parking lot.

It was about ten-thirty, a half hour before my interview. A terrible night's sleep in a terrible motel along Highway 101 meant that I didn't have a plan, and I hoped that sitting in the parking lot would clear my thoughts. No such luck. Every time I found my train of thought, Brooke would walk in and derail me. Useless.

I quit the parking lot, figuring that some time inside Tetra might give me a better idea of its layout. I walked through a sea of sun-blasted cars, toward the place where, a week before, Paul Murphy had been punching his time clock. My heart thumped more than it should have as I passed under a glass-and-steel canopy that bathed the walkway underneath it with a weird oceanic light.

My shoes clacked across the polished granite floor of the atrium. Inlaid into the granite in brass was the Latin phrase *nosce te ipsum*. My education may not have been Ivy League, but I did recognize the words: *Know thyself.* The same words had been chiseled over the entrance to the Oracle of Delphi. They were recycled centuries later in the frontispiece of a book by the Renaissance anatomist Vesalius, recycled again in early-twenty-first-century California. These Tetra guys were lucky copyright laws didn't extend to wise old sayings.

I introduced myself to a security guard perched behind a high-concept metal desk, told him I was here to see Francine Hartman. He took my Georgia driver's license, gave me the once-over, called someone. After a few grunts, he hung up the phone and pointed to a computer at the periphery of the atrium.

"She'll be down in a few minutes. You can sign in there. Fill out the NDA and you'll get your visitor's badge."

At the computer, I typed in some personal information—name, organization, Social Security number, genetic code—and up popped Tetra's Non-Disclosure Agreement. These things were mandatory for any tech company, and life sciences companies were among the most skittish about their intellectual property.

I read through the form, peppered with words like "confidential" and "proprietary," "injunction," and "arbitration." If you read these things closely—and I didn't anymore—you might start to worry about spending twenty years in the clink if you accidentally disclosed some trade secret like, say, the color of the bathrooms.

I hit "Agree" at the bottom of the form. From a printer below the computer, an ID badge was born. I peeled the ID from its backing and stuck it on my jacket. Thus identified, my civil rights curtailed, I found a seat.

Francine Hartman didn't appear, and after nine minutes my ass began to ache on the hard marble bench. I adjusted and readjusted and got so involved in my posterior discomfort that I didn't notice the woman walking toward me, watching me grind my butt into the marble like a hemorrhoidal chimp.

"Dr. McCormick?"

I looked up and saw a primate female, about thirty-five, too stylish to be anyone but Human Resources or Marketing. Francine Hartman. She introduced herself; I shot to my feet and shook her hand.

"Those benches, they certainly need a little padding, don't they?"

I felt my face go red.

As we walked through the glass doors to the elevators, Francie, as she insisted she be called, brought me up to speed on Tetra Biologics. She spun the humdrum corporate line on the trip to the sixth floor. Nothing more than I'd already gotten from the website, I thought, as the doors opened.

The area was carpeted, which immediately signaled to me that not too much science was conducted on floor six. You don't carry trays of cell cultures over carpet. If you drop them, the cells really are a bugger to tweeze out of the fibers.

This floor was obviously the provenance of the corporate guys, the suits, the parasites on the backs of good scientists like Paul Murphy. Okay, I might be doing a little demonizing and romanticizing, but I know where my loyalties lie.

Francie pointed down the hallway. "That's where all the head honchos are. We're down here."

"Dustin Alberts is still CEO?"

"Last I checked. You do your homework, Dr. McCormick."

If that was doing my homework, then the bar for entry to Tetra was, indeed, very low. I said, "I always do my homework. Ever since third grade, when Mrs. Dunn gave me detention—"

I stopped myself when I realized Francie was not paying attention.

We continued down the corridor. Along one wall were

the offices with windows. Along the other, offices with walls. Many of the spaces seemed unoccupied.

Francie led me to her office, which, I noticed, had windows.

She sat. I sat. She handed me Tetra's press kit, a glossy folder emblazoned with the company's logo.

"Your schedule for the day is in there. You'll meet with Dan Missoula and Alexandra Rodriguez from our antivirals division."

Francie leaned back in her expensive chair, prattling on about Tetra, giving me a good glimpse of the high contrast between her bleached choppers and her too-tanned skin. She wore a black blouse, opened one button too far, exposing more nut-brown epidermis. As a former public health official, I wondered if I should have a talk with her about the dangers of sun exposure.

She sprayed the press packet verbatim, not giving me much new information.

"And how old is the antiviral division?" I interrupted.

"Oh, relatively new. Three to four years. We just got through Phase 2 with the product, and we're going into Phase 3 sometime soon. That"—she stabbed a manicured fingernail at me—"is why we need a new Medical Director."

"What is the product?"

"Very good question, Dr. McCormick. Direct. I like the pizzazz. Dr. Missoula and Dr. Rodriguez will fill you in more, but it's called Multavirin. It was one of Getra's"—a big multinational pharmaceutical company—"orphan drugs which we licensed a while back. It seems to have some efficacy against hepatitis C."

Orphan drugs are the cast-offs, the ones that don't

make business sense anymore for mammoth companies interested mostly in billion-dollar molecules.

"Just like ribavirin," I said, "cor—"

"Enough!" She splayed her fingers in front of her face and wiggled them around like she'd just been attacked by bats. She began to laugh like an orangutan. "Stop! I'm at my limit! I came from Yahoo! three months ago and just learned that transcriptase isn't chat software."

Well, that was a good one. We both laughed—har har har—about it. God, this woman was wired. Maybe I didn't need to talk about skin cancer, but about caffeine toxicity.

Francie continued on about some of the other products in the pipeline: a diabetes drug, one for cancer of the gut. It struck me that Murph must have been managing the cancer drug.

Surprisingly, Francie said something interesting.

"But what I'm most excited about is something called Regenetine." She must have seen my eyebrows jump, because she said, "Uh-huh. Regenetine. Not wild about the name, but that's what Marketing stuck us with. It's some recombinant something or other."

"That's your wound-healing product?"

Francie looked at me with a deer-in-the-headlights glaze, those bleached teeth shining back at me like the face of a glacier. "I saw it on your website," I explained.

"Right. Of course. Wound-healing. Yes."

"Wow," I said. "That sounds pretty . . . cool."

"Very cool, Dr. McCormick. Very cool. Regenetine might be our blockbuster."

"Congratulations."

"Well, thank you. We're hopeful, but we don't want to be *too* hopeful. Like they tell me: a snowball has a better chance in you-know-where than a drug getting approval from the FDA. Things are going well, though. Knock on wood."

She rapped on her head three times, blazed those choppers again, and stood. I didn't. Instead, I said, "I have—had—a friend who worked here. Said it was a terrific place to be—"

"It is."

"—which is why I'm here. Paul Murphy?"

Her smile faltered. "Oh, God, you were a friend of Dr. Murphy's?"

"I knew him from grad school."

"How awful . . ."

"I was wondering if you knew who his friends were, here. It was a long time since we were close, and I wanted to connect . . ." I trailed off.

"I'm sorry. I don't know him—didn't know him—well. Maybe you should ask Dr. Missoula. Or Dr. Rodriguez. God, it's been a rough week. It's been really hard for us here. His poor little ones . . ." She looked at her watch. "Oh! How time flies. I have to get you down to Dr. Rodriguez's office. She'll be waiting."

19

DR. RODRIGUEZ, DIRECTOR OF RESEARCH for Multavirin, made me sit for thirteen minutes in a shotgun waiting area outside a locked door. Again, my glutes were being assaulted, this time by a hard plastic chair next to a tiny table covered in scientific journals. I rolled my rump left to right and failed to get comfortable, finally standing up to avoid any misinterpretation about my movements. One Tetra employee suspicious of an itchy ass in Dr. McCormick was enough.

There was no carpet on the floor. Actual work took place here.

Brushed-metal double doors opened, and I turned to see a woman who I hoped was Dr. Rodriguez. "Hoped" because the woman was quite a looker, to put it mildly, and I wouldn't mind spending thirty minutes of quality time with her.

"Dr. McCormick?"

"Yes. Dr. Rodriguez?" I hoped, I hoped.

She nodded. Excellent. It's the little things in life that count.

"Follow me, please," she said coolly.

I followed her—thirties, olive skin, shoulder-length black hair, copper lips that begged to be kissed and bitten—

through the doors and down a long white corridor, each side flanked by antiseptic-looking labs.

"You're from the area?" she asked.

"No. Pennsylvania. But"—I didn't see the need to discuss my problems in "the area" from years before—"I live here now. Before that, I worked all over."

"I saw that on your résumé."

Dr. Rodriguez opened a door and led me into a small office suite—an administrative assistant's desk with a male administrative assistant behind it, gray carpet, white walls, four doors leading to individual offices. We walked to the far door, to a modest office with a good view. There was a single, framed picture amongst the reference books: a black-and-white of a woman, hands jammed into a thin crack on a sheer face of rock.

"Please, have a seat, Dr. McCormick."

I sat. She took off her lab coat, revealing a short-sleeved blouse and well-muscled arms. "That's you?" I pointed at the picture.

"Yes," she said, and gave me no more detail. If I'd been hoping for a little light flirting, I was disappointed. Dr. Rodriguez was all business. She began flipping through my CV.

"Peace Corps. Medical school at the University of Maryland. Internal medicine residency at the University of North Carolina. CDC for two years. What did you do between college and medical school? I don't see it here."

Ah, The Question. Since it had been a long time since my last job interview, I hadn't thought about my approach to the inevitable inquiry concerning that big, four-year gap. Come clean about it? Tell her I'd been kicked out of the med school thirty miles south of here for cheating and fighting? Do what I did for my CDC interview and spin it, tell her I just wasn't ready for medical school at the time, took a leave of absence, then headed to Maryland to finish?

Since I didn't want her to throw me out of the building before I got some information, I took the CDC approach. Hey, it worked in the past.

"So, you were here for your first two years of medical school?" she asked.

"And two more years in a PhD."

She paused for a moment, thinking. "And you left."

"I did. I was too young. Too stupid."

"Well, I have to assume you're older and wiser now. You did quite a job for the CDC." She must have seen my surprise. She said, "I read the papers about your exploits here last year. And I have to tell you, what you did for Chimeragen didn't help the industry much in the short term."

I didn't know how to take that.

"But we're much healthier now," she said. "Much more by-the-book."

"Good to know."

She tucked the résumé back into its file. "For someone from the public sector, for someone who had such an exciting job and who seemed to be doing so well in that job, why switch now?"

I wanted to say, *Because I'm here to figure out what happened to the employee who had his throat cut.* But I didn't think that would fly on a first interview. I said: "I burned out with CDC. And I've always found research fascinating." I realized how lame I sounded, so I added, by way of credentializing myself, "In my PhD, I worked on hepatitis C."

Research might be fascinating, but this interview wasn't. I talked about my decade-old hep C work, she talked about the antiviral project. Twenty minutes after the interview began, Dr. Rodriguez asked me if I had any more questions. Well, you know what? I did.

"Did you know Paul Murphy?"

The beautiful round face froze.

"Yes," she said. "Why do you ask?"

"I was a friend of his."

The frozen look again, then Dr. Rodriguez blinked. "I'm sorry for the loss," she said woodenly. Then she ended the interview.

20

ALEXANDRA RODRIGUEZ STEPPED OUT OF the office, returned a minute later, telling me to follow her to meet Dan Missoula. As it turned out, Dr. Missoula made his home fifteen feet away. At the doorway, the beautiful Dr. Alexandra Rodriguez and I shook hands. Her fingers were cold.

"We'll be in touch," she said.

Dan Missoula's office was relatively large with relatively large windows. Dan Missoula was a relatively small man with a questionably sparse beard and an unquestionably fierce grip. He squeezed the living hell out of my hand, like he was trying to make up for five lost inches by bringing me to tears. I instantly disliked the man.

We had another pro forma interview. Actually, it wasn't as much an interview of me as it was a narrative of Dr. Missoula's spectacular career—in his mind at least—from early days as a Harvard undergrad and Harvard grad to a UCLA postdoc to a number of forgettable biotechs to his current post as head of the antiviral division of Tetra. He didn't get to the part about why he was still upper-middle management at a second-tier company.

When Danny Boy did actually get around to asking me about me, he zeroed right in on that damning chasm in my résumé.

"So, you just—as you said—you were just too young?"

"I think so."

"Weren't there a lot of young people there? In your class?"

"Yes."

"You weren't any younger than they were, though."

"Not most of them, no. I was immature. Maybe that's a better word."

"It was *hard*?" he asked with mock innocence. "That's what you're saying?"

"It wasn't the right time for me. I should have waited a year."

"I see. Well, *Harvard* was hard, my friend. You heard of—?" He mentioned a brand-name chemistry professor up at the big H, a Nobel laureate, who was famous for having had a few grad students and postdocs commit suicide. "My PI made that guy look like a Girl Scout." Missoula said it as if it were something to be proud of.

Okay, I knew why I was there, and it was not to shoot off my mouth. I was there to infiltrate the organization, to talk to people who might know something about Paul Murphy and why he died. But how long would that take? How long until I wended my way through the hiring process? And how in the hell would I be able to work with someone like Dan Missoula?

But I'm rationalizing. Truth is that Dan Missoula had picked at a scab and broken through to the raw parts underneath. Truth is that Dan Missoula was an intolerable fuck. So I lost my temper and shot myself in the foot. "Your lab sounds worse than Jonestown. How many suicides?"

"That's not the point."

"Oh. Well . . . what is the point?"

Dan Missoula huffed once. "It was a damned pressure cooker is the point."

"Gosh," I said, "Harvard sounds like it was really super tough."

"You have no idea."

I did, in fact, have an idea. Most academic science is a damned pressure cooker. The pressure in my lab in school was enough to make me crack, to make me cheat and lie, to get me kicked out.

"Tetra's a pressure cooker, Dr. McCormick. We work on tight deadlines."

"Not pressure like Harvard, I'm sure."

Dense as he was, Dan Missoula began to understand I was busting his balls. I should say something here in defense of my sabotaging any chance at a job: Harvard people generally annoy the shit out of me. Their self-serving sob stories, like theirs is the only institution in the world that breaks their students. The annoying trait where they can't let five minutes pass without letting you know they studied "in Cambridge."

"Pressure like that," he said. "Survival of the fittest."

"Good. I've been doing a lot of push-ups lately and—"

"Okay, Dr. McCormick. That's very funny." He smiled broadly as if everything were actually okay, which, of course, we both knew it wasn't.

"Sorry," I said. "I tend to be a joker sometimes. I find it lightens the pressure in the labs."

He stood. *Crap.*

"We do serious business here, Doctor."

"Exactly why I'm here."

"Exactly why you're *not* here, Dr. McCormick. I'll show you out."

If I'd had Murph's gun just then, I would have kneecapped myself just for being so stupid, so aggressive.

I stood, shuffled at a desultory pace out the door. My big day—my chance to find something useful—was a bust.

At least when we shook hands in the atrium, after he'd safely seen me through security, I'd be ready for the killer handshake. I flexed my fingers.

But we didn't get that far.

"Dan?" It was Alexandra Rodriguez, making her way from her office toward us. "I thought I'd give Dr. McCormick a little tour of the labs. Give him a sense of what we have to offer here." She didn't look at me, but kept her eyes on Dr. Missoula. "He spent some time in the lab, after all."

Dan Missoula looked at me, then at Rodriguez. "I don't think that's necessary at this point—"

"Of course it is," she told Missoula. "It'll give us a chance to show off."

"Alex—"

Without giving Danny the chance to continue, Dr. Rodriguez opened the outer door of the office suite and held it for me. "Dr. McCormick, please follow me."

21

"HOW DID IT GO WITH Dan?" she asked, leading me down the hallway. Her tone was weirdly informal, like somehow in the past half hour she had had the chance to think and decided we'd become friends.

"You heard of Waterloo?"

She didn't laugh. "He can be a little intimidating."

"I guess that's the word."

There was an ID card hanging from a lanyard around Dr. Rodriguez's neck; she swiped it against a black panel next to a metal door. There was a click.

"This is where we do our cell cultures, transfections and the like. I'm going to have to ask you to stay near the door. We're absolutely freaked about contamination."

I liked the way she used that phrase—"absolutely freaked"—it made her sound more human, or at least more like the humans toward whom I gravitate.

The facility was huge, extending forty feet in either direction from the door. There were three banks of lab benches, three separate cell culture rooms. On a bench near us, a small PCR machine cycled away.

"This is just for the antiviral drug?" I asked her.

"We share it with the cancer group." There were a few researchers milling around the space. One of them, a guy with dyed blond hair and two of those big, round earrings expanding his earlobes, walked in front of us, pipette in hand. He was wearing shorts and a T-shirt under his lab coat.

Unexpectedly, all of a sudden, I missed the lab. I missed the camaraderie. I missed the oddball, smart people.

But I wasn't going to be part of a lab anytime soon. Not at Tetra, at least.

"How well did you know Paul?" I asked Dr. Rodriguez.

"Pretty well," she said evenly.

"Did he ever say anything to you? About . . . well, about anything?"

Alexandra Rodriguez was silent for a moment. Then she said, "Let me show you what else we do here."

22

WE SPENT THE NEXT TWENTY minutes on a whirlwind tour of Tetra Biologics. We hit the diabetes labs, then the tissue regeneration labs. All I got from Dr. Rodriguez was that these two products—for diabetes and tissue regeneration—were going well. The diabetes trials were in Phase 1, which meant Tetra was testing safety in humans. The tissue regeneration project—Regenetine—had passed Phase 1 and was in Phase 2, which established efficacy. "Regenetine is going very, very well," she told me.

"Your blockbuster," I said, recalling what Francie Hartman had said.

"We hope."

In the Regenetine labs, Dr. Rodriguez introduced me to one of the lead scientists on the project. Jonathan Bly was a tall, sallow man with thinning hair and an exhausted stoop. We shook hands. His long cold fingers wrapped loosely around mine. I felt I was shaking hands with a corpse.

"Dr. Bly is going to make us the next Genentech," Alexandra Rodriguez told me.

"We'll see," Bly murmured. He seemed about to keel over.

"I was telling Dr. McCormick how well everything was going."

"Yeah. It's going well."

Alexandra Rodriguez lowered her voice. "Dr. McCormick was a friend of Paul Murphy's."

Bly's eyes flicked toward mine, then away. "I'm sorry about your loss," he said mechanically.

"Thanks," I said.

"Excuse me," he said. "We have a lab meeting in ten minutes."

And with that, he turned from us, his white coat fluttering behind him.

"I guess I'm not understanding something here," I said to Dr. Rodriguez as we watched Bly push through the thick white doors to the hallway.

"What's that?"

"How is a wound-healing drug going to be a blockbuster? I mean, it's wound healing, not heart disease or depression. Seems like the market would be relatively limited." I started thinking out loud. "Postsurgical. Trauma. Battlefield."

She cut me off with a look that I couldn't quite place. Not an unpleasant look, but not nice, either. "There are a lot of wounds in the world, Dr. McCormick. Lots of them."

23

WE WERE IN TETRA'S CAFETERIA, a big, airy room with long white tables and hard—what else?—white chairs. Both of us had our coffee. It was, to say the least, very weird. Tetra wasn't going to hire me, that much was clear. And yet I got the whole dog-and-pony show. I couldn't make sense of it.

"Thanks for the tour, Dr. Rodriguez."

"Please. It's Alex."

"Alex? Like—?"

"Yes."

I smiled. "Anybody call you A-Rod?"

"A lot of people call me A-Rod. I hate the name A-Rod. I'm older than that overpaid jerk. I've always been 'Alex' and refuse to change it no matter how much crap I get."

She took a sip of the coffee, somehow making it look sexier than if she were unhitching a garter belt. She really was a beautiful woman. "I suppose we should talk about Paul."

That conversational shift happened so abruptly, I sloshed scalding coffee into my mouth. Pain is for the weak, though, and I swallowed the bolus, blistering my esophagus. "I suppose."

She leaned close. "Tell me, Dr. McCormick—"

"Nate. Please."

"Tell me, Nate: how much of this was about a job, and how much about Paul Murphy?"

I tongued the raw parts of my mouth and sized her up. I'd be lying if I said I wasn't taken by her looks, by the change from schoolmarm to buddy-buddy. "About fifty-fifty."

"Phooey."

" 'Phooey'? No one says 'phooey' anymore."

"I'm an old-fashioned gal."

"Yeah. The old-fashioned rock climber." I smiled. "Sixty-forty. Maybe seventy-thirty."

"Now we're talking. Let's discuss why seventy percent of you is here. I have to tell you, though, we already talked to the police about what happened."

"We?"

"Me. Others who work here. People who knew Paul."

"Did he have many friends here?"

"I don't think he had any bosom buddies or anything like that. He seemed very involved with his family."

"You? How well did you know him?"

"About the same. Maybe a little better."

Call me old-fashioned, but I found it hard to believe that a man like Paul Murphy and a woman like Alex

Rodriguez would be anything but acquaintances or lovers. Nothing in between. "Just friends, huh?"

"Yes, Nate. Just friends."

"I wanted to know," I said, "if there was anything you noticed. Or anything anyone here noticed."

"Nothing strange, which seems very strange, doesn't it?" She took another pull on her coffee. "Like I said, though, we were work friends. Nothing ever seemed to change with Paul. Came to work, left work, went home. A good-humored, stable rock." She turned from me, looked out the cafeteria window to a brilliant September day. "A good-humored, stable rock who's now—I still can't believe what happened." She swiveled her head back toward me. "Why are you doing this?"

"What?"

"Going through the trouble of an interview. Asking those questions."

"I'm an investigator. It's in my blood."

"You investigate things ten microns across."

"So maybe I'm tired of looking for things I can't see." A-Rod, by the look on her face, was not satisfied with my answer. "And I feel I owe something to Paul. And his kids and wife."

"Why?"

"He asked for my help."

"For what?"

"I don't know. Which is why I'm here."

Alex stared at me.

"He thought he was being followed," I said. "I mean *I* think he was being followed, too. I saw the car."

"Who was it? Why?"

"I don't know. Which is—"

"Which is why you're here. I got that." Alex began aimlessly swirling the cup in her hand. "Isn't this great? A man and his family are murdered and nobody knows anything."

She leaned back in her chair, ran her fingers through the dark hair. "I need to stop obsessing about this. I have a project to run. When I found out you were a friend of Paul's, I wanted to know if you had any new information, and now I do, and it helps me settle down not one little bit."

"Sorry."

"No. It's not your problem. As you can imagine, everyone here is very upset."

"I'm sure."

"And yet you still want to work here?"

"Who wouldn't want to work at the next Genentech?" I smiled. "Which is not going to happen. Did you know Dan Missoula went to Harvard?"

"Of course. So did I."

"Sorry to hear that."

"Dan and I sing fight songs over gels. You know, *Ten thousand men of Harvard want vict'ry today, for they know that o'er old Eli, fair Harvard holds sway.*"

"I don't know, actually. I went to Penn State. *Hail to the Lion, Loyal and True.*" She smiled. "Okay, so we didn't have a lot of poets up there in State College. We would never use the word 'o'er.' We shot people who used the word 'o'er.'"

"You're a pretty funny guy, Dr. McCormick. Weird that Paul never mentioned you."

Weird that Alex thought it weird. Why would "just a

friend" talk to her about a guy who freefell out of his life ten years before?

I stood outside Tetra, outside the glass building's glass doors, and watched the femme fatale A-Rod disappear behind the security turnstiles. What an odd and thoroughly disappointing day, I thought. And what a naive and utterly stupid strategy. Apply for a job and insinuate yourself into Tetra's culture? Question all his colleagues more effectively than the police had? Get real, Dr. McCormick.

I needed to leave this place. Find a job in Philadelphia or Boston or call up CDC, hat in hand, and beg to get in there again. Or even, God forbid, make a real effort to find a job in the Bay Area. Brooke was right: I don't do well without a job, without direction. And with my hopes dashed of getting anything—anything at all—out of Tetra, I had neither. Short of joining the San Mateo Sheriff's Department, I didn't know what else I could do for Murph.

But I could do something for my soul. There had to be a bar close by.

I crossed the lot to the Corolla, got in, closed the door, and started the monster. But I didn't go forward; I didn't even put the car in gear.

As if materialized out of nothing, a man appeared, leaning over the front of the Corolla, hands resting lightly on its hood.

He was of Asian descent, wearing sunglasses, a suit that cost more than my car, and a broad smile. I couldn't put an age on him.

He stood there like a strong man daring me to put the

car in gear and try—just try—to run him over. The smile didn't change, the gaze didn't waver.

I didn't waver either. Instead of stepping out of the car, asking the guy what he was doing, who he was, why he was daring me to move, telling him he was leaving handprints on an exquisite twenty-year-old paint job, I held the gaze. It was clear this was a standoff, and I'd be damned if I was going to blink. It was also clear I had no idea what to do.

During our quality time with one another—two grown men making googly-eyes at each other—I noticed a large mark on his neck. Black and red ink, crawling up the side of his neck and disappearing around the ear. A tattoo. Looked like the end of a dragon's tail. Fabulous, I thought, some Yakuza fuck is carjacking me for my classic wheels. Maybe he was one of those California fast-and-furious types who had a hankering to redo an old Toyota.

But he didn't carjack me. He didn't even move for a good forty seconds. When he did, he simply broke the stare—no nod, no words, no threats—and stepped away from the car, walked purposefully across the lot. I got out of the car and watched him. I had no trouble imagining him moving across the hardwood floors of Paul Murphy's home, the cries of children and screams of adults bouncing off the walls.

A big black Lincoln Navigator sat waiting for him—the same type of vehicle I'd seen on my run yesterday. I couldn't see the driver. My threatening friend made no attempt to hide where he was going, sauntering across the tarmac like he owned the freaking place. One last look at me, that same cocksure smirk on his face. He stepped into the SUV, and the two men motored off at a slow, deliberate pace. It was like they wanted me to feel how little they cared for me, like they wanted me to know they could find me anywhere and squash me like a bug.

And I had the sick feeling in my gut that they could.

24

TWENTY-FIVE MINUTES OF INCONSIDERATE driving later—dipping into parking lots, quick turns here and there—I felt I was probably free of any tail. Only then did I pull my car into the parking lot of Mid-Peninsula Regional Gun Club. As luck would have it, Dale Connolly was behind the desk.

"You're the doc, right? Friend of that big guy."

I wondered if he knew the big guy was dead.

"You have a good memory," I said.

"Helps in this business. We get questions about some of the people who come through here, know what I mean?" He looked at me as if I might be someone he'd have to answer questions about. Or not. Maybe I was just being paranoid.

"I need a gun," I said.

"We have guns."

"I see that."

"What do you need it for?"

As a first-time gun buyer, I was a little nervous. I mean,

I didn't want to tell him I needed it to drill holes through the engine blocks of big SUVs, did I?

"Uh, for protection."

"We got those. What are you thinking about?"

I didn't know. So Dale brought out enough small arms to outfit an insurgency. I settled on a Sig Sauer P229 semi-automatic. It felt the best in my hands and, according to Dale, had become the standard weapon for the U.S. Coast Guard and Homeland Security.

"This, Doc, is the weapon of choice for the War on Terror."

If it's good enough to protect the land of the free, it should be good enough to protect me, I thought. I asked him if he had a demo model I could shoot.

Of course he did.

So I spent the next forty minutes plugging away at silhouettes. Now, if I could only have gotten them to put some fancy Revo shades on the target, give it a neck tattoo, then we'd be in business.

I was becoming reasonably comfortable with my new toy, though I'm not sure my aim was improving that much. Still, I managed to perforate quite a few vital areas on the paper.

"I'll take it," I said to Dale, after I got back to the counter.

"You have a basic firearms safety certificate?" he asked. He saw the look on my face.

"You'll need one of those before you pick up the weapon. Here." He handed me a Xerox with a list of places where I could get the certificate. "You want to carry it, you got to go to the sheriff's, get a special license to carry."

This was becoming complicated. I was a healer, for God's sake, I wasn't about to go blast some guy who slept with my wife. "Okay," I said, and I handed over my credit card and driver's license. "So if I get the certification, I can get the gun tomorrow?"

Dale smiled at me with a big set of yellowed teeth. "Where you from, Doc?"

"Georgia."

"Well, my friend, this ain't Georgia. California's got a ten-day waiting period for handguns. I know, I know. The flipping gestapo in this damn state wants the gangs and thugs to have weapons, but not good citizens like yourself. Really burns my butt."

"That's not soon enough," I grumbled.

"You're darn tootin' it's not soon enough, but those liberal, gestapo, tree-hugging, fascist—" The tangled, Limbaugh-soaked logic poured forth from the flapping lips of Dale Connolly.

Politics aside, gun control was throwing a serious wrench into my plans for self-protection.

Dale Connolly ended with "Wish I was in Georgia sometimes."

Me, too, I thought. I looked longingly at the Sig Sauer. "Cancel the order."

Dale Connolly shrugged, silently acknowledging those tree tugging fools who stripped us of our rights to mow down our enemies. I said, "And get me one box—no, two boxes—of the .357 Magnums."

He went to the case behind him and removed two boxes of ammunition, placed them on the counter in front of me. He kept his bloodshot eyes fixed on me. "Don't do nothing stupid, Doc. They got real penalties in this state for firearms violations."

"For my mother," I said, handing over my credit card and scooping up the shells. "She's got a helluva raccoon problem."

25

THE DRIVE TO MURPH'S TOOK almost an hour, twice as long as it should have, as I shucked and jived my way south, trying to lose anyone who did not want to be lost, someone I couldn't even see. Driving like this was becoming a pain in the ass, as well as a pain in the wallet, considering gasoline prices.

Strange how an hour before, I was ready to give it all up, to throw up my hands because the next steps were so obscure and hidden. Be careful what you wish for, right? Now, whatever it was had come to me. And I wanted to be ready for it.

At Laurel Road, I pulled up the long drive half expecting to see the area still choked with emergency vehicles. Fortunately, the place was deserted. The cops had left only fluttering crime-scene tape.

At the front door, I glanced at the notice threatening jail for a very long time if I entered the house. I reached through the lattice of yellow tape to find the door, predictably, locked. That would have been too easy.

I spent the next few minutes pawing around the front stoop, under the doormat, under the potted plants, on top of the beams that ran under the awning. No luck. I stepped off the porch, hunched down, and made my way through the dirt and rocks of the garden that bordered the house. The last thing I wanted to do was break through a window, but I was in serious violation of some law here and would be in violation of another soon enough; broken glass would just be icing.

As it happened, I didn't have to smash a window. Next to some succulent-type bush, I found a little plaster rabbit. On its underside was a small door that pivoted to reveal a key. I took the key, replaced the rabbit, and unlocked the front door.

Squeezing through the yellow tape, I stepped into the house. It was too quiet, like a morgue. My dress shoes—I was still in my interview uniform—made a racket on the floor. All I needed now was the ghost of Paul Murphy to come lumbering at me like Hamlet's dad, spouting something about spilt blood. I would have wet myself, then told him I was working on the revenge thing.

On the way down the hall, I passed by Drew's, the boy's, bedroom. The mattress was gone and the room smelled of cleaning fluids. Barry Bonds was still there, looking up toward the ceiling for his homer. How scared do you get, I wonder, if you're five years old and a man puts a knife to your throat? How frightened are you when you realize your parents were mistaken all along and the monsters are real?

I pushed the sight of the dead kids out of my head, and kept walking to Murph's bedroom. The scene had been cleaned up, not too well, I noticed. There was still blood caked in the cracks between the floorboards. The bed had been stripped, and brownish stains marred the fabric of the mattress.

And the goddamned images would not leave me alone: the tongue on the floor, the ears next to it. The dead wife loosing her last breath . . .

My phone rang and I jumped.

Okay, so I wouldn't need a ghost to make me wet myself.

"We need to talk," Brooke said.

"I can't right now," I said.

"Not now. Later. What are you doing?"

At that point, what I was doing was walking over to the wardrobe, examining it. Heavy dark wood. Chinese designs all over it. About seven feet tall, I guessed.

Suddenly, I remembered Brooke's reproach about growing up and felt irritation fill me like a hot liquid. "I'm kicking around in the sandbox," I said. "That's what children do."

"I'm sorry about that comment."

The hot feeling passed. "You were angry," I said.

I ran my hand along the wood of the wardrobe, opened the doors. It was filled with pressed dress shirts that would likely never be worn again.

"I was angry. I still am. But more than that, I'm worried," Brooke said. "I'm very worried about you, Nate."

I looked at the bottom of the wardrobe, a few pairs of shoes in it. One was the pair that Murph had worn in the café, on the first day I'd seen him in ten years.

"There's nothing to be worried about," I lied.

"Nate, whatever you're doing, please stop. You're all caught up in revenging Paul. You're losing your head over it. We'll talk and—"

"I miss you. I'll call when I can." I pulled the phone from my cheek and held the End button until the power went off. I looked at the dead phone for a moment.

"Damn it," I said, and left the bedroom. I walked down the hallway, past the kids' bedrooms, to the front door. I stopped there.

Brooke was right. This was the time to get off the merry-go-round. That's what the jerk in the parking lot was telling me, wasn't it? *Get out now, Doc, while you still can suck a breath. Get out now and make sure you and yourn are safe. Protect the womenfolk. Save your ass.* The logic seemed irrefutable.

But what, then, did that make me? How did you go about your life—getting a job, getting hitched, tending your garden, tending your flock—knowing that you let the ball drop for a guy who, even then, was reaching a hand down from his celestial haunt to clasp your shoulder and remind you what a strident twit you'd been for most of the past decade?

"Damn it," I said again.

And what did that mean for "the really bad stuff" that Murph was caught up in? I'd spent much of my life trying to help people. Maybe I didn't care too much about people, as Brooke insisted, but I sure as hell tried to help them. And I didn't for one moment believe that "the really bad stuff" stopped with Paul Murphy.

And, importantly, I didn't believe it started with him. He'd been trying to do the right thing, I knew that in my bones. And somehow that killed him. I could not turn away from this.

In the end, you do what you have to do.

I don't know how long I stood at the door to Paul Murphy's house, having it out with myself. In the end, though, I won. I also lost. Put that in your philosophical pipe and smoke it.

I walked back to the bedroom.

To get to the top of the wardrobe, I found a chair and pulled it across the room. It was a sturdy thing, the same one, in fact, in which Murph was murdered. I could see the gouged wood and scratches where the handcuffs had torn off the finish. *Revenge,* Brooke had said. Bad word. *Justice.* Better.

Climbing onto the chair, I slid my hand over the top of the wardrobe, collecting a colony of dust bunnies on my palm. Then I hit something metal, flat. The key. Murph was right, no way a kid would be able to climb up here.

Key in hand, I went to the nightstand with the door in it. A Thomas Friedman book sat on the top, the cover flap sunk somewhere in its middle, marking the last page Murph ever read. I opened the book, read a few sentences about the need to bolster the sciences, and felt sadness wash over me. We'd once had a scientist in Paul Murphy. All that brainpower, all those years of training, all that determination to improve people's lives, had drained out and coagulated on the floor.

Inside the nightstand were a few books sandwiched next to a metal box.

There, I found what I was looking for: the gun case for

Murph's recently purchased .357. There, too, was a manila envelope and a box of ammunition. Strange. But first things first. I opened the pistol case and took out the Distinguished Combat Magnum, looking something other than distinguished. I spun the cylinder. The gun was loaded, ready to use. But that night, the key had been too far away, or Murph had been too slow, or any number of things.

The gun went back into its case. Now, to the envelope, which I expected to contain warranty and liability information for the weapon. It did not.

Ho-ly shit.

26

INSIDE WERE TEN COLOR PICTURES, close-ups of faces. Eight female, two male. The pictures, to put it mildly, were grotesque.

Holding them by their edges so as not to clutter them with my prints, I spread the photos across the bare mattress.

With the glossies fanned out in front of me, I stared, sickened, trying desperately to see the human features beneath the explosions of flesh that marred these faces. There were tumors—or what looked like tumors—everywhere, so that each face looked like a grisly latex mask. One woman had eruptions through her face, as if a hundred spiders had laid a hundred egg sacks under the skin. A golf-ball mass of flesh near her right eye had begun to ulcerate, leaving a red, glistening crater. What looked like a stick of melting butter sludged over her cheek.

Another woman had a lime-sized tumor at her nasolabial fold, the crease between the side of the nose and the corner of the mouth which is euphemistically called a "smile line." The tumor lifted the flesh of her left upper lip, splitting the skin and twisting her mouth into a sneer.

In another, a man's eyes were pushed shut by cauliflower masses on both lids. Another woman had actually lost an eye; the tumor seemed to have invaded the orbit and eroded into the sclera. And another, and another, and another. Ten, all together.

Something slammed.

Quickly, I slid the pictures back into the envelope. Doing so, I noticed a small jump drive in the bottom. I fished it out, stuck it into my pocket. Then I shoved the envelope into my pants. The gun? Loaded, good. I stuck that in the small of my back, under my belt, under the jacket. I pulled my belt tight, jamming the metal deep into my sacrum.

I closed the empty pistol case, shoved it into the nightstand. The key went into my pocket.

Feeling like I was about to spill weapons and photos out the legs of my pants, I walked to one of the kids' rooms, pushed the curtain aside, and peered out toward the driveway. No Navigator. No machine-gun–toting, shades-wearing refugee from a John Woo film. Just a sandy-haired white man and a brunette woman, looking confused and a little worried, speaking to each other, scanning the area, fixing on my car.

I recognized the couple from the funeral.

I walked to the living room and to the opened front door.

"Hi," I said, standing behind the yellow tape. The couple practically jumped out of their skins. "Bill, right? Paul's brother?"

"Who are you?" he asked warily.

Just your friendly neighborhood home invader, I thought. I said, "Nate McCormick. I'm a friend of Paul's. We didn't meet at the funeral, but I saw you there."

The couple looked at each other. "Why are you here?" Bill seemed to relax a bit into his mesomorph frame. His wife stepped behind him slightly, eyes narrowing at me.

"Paul gave me a key," I said, pointedly not answering the question.

"Yeah," he said. "I think I recognize you. This is Tina." His resemblance to Murph was striking. Both were big, both had those oversized hands, the stubborn jaw. Bill, however, was a little more stick-in-the-mud than his brother. Razor-cut hair parted to the side, glasses, a trimmed beard. He wore pleated khakis and a blue oxford shirt under a sweater vest.

"Honey," Tina said urgently, "the police should know."

Bitch.

Bill Murphy took a second, then said, "Mr. McCormick, I'm going to have to call the police."

The gun in my back was killing me. If I'd been a bloodthirsty lunatic, I could have used it to waste the couple. Couldn't they see I was a good guy?

"Fine," I agreed. "Please do."

And you know what? The bastard did. He spoke softly into the phone.

I tried to crawl between the police tape, got tangled up in it. "Damn it," I said, ripping plastic.

"Whoa, whoa," Bill Murphy warned. "Just stay there."

"I'm just going to sit here on the porch. You don't want me running around inside, right?"

He looked dumbfounded for a second, which I took to mean he didn't mind if I sat. I tore through the rest of the tape.

As I took my seat on the flagstone steps, the gun's cylinder shifted and dug out a couple pounds of flesh from my back.

After too many minutes waiting for the cavalry to arrive, I decided to try to break the ice. "Where are you from?" I asked. Tina was in the car by that time; I could hear the local NPR station pumping from the speakers.

"Wisconsin," Bill Murphy said. "How do you know Paul?"

"We went to school together."

"College?"

"Grad school." That seemed to satisfy him a little.

Birds twittered in the background.

"Sorry about calling the police." He shrugged. "But, you know . . . With everything that happened . . ."

"No problem," I said as I pictured what life would be like sleeping in a urine-drenched holding tank, trying to keep some doped-up hulk from taking my virginity.

"Why'd you come here?" Bill asked.

"I was the one who found Paul and the family that night."

"Oh, right. That's you." He turned that over for a second. "So why are you here now?"

"Paul left something for me."

"What?"

I didn't see any reason not to tell him; I was in deep enough shit as it was. "I'll show you."

I stood. "I'll come up there," he said hastily. He walked toward the porch, placing his body between me and the woman in the car.

I reached into my pants and pulled out the envelope, held up the photos. Let Bill see the freak show.

"Holy Lord Jesus," he said, eyes on the photographs, and crossed himself. Was this guy for real? "What is this?"

"I was hoping you might know."

"Of course I don't! Why'd he want you to have this?"

"He wanted me to help out with something. He was worried about it. Murph—Paul—ever say anything to you?"

"No. He never—"

At that moment, a car raced into the driveway, dashboard light flashing, and screeched to a dramatic stop. A woman sprang from the driver's side. Detective Bonita Sanchez. Wonderful.

"Well, hello. Hel-lo, Dr. McCormick. What on God's green earth are you doing here?"

"Hunting for chanterelles. This is the season—"

"It's not the season," Bonita Sanchez snapped. "You are damned lucky Mr. Murphy called me and not 911. And you're damned lucky I was coming here to meet him. Your lily ass would have been in jail, Doctor, quicker than you can say 'chanterelle.'"

Bill Murphy looked horrified. "You know each other?" he asked.

"Dr. McCormick was first on the scene." Sanchez

pointed at the open door. "You see that sign, Doctor? You see all that tape? You go in there?"

"I did."

"Well, it is not a goddamned welcome mat." Bill Murphy winced, probably at the profanity; she ignored him. "This is still a crime scene. You broke the law."

"I know," I said. If she frisked me, I was sure I'd find out how severe were the firearms violations Dale Connolly had warned about.

"I'm going to have to take you in, Doctor. I'm going to have to take you down to the station and— What's that?" She gestured at the pictures in my hand.

"From inside," I said.

She swore softly, then turned. "Mr. Murphy, would you give me a minute alone with Dr. McCormick?"

"Sure." He sounded relieved that he was about to escape the blasphemy and any attendant lightning bolts that would surely follow. He walked back to his car, his wife, his NPR.

"Dr. McCormick. You screwed up here."

"I know."

"I should take you to jail."

"Uh, I don't know about that."

Her eyes shot toward me, then to the pictures. She pulled a pair of latex gloves from her pocket, snapped them on, then took the glossies from me.

"Mother. Of. God. What are these? Where did you find them?"

The gun dug painfully into my back. I grabbed my belt and hoisted it. Repositioning helped the cylinder slip down a few centimeters. The grip snagged on my belt. I pushed out my gut to tighten everything.

"Inside. In the master bedroom."

"We processed that room."

"Not well enough, I guess."

"Try not to be a pain in the ass, just for once, okay? How did you know about these?"

"Paul told me."

"And I suppose you have a real good reason why you didn't tell us about them?"

I didn't, so I kept quiet.

"We're the police, Dr. McCormick. We conduct *investigations.* We collect what's called *evidence.* These are evidence. You are not police. You have no business breaking and entering. You have no business getting your greasy-ass fingerprints all over our evidence."

"I was careful."

She batted me on the chest with the back of her hand.

"Police brutality," I said.

"I'll show you brutality. I will show you brutality, Doctor. Ugh. These are disgusting." She shuddered.

27

IN THE COROLLA, THE FIRST thing I did was to pull the gun out of my ass and stick it under the seat. The second thing I did was to freak out.

Ten people, their faces blasted with what looked like tumors.

Please don't let this be big, I prayed. *Not here, not now.* Two years at CDC had taught me to dread the early signals: the reports of a few suspicious deaths in Angola, the word that a few women in Baltimore were coughing blood, the sketchy information that portends death and misery or portends nothing. *Dread.* The perfect word for it.

The subjects had all been older, forties through sixties. All were Asian, and all were in street clothes, not hospital gowns. There were no identifiers anywhere on the images.

No idea who these people were, where they were, what was destroying their faces. Ten of these people scattered across the world was not a big deal. Ten of these people in the Bay Area would be. The former was a collection of case reports, rare cancers or infections, the one-in-ten-million type things. The latter was an outbreak, a cluster, a real problem.

Damn it, I thought. Damn. It.

I followed Bonita Sanchez's car to the forensics lab for San Mateo County, where she had agreed to make copies of the pictures for me. I told her to contact San Mateo Public Health immediately about the images. As to what I was going to do with them, I left that undefined, vaguely referencing my deep contacts with local and state departments of health.

An outbreak on top of Murph's murder? Things just kept getting worse and worse, didn't they?

I put my eyes on Sanchez's blue sedan, then, to calm myself down, I began to flex the old diagnostic muscles. What did we have so far? Pictures of ten different people with what looked like tumors all over their faces. It didn't look infectious—no frank pus, no large swaths of red, inflamed skin.

Not infectious, not an outbreak. A cluster perhaps, but not an outbreak. Good so far.

What could have caused this? Could be a genetic problem, say, something like neurofibromatosis. Possible. But these people were older; a genetic problem would have shown up much earlier in their lives. So why, then, no pictures of children? Could be autoimmune, but which one? Discoid lupus? No. Polyarteritis nodosum? No. I tabbed through the autoimmune problems I knew but could not think of a match. I couldn't think of any autoimmune problem that would produce what I'd seen.

If I hadn't seen the blue municipal signs, I would have thought we'd arrived at the headquarters of a tech company rather than the San Mateo forensics labs. The low steel exoskeleton of the building supported a carapace of solar cells on the roof. The architects had made sure the lab integrated well into the rolling hills and amber grass. The complex didn't sit on the environment as much as sprouted from it. The interior looked as if it had been plucked from a catalog.

"We need to process these." Detective Sanchez flicked a finger at the pictures, now encased in an amnion of plastic. "And we need to get one thing straight."

"Sure."

"This ain't no two-way street anymore, Doc. I give you these, you tell me whatever you and your public health buddies find. It's one-way from now on: you to me. Understood?"

That didn't sound fair, but I nodded anyway. Sanchez

gave me a hard look, then left me sitting in a single chair pushed against the receptionist's desk.

I waited for two hours while the forensics folks took digitals of the pictures to give to me. The wait gave me time to feel guilty about the jump drive I'd dropped into my pocket—and which I'd failed to mention to Detective Sanchez. But my "greasy-ass prints" were all over it now, and I didn't think the geniuses here would pull anything useful from its surface. That's what I told myself, anyway.

I forced myself to think about the subjects of the photos.

Not an autoimmune disease. Definitely not. More likely tumors. Neoplasms. Could be a collection of cases of naturally occurring cancer, and not actually a cluster. Histiofibrosarcoma. Dermatomyofibrosarcoma. Extensive basal cell carcinoma. But why would Murph have collected the photos of a bunch of folks with cancer? He was working on cancer, sure, but why pictures of something so rare I'd never seen anything like it?

There was only one thing I was sure of at that point: the images had to be part of Murph's "really bad stuff."

Which meant what was on the jump drive had to be part of it, too.

A good citizen would have handed the drive over to Sanchez and been done with it. But breaking into the house of a dead man and stealing evidence did not a good citizen make. Or so I was rationalizing when a middle-aged guy with a Van Dyke goatee shuffled into the reception area. "You Dr. McCormick?" He carried a large envelope.

I told him I was.

"These are for you."

I took the envelope and thanked him.

"What's wrong with those people?" he asked.

"I don't know," I said. But one thing I did know: I'd finally found myself a job.

28

BACK IN THE COROLLA, I groped under the seat to make sure the gun was there, that it hadn't gotten up and walked off. The gadget was a weird introduction into my life, both empowering and disturbing. Like taking on a mistress, I suppose.

I turned on the cell phone, which chirped merrily to let me know some messages were waiting. It irritated me, and I thought about using my new gadget to blast the old gadget to pieces.

From the back of the car, I got my laptop, popped in Murphy's jump drive. After the computer scanned for viruses, a folder appeared on the desktop. Surprisingly, it was called "NateMcCormick." I double-clicked it and revealed another folder: "DorothyZhang."

In the second folder, I found ten image files. They were labeled "Pt 1," "Pt 2," etc. I opened "Pt 1." A picture of a disfigured woman. I selected and opened the nine other images. All disfigured individuals. All different. All familiar.

I pulled the copies given to me by the forensic tech from their envelope. The pictures in my hands matched the pictures on the screen perfectly.

So, Murph was worried about this disease, whatever it was, which is why he wanted to contact someone in public health. Not someone. Me. And I was now connected to someone named Dorothy Zhang. Whether or not she was one of the women in the pictures, I didn't know.

After copying the images from the jump drive to my computer, I dropped it into the manila envelope. I found a piece of scrap paper and wrote *From Paul Murphy. Forgot to give to you*—and dropped that inside.

Back in the building, I handed the envelope to the receptionist, feeling dirty for keeping the drive from Sanchez but elated that now, finally, I had a name.

But that name meant nothing to me. Who the hell was Dorothy Zhang?

29

THE MESSAGES ON THE CELL phone—three of them—were from Brooke. No matter that we weren't really that involved anymore, we were still, well, involved. Anyway, all of the messages were short and their tone progressed something like this: First, worried. Second, worried and annoyed. Third, royally PO'd.

Because I am an honorable man and because I cared for her, I called Brooke.

"I'm sorry I turned off the phone."

Silence.

"I was in the middle of something and . . . well, I couldn't talk."

Silence.

"Brooke, come on. Say something."

She said nothing.

I continued, "I was at Paul Murphy's house . . . I found some pictures. Eight women, two men. Horrible pictures, actually." I waited for any flicker of curiosity from her, got none. "Have you guys had any reports of disfigurement at the Department of Health? It looks like basal cell carcinoma, but it's everywhere over the face. Maybe like a really bad case of neurofibromatosis. Best guess is that it's a neoplasm. Brooke?"

Again, I waited, but she said nothing.

"Tumors. Faces."

Silence.

"They could be isolated cases, and all of the individuals are Asian, so maybe it's something that cropped up over there. But I think they have to be connected somehow, or Murph wouldn't have gathered them together . . .

"God, this is wonderful," I prattled on. "Just like talking to a shrink . . . You know, when I was eleven, my cousin and I went out to the barn. She made me show my stuff, then she showed me her stuff. I think it scarred me for life . . . Sometimes I think I'm secretly a woman trapped in a goat's body trapped in a man's body."

If that didn't get her, nothing would.

It didn't get her. She broke the connection.

30

I CALLED DIRECTORY ASSISTANCE AND got the number and address for a gun shop in Redwood City. There, I bought a shoulder holster from a guy who must have purchased his clothes and his politics from the same place as Dale Connolly, up at Mid-Peninsula.

"You have any trouble getting your concealed license?" he asked.

"Not a bit," I assured him.

"Good. Sometimes the police can be Nazis about these things," he said, and I tried not to let myself start stereotyping gun shop owners. I also tried not to get freaked about the growing list of firearms laws I was violating. Concealed weapons license? Who knew?

Back at the university, I slid the Corolla into an open parking spot near the library and cracked the windows. It wasn't boiling hot, but I didn't know the flashpoint of .357 shells. I didn't want to come back and find a gaggle of wounded, bleeding undergraduates encircling the car.

In the library, first thing I did was to grab a dermatology text and compare the pictures from Murph's with the images in the book. I double-checked basal cell carcinoma and neurofibromatosis to make sure my recollection of those two diseases was in line with what I told Brooke.

Well, I was in the ballpark. The pictures of basal cell carcinoma, or BCC, showed a few small tumors and a few monsters. The biggest ones—invading the eye socket, gnawing on the skull—had morphed into what the dermies called "rodent ulcers." As the cancer grows and outstrips its blood supply, the tissue dies and the tumor ulcerates. Someone thought it looked like a rodent had been chewing through the flesh. The name stuck.

Neurofibromatosis is a condition of tumors of the nerve sheath. Some of the more severe cases looked like what I'd seen in Murph's pictures—bumps everywhere. No ulcerations, though. What I saw was like a hybrid: basal cell carcinomaneurofibromatosis. There was no entry for that in the textbook's index.

I leafed through page after page of revolting imagery—mycosis fungoides, toxic epidermal necrosis, dermoid cysts, and any number of carbuncles and furuncles. After having my fill of pus, seepage, and scale, I closed the book and went back to pictures from Murph's place. I stared at this misery, one image after the other, hoping that something would pop.

And it did.

It was the site distribution of the lesions. Most of the folks seemed to have higher concentrations of lesions in certain areas: along the nasolabial fold, at the corners of the eyes, between the eyes. Conversely, some areas seemed spared: the neck, the ears. But the pattern didn't hold for all of them. And I didn't have full-body shots to know if the lesions were distributed elsewhere.

I walked to a computer, took a seat, and placed the pictures facedown on the table. Next to me sat a woman in scrubs and a white coat. She hadn't bothered to remove her cap or her shoe covers from the OR. Gross.

I felt her eyes bore into me.

"Well, isn't this a surprise?"

I turned, glanced quickly at the ID badge, then back up to the toothy smile. *No,* I thought, *no, no, no.*

"Hi, Jenna," I said.

"Nate . . . I can't believe . . . What are you *doing* here?"

"My wife blocked my Internet and I still have two weeks' subscription left on Tasty Teens."

She laughed. "That's funny." Then her tone turned grave: "Seriously?"

"No. I lied. The subscription is actually for Bestiality .com."

When you return to old haunts, you always run the risk of running into old ghosts. And I'd had the misfortune, a year before, of bumping into Jenna Nathanson, a former classmate and perennial pain in the ass. The woman seemed to be assigned to me somehow.

"So," I said, "you're on faculty, right? Neurosurgery?"

She pointed at her ID badge: *Assistant Professor, Neurosurgery.*

"Congratulations," I said.

"Congratulations to you. You're famous. That thing last year, what was it called?"

"Chimeragen."

"Right. Well, you sure cracked the case, to use a phrase from your line of work."

Cracked the case? Lord, deliver me.

"It's not something you want to be famous for. People died, Jenna."

"Oh, I know. I'm so sorry." She reached out and

touched my arm, and I felt my life force drain away. Maybe she really was a ghost. Or a vampire. "You dated that girl—"

"Alaine Chen."

"Right. In med school. I *knew* you two dated."

"Good memory."

"Well, it's par for the course. Don't let them fool you: half of neurosurgery is just remembering things."

I'd never been fooled, Jenna.

"So why are you back here?" she asked. "Another big investigation?"

Just then, her pager went off. My prayers had been answered.

"Darn, I have to get this, Nate. I'm sorry."

"Please do." *Please, please do.*

"Here." She popped a pen from her white coat and scribbled a number on a scrap of paper. "Page me when you get some time. I'd *love* to catch up."

And I wouldn't. I nodded and took the paper and watched Jenna as she scuttled across the library, those OR booties dragging along whatever brain material still clung to them. The screen on her computer was still up: a wedding rental page for a vineyard up in Napa. Price tag: thirty grand. I wondered who the unlucky guy was.

Back to more pleasant tasks—hunting down Dorothy Zhang, whose name was on the folder on Murph's jump drive. I began with an informational shotgun blast: Google. As you'd guess, there were thousands and thousands of references. Bingo.

From a two-year-old press release of the San Francisco Chinese-American Association:

> Native daughter Dorothy Zhang, an anchor for ABC-affiliate Channel 7 News, returned to her community yesterday as a judge for the Bay Area Miss Chinatown beauty pageant. Ms. Zhang, herself a winner of the pageant in 1988, said that the pageant was "a wonderful builder of self-confidence" and gave her the self-esteem to involve herself in broadcast journalism.

But she was no longer a broadcast journalist, according to a local news story.

> Dorothy Zhang, the striking co-anchor for Channel 7 Evening News, made the surprise announcement on the air yesterday that she would be taking an indefinite leave of absence from the station. "I need to spend more time with my son," she told viewers. "He's changing every day, and I feel I need to be there to see the changes. Though I love my job, I cannot sacrifice watching my son grow up."

The story was dated over four months before. Eight other stories said more or less the same thing.

Incidentally, I could see at least part of the reason for Dorothy Zhang's success: the woman was stunning. Sculpted face with high cheekbones, taut skin, almond eyes. Her most recent pictures were her best, a combination both of the youth she'd shown in her early photos and the maturity of someone who'd grown into full professional confidence. In a word, flawless.

I double-checked the picture of Dorothy Zhang on the computer against the pictures of Pt 1, Pt 2, and all the others. Since the flesh was so distorted, I concentrated on bone structure and facial dimensions. None seemed to match Zhang's picture.

After a half hour, the Google search was producing pretty picayune stuff—charity events and such—so I switched to LexisNexis to check out what the papers and magazines had to say. Two hours later, after my eyes had dried out and I felt disconnected from my body, I took a breather. By then, though, I had pieced together something of a biography for the "striking" Ms. Zhang.

She was born thirty-five years ago in San Francisco to parents who'd emigrated from southern China. Dad was a gift shop owner on Grant Avenue, mom stayed at home. One brother, a year older. She graduated from Galileo Senior High, went on to win the Bay Area Miss Chinese contest. Then to UC Berkeley, where she studied political science and Asian history. She spent a year working for an East Bay newspaper, then returned to Cal to their journalism school. Two more years working for newspapers in the area, before she broke into broadcast journalism as a reporter. From the look of it, her beat was just about everything. I found references to stories on real estate, political campaigns, snakeheads, and immigrant smuggling in Chinatown. Three years ago, Dorothy won the plum job of anchoring the weekend spot on Channel 7. A year later, she was warming the station's co-anchor's chair.

She married in grad school, an ear-nose-throat surgeon named Kendall Kim. They had a kid a year later. She divorced within two months of getting the anchor's job. Dr. Kim, a little research showed, fled to Chicago.

Dorothy Zhang's life was very publicly sprinkled through the web pages and databases; she even had a little fan club online. But something odd happened. Four months ago, after her announcement of a leave of absence, everything stopped. No charity events, no public appearances, no speeches. No mentions of death or trips to rehab. A few blogs wondered about her, but their interest only lasted for a couple weeks before even the most devoted Dorothy Zhang fans got tired and switched allegiance to another minor celeb.

The whole situation struck me as weird. And a little disturbing, too. How do you go from something to nothing? From the glare of TV lights to nonexistence?

And how was it that her name appeared in a folder with my name on it, on the storage device of a dead man?

31

I FLIPPED THROUGH THE PICTURES again, one after the other, struggling to make a diagnosis based on two dimensions and little else. By that time, I was liking some of the soft tissue cancers, the cancers of muscle and fibrous tissue. I was way out of my league on this, though. Cancer wasn't my thing.

CDC was the natural place to call. I still had friends there, believe it or not, and could get a relatively quick read on the images. But I could get a quicker read in California. And I could put out feelers to see if this was happening in my backyard. If Brooke wouldn't help, I knew someone who would.

On the Web, I found the number for the California Department of Health Services in the East Bay, and punched it into the phone. The operator patched me through.

"Ravinder Singh."

"Ravi. Nate McCormick."

There was a pause.

"Jesus Effing Christ, Dr. McCormick. You're calling me."

"I am, Dr. Singh."

"Your raggedy-ass car leave you stranded in Grand Junction, or did you make it out here?"

"I'm out here."

"And I bet you've been out here for two months now, and just finally got around to calling your old buddy."

"I've been busy, Ravi."

"Doing what?"

"You know, kicking ass, taking names."

"Man, that's exactly what *I'm* doing. Way to go, EIS alumni."

Ravi Singh had been one of my better friends at CDC. An EIS officer in my same year, he'd been with the National Center for Infectious Diseases, working on meningitis outbreaks in this country and in Benin. He was whip-smart, didn't wear a turban, and had enough energy to light a small city. In an informal poll at the end of our tenure, Ravi was voted "Most Likely to Stroke Out Before Forty." It didn't help that he never exercised, ate only saturated fats, and, until he got the word from our bosses, smoked like a dragon.

"Ravi, I got some questions—"

"And the answer is yes, I'm still single, so feel free to give me her number—"

"I have some real questions."

"This sounds serious." He cleared his throat. "Hit me. I got answers. I am the answer man."

"I have some pictures of women and—"

"Good, good. You finally discovered the power of the Internet. Hey, how's things working out with that fox you came out here for?"

"Fantastic. Everything's great. So I got these pictures and—"

"And when you saw the women, you became excited . . . I have to tell you, Nate, that's normal."

You can see the character of Ravi's and my relationship.

I tried again. "The pictures are of women *and* men, Ravi. Eight women, two men. They show severe tumor-like involvement of the face. I only have head and neck shots—"

"Okay, so now we're talking kimchi."

"We're talking kimchi."

"Okay. Tumors on the face."

"Some are just nodules, others look like frank tumors with involvement of the orbit, gums, and teeth. Some are ulcerated. Distribution generally follows the NLF, around the eyes—"

"I'm not a dermatologist, man."

"You have people there, though."

"Why didn't you call CDC?"

"I don't want some people there to know what I'm doing."

Ravi was silent a heartbeat, taking this in. "You going off the reservation?"

"I'm between jobs. Plus, I'm wondering if you guys picked up anything like this, if anything came over the transom from local docs or county health departments."

"Hold on. You're in luck. I sit right next to our in-house disgusting-skin maven." I heard the phone hit the desk and then Ravi, in a full voice, say: "Yo, Monica, you get wind of any reports of lumpy-bumpy things popping up on *faces*?" There was a pause, then Ravi said, "Not acne, tumors." Another pause, then he came back to the phone. "Hey, Nate, you sure they were tumors and not infectious?"

"I think they were tumors. Maybe with something like dioxin poisoning thrown in." Dioxin was the substance that purportedly caused the disfigurement of Viktor Yushchenko, the Ukrainian president, a few years back.

Ravi belted, "Tumors with some dioxin thrown in." A pause. "No?" He picked up the phone. "We haven't heard anything."

"Good."

"You think it's here?"

"If there was a cluster here, you guys would have picked it up. The pictures are . . . they're pretty dramatic."

"Yum. Send them."

"As soon as I'm off the phone."

"These pictures," Ravi said, "where'd they come from?"

"A friend."

"Ask him about 'em."

"I can't."

"Why not?"

"He's dead."

There was a silence on the phone, and immediately I

regretted what I'd said. Pictures of disease don't necessarily arouse suspicion. Pictures of disease from a dead man do. "What's going on here, McCormick?"

"I'll fill you in when I can. Right now, I just need this little favor. Some diagnostic help, a little surveillance."

Another lull in the conversation. Ravi, I assumed, had just realized the pros and cons of helping out his old pal. This was not a decision to be made lightly, and he knew it. As he said, I was off the res, and I hadn't gone quietly.

"Ah, McCormick. Skin stuff gives me the creeps. I always start itching when I hear about these things."

"That's the crabs, Ravi. Watch what you do with your free time."

He guffawed into the phone, and I was happy to have crossed back into chummy ball-busting. "Okay, keep us informed about tumor faces. And let's get beer. I can't believe you didn't call before you needed something from me. It hurts, McCormick. It hurts."

I hung up the phone, went back into the library to e-mail the pictures to Ravi and make him itch. Then I got into the car and drove north, to try and make someone sweat.

32

THE DRIVE TO TETRA SHOULD have taken me forty minutes, but took over an hour. Wanting to avoid any run-ins with a dragon-necked thug from central casting, I was more careful in my journey this time: parking lots were cut through, red lights run, double-backs doubled back.

Alex Rodriguez stood at the far end of the lot at Tetra. I pulled up in front of her and popped open the passenger-side door.

"I can spare about fifteen—"

"Get in," I said.

She didn't move.

"Get in," I repeated. "I don't want anyone to see us together."

Something crossed her face I couldn't read. I softened my voice. "Trust me, Alex. Just get in."

After a beat, she did.

I tossed the envelope of pictures in her lap, then left the lot. "Look at those. Tell me if they seem familiar."

"Oh my God," she said, unsheathing the photos. "Oh my God. What is this?"

"That's what I need to ask you. Paul left them for me."

"I have no idea, Nate."

"He didn't say anything about this to you?"

"Of course not." We stopped at a light and I leveled my eyes at her. "What? Oh, come on, Nate. I told you. We were just friends."

A car—a big black American behemoth—rolled to a stop behind us. "Friends," I repeated, keeping my eyes on the rearview now. There was no cross traffic, and I accelerated through the red light.

"What are you doing?" Alex yelped.

"Being paranoid. Nothing at Tetra like those?"

"These photos? Good Lord, no. What would make you think that?"

The black car hadn't followed.

"Murph got those pictures from somewhere."

"But not from Tetra. Slow down."

"Aren't they part of his cancer research?"

"No. Why would they be? He's a basic scientist—he *was* a basic scientist. He never even touched a patient. Besides, he was working on cancers of the gut, not this."

"Look at the pictures, Alex—" I careened onto the freeway, screeching the tires a little.

"I have been— Jesus! Are you trying to scare me with the driving?"

"I'm trying to scare you with the damned pictures," I answered. "Whatever this is is bad. I don't know what it is, I don't know where it is. All I know is that Paul wanted me to know about it."

"Which doesn't mean that Tetra had anything to do with it."

"Why are you so sure of that?"

"Because I've been asking around. The police have been asking around."

"You've been asking around?"

"Someone at your company is killed, you start poking around a little. At least I start to." I ripped past a semi and Alex gripped the seat. "Don't believe me, then. Go crawling around the company and my friendship with Paul. Waste your time if you want. Slow *down*!"

The sign for the next exit appeared, hanging over the center of the freeway, and I slanted us into the right lane, back toward Tetra. "Okay, Alex," I said, slowing the car. "Like you said, Tetra had nothing to do with this."

33

IN THE TETRA PARKING LOT, I dropped off one attractive woman and called another.

"Brooke, it's me," I said. "I checked Tetra to see if anyone there knew about the people with the tumors. They didn't." She gave no response. "I've got a bad feeling about this. These people look awful. Not the kind of stuff you recover from." Nothing. "You've got to be kidding me with the silent treatment." Brooke was not kidding with the silent treatment. "Okay, cupcake, I have a question for you: You ever heard of a newscaster named Dorothy Zhang? She fell off the radar a few months ago. Doesn't seem like there was any manhunt or anything, more like she just up and left." Nothing. "Can you use your contacts and see if anyone knows anything?" I waited for any sign of life. "And I don't want any questions." She didn't have any questions. "Good."

Quiet except for the muted conversation of a couple of passing physicians.

"If you want to meet me . . . If you want to talk about things, I'll be at the campus coffee shop in about an hour. I'll wait there for you. We should talk about things."

Brooke obviously didn't want to talk about things, since she said nothing.

"My aortic aneurysm just dissected. I'm bleeding out right now."

I couldn't even hear breathing. There was a good chance Brooke had set the phone on her desk and I was chattering away at a couple of paper clips.

"If I live, I'll call you from the hospital."

One of the many problems with cell phones is that you can't slam them down. But I hit the End button extra hard.

34

TEN YEARS AGO, WHEN I had that short-lived job at the place, the campus coffee shop was dark and cavelike, a strange venue to grab a cup of joe when the California sun glittered outside nine months out of the year. Now, however, it looked like even the CoHo wasn't immune from a sublethal marketing virus that had softened university hosts around the country. Colleges boasted fully outfitted "fitness complexes," "student centers" with big-screen TVs and plush couches, cafeterias with menus dreamed up by brand-name chefs. When I was an undergrad, we slept in mud huts and ate cockroaches. We studied by moonlight and wrote essays with blocks of charcoal. Really.

I grabbed a coffee and found a seat on a new but drink-dappled Scandinavian couch.

Wall hangings, a nice lamp or two. The biggest and most irritating change, though, was that they changed the name from Coffee House to CoHo. What had been affectionate slang for the place was now its official name, which made it *très* uncool. Kind of like when your parents start trying to speak your language, when they tell you to calm down and stop being so "hyphe." No quicker way to get you to stop using the word "hyphe" than for Dad to start dropping it into conversation around the dinner table.

Anyway, the place was still dank, thank God, still smelled of stale beer. You can give the girl a face-lift, pump Botox into her brow, but you can't change the bones. And the CoHo's bones were still there, underneath the new paint job and the art student scribblings on the walls. I was glad about it. But I wasn't glad about the painful memories it dredged up. And I definitely wasn't glad about the band, a foursome calling themselves "Organic Whine."

God, I am old, I thought, as the drummer began pounding out a cardiac rhythm. Best I could figure it, these guys were into acid jazz and tribal grooves.

Fifteen minutes later, my foot was tapping away to the music. So, maybe not that old, then, but did they have to be so *loud*?

An hour passed, and I shifted from coffee to beer. A bevy of young women sat at a table in front of me, in jeans so tight I worried for their circulation. One, a cute brunette in a revealing halter top, shot me a look, and I wondered if it wasn't too late to do a little more undergraduate work.

Organic Whine took a set break to suck beer; the pretty brunette split to go study, or pole dance, or whatever it is undergrads do these days. I'd been there nearly two hours. Brooke wasn't coming.

I'd decided to leave, go try to find the brunette and help her with her anatomy homework, when I saw a tall blonde walk into the joint. Conversation stopped, men gawked, and the band started to play "You've Lost That Loving Feeling." Actually, the conversation was in full swing, and the band was getting shit-faced in the corner. A few guys did look, though.

"Going back to your roots?" Brooke asked.

"Reliving my glory days."

"Isn't this where you punched that guy? Didn't you get thrown out of school for that?"

"Like I said, glory days. Beer?"

"I'm okay." She took a seat on the couch next to me.

"I'm happy to see you still speak."

"And I'm happy to see you still make incredibly insightful observations."

That was funny—so funny, in fact, I took a sip of the beer for clarity and courage. "We're not getting off on the right foot here."

"We're not getting off on any foot, are we? Why on earth did you want to meet here? There's a band, for God's sake."

I sighed.

Brooke said, "You know, I can't help but see this as just

another indication that part of you stopped developing around age nineteen. So, where are the pictures?"

The change to all-business-Brooke was disconcerting. I expected the anger; I didn't expect her to want to get down to brass tacks right away.

"You don't want to talk first?" I asked.

"Do you, Nate?" she challenged.

I took her in for a moment, then said, "You know what? I don't think now's the right time."

"Why am I not surprised?"

In silence, I pulled the laptop from my bag, roused it from sleep, and opened the image files. I handed it to Brooke. The screen illuminated her face a pale blue. A little twist of her lip was all the reaction she showed, the only thing that indicated she wasn't just looking at e-mail.

I reminded myself that this woman had been through all the courses and had seen all the slides that I had. She knew disease and morbidity and mortality. I reminded myself, too, that she despised me right now, and she was taking it out on me by being totally and irritatingly professional.

"You found these at Paul Murphy's?" she asked.

"Yes. They were in a file marked with my name. Dorothy Zhang's name was there, too."

"And you don't know where he got these or where these people are?"

"No. That's the problem."

"And you don't know what it is, either."

"That's the other problem."

"You have a lot of problems, Nate."

"Yes, I do." I took the computer back from her. "Ravi Singh knows about this. He's helping out."

"You just pull everybody in on the adventure, don't you?"

"What's that supposed to mean?"

She didn't even look up at me, just produced a folder from her shoulder bag. She began leafing through the pages inside it. "I pulled some cases we had matching anything like what you described over the phone. Some basal cell carcinoma, neurofibromatosis, other things. This is *not* BCC or NF, Nate."

I let the jab at my diagnostic abilities slide.

"None of those match, except—" She flipped through a few more pages, then stopped. She took out a sheaf of three pages, stapled together, and handed it to me. On each page was a color printout of the same woman's face—one a frontal view, the other two in profile. Nodules, ulcerations. A battlescape across her flesh.

"This is it," I said. I held Brooke's pictures up to the computer screen and toggled through the images. Though I couldn't be sure, one seemed to fit.

"We have a match, I think," I said. "Who is this? Dorothy Zhang?"

"It's not her."

"Then who is it?" Brooke didn't answer and didn't meet my eyes. "*Where* is she, Brooke?"

"I work in Santa Clara. That should tell you something."

"Where *exactly* is she?"

Brooke looked back to me, then shook her head. "HIPAA."

I was incredulous. HIPAA was the privacy law governing health care information. Generally, it made life hell for doctors trying to find out anything about any patient.

HIPAA was supposed to give patients control over their medical information, but it's become so burdensome, it's begun to affect care. Good intentions paving the road to hell and all that. But HIPAA didn't apply to public health investigations. Problem was, I wasn't public health anymore.

"What's this about, Brooke?"

"I am not your sidekick here. Not this time."

"I'm not asking you to be my sidekick."

"Right. 'Find out if there are any cases, find out what you know about Dorothy Zhang,'" she was mimicking me. "I found you a case, Nate. She's not Dorothy Zhang. But you'll have to go through the proper channels to get more information on her." What Brooke left unsaid was that there would be no proper channels open to me. Not to a guy without a job. Not to a guy with a hunch and a mission and little else.

"Just tell me where she is, Brooke. I need to make sure we're not dealing with a cluster here."

"Don't lie to me. It's because you think it might help you find out what happened to Paul."

The band was staggering over to the stage, the drummer crawling behind his trap set with a pint glass in hand. I was silent.

Brooke leaned forward. Two feet between us, but she might as well have been shouting across a canyon. "I fell in love with you, Nate. I fell hard. I fell in love with the guy who I'd see two weekends a month, who I could talk for hours with on the telephone. The guy who I cried for hours over when he went to Angola. The guy who used to be fun, who used to be in love with me—"

"There's more to it now. These people."

"And what does that mean? So maybe we know where *one* of these people is, that's it. And maybe she's sick. That doesn't make a cluster, Nate. It doesn't make it anything more than normal, tragic life. A weird cancer that popped up in one case in California. Paul Murphy somehow found this person. We found her."

I looked at the pages, looked back to Brooke. "Where is she?"

"This is *not* a cluster. Be realistic." Brooke put her hand on my knee. "Something like this would rise to the surface if it was anything more than a sporadic case."

"It's not a reportable condition." Some infectious diseases—meningitis, TB, rabies, syphilis, AIDS—must, by law, be reported to health departments. Facial tumors is not one of them.

"But it's dramatic, Nate. Public health would know about something so dramatic. Your friend probably collected cases from all over the world. It was his pet proj—"

"Brooke, *where is she*?"

She leaned back abruptly, her hand sliding limply off my leg. The drummer had started to beat the skins. A bass guitar joined a few bars later.

"You're making a choice, you know that." I could hardly hear her over the music. "If you ask for this again, I'll tell you. But after that, I will not help you, Nate. And I don't want to see you again or hear from you. I'll store your things if you want. But until this is resolved, I want you out of my life."

Her hands came quickly to the side of my head, pulled it close to hers. Her words were urgent. "Nate, I'm asking you to let the police deal with this. Let public health deal with it. Ravi knows now, let him do it. Please. For me."

The music was picking up steam now. The guitar chimed in, broken chords from a musician too drunk to find his groove.

My hands went to Brooke's; I laced my fingers in hers, held them. Then, gently, I asked, "Where is she?"

35

THE NEXT MORNING STARTED WITH the electric shriek of a cheap digital clock sitting on a cheap nightstand in the cheap motel in which I'd found refuge. Clouds hung low in the sky above the South Bay town of Milpitas. They would burn off by afternoon, the weather in this part of California in September being about as variable as the Earth rotating on its axis. What I wouldn't give for a surprise hailstorm once in a while.

Then again, I guess I'd been hit by one last night in the coffee shop. Be careful what you wish for.

Brooke had given me the address of the house before which I now stood: a three- or four-bedroom with a stone skirt and beige vinyl siding. Sprinklers tittered over the tidy lawn and wet the fender of an older-model Mercedes sedan in the drive.

It was six-thirty a.m. Not wanting to lose any advantage, I hadn't called ahead. I unsheathed my laptop, stuck it under my arm with the photos Brooke had given me, and walked to the house.

The curtains were drawn. I paused before ringing the bell, tried to set my priorities straight. *This is important,* I told myself. *A possible health nightmare. A key to a family's murder. Brooke is wrong. This is important.*

My finger went to the bell. The door opened within seconds.

The crack between door and jamb revealed a girl, sixteen maybe. Her hair was wet and hung in long, dark tendrils.

I introduced myself. I asked, "This is the Yang residence, correct?"

Quietly, she said, "Yes."

"Could I speak with Cynthia Yang? Is she your mother?"

A man shouted in the background, his voice loud and angry. The girl studied me for a moment, then slammed the door in my face.

Stunned, I stood there for a moment. I rang the bell again. And again.

The door opened a crack. An Asian man, no taller than the girl, now stood behind the door. His left hand rested on the jamb; I could not see his right.

"What do you want?"

I leaned back to show I meant no threat. "I'm Dr. Nathaniel McCormick. I work with the health department in Santa Clara." I was doing my best not to lie, to avoid the phrase "work *for.*" "I need to speak to Cynthia Yang," I said.

If he was surprised to see me, his face didn't show it. "You can't speak to her."

"Are you her husband?"

"Yes."

"I need to speak with her."

"You cannot speak to her. Please now. Thank you."

The door started to close. I put my free hand on the wood to stop it. Fear lanced across his face.

"Mr. Yang, I'm worried your wife may be very sick."

"You go now." He was almost pleading, pushing the door against my resistance. I stuck my foot at its base and fumbled through my jacket pocket, doing my best not to drop the damned computer.

"I'm with the Centers for Disease Control. The federal government." I got hold of my old plastic badge and flashed it. "I'm a doctor. I work with the health department here." I stood there, the invalid CDC ID dangling.

A year before, when I'd lost all my identification in the mayhem surrounding that Chimeragen thing, I was issued new papers, a new ID. When the old ones were discovered and returned to me, after the investigation, I had two sets. When I left CDC, I returned only the reissues. Lucky for me. Now I could commit a crime by impersonating a federal official.

"Mr. Yang, I really need to talk to your wife."

I felt the pressure on the door ease. "She dead. My wife dead," Yang said softly.

I lowered the badge. "I'm sorry."

The door opened a bit farther. Behind him, I could see the girl, standing stiff in the hallway. Her arms were crossed protectively over the chest of a younger boy who pressed against her. Their father looked back at them. Then he stepped outside.

In his right hand was a large kitchen knife.

* * *

"When did she die?" I asked. The two of us stood on the stoop, looking out over the waking neighborhood.

"Month ago."

I handed him the pages from Brooke, the ones showing the disfigured Cynthia Yang. "This is her? Your wife?"

Yang stared at the printouts. "Yes."

I opened the laptop, which came to life with the face of one of the women from Murph's jump drive. Yang looked at the screen, nodded. "We try to get pictures back, but Dr. Wu he say they already with the government."

I closed the laptop and took the pages back from Yang. "Dr. Wu was your primary care physician?"

"Yes."

"He did the right thing. Why did you want the pictures back?"

Mr. Yang looked at the knife still in his hand. He said nothing.

"Did you ever see him again?" I asked.

"We use Chinese medicine, not Dr. Wu."

"What were you told was wrong with her?"

Yang looked at me, not understanding.

"What was her sickness?"

"Cancer."

"How was it diagnosed? Did anyone take tissue? Cut out a little piece of Cynthia's skin?"

Yang shook his head.

"Where were the tumors located? On her face only? Or were they elsewhere on her body?"

"Face only."

"Do you know if your wife had any exposure—did she touch or come in contact with—any chemicals?"

Yang didn't answer.

"Did she have contact with anyone who was sick?"

He stared at me.

"When did her cancer start?"

"She in much pain, Doctor. She in so much pain."

He bent his head, and I knew the interview was over. I'd gotten what I would get. "I'm sorry for your loss," I said, then stepped to the sidewalk.

After a few paces, I turned back. One last question I needed to ask, but the words never got out of my throat. I could see the curtains drawn back slightly from a first-floor window, the teenage girl and her younger brother watching, their eyes wide with fear.

36

"YUCK! YUCK, YUCK, YUCK."

Ravinder Singh's voice nearly split the speaker on the cell. I braked hard to avoid smashing into a car in front of me and becoming another reason for delay in the San Jose morning rush.

"You got the files," I said.

"You are a sick, sick man, McCormick. You didn't get my e-mail?"

"Ravi, everything from you goes into the junk folder."

"Don't tell me I'm in there with the penis-enlargement spam . . ."

"Penis enlargement doesn't go in my junk folder." Enough of the small talk. "You got the pics . . ."

"Disgusting, man. I've showered four times in the last thirty minutes."

"Maybe that will help with the smell." Oh, boy, will the fun never end? "How's it going with diagnosis?"

"I put Monica on it. She loves skin."

"My kind of girl."

"My kind, too. Thirty-two, single, absolutely no interest in me. Anyway, we've narrowed it to a sarcoma or carcinoma."

"Cancer. Wow. I figured that out by myself."

"Beggars can't be choosers. Get me some tissue, I'll get you a diagnosis."

Tissue would be stellar, I thought. "Did you notice the distribution? Along the NLF, around the eyes?"

"No, but I'll put Monica on it. Anyway," Ravi said, "we got nothing on cases here. If the local health departments saw anything like this, they haven't punted it up to state. There's a chance they're just sitting on something, shelving it. Monica and I are going to call around, see if anything surfaces. But I got to tell you, man, this doesn't look like a communicable disease. The chances of it being reported to us are slim."

Ravi had hit on one of the problems here. Investigative public health is most concerned about infection—from HIV to TB to hepatitis to salmonella. What we were dealing with here really didn't look infectious. It was entirely possible that a dozen cases could have popped up over the Bay Area, and unless they came to the same hospital, the same service, the same doctor, it probably wouldn't cause alarm. Rare, one-off cancers find their way into journals as case reports; they don't find their way to public health.

"Ravi," I said slowly, "it's here. One case at least."

"You serious?"

"Milpitas, just north of San Jose. Died a month ago."

Ravi was quiet, thinking. "So we got one here. Doesn't mean it's a cluster."

"No. I got a feeling, though."

"Spider-sense is acting up again?"

"I have a gut on this one."

"Did your gut tell you to contact the coroner down there?"

"Gut said to have you do it. I don't have official status, remember?"

"What about your flame? She's there."

"She's busy," I said.

Ravi, picking up on something for once, let it drop. "I'll get back to you," he said.

37

I WAS DRESSED IN THE sort of official-casual I often used for field interviews: blue sport coat, khakis, blue shirt, no tie. And though I tended to gussy up a little more than my public health colleagues—most of them didn't go for the jacket—I definitely wasn't *GQ*. You want to look stand-up, but not too good. A public health doctor in the field is not the same as a private-practice cardiologist in his clinic. You don't want the public to get the wrong idea about how much it pays its employees, which, for the record, is peanuts compared to the private-practice guys. Besides, good clothes put distance between the average joe-on-the-street and an investigator. The goal is to minimize distance between you and the interviewee while still looking formal enough to engender some respect. In any case, all this costuming had been wasted on Mr. Yang; I would have gotten the same information from him if I'd been dressed in three-piece Brooks Brothers or one-piece leotard.

As I pulled the Corolla into a Denny's, I looked around the lot. Nothing out of the ordinary. No SUVs, no Caddies. Just the same, I reached under the passenger seat and pulled out the Smith & Wesson, then slid it back. If someone wanted to dust me at a Denny's, to scramble my brains with the Grand Slam, they could damn well be my guest. I should have eaten four hours ago. I was starving.

I went into the restaurant sans weaponry. The pancakes, eggs, and bacon went down without incident.

During coffee, my phone vibrated.

"Coroner in Santa Clara called it cancer NOS," Ravi reported. NOS meant Not Otherwise Specified. It meant the coroner hadn't biopsied anything. It meant they didn't know.

"Anything helpful?"

"They pulled the report for me, 'Extensive involvement of the face.' "

"Only the face?" I asked.

"Only the face."

"That's something. So now we can hope the pictures

are showing us the whole story and these people aren't lit up over the rest of their bodies."

"We can hope, sure. Anyway," Ravi said, "I'm still not convinced we have anything more than a rare case here. Probably just some weird sarcoma. Just one of those things."

"Just one of those things . . ." I let the sentence trail. "All right, Ravi. Keep an eye out for me."

"You got it, boss." He laughed. "I love this, McCormick. You owe me more and more each phone call. Hey, did you really have some ceremony with Hillary Schaffer last year?" Schaffer was the Director of CDC.

"Not by choice."

"Damn it, man. You lucked out with that Chimeragen thing. Lucked *out.*" He hung up.

Luck, I'm pretty sure, would be the last word I'd use to describe it.

There was something rotten in my gut, and I realized it was more than the grease I'd just ingested: that other thing, the feeling I'd told Ravi about. I focused on the sensation. Anxiety. Anxiety about what might be blossoming on the faces of people out there in the community. Anxiety that whatever and whoever had killed Murph might zero in on me.

I wanted to tell myself that I was losing it, that I was being irrational and paranoid. But I couldn't totally convince myself of it. We spend our lives worrying about the terrorist attack while we drive to and from our suburban home to our suburban job. We worry about the nuke sailing into San Francisco on a container ship. We worry about hurricanes and earthquakes. Low-level worry. Harder to deal with the threat of shadowy, threatening guys in vehicles with tinted windows.

I finished my coffee, signaled for the waitress to fill me up again. While I waited, I called directory assistance for Dorothy Zhang's number. Predictably, there was none. I asked for the number to Channel 7, the local ABC affiliate. Predictably, there was a listing.

I scrolled through the numbers on my phone, stopped on Brooke's, stared at it, and closed the phone.

As I paid my bill, I asked the girl at the register if they had a pay phone. She looked at me as if I had just spoken through my navel.

"You have a cell phone," she pointed out. "I saw you using it."

"That's true. But I'm calling my hit man, and I don't want them to trace the call."

She grimaced, bored, pointed to the sign that said "Restrooms."

Truth was, I really didn't want the call to be traced. No need to let some nosy news hack from Channel 7 finger me with caller ID. Truth also was that I'd forgotten you actually needed to pay for a pay phone, so I had to return to the helpful young lady at the register and get some change. I handed over four dollars.

"My hit man's in France," I informed her.

Back at the restrooms, I dropped an avalanche of coins into the phone, got through reception to the newsroom. Then I began to lie my ass off.

"Hi, uh, this is Bert McBrooke from McBrooke and Filbert," I said. "Is Dorothy Zhang available?"

"She doesn't work here anymore," the woman said. She sounded like she was twelve.

"Do you have her current contact information?"

"Hold on."

There was a click; I took advantage of the moment to pump a few more coins into the phone. No self-respecting partner from the esteemed law firm of McBrooke and Filbert would ever use a pay phone.

"This is Andy Thomas," a crisp male voice said.

"Bert McBrooke of McBrooke and Filbert, Mr. Thomas. I'm trying to get in contact with Dorothy Zhang."

"She's on leave from the station."

"I realize that, but I very much need to get in touch with her."

"We don't give out that information. What did you say your name was?"

"Bert McBrooke." The name was sounding more and more stupid each time I said it. "This regards a financial matter. I represent the estate of Jerry Bang"—*Jerry Bang?*—"who recently passed away. He was her . . . uncle . . . and left a substantial amount of money to Ms. Zhang."

"Why are you calling us?"

"Because her number is unlisted."

There was some silence as Andy Thomas weighed and reweighed. A voice came on, informing me I had one minute left for my call. I fumbled for more coins. "What was that?" Andy Thomas wanted to know.

"I'm driving to a meeting. I don't want to drop the call, Mr. Thomas."

"You said the name was Jerry Bang?"

"I've given you too much information already."

Sounding peeved that I didn't give him more of a scoop, he spoke brusquely. "We don't know how to get in touch with Dorothy. She didn't leave any forwarding information and I haven't seen or talked to her in months. If you want, I'll take your number and, if she calls, I'll let her know."

I gave him a fake number. He made me spell out McBrooke.

38

SO, DOROTHY ZHANG HAD DONE gone and dropped off the face of the planet. And her name was the strongest thread I had left at that point. All I could hope to do was yank, pull, and tease at it, hoping to unravel something I knew nothing about.

I was in the parking lot again, in my car. I felt more comfortable there. The gun was near me, the sight lines good. It was only eleven and I had a full set of bars on my cell phone. Things were going well.

Since I was going to be mostly honest on this one, I didn't care about my number showing when I put in a call to Lane, Battle & Sim, a law firm in San Francisco with an intimidating polyglot name, and asked for Daniel Zhang.

Dorothy and Daniel, I thought. Cute.

When he got on the phone, I introduced myself.

"What do you want?"

Okay, I thought, not cute, and I immediately disliked the guy. Hoping to appeal to his fascination with the morbid, or to his sympathy, I told him about a "worrisome development in public health," and about Murph's and his family's murders in Woodside.

"I heard about that. What's it got to do with me?" He had the disconnected tone of someone otherwise engrossed—reviewing depositions or editing a motion or another fascinating task—while talking to me.

"You're Dorothy Zhang's brother, right?" I asked.

He hung up the phone.

Touchy, touchy. But at least now I knew that Ms. Zhang, or at least Ms. Zhang's disappearance, was of some importance to her brother.

I sifted through my other contacts, found the number for Dorothy Zhang's mother, and dialed. After a couple of rings, I heard a female voice utter a staccato "Hello."

"Wei-Ching Zhang?"

"Yes?"

My introduction this time focused on doctor things, public health things. You know, "This is Dr. Nathaniel McCormick, I'm a public health physician"—I didn't tell her with whom—"I'm concerned about some public health activities"—I didn't say what—"that have some of us concerned." I asked if I could speak with her daughter.

A burst of Cantonese. Or Mandarin. I sure as hell couldn't tell the difference as the voice squawked out over the phone in a tumble of unfamiliar syllables, conveying either annoyance or confusion. Maybe Mrs. Zhang didn't speak English. Maybe her son had already called her and told her not to talk to me. Either way, I wasn't going to make any progress. Through the stream of words, I thanked her and hung up the phone.

So far, Nate McCormick: nil; forces of evil and confusion: more than nil.

Maybe not a total wash, though. Daniel Zhang's motor had clearly shifted into Drive, and he was beginning to move through his speed-dial, then his address book, warning whomever not to speak to a Dr. McCormick when he called asking questions about Dorothy. The whole situation started to bug me.

Anyway, it was still early in the day, which left more than enough time to head to the City by the Bay, to kick over rocks at the law offices of Lane, Battle & Sim.

39

THE EMBARCADERO IS SAN FRANCISCO'S answer to Wall Street, a clutch of tall buildings crammed with law firms, investment banks, management consultants. And, like downtown Manhattan, it's a cold space dominated by enormous complexes with inventive and creative names like "Embarcadero Center 1" and "Embarcadero Center 2." Besides the big, steely numbers stuck to the buildings' granite façades, the only thing that truly differentiated one from the other was first-floor retail, but even that looked like it was manufactured on the same assembly line that puts together malls and shopping centers around the country. The Embarcadero was the kind of place that died every night and every weekend, only to be resurrected again at eight a.m., Monday through Friday.

Lane, Battle & Sim was shoehorned into two floors in

Embarcadero Center 4. I got off on sixteen, and found out from the receptionist there that Danny Z. was one floor up. The very put-together thirty-something asked if Mr. Zhang was expecting me, and I assured her he was. She pointed to an internal staircase, told me to walk up the steps and she'd let Mr. Zhang know I was here.

The reception area in which I now found myself was armored with rosewood paneling, matched to the rosewood coffee table in front of me, the walnut-caned chairs, and the rosewood end table next to the couch on which I parked myself. For someone who spent a good deal of his life in labs and hospitals, the sheer amount of biomass that surrounded me was off-putting. We don't like wood in medicine. It's hard to clean, its porosity hides a lot of germs, and it's expensive. None of this seemed to concern the esquires.

I waited for a few minutes, got so bored I picked up the *Wall Street Journal* and read about rising interest rates, a falling dollar, a ballooning deficit, and any number of indicators that said the economy was getting the shakes. Thank God I didn't have any money; I might actually have been worried.

Twenty minutes later, I was deep into the editorial page of the *Journal,* passively absorbing the opinions of guys who thought the country had gone to shit with the New Deal. I needed to get out of here before I started writing my congressman to gut the commie FDA.

Five more minutes passed. Ten. The Denny's coffee continued to work its magic, and I'd soon need a bathroom.

I got out of the chair and started walking. At one of the cubicles I saw a woman on a computer, scrolling down through a long list of handbags. For the dedicated, it seemed, there was always a deal to be had on eBay. She clicked on a picture of a Marc Jacobs number, most recent bid at $325. I thought I heard her coo.

"Nice bag," I said.

Startled, the woman wheeled around.

"I'm here for Daniel Zhang," I said.

She answered with a glistening smile, the kind of smile that made men like me—men not used to the aggressive mating dance that takes place in the glammed-out corners of society—nervous. Guys I went to college with, guys who went to trade on Wall Street after graduation, would probably take that smile as the opening step in some combative *pas de deux,* one that ended hot and huffing in a broom closet on floor sixteen. Me? Well, I'm not proud of it, but I felt certain parts of my anatomy shrink.

"Who are you?" She uncurled her talons—bloodred from the young lawyers, copy boys, and whomever else she'd devoured in the past few days—and thrummed them against the desk. "You're not new here, are you?"

"No." I stuck out my chest a little to show that I wouldn't be intimidated, that I could play this game. "My name is Nate McCormick."

"Mr. Zhang's expecting you?" *Click, click, click* as the claws tapped across the desk.

"I've been waiting here for nearly an hour."

"Are you a lawyer?"

"I'm a doctor."

"Oh, really?" she asked with interest. "What kind of doctor?"

Before I could reply, I felt a presence behind me. I turned to see a guy about my height, about my weight, my age, head buried in a document. "Stacey," he said, "I need you to get in touch with Sam Veatch's office—" He looked up and saw me and stopped speaking.

"Mr. Zhang, this is Dr. McCormick. He says he's been waiting to see you."

His greeting had all the warmth of the lupine growl. Incidentally, I've heard that lawyers, like dogs, can smell fear. My deodorant, I hoped, was extra-strength. I said hello.

"Yeah," he said. He looked at Stacey. "I'll be back in five minutes." He cast his eyes back to me. "Follow me, please."

Stacey gave a little flutter of her fingers. "Bye, Dr. McCormick."

Daniel Zhang wore a jacket and tie, and I was reasonably sure his duds didn't come off the rack at the Gap like mine did. The cut hugged his wedge-shaped body, leading this disease detective to believe that Zhang spent his free time heaving weights around in some expensive gym. He threw his document down onto his desk, sat in the chair behind it, and indicated a chair across from him. I took it.

With my first good look at his face, I could see the resemblance to his sister. His bone structure was more prominent, giving him a predatory look. Good teeth. Perfect for a lawyer. Perfect for sinking deep into the flesh of a physician unfortunate enough to be on the wrong side of a malpractice suit. But the guys at Lane, Battle & Sim weren't into malpractice. Too small-potatoes. These guys were *corporate.*

Daniel Zhang leaned back in his nine-hundred-dollar chair and spread his hands. "What?"

I wasn't going to do well with such an open-ended question, so I parried with my own inquiry. "You're Dorothy Zhang's brother, correct?"

"Maybe we should begin by you telling me who you are."

"I told you. On the phone."

"Refresh me."

As I geared up for the refreshing, I keenly understood the liability of not having a job. Who was I? A doctor who wasn't working, who had no vocational peg? Who was I without a job? Basically, a guy with girl trouble, a citizen concerned about some wacko cancer running roughshod over people's faces, a man who was furious about his friend's death and foolhardily trying to "get to the bottom of things." None of this would impress the man across the desk from me.

So I fudged. "I'm a doctor with the Centers for Disease Control." Once a CDC doc, always a CDC doc, right? "I told you over the phone about the deaths of Paul Murphy and his family. I'm working with the investigation."

"Why is the CDC involved in a murder investigation?" Zhang took a long look at me. What he saw did not appear to thrill him. "You have identification?"

I fished in my pocket and pulled out the badge, handed it across the desk. I hoped he didn't look at the expiration date.

Zhang eyeballed the plastic, then handed it back to me. "I thought it was clear from our conversation this morning what I wanted our relationship to be."

"I'm not good at interpreting signals," I confessed.

"Well, that would seem to place you at a competitive disadvantage in a homicide investigation."

Touché. "I need to talk to your sister."

"What sister?"

I made a big deal of sighing, reached into my shoulder bag and took out a folder. I leafed through for one of the printouts I had, one mentioning Daniel and Dorothy, and slid it across the desk.

The lawyer looked at the page, looked up. "I don't know where she is."

"Your sister's name was given to me by a man whose whole family was murdered," I improvised. "Your sister may be in danger."

Zhang held my gaze and didn't blink. "Our family can take care of itself." He looked down at the documents on his desk. "I trust you can find the way out."

Unable to think of a way around his impassivity, I stood. "I found the way in."

"And I'd appreciate if you didn't contact me or my mother again. I don't want to have to call your superiors."

"Tattling is for those who can't take care of themselves. Right, Mr. Zhang?"

On the way out of the office, I passed by the terrible Stacey. Without looking up from the computer, she said, "Done so soon?"

I wanted to be out of there, before my civil rights were threatened or my bank account seized or my manhood devoured, but I also had to attend to certain biological imperatives.

"Can you tell me where the bathroom is?"

Stacey turned. She smiled in a way that sent me back to

age thirteen, quivery and unsure. Those nails flared again. "Around the corner. To your left."

At least she didn't offer to help me.

On my own, I found the gents', all dark granite and sparkling white porcelain. I didn't aim well and I didn't flush.

40

"YES, YOU HAVE THE RIGHT Dr. Kim." Somehow I'd managed to reach Kendall Kim—Chicago otolaryngologist, former husband of Dorothy Zhang, father to their son, Tim—on the first call. This was a feat and a miracle and a good omen, since the odds of reaching a busy doc in the middle of the day are only slightly better than hitting the winning Powerball numbers. "But I haven't spoken with Dorothy in over six months."

Or not such a good omen.

I stood outside the offices of Lane, Battle & Sim, fumbling with the phone and with the computer printout with Kendall Kim's number on it.

"Do you know where she is?" I asked.

"Who are you again?"

"Nathaniel McCormick. CDC."

"Why does CDC want to talk to Dorothy?"

"I really can't get into that."

"Whatever. No, I don't know where she is. And I don't really care where she is."

I got the sense that I'd trod on the very sensitive turf of a very messy divorce. Nevertheless, I pressed on.

"She has custody of your son?"

"Yes, she has custody. And no, I haven't seen Timothy."

"When was—"

"Six months go. Last time I saw Dorothy." Kendall Kim sighed. "Look, Dr. McCormick, if you want to keep talking about this, I'm going to ask you to set up a telephone appointment, fax over your credentials. Don't mean to be rude, but I'm busy and this isn't really a topic I like to discuss with anyone who's not my lawyer. You understand."

He hung up.

I did not understand, however. People don't just disappear. And if people do just disappear, other people get concerned about them. They search for them, they raise a stink. I could understand Kendall Kim and his messy divorce. With a stretch I could even understand his not knowing where his son was—maybe he wasn't meant to be a father, maybe he'd taken on a new family and didn't care, maybe the lawyers had gotten into things and really messed them up. But that *no one* knew where Dorothy Zhang or her son was, and no one seemed to care, disturbed me to the core.

How do you just evaporate into nothing? How do you do that with a child in tow?

I cut my way through the Embarcadero Center, walked quickly up steps and down, took elevators up one floor, only to take them down again. My paranoia was in high gear. When I was finally satisfied no one was behind me, I walked east toward the bay, toward the actual Embarcadero and the Ferry Building. Before the Bay Bridge was built, the Embarcadero was the nexus for ferry routes across to Berkeley and Oakland; it had some of the highest foot traffic in the nation. People used to "embark" on their trips across the bay, I suppose. Or maybe the word was Spanish for wharf. In any case, a few ferries still left from the Ferry Building, and cafés there produced ten-dollar sandwiches. What they call progress.

I coughed up a Jackson and took my aged-prosciutto-provolone-avocado-sun-dried-tomato-organic-sprout concoction to a bench outside. Seagulls gathered, eye-balling me, bent on murder. Barring my asphyxiation on the twelve-grain bread I was eating, the bastards would have to go hungry. It's gotta suck being a seagull.

The sandwich and drink had been financially devastating, and I found the nearest ATM. Plus, I was a guy on the run, right? Cash only from here on out. I took out two hundred dollars from the machine and saw that I had just under two thousand left. Not much, considering the security deposit for my nonexistent apartment was supposed to come out of that. I thought about the number of meetings with landlords I'd blown off since Murph died. Two? More?

Considering the events of the day, I decided the best way to find Dorothy Zhang would not be to go pawing around family and friends.

I called Bonita Sanchez.

"I hope you're calling me to tell me something," she said.

"Um, it's a really nice day where I am."

"And where exactly are you?"

"Are you going to arrest me?"

"If I can."

"Okay, I'm in Phoenix. And I do actually have a question." I heard her say something in the background. "If you're tracing my call, I'm calling from my cell in San Francisco."

"Don't flatter yourself."

"Have you heard of a woman named Dorothy Zhang?"

"Oh," Sanchez said. "Oh, my, Dr. McCormick. And here I was, wondering how a little jump drive found its way onto my desk. All packed up in its little envelope. Where did you get it?"

I toyed with playing dumb, but I was already in enough trouble with her. "Murph—Paul Murphy—gave it to me."

"Not mentioning it to me seems like a teeny-weeny oversight on your part, don't you think?"

"Oversight or not, you have the drive now. The pictures are the same as what you got yesterday. And you saw *my* name in there, so you know it was intended for me." I plowed ahead. "I just wanted to know about Dorothy Zhang," I said, and then waved the olive branch. "And I wanted to let you know I found one of the sick people."

"Where?"

"Milpitas. Public health is investigating." I told her the woman was in the photos, that she was dead, that we knew nothing else. That Santa Clara and California State were chasing it down. "The woman's name is Cynthia Yang."

"And your contacts in the health department?" she wanted to know.

I gave her Brooke's and Ravi's phone numbers. "Now, can we please talk about Dorothy Zhang?"

Sanchez sighed. "She was a newscaster—"

"—who vanished. I know that. Was there ever a missing persons report filed on her?"

"No. We checked that out with San Francisco PD, which means, Doctor, she's not technically missing. Or it means that the people who could file a missing persons report—family, close friends—haven't done so."

"So they know where she is."

Sanchez sighed again. "Look, Dr. McCormick, I appreciate the information about the woman in Milpitas, I'll follow up. As for the Zhang thing, I'll follow up. But I have to tell you that manpower is limited."

"Limited?" I wanted to know exactly what that meant for a quadruple homicide, but she'd already hung up the phone.

41

IT WAS SURPRISINGLY EASY TO find out where Daniel Zhang lived. A call to 411 produced nothing, but a call to Ravi Singh, with his easy access to big databases, produced a hit.

"Another one you owe me," Dr. Singh reminded me before signing off, collecting these favors like interest on a bank account.

I pointed the mighty Corolla toward the far-flung, foggy districts of western San Francisco, where the skyscrapers and Victorians give way to block after block of two- and three-story residences and businesses. Suburbia spread like mortar between the city and the ocean.

I drove past the house at 2387 Irving. It was only three p.m. and I couldn't imagine any firm lawyer home that early, so I continued out to the coast. The parking lot at Ocean Beach was a quarter full. Fog blocked the sun, and wind ripped at the sea grass on the dunes and at the low buildings. This part of San Francisco had the look of always being in the off-season. A handful of people moved along the sand like seabirds. A beach on the edge of a city, and somehow so desolate.

The wind and the fog made me cold, and I decided this was not a place I wanted to be. It was a place for lovers or misanthropes. I was no longer the former, and I wasn't ready to admit to being the latter.

A last look at the steely, white-flecked Pacific, and I returned to the car. East then, to the Sunset district. I parked down the street from 2387 Irving and settled in.

The Sunset was a residential neighborhood with single-family dwellings that housed, it seemed, much of the Chinese community in the area. The name was odd, considering the area labored under one of the foggiest microclimates in the city, and actually seeing the sun set was the exception rather than the rule here. But it was family-oriented and cheap, at least compared to the rest of the city. Incidentally, most of the homes in the area were yawners—stucco things with paneled wooden doors and tiny, manicured lawns—but Danny Zhang's place was modern, looking as though it were composed of big white cubes set haphazardly atop one another. The windows were dark.

I waited. Cars parked. Cars left. I fiddled with the radio

and decided that stakeouts had to be one of the most boring ways to spend your time.

At around eight o'clock, I closed my eyes.

Next thing I knew, I was awakened by the sound of a car door slamming and an alarm system arming. A bright red Mercedes was now in the driveway, and Daniel Zhang was striding to the front steps of his home.

I got out of my car, then stopped.

Three men had rushed toward Zhang. One swung at the back of his legs with a baseball bat, bringing him to the ground. The bat fell again, kicks flew. I could hear the muffled grunts of effort and pain.

I dove back into the car, scrabbled under the seat. My fingers found the grip of the Smith & Wesson, closed around it. The thing felt heavy and unfamiliar. It felt very wrong.

What was I going to do? Blow the three guys away? Right.

"Shit," I spat. *"Shit."*

I dropped the gun on the seat and grabbed my cell, punched in 911. I stole a glance over the backseat—one of the guys was on top of Daniel Zhang, saying something in his ear, pressing his face into the grass.

It seemed like ten minutes until the dispatcher picked up. When he did, I barked the situation and the address into the phone.

The guy on top of Zhang rammed his face into the turf. Then he rammed again.

I couldn't watch this anymore.

I dropped the cell in the car and walked quickly toward the melee, my hands raised in an "it's-all-over-now" gesture. "Hey, hey," I said.

Three heads swiveled; six eyes fixed on me. The attackers were Asian, dressed in good—if flashy—suits. One of the men had spiky blond hair; another, the one with the bat, sported a black baseball cap.

"The police are on the way!" I shouted. "Get off him!"

For a moment, no one moved. My eyes darted from one face to another. The man with the blond hair and the one with the baseball cap, I didn't recognize. But the one whose knee was stuck into the middle of Daniel Zhang's back, whose fingers were laced into Daniel Zhang's hair . . . feline eyes, tattoo. My buddy from the Tetra parking lot.

He barked something I couldn't understand. Suddenly, blondie and his friend with the bat grew animated, stepped toward me. I realized I was not prepared for this. I realized I'd thought the mention of police would cause everyone to scatter.

My legs went weak, and I began shuffling backward. The pace of the two men quickened. The bat in the ball cap's hand lifted. He was fifteen feet from me.

"The police . . ." I stammered. All I could think of was the bat crashing into my skull.

I turned and ran to the car.

I ripped open the door and grabbed the Smith & Wesson. I didn't feel its weight this time, and whirled around, pointing it toward the two men. Even though the end of the barrel quivered and shook, I thought the sight of the cannon would stop them.

It did. For about three seconds.

Ball cap dropped his bat and reached into his jacket. The blond reached into his. Next thing I knew, I was staring at the business end of two black automatic pistols.

The men began to advance slowly, tiny expert half-steps, as if they'd done this many times before. Thirteen feet, eleven, ten. My gun had begun to feel heavy again, and the shaking had gotten so bad I couldn't be sure I'd hit a barn door from a yard.

"Just leave," I begged. "The cops are coming."

In the background, I caught a glimpse of tattooed man. He was standing now, watching us, towering over a limp Daniel Zhang like a hunter after the kill.

From up the street, I heard the sound of a car.

Light illuminated the faces of the two men, now seven feet in front of me. Shadows shifted and intensified as the vehicle approached. The blond cut a look to his comrade, then stepped to the middle of the street and pointed his gun. From the sounds—the brakes, the high-pitched reverse, the brief squeal of the tires—I figured the car got no closer than forty feet.

The blond turned to me, the gun following his gaze.

In the distance, a siren wailed.

The tattooed man shouted something. The words were terse, like a battlefield command. The blond and the ball cap stepped backward until they were fifteen feet from me, then they turned and holstered their weapons. The ball cap picked up his bat. They made their way toward a white Cadillac sedan parked behind me, thirty feet away.

The siren grew louder and the men picked up the pace.

"Next time," the inked asshole said. He glanced down at Daniel Zhang, then turned on his heel and followed his henchmen.

The men reached the car: blondie to the driver's side, ball cap to the back, tattoo to the passenger's side. I felt myself begin to relax and let the gun drop to my side.

But it was too soon. As he reached for the door handle, the tattooed man wheeled around, tore a pistol from inside his jacket, and leveled it at me.

"Bang," he said, grinning. Then he slipped into the Caddy, closed the door quietly, and rolled away.

42

AS THE SIRENS GREW LOUDER, I stepped to the hedges surrounding the house and dropped the gun behind them. Daniel Zhang pulled himself upright, sat slumped on the stoop, head hanging. He spit a drool of pink saliva between his legs.

"No gun," I told him. "I didn't have a gun."

He looked up at me. The blood on his face was turning dark now, sludged in the creases of skin. "What is *wrong* with you?" he spat.

"What?" I asked, surprised. "I do not want to get into a discussion about where I got the—"

"This is so fucked up. *So fucked up.*"

I was a little irritated at the ingratitude. "I just saved you from getting the living crap beaten out of you."

"You just killed me, you idiot. Fuck. *Fuck.*" He spat and put his head in his hands. "You just killed yourself."

* * *

We spent an hour in the modernist house, filling the cops in on what happened, or at least on the new version of what happened. Descriptions of the men, details of the events. Zhang, to his credit, didn't mention the pistol.

"You want I should call an ambulance?" asked the red-faced bull of a man whose nameplate read "Polaski."

Daniel shook his head.

"You sure? You got quite a knock—"

"He's fine. I checked him out already," I lied. By that time, Polaski knew I was a doctor.

Polaski asked more questions and jotted more notes. I heard the name Wah Ching, Jackson Street Boys, Wo Hop To. The names didn't mean anything to me, but they seemed to mean something to Daniel. He said "I don't know" a few times, then snapped: "I am not in a gang. I have never been in a gang. I will never be in a gang. I have never been associated with a gang."

Polaski decided to give up on helping those who didn't want to be helped. He handed us both follow-up forms, pointing to two boxes that had been checked. One read, *General Works*; the other, *Gang Task Force.* Below each was a telephone number.

"You call one of these you remember anything," Polaski said.

"What's General Works?" I asked.

"Like it says." Polaski was becoming less friendly with each sentence. "General things, assaults and the like."

I didn't need to ask what the Gang Task Force did.

Before leaving, Polaski delivered his parting shot. "You know, you guys are the ones who can prevent this from happening to someone else." He looked suddenly tired, as if he'd seen this a thousand times before.

Once the front door closed, Daniel and I sat at the dining room table in his sleek, spare home. An enormous plasma screen TV was affixed to the wall in the living area, which was open to the dining area and kitchen. White walls, white carpet. Black, chrome, and glass furniture. Except for the TV, the place looked very hip for 1988.

"You should get to a hospital," I said.

"I'm fine."

"You feel nauseated?" I asked.

"No."

"Vision okay?"

Daniel Zhang smiled dismissively.

"You might be bleeding into your head," I explained. "You should get a CT just to be sure—"

"Look, a little bleeding in my head is the least of my worries."

"Who were they?"

"Forget it, Doctor."

He swept one of the cop's follow-up forms into his hand, regarded it. "You couldn't let this go," he said. "You had to visit me at work. You had to come *here*."

"I need to know where your sister is."

"Well, I don't, okay? I don't know where she is and I don't want to know where she is." He crumpled the form and dropped it back to the glass table. "And now these bastards think I know."

"*Who* bastards? Gangs?"

He shook his head.

"Did your sister tell you about sick people? People with disfigured faces, looks like growths under—"

Zhang's eyes locked on mine.

"What?" I persisted. "She told you, didn't she? What did she tell you?"

"She didn't tell me anything."

"Did she ever mention a man named Paul Murphy?"

He looked away. I grabbed his arm. "She mentioned him, didn't she? She said something about—"

He wrenched his arm away and stood. "I need to get out of here. I need to get my mother and myself out of here."

"And what about your sister?"

"My sister can take care of herself. Let me give you some advice, Doctor: Get yourself gone. Forget you ever heard of my sister."

"I can bump this up to the next level, you know. I can keep this going with the police."

"Right." He forced a sour laugh. "You do that. See how much it helps you."

I held his gaze for a moment, then scooped my copy of the follow-up form into my hands.

"They know about you." Zhang watched me fold the form. "If you stay in this city . . ." He didn't finish the sentence. "This is the beginning of the end, Doctor," he said. "Get out of here."

And I did.

In the car, I slipped the Smith & Wesson under the seat. I brought my hand in front of my face. It trembled. *The beginning of the end,* Daniel had said. What beginning? What end?

I tried to steady my hand. I couldn't.

Daniel Zhang came out of his house. He threw two black duffels into the trunk of the red Mercedes. He climbed into the car. A moment later, he was gone.

43

FIVE AND A HALF MILES east of Daniel Zhang's place, I parked the car as close to the entrance to the bar as I could get. In the sideview mirror, I watched headlights loom and zip by, fully expecting to see a white Caddy lumbering along, machine guns bristling from its windows.

The neighborhood, called South of Market—SoMa—had forever been changed in the 1990s-dotcom convulsion. Clubs with names like "DaDa" and "Playbar" had muscled aside the auto shops and warehouses and artists' studios. Though the bubble and its burst were now distant memory, the gentrification remained, poised to siphon dollars from a resurgent Internet economy.

I exited the car, slammed the door, looked around. Vehicles whisked by, a few pedestrians sauntered. Everything—the cars, the people, the shuttered buildings—seemed to hide a threat. 750,000 people in this city, and I felt alone and pursued by every one of them. My heart would not stop thumping, my hands would not stop sweating. I circled to the trunk of the car and unboxed the shoulder holster.

It took me a few minutes to deal with all the straps and configurations. My arm, it seemed, could not find the right hole, and the thing wrapped around me like a net. A metaphor if ever there was one. But I wanted to make sure that if I went down, at least I'd go down with a Smith & Wesson blazing. If not blazing, then I'd go down struggling to get the damned thing out of the holster.

Finally, I worked out the logic of the contraption. I traded my sport coat for the windbreaker I'd fished out of my duffel. Zipped up, it hardly showed the bulge of the holster.

At the front door of the car, I paused.

Screw it, I thought.

And that's how I—the former public health official who chastised Paul Murphy about having a gun in his home—carted a loaded firearm into a bar.

The Grand Junction had weathered the neighborhood's changes better than most. And though I hadn't been there for ten years, I was pretty sure it was not the type of place where you'd ever find Asian guys with big tattoos. Asian guys with small tattoos, sure, but they were mostly hipsters and software guys looking to hear a band and tie on a buzz. It seemed, in short, safe.

Making sure I had a good view of the door, I took a seat at the end of the bar. The place had a vaguely Western decor: a stuffed elk head, a Remington sculpture knockoff collecting dust, a couple of battered license plates from Colorado. From the female bartender, I ordered a beer. Without any problem, it was provided to me. Small victories, I thought.

There was a baseball game on the television, and the place was maybe half full. I grabbed a handful of pretzels, chewed them into mush, and washed it down with a gulp of suds. The guy sitting next to me—thin, mid-forties, long wispy hair, some rock concert T-shirt under a corduroy blazer—was chowing his way through what looked like a veggie burger. I realized I was starving, so I ordered one. I ordered another beer.

"You look tired, dude," the guy mumbled at me through his burger.

"I am tired, dude," I said. I can give it as good as I can take it.

"Yeah. We're all tired. The country's tired, man, you can feel it. It's 'cuz we're holding on by our fingernails above the abyss. You work around here?"

I should've known that a bar, in the late evening on a weekday, didn't attract the solitary types who wanted to keep their shit to themselves. It would attract socially outgoing misfits like my neighbor here. Folks who had a desperate need to *connect.*

"I don't work," I said.

That should shut him up.

Or not.

"Yeah. And they say the economy's on the mend. Bullshit, I say."

"Look, man, I really am tired."

"Okay. That's cool, dude."

I took a long pull on the beer. I held my hand in front of me. Steady as a goddamned *rock*.

"You're not a software developer, are you?" the guy asked. "You're—"

"No."

"—you're more the business-development type."

"I'm a doctor," I said. Where the hell was that veggie burger?

"Oh, yeah. The hand thing. Surgeon?"

"No."

"What kind?"

"Public health."

"No shit? We just did a big database project for Georgia State Department of Health."

"No shit," I said. For the first time, I turned to look him in the eye. "I used to work in Georgia."

And that is how I met Miles Pikar, Chief Technology Officer for Paladin Software, my new best friend.

Two hours and five beers later, I had disgorged to Miles pretty much everything that had happened in the previous week. I told him about Murph. I told him about Dorothy Zhang. I did not tell him about the gun.

He took a sip of beer. "The Zhang woman just vanished?"

"Looks like it," I said.

Miles rattled on about some database, something about deadbeat dads and child support and tracking employment. The dads talk got me thinking about parenthood, which got me thinking about children, which got me thinking again about one particular child: Tim Kim.

I interrupted Miles. "The missing woman's got a kid. A boy."

"He's probably with the dad."

"He's not with the dad. Dad doesn't know where he is. Besides," I said, "it makes sense, right? If she's hiding out from something, she wouldn't just leave the kid with him. Whoever's pressuring her would be sure to guess where the child is. It'd be too easy to grab the kid from his dad and use him as leverage."

Miles shrugged. "It would be pretty good leverage. A kid. You got kids?"

"No."

"Me neither. You got a partner?"

I told him about Brooke Michaels; I told him she was the third most important thing in my life, after Murph and after finding out what happened to the people in the photos.

"Your priorities, my friend, are a bit fucked up."

You said it, dude.

He patted me on the shoulder. "I gotta go, Nate."

"It's only midnight," I said pathetically. I was, needless to say, pretty far gone by this point.

"Have to wake up early tomorrow, get a little yoga in before I genuflect for The Man."

"Yeah, yeah."

Miles Pikar looked at me with something like pity in his eyes. "Where're you crashing?" he asked.

"Dunno. There's got to be a motel around here somewhere." I snapped my fingers at the bartender, who pretended not to hear. In my inebriated state, I was becoming *that guy,* the drunk jerk way past his tolerance.

"Look, dude, I got an extra bedroom. You want, you can stay with me."

"No," I said. I turned to the bartender again. "Excuse me? Is there a motel around here?"

She didn't answer me, but looked at Miles instead. She drew her hand across her neck in a "he's cut off" motion.

"Avoid interaction with Brenda," Miles advised. "She hates you. Come on, you stay at my place."

"I can't," I replied.

"Why?"

That was a stumper.

Miles laughed, stood up, and helped me out of my chair.

44

WHEN I WAS FINISHING MED school in Baltimore, I did a month in the Emergency Department, tending to a constant stream of gangbangers with gunshot wounds, homeless guys who drank themselves into comas, motor vehicle accidents, and, it being Baltimore, heroin addicts who'd gotten a little enthusiastic with their fix. One afternoon, a black guy in baggy jeans and a Wu-Tang T-shirt came in with a gunshot wound to the abdomen. We all assumed some brawl over girls or drugs, just another slab of bad urban meat across the table. Turned out, though, it wasn't a brawl. Turned out that the weapon that injured the guy wasn't a TEC-9 or a MAC-10 or anything with millimeter behind its caliber. It seemed Alphonse Durrin—I still remember his name—spent his weekends as a Revolutionary War reenactor and had accidentally shot himself. He'd been readying the gun for a big get-together in upstate New York and it went off.

To recuperate, he had to take two weeks' leave from his job as a senior VP at an investment bank. The pistol, he told me later, was authentic. Three grand from a dealer in Tampa.

I remembered that story as I walked with Miles back to his apartment. I remembered it because appearances—the trappings of fashion, the inkings of race—are so insidiously deceptive, most of the time you hardly see their handiwork. So, it's a shock when what you didn't even know was there is dismantled. It's a shock when the urban thug turns out to be a history nut and a veep at a bank. It's a shock when the guy whose hair and vocabulary scream "society dropout," whose Pink Floyd T-shirt consisted of little more than threads and flecks of color, turns out to be the CTO of a tech company. When that CTO owns an enormous flat. When that dropout CTO owns the whole building.

Miles's large, open loft with hardwood floors, exposed beams, exposed brick was a surprise. The cleanliness was a surprise, too. Spotless almost, except for the squares of sod on the counter.

"Wheatgrass, man. I just started growing it. For the smoothies."

Smoothies whipped up in the three-hundred-dollar blender parked on a granite counter next to the big Sub-Zero refrigerator.

"This place, man . . . this place is *cool,*" I said lamely.

"The revolution starts here. In the quiet comfort of Casa Pikar."

Miles kicked off his flip-flops, hiked up his jeans, and led me to a room off the kitchen, a tidy place with its own bathroom. "Your fiefdom."

It looked to me like this was the only separate room in the place. "Where do you sleep?"

"Over there." He pointed to a bank of computers and flat-screen monitors. Next to them was a bed. "I sleep next to my babies."

In my deeply inebriated state, it all made sense.

"You got to get to sleep, dude. Big things in store for you."

I nodded and turned unsteadily toward the bedroom.

"Un momento, señor. You said the kid's name was Timothy Kim?"

"Who?" The synapses that hadn't been completely numbed by the alcohol made some connections. "Yeah. Tim Kim. Dorothy Zhang's kid. Yeah."

"You got a middle name?"

"I don't . . . I can't remember. Why?"

He patted me on the shoulder again. "Get some sleep, Doc."

45

I OPENED MY EYES, AND the hangover slammed into me like a meteor. I closed my eyes.

Morning.

There are times in my life in which I do stupid things. Hard to believe, I know, but fully three-quarters of my time on this planet has been spent with my head at various distances up my ass. Ask Brooke. For example, taking a gun to a bar was not smart. Getting drunk in the middle of this—of figuring how to deal with a slaughtered family and a possible public health nightmare—was not smart. That not-so-smart bout with alcohol got me thinking of other not-so-smart bouts with alcohol. In particular, I was thinking of one evening years ago when I decided to let Murph talk me into a drinking game. Poker. Head-to-head.

The Boy Scout outweighed me by a good fifty pounds, but, with pressure mounting in my lab, I'd recently begun to strengthen my liver with nightly challenges of bourbon. That night's match with Murph, I figured, was even. What I hadn't counted on was that Murph was one hell of a poker player.

We thought about betting shots of vodka, but, being PhDs, we realized that would make the game very short. So we opted for shots of beer. You win the hand, the other guy drank the collected "bet."

It was just us, two cases of Busch, and a steady stream of classic rock from the stereo. Friday night, gambling, drinking, and Credence. An alpha male's dream. Well, all dreams come to an end, and this dream ended four hours after it began, with me in Murph's bathroom, heaving out my guts. Naively, I'd also agreed that the first one to vomit had to pay for the beer. So, after crawling out of the bathroom, I peeled off some bills, thrust them at Murph, and passed out on his couch.

The following morning I awoke under a blanket that had somehow found its way onto me. The coffee table next to me had been cleared of its beer cans and shot glasses and cards. There was a glass of water on the table, and two Tylenol. The money I'd given to Murph lay on top of a scrap of notebook paper which read: *Blackjack tonight???*

For me, the more primitive senses—smell, pain—bring on memories with more intensity than sight or hearing. A hangover was kind of a sixth sense, and I was unprepared for the rush of Paul Murphy that flooded into me. Lying in Miles Pikar's swank guest bedroom, eyes squeezed tight against a new day, I missed the Jolly Giant. I missed the years in which we hadn't seen each other, the marriage, the kids, the changes of jobs. I missed never having played that game of blackjack with him.

I opened my eyes and felt like death.

The granite floor of the bathroom was cold under my bare feet, but the water gushing from the brushed-steel faucets turned hot instantly. I spent a good amount of time scrubbing my face, as if cleaning it would somehow erase the hangover. It didn't, and I caught a whiff of my own musty odor. I really needed a shower.

First, though, I needed to give some salutations to my host, make sure it was okay that I dirtied towels and scummed the model-home bathroom. I pulled on clothes, made sure the gun was balled up in the windbreaker on the bed. I checked the cell to see if Brooke had called sometime in the previous ten hours. Not that I would have called back, but it would have been nice to know she'd blinked before I did. She hadn't. There were, however, two missed calls logged on the phone. Both from a blocked number.

The massive loft space was dully lit by huge windows and, it turned out, by three flat-screen monitors and a single desk lamp at the far end of the room. I walked in my stocking feet over to the monitors. There were lines of text on two of the screens, a bunch of collapsed files on the other.

"There's coffee in the pot," Miles Pikar said without turning around. "Sleep well?"

"Well enough. You?"

"Two hours, dude."

"Two hours? You under deadline or something?"

"Doing my part to aid the forces of good. Get your coffee. I got something to show you."

I crossed the quarter mile of apartment to the kitchen area, found a cup that said "National Institute of Standards and Technology," and filled it with the inky fluid. The coffee was dark as Texas crude.

When I returned to Miles and his toys, his knee was hopping up and down like a grasshopper's.

"Not in Chicago," he said, eyes on the computer. "You were right. Not with the dad."

On the screen, he opened a file that looked something like a spreadsheet. At the top, I saw a field entitled "Last Name." Under it was the name "Kim." First name "Timothy," middle name "Dong-wei." The boy was eight years old. Race, immunization status, address were listed.

"How'd you get this?" I asked Miles.

"Database magic, my friend. And some early work with the California Basic Education Data System, which gathers stats on kids and their curricula. There were a bunch of changes to the database since then, but my guys laid down some of the original architecture."

"And this is open to the public?"

He looked at me with a crooked smile and said nothing.

I smiled back. "You hacked in?"

"'Hacked' is such an ugly word, Doc. Ugly, ugly word. Let's just say I let myself in through a back door. And remember I worked on this a long time ago, so I feel I have some ownership over it."

"Sure."

"Got to justify," he said. "Lets me sleep better at night."

"Your two hours."

"It was a *good* two hours."

He clicked more keys; a long list of names popped up. Timothy Kim's was highlighted in yellow. "This is the data from the San Francisco Unified School District. Young Timothy was pulled out of the system in June of this year." He flipped back to another page. "He was enrolled in an alternative school in Berkeley for the summer, some arts and sciences summer program. He left in August and"—he brought up the first page—"enrolled at Glenfield Elementary School in the Napa Unified School District."

"And that's his current address?" I pointed to the screen.

"Current as of a few weeks ago."

In the field entitled "Parent/Guardian" was the name "Dorothy Zhang" followed by "(mother)."

"Nifty," I said.

"Dude, data is nifty. Databases are divine."

I took a sip of coffee, felt a few neurons wake up and flash to life. "Isn't this illegal?"

"Highly. But I covered our tracks. Besides, for the forces of good . . ."

"Right."

Just then the telephone on the desk rang. Miles popped on a headset, spoke rapidly into it. "Up. Been up. Been helping out a friend . . . Dude I met in a bar last night. No, not like that. He's a doctor. Don't sweat it. Just come up."

He took off the headset and Miles Pikar, database guru, surprised me again.

"You're gonna meet the boyfriend. He's cool, but kind of the jealous type. You're not bi or anything, are you?"

"No."

"Didn't think so. You didn't trip the gaydar. But sometimes Angel's gaydar gets confused if he's irritated. Just warning you."

Better and better, I thought. Hungover and caught in the middle of a lover's quarrel.

"Spend some time with this," Miles told me, gesturing at the computer. "Get what you need to find that kid. Gotta go change."

Miles disappeared, and I squinted at the information, half distracted by the imminent arrival of the irritable Angel.

And arrive he did.

"Hi," I heard someone say from across the room. I turned and saw a tall, well-built guy with a shaved head—kind of a point-guard type a dozen years past his prime. He was wearing sweatpants and a puffy vest, clutching a fruit drink and a small brown bag.

"Hi," I said, dragging my corpse and my coffee over to greet him. He set down the bag, then shook my hand.

"You're Miles's friend from the bar?"

God, he made it seem so sordid. "Yeah," I said.

"Where's Miles?"

"He's getting changed, he said."

"Of course he is."

We stood like that for a few painful moments. I ran my hand over the wheatgrass. "You want some coffee?" I asked.

He laughed sarcastically, like who was I to be offering the coffee. "So you two met last night?"

"Yeah. At the Grand Junction. Miles is helping me out on some things."

"Oh. What?"

"Some public health things. I'm a public health doctor."

"Well, Miles certainly knows about that. You two are birds of a feather."

"Yeah. So, what do you do?"

"I'm a writer. Cyberpunk. You ever heard of *The Electric Fountain*?"

"No."

"Spraybots?"

I guess I needed to get out more.

Thankfully, Miles appeared at that moment, his pale skinny legs poking out of the bottom of cut-off sweatpants, a disintegrating Grateful Dead T-shirt on top.

"Yoga time," he announced. "You guys met. Cool."

Miles kissed Angel briefly and scooped the bag off the counter. "Blueberry bran. Awesome. Nate, you up for some Ashtanga?"

"No thanks."

"That's cool. You should work some poison out of your system, though."

"My brain works best on poison."

"Work some poison out of your soul."

"Soul likes poison, too."

Miles put a hand on Angel's shoulder, asked, "What time do you have to be at work?"

"Nine-thirty," Angel said. He caught me looking at him, perplexed. He smiled. "I'm a partner at a law firm, honey." Then, as Miles slipped a DVD into the player and switched on the plasma screen TV, I heard Angel mutter, *"Spraybots."* He chuckled.

So there I was, taking notes on a scrap of paper. It would have been easier to print everything out, but I didn't want to interrupt the yoga master. *"Chataranga and Upward Dog . . ."* and so on and so on.

In ten minutes, I'd written down Tim Kim's current address, as well as the contact numbers for his old school in San Francisco and the summer program in Berkeley. I hopped on the Web, and got directions to the address in Napa.

It wasn't lost on me how odd it was to find this information. I mean, it wasn't easy to get—Miles did, after all, have to crack into a government database—but it wasn't impossible either. Anyone with some diligence would have been able to find Timothy Kim. And if it was possible to find him, my theory about why the kid wasn't in Chicago with his dad was crap. He wasn't being hidden, not very well anyway. By extension, Dorothy Zhang wasn't being very well hidden.

If she was with her kid, that is. If she hadn't jetted off with Moonies or the Zapatistas.

So, she was with her kid? Or on the run? And if she was on the run, was it from her former colleagues at work? From her brother? Why would she want to hide from her brother? Why was her brother beaten to a pulp? Who were the men who had so frightened him?

Was his sister under threat by the same man? Was she even still alive?

"Shit," I said to myself.

"Step forward to Warrior One," said the man on the DVD. *"Warrior Two."*

Dorothy Zhang dead? I didn't want to think about another body now, and tucked this in with the hundred other unknowns. I looked back to the computer.

Now, no one's ever accused me of keeping my nose where it's supposed to be. I didn't see any No Trespassing signs on Miles's desktop. I wasn't going to dig through private folders, but the desktop . . .

"As you breathe out, think about your shoulder blades coming together . . ."

The desktop was unfamiliar territory—seems Miles had split his hard drive into about a half-dozen other drives: "THX Code," "Brk Code," and something wild called, well, "Smthg Wld." I avoided them all, not needing to see any high-level coding and not wanting to see what Miles considered "wild." A desktop folder caught my eye. "NMcC." Those letters seemed familiar. I opened the folder.

"Downward Dog. Lift your tailbone to the sky. Stay rooted in your forefingers and your thumbs. Breathe in. Slowly release the tension from your body . . ."

At that point, I was rooted in the fifteen files contained in the "NMcC" folder. All were Web pages—articles, a few blurbs from CDC.

All were about me.

46

I CLEANED OFF IN A marble shower the size of my first apartment. The stink of alcohol still clung to me like a skunk's spray.

Pants went back on. Shirt. I stared at the balled-up windbreaker with the gun nestled inside. Nate McCormick and Smith & Wesson? I did not want those names to be in the same sentence. I did not want to be the man who felt so threatened he needed a goddamned weapon. But, hell, I was threatened. Disgusted with myself, I strapped on the gun. Zipped up the windbreaker.

I emerged from the bedroom into a modern domestic tableau: Angel, pureeing some deeply purple concoction; Miles close behind him, arms around his waist.

Angel cut the blender.

Miles turned to me. "Smoothie? Blueberry and wheat-grass. Full of antioxidants."

I said sure, and Angel tipped the carafe to fill three glasses. He handed me one, and I saw his eyes linger.

The two were dressed for success. Angel in his trendy business casual, Miles in a suit and tie. His hair was pulled back in a ponytail.

I felt Angel staring at me.

"Going to a funeral?" I asked Miles.

"Got a meeting with Whitey McWhite today, Nate.

Pitching our services to the Empire." He named a huge software firm in the area.

"Why the jacket, Nate?" Angel asked.

"Uh, I'm a little cold."

"It's not cold," he said, and continued staring. I took a sip of the smoothie, trying to be as nonchalant as possible.

"Get out of here," Angel said.

"Angel—" Miles looked shocked.

"Get out now," his lover repeated.

I stammered, "What's—"

"He has a *gun,* Miles," Angel spat. "You invited someone with a gun here."

"I don't know what you're talking about," I said.

"Under your left arm. I didn't spend two years as a prosecutor and not know what a shoulder holster looks like."

There was a long moment in which no one said anything. Miles's face was a mixture of confusion and disappointment. Finally, he spoke. "You should go, Doc."

I set down the glass with the smoothie. "Thanks for . . . thanks for everything." I felt like a schoolboy caught in the act of cheating, stealing, lying. There was nothing really left to say, so I began to slink toward the elevator.

"What are you *doing,* dude?"

"He's leaving, Miles," Angel said. "Let him go."

"What are you doing, Nate?" Miles repeated. "You think you're going to work this out with a gun? What world do you live in, man? You're going to go toe-to-toe with these guys who you say sliced up your friend? You a good shot, Nate?"

Angel sighed. "Miles—"

"Quiet, sweets." He turned back to me. "This ain't you, Nate."

"You don't know who I am."

"And obviously neither do you. You want to find out what happened to your friend, you want to find this Zhang woman, this isn't the way to do it."

"It's just for protection," I said weakly.

"Let him take his popgun, Miles."

"Angel," Miles said sternly. "Play out the scenarios, Doc. These guys find you, you have a gun, you pull it, you shoot once, then you're dead. These guys find you, you *don't* have a gun, you have a spitting chance."

"I don't have a chance either way."

"Come *on,* dude. You got your brain. You got your wits. You got a chance. But not with that." He pointed to the slight bulge under my arm. "Look, I didn't pull an all-nighter so you could get yourself killed. You owe me. I don't want to read about you in the paper. Screw the weapon."

I stared at him and did, for a moment, play out the scenarios. Then I unzipped my jacket, and Miles took a step back.

"I'm making sure I don't backslide," I said. I unholstered the pistol, fiddled with the cylinder, and popped it out. I handed it to Miles. "I owe you."

"You're doing the right thing," Miles said. He balled the cylinder in his fist, smiled, and clapped me on the shoulder. "You let me know whatever else you need. We don't want more people getting nasty tumors, do we?"

* * *

Outside, I trawled around until I found a small pile of gravel. I worked the grit into the action of the gun. Satisfied that no industrious kid or jonesing addict would ever be able to make the thing work, I dropped the Smith & Wesson into a storm drain.

From the trunk of the car, I retrieved the box of bullets. I dumped them in a trash can. I threw the holster in after them.

There. All done. I now had nothing but my wits. And I hoped they were enough.

The cell shook as I approached my car. A blocked number. I picked it up.

"You don't answer your phone? I called you twice this morning, McCormick."

"And didn't leave a message, Ravi."

"Because I'm at the General and I'm using their line, and I'm telling myself that if you don't pick up the goddamn phone I'm taking this case all for myself."

"What are you talking about?"

"We got one, man," he said. "We got another one."

41

FOR ALL ITS SHINE, SAN FRANCISCO has an underbelly. And when the underbelly gets sick, it comes to San Francisco General Hospital.

The General backed up to a gritty neighborhood called the Mission, just northwest of grittier Bayview. The hospital was aging, publicly funded, and hemorrhaged cash as fast as its trauma patients hemorrhaged blood. Every year, the overseers at the hospital would trudge to City Hall, hats in hand, begging for scraps from the budget table. I don't think the phrase "in the black" was ever used to describe the place. "In the red" was far more apt—literally and metaphorically.

I drove along Potrero Avenue, in front of a phalanx of buildings that composed the oldest part of the campus. The buildings smacked of the East Coast. They were brick, not something you often see in earthquake territory, and they had a Gothic flair, not something you often see west of the Rockies. The whole layout had a sinister vibe, evocative of straitjackets, transorbital lobotomies, and other miseries. I passed a small sign that said "Emergency Services" and "Physician on Duty 24 hours." In these days of nonstop medicine, the sign itself seemed like a throwback. From the faded colors, I figured it had been there since the Eisenhower administration.

The main hospital was a hulking gray edifice. Very Soviet, and not very welcoming, despite the small circle of flowers planted outside the entrance, despite the brightly colored heart sculpture rising up from the flowers.

Weird aesthetics aside, I liked the General. The grounds of public hospitals, county hospitals—big or small, rural or urban—fill me with a glimmer of optimism, that maybe some part of our anonymous, anatomized society still gives a shit. Give me your tired, your poor, they say. But please give us your tax dollars to say it. In the case of the General, the offer to be taken in is extended to more than sixty-five thousand people a year, ninety percent of them low income or indigent, and who were nearly equal parts white, black, Asian, Hispanic. In that way, I think, places like the General are the true monuments to our best qualities; they mean more than promises stamped into copper on some statue in New York Harbor.

There was another reason I dug the General. It was operated by the Department of Public Health for San Francisco. Public health. My kind of people.

The visitors' desk was staffed by one volunteer and two sheriff's deputies. The volunteer, a birdlike septuagenarian, pointed me to the elevators, and I rode skyward with an orderly who needed a bath and a cluster of harried-looking residents from UCSF. They spoke in hushed volume about some "brain-dead ER doc."

Fourth floor.

I walked over the scuffed linoleum, past the whiteboard with patients' names, past a patient dragging an IV pole, toward Ravi, who waited at the nurses' station, standing beside a petite woman with frizzy blond hair and heavy glasses. Ravi's clothes weren't what you'd call standard health department: black pants, cream silk T-shirt, blazer. The guy looked like a shorter, squatter, swarthier Don Johnson. He even sported the two days' growth of beard.

"You walk here?" he asked impatiently.

"I walked to my car, drove here, and walked from my car."

"You look like shit."

"Great to see you, too."

He grunted. "Long time, McCormick." Ravi turned to the woman. "Monica, this is Nate McCormick. Bane of disease and bad guys everywhere." To me, he said, "This is Monica Evans, bane of skin disease and cystic acne." Monica blushed. I noticed she had perfect skin, creamy and glowing under the sudden rush of red. I shook her hand, keeping my eyes glued to hers so as not to signal I noticed her embarrassment.

"What's up?" I asked.

Monica opened her mouth to speak, but Ravi bowled her over. "After we put out the quiet word, Monica got a call from a pal of hers in the San Francisco Department of Public Health."

"It was off the record," Monica said.

"Yeah. Anyway, she got a call about it, so we decided to come down here early to take a look. It's *it,* man. Extensive involvement of the soft tissue around the mouth and eye. Woman's here because she began to bleed from one of the sites."

"Where is she?"

Monica pointed to a room down the hall. "In—"

Again, Ravi cut her off. "That's a problem."

I waited for an explanation.

"SF Public Health is with her now. Monica's pal, it seemed, didn't realize there was anything to get excited about until we acted excited." He shot a scathing glance at his co-worker, who blushed again. "Now we've got jurisdictional bullshit to contend with."

"They wouldn't have invited you guys?"

"San Francisco never brings in state. They think they're so damned competent they never invite us in."

One thing I didn't miss about working in public health were the pissing matches between agencies. The normal flow of involvement was from local to state to the feds. Normal flow, though, implied there was a set protocol for bringing in bigger guns. However, some of the monstrous locals—San Francisco, LA, New York—were so sure of themselves, they often handled *everything* locally. If it got too big for them, they leapt over the state authorities and went straight to CDC. Public health, in general, is an invitation-only affair. And if the locals don't invite the state or the feds in, they usually stay out.

To be fair, SFPH did have the reputation of being highly competent. As such, they rarely placed calls to the state offices across the Bay. The problem here was that the call had been placed on the down low. But Ravi Singh was not a down-low-type guy. He was ambitious. He smelled glory, and he was going for it.

"They'll screw the pooch on this one, if we let them," he said unhappily.

"We can't keep them out of this," Monica replied.

"I know that, Monica."

"Okay," I said, tired already of the bickering. "What's the story?"

Looks were exchanged between the two state docs. "Go ahead," Monica told Ravi.

"Beatrice Lum, forty-three, Asian," he said. "Came to the ED two days ago because she was bleeding from a wound in her face and the family couldn't get it to stop. Ulcerated mass. ED docs applied pressure, but couldn't stop the bleeding, which they thought was coming from the maxillary artery. She was crossed and matched, and got a unit of blood in the emergency room. ENT was consulted. They took her to the OR, gave her another unit there, and ligated the artery, debulked what they could of the mass."

"You said extensive involvement?"

"You'll see her. It's extensive." He cleared his throat. "They did an MRI yesterday. It showed multiple soft tissue masses through the face. There are two large lesions. One on her maxilla, which eroded into the maxillary artery—debulking probably got about fifty percent of it. There's another big one lateral and inferior to her left eye. That's wrapped around the temporal nerve and involves the orbicularis oculi muscle. The smaller tumors seem to be staying in the skin and subcutaneous tissue. The bigger ones aren't respecting tissue planes."

"Sounds bad."

"It is bad. Her whole freaking face is becoming a tumor. And it hurts her, man. It's in the nerves."

I sighed. "So, the big question: What does path say?" Pathology would clench it. Tissue, as they say, is the issue.

"Monica can take that."

I smiled. "Ravi said you like skin." As soon as the words were out of my mouth, I wished I could pull them back. Monica turned red again.

"She's the only person in the world who did a derm residency and still ended up in public health," Ravi said. "That's why I love her."

"Ravi . . ."

"See? She loves me, too."

"What's the path say?" I asked again, wanting to get a diagnosis on this thing that was turning entire faces into tumor.

"Histologically, it looks like an extremely aggressive dermatofibrosarcoma protuberans, with areas of fibrosarcoma," Monica said, sounding relieved to be moving to more professional topics. "That was my read and the pathologist's." Dermatofibrosarcoma protuberans is a rare cancer of fibroblasts, a soft tissue cell type ubiquitous through the body. She gnawed her lip. "I suppose the fibrosarcoma elements could account for the involvement of deeper structures, but clinically, it's acting very weird . . ."

"More like run-of-the-mill fibrosarcoma maybe?" I asked.

She shook her head, looking worried. "But that doesn't usually involve the head and neck. It's being classified as DFSP-FS. Dermatofibrosarcoma protuberans–fibrosarcoma. But if it's a form of DFSP-FS, and I guess it is, I've never seen anything this invasive. Or this extensive."

"That's because you were too busy removing moles."

"Shut up, Ravi."

"History?" I asked.

"Negative personal history for cancer," Ravi answered. "Negative family history. Negative for exposure to toxins or chemicals. Travel history is significant only for a trip to Hong Kong last year."

"What happened in Hong Kong?"

"Family and patient said nothing. The Lums visited family."

"No visits to shamans? No tours of toxic waste dumps?"

"Nothing notable."

I asked Monica, "What are the risk factors for fibrosarcoma?"

"Radiation, chemical exposure, genetic risk."

"And Beatrice Lum has none of these," I said.

They shook their heads.

"So," I said, "we have one confirmed case of the fibrosarcoma in San Francisco, Beatrice Lum. We have one suspected case in San Jose: a woman named Cynthia Yang, deceased. Lum's disease is more extensive than anyone's seen, correct?"

"She's been seen by ENT, plastics, dermatology, oncology. Ophthalmology even. No one's ever even read a case report of these cancers being so aggressive. Like I said, its presentation is really weird. Multiple foci. It's not looking as if she had one tumor which metastasized to other sites. It's like they *all* popped up at once."

"Clonality?" Genetic analysis of the tumors would tell us if the cancer sprouted from the same cell or arose from different ones. If all the cancerous cells were clones, that suggested metastasis—spread—from a single cell and tumor.

"That's another weird thing," Monica said. "They're clones."

I thought for a moment, then asked, "Did you match her to the pictures I sent?"

"Yeah," Ravi said. "We got what we think is a match." He reached into his shoulder bag. "Here—"

He stopped abruptly and slid the folder back into his

bag. His eyes and Monica's moved to something over my left shoulder.

"San Francisco," Ravi said under his breath. I turned.

Behind me stood a tall, gaunt man. Thirty-something, balding, bespectacled, a stethoscope slung around his neck. His khakis and frayed oxford shirt—his general inattention to fashion—screamed public health.

"I don't think there's a lot here for us," he said, by way of greeting. I caught Ravi's eye; he looked relieved. "It is bad, though. She's bad." The man stuck out a hand sprouting long, thin fingers. "Giles Spangler, San Francisco Department of Public Health."

"Nate McCormick." I shook the hand.

Ravi spoke. "Dr. McCormick worked with me at CDC."

Dr. Spangler, instead of being impressed, scowled. "CDC is here? This is—"

"I no longer work for CDC," I said. "I'm . . . freelance." I should clarify: there are not a lot of unaffiliated, freelance public health doctors out there. In fact, I might have been the only one.

Spangler stared at me for a moment. His eyes were a green so pale they were almost colorless.

"Nate's helping out," Ravi told him.

"Fair enough. 'Freelance.'" Spangler sighed. "Like I said, I don't know what we can do about this. Not a lot there. Didn't get a significant exposure history, no family history. Thanks for the heads-up, Monica, but I think we'll just stay out of this for now."

I could see the gears and cogs whirring in Ravi's brain. He was happy that the local boys weren't going to jump all over this. At the same time, it put him in an odd position:

trying to play in a game it didn't look like state would be asked to join.

But I didn't have any institutional loyalty. I didn't care who took ownership of this mess. I just wanted some get-up-and-go from someone.

"There was a case in Milpitas," I said.

Ravi looked as if I'd just blurted out his SAT scores to a room full of strangers.

Spangler blinked at me, surprised. "The dermatofibrosarcoma?"

"Looked like it," I told him. "That patient is dead."

Spangler absorbed the information. "There are seven million people in the Bay Area, Dr. McCormick. Statistically, there are likely to be a few cases—"

"This patient had the same multi-centric, extensive involvement," I interrupted. "We have reason to believe there may be more cases."

Ravi was trying to waste me with his eyes.

"What reason?" Spangler asked.

"I can't say now."

"Are these other cases in the Bay Area?"

"We don't know."

Spangler scratched his chin, thinking. "I'll take this to my boss. But I have to be honest, I don't see the public health angle yet. I don't see a cluster."

He was right. Two people were not a cluster. Ten people—those people in Murph's pictures, if they were all in the Bay Area—*that* would be a cluster. And we didn't know where those ten people were.

"Surveillance?" I asked, already knowing the answer.

"We won't be able to justify it," Spangler replied, pale eyes on me. He looked at Ravi and Monica. "State?"

"Nothing official," Ravi said.

Setting up disease or syndrome surveillance isn't as easy as flipping a switch. It involves bulletins, faxes, and e-mails to thousands of hospitals, clinics, and doctors' offices. It's very official, and the threshold to put the word out is high. The will to set up a surveillance program for anthrax is easy after the stuff turns up in envelopes around the country. The will to set up a surveillance program for a rare form of cancer that cropped up in two people in a population of seven million is nil.

"So," I said, "we wait."

"Yes," Spangler replied. "We wait."

"We wait," Ravi echoed unhappily.

I stood there, watching our highly trained, over-educated band of do-gooders shuffle their feet impotently. In our foxholes, in our bunkers, waiting.

"I'm going to see her," I said.

48

"WHAT ARE YOU DOING, McCORMICK?" Ravi muttered as we walked to the patient's room.

"We want the locals involved."

"No, we don't. Not yet."

"Well, you got your wish. Everyone's staying out of it."

"Just check things out with me before you blab, will you?"

"Ravi," I said, "no one's going to touch this. I *want* people to touch it."

"We are."

"No, *you* are. And somehow you roped Monica into it. Who else at your office knows about this?"

Ravi said nothing.

"Exactly," I said. "I appreciate the help. I do. But you're walking a fine line. Keeping this unofficial and quiet as long as you can so you have ownership over it when it pops could kill people."

Ravi refused to be provoked. "It's unofficial because we're maxed out now. State and CDC have their hands full of flu and another *E. coli* outbreak. You saw local's response."

"Why do you want to deal with it?" I asked.

"Because we're buddies, right, McCormick? And because you got a nose for the big thing, right?"

A nose for the big thing. I felt a spurt of anger, thinking of the ruined faces in Murph's photographs, of the dead woman, of the woman in the room we were about to enter. "Just stop playing games, okay?"

Ravi didn't answer me, just pushed forward into Room 15.

Beatrice Lum was awake. She occupied the bed close to the door, a curtain separating her from the patient in the window bed. A man sat holding her hand. Her husband, I guessed. The television played what looked to be a soap opera. Unfamiliar language squawked from the TV remote control/speaker on the bed next to her. Her face was heavily bandaged above the lip on the left side and on the lower jaw. An egg-sized mass rose from the area around her left eye. She looked like she'd been smacked with a baseball bat.

The distribution of Beatrice Lum's tumors—along the nasolabial fold, at the corner of the eye—was identical to the distribution of tumors in the pictures.

I noticed a morphine drip hung next to saline.

"You're popular today," Ravi said, smiling. Mr. Lum forced a smile. The bandages on his wife's face shifted; I assumed underneath she was trying to smile, too. Both looked exhausted.

"This is Dr. McCormick from the Centers for Disease Control," Ravi told them. I shot a hard look at him. I was getting sick of the lying. Bad enough when I did it myself; worse when it was done on my behalf. "You've heard of the CDC, right?"

Mr. Lum nodded.

"Pictures?" I asked. Ravi produced his folder and slid out a blowup. He handed it to me and I held it up to Mrs. Lum.

When they saw the picture, the Lums' faces contorted; you'd think I'd just dropped my pants. "I showed them before," Ravi said in a low voice. "They don't seem to like the photos."

"Why?"

"They won't say."

I handed the reproduction back to him and it disappeared into folder and bag.

"Now," Ravi told the Lums, "I know we covered this before. But I was hoping you could tell Dr. McCormick when you first noticed anything wrong."

"We noticed a little bump about five or six months ago.

It was here." Mr. Lum pointed to the left side of his upper lip. "It grew bigger and then we saw other bumps here"—he pointed to his left eye—"and here." He touched his jaw.

"Did you go to the doctor at that time?" I asked.

Glances between the two. "No."

"Why?"

"We couldn't go, Dr. McCormick."

"Why not?"

"We answered these questions for Dr. Singh before. And for Dr. Spangler after that—"

"Sorry. This is something doctors do," I said, trying to win him over with a smile. "We ask the same questions over and over. But we're very concerned for your wife, and for you, and we need to make sure all the questions have been asked. There may be other people who have what your wife has."

Mr. Lum's lips pressed together. I persisted, "Was your wife feeling well otherwise?"

"Yes."

"Any recent sicknesses?"

"No."

"Any sweating during the night?"

"No."

"Any contact with sick—"

"We did not have contact with any sick people. She did not have exposure to any chemicals. We have taken one trip in the past year, to Hong Kong. She was not sick then. We do not have any pets. She works as an accountant—"

"Okay, Mr. Lum."

"—in a software company. We have two children. They are fifteen and seventeen. She takes no medication—"

"Mr. Lum—"

"—except for multiple vitamins. She has never been exposed to radiation. She has always been healthy except for a hysterectomy for benign fibroid tumors—"

I put my hand on his shoulder, silencing his volley of bitter answers. "It's okay, Mr. Lum. Mrs. Lum? Are you in pain?"

"Yes," Mr. Lum said for his wife. "She's in great pain."

"Your wife speaks English?" I asked him.

Something I'd swear was hatred sparked in his dark eyes. Mr. Lum said, "Of course."

"Then, I'd like to speak with her. Alone, if you don't mind."

"I don't think—"

Mrs. Lum said something—tired and sharp—in Chinese. Her husband's face darkened. His response was in Chinese, but I could guess the meaning; it sounded like "Do whatever the hell you want."

"I am going for coffee," Mr. Lum announced.

I turned and caught Ravi's eye, nodded. "I'll get some coffee, too," Ravi said. When they left the room, I sat in the chair, still warm from the husband's body.

"I'm sorry to send everyone out. I just wanted to talk to you." I spoke softly, so as not to disturb—or interest—the patient on the other side of the curtain.

The bandaged woman nodded.

"You're still in pain, aren't you?"

"No," she breathed. Because of the surgery near her mouth, her words were indistinct. "Not now. The morphine . . ."

"Good."

The pain was a thread. I followed it. "Were you taking pain medications before you came here?"

"Yes . . ."

"What medicine?"

"Vicodin. Percocet. We told the doctors this."

"Who prescribed the medicine?"

Mrs. Lum sighed, shook her head slightly.

"Who wrote the prescriptions?"

"No prescriptions."

"Who gave it to you?"

She said nothing.

"Mrs. Lum, you need to talk to me. Otherwise, I can't help you."

I wouldn't have been able to tell she was crying if not for the tears draining slowly from her eyes, across the bumps on her face.

"It's okay," I told her, though we both knew it was not. "I'd like to take a look at your wounds, if you don't mind."

"I don't mind," she said softly.

Carefully, I undid the tape that tacked down the gauze over her lip. I looked first at the surgical site. The wound was enormous, raw and glistening, about four centimeters square and crossing the vermilion border of the lip. I could see the contours of bone and muscle, what was left over after the tumor's excision. I assumed the plastics folks were talking skin grafts at this point. Even with the best reconstructive medicine, Mrs. Lum would never look normal again. Whatever normal meant.

I sat back in the chair, reached into my shoulder bag, and retrieved Murph's photos. "These are people who have what you have," I told her. I paged through them, one after the other, trying to match Lum's face to a face in the ugly images.

She was not there.

"There are others who are sick," I said.

"Yes," she agreed.

I felt my heartbeat quicken. "You knew there were others?"

Mrs. Lum stared at me.

"Where? Here? Hong Kong? You recognize these people?" I held the pictures up to her.

"There are so many . . ." she whispered. Then, "Please. Stop."

I did. I sheaved the pages. "What happened to you? Do you know why you are ill? Mrs. Lum?" My gaze drifted to the mound of flesh heaped next to her eye, to the gaping wound at her mouth that would forever change the sound of her voice.

"I don't know," she said.

"What happened in Hong Kong?"

"I cannot help you," she said.

"I need to know what's going on. I want to keep others from getting sick."

"I know," she said. "I cannot help you."

Hundreds of patient interviews taught me to know when the end has come, when one more question would be nothing but wasted breath.

Gently, I reattached the bandages to her face and sat. I picked up her hand and held it cupped between mine. We sat in silence, listening to the faint sounds of the Chinese-language soap opera on the television. The skin of her hand was smooth, perfect.

"I'm sorry," she said. Her eyes met mine. She was asking for help that I could not give her.

I looked at the undulating landscape of her ruined face, at the serum stains seeping through the gauze. "So am I," I told her.

49

I STAYED WITH BEATRICE LUM for another ten minutes, doing the only thing left to me at that point: to give a little comfort. No more questions, no discussion of what protocol—surgery? radiation?—to evaluate or follow. I held her hand and watched a television show I could not understand.

Perhaps Brooke was right. Perhaps I don't like real people. Perhaps I only like the sick, the desperate. So be it.

The gaze of the bandaged woman in the bed unnerved me. It was the look of someone who knew she was dying.

I felt my anger rise.

I tore off a corner of the folder that contained the photos and scrawled my contact information on it. "My business card," I said, and smiled. Mrs. Lum smiled back and broke my heart.

"I'll come back tomorrow," I promised. "Maybe we can talk again then."

Mrs. Lum surprised me. "Yes," she said. "Yes."

My spirits lifted for the first time in days.

* * *

"We're trying to save her life—"

"Dr. Singh, I—"

"—and you're not telling us squat."

"I know nothing. I am not a doctor."

I was in the hall outside Mrs. Lum's room watching Ravi seriously invade Mr. Lum's space. Ravi, two inches shorter than the other man, had his finger pointed like a stiletto.

I realize that I am not the most politic when it comes to dealing with people, that my *savoir faire* leaves a lot to be desired. But I'm an angel when compared to Ravinder Singh. While my evaluations at CDC always suggested the need for improvement in professional relations, Ravi's, I believe, implored him to learn the definition of the phrase. The man was insane.

"Bull. *Bull,* man," Ravi said in a harsh whisper. "What was your wife *doing*?" Two nurses down the hall stared.

"I don't know anything. I am not a doctor."

Let's fill in that bright line between Dr. Singh and myself. I can be pretty compelling when I need to be; I'm a pain in people's asses, I can twist an arm or two when needed. But in an investigation, Ravi is a cluster bomb. When he was in Benin doing his meningitis work, rumor had it he'd come across a corrupt headmaster at a boys' school there. The man denied any outbreaks at the school, unless, of course, a donation was made to the school's "scholarship fund"—in which case he might be able to give the ballistic CDC investigator access to the boys. Ravi, who'd contracted malaria a few days earlier, was in no mood to haggle. He grabbed the guy by the shirt, dragged him over his desk, slapped him two or three times across the face, broke his glasses, then asked the questions again. This time, the headmaster seemed able to produce information, and Ravi ended up making a small donation to the Headmaster Spectacles Replacement Fund.

Thank God, I thought, we're not in Benin.

"Hey. Don't say that to me again, because I know it's not true," Ravi said. Just so you know, this—this browbeating—is not the approach you would take with ninety-nine percent of people you interview on an investigation. But for some reason we didn't know, the Lums were lying low. They would not complain to Ravi's superiors and we all knew it. "Let's go through it all again," he insisted. "Does she use any cosmetic products? Creams, soaps, astringents—"

"I already told you, no."

"Bull. All women use that stuff. Has she had any exposure to chemicals? Arsenic? Polyvinyl chloride? Something called TCDD?" These were some of the chemicals known to cause soft tissue tumors.

"No."

"Did she get any procedures done in Hong Kong?"

"Procedures? No."

"Bull. Did she do anything out of the ordinary in the last year?"

"No."

"Bullshit. Bullshit. Bullshit."

"Ravi—" I said.

"What?"

"—Lay off." I could tell this was going nowhere. Ravi, in the thick of battle, could not. "Mr. Lum doesn't want to talk, it's his right."

"It's *not* his right, *Doctor.*" Ravi shot a look at me like he wanted to kill. For his part, Lum looked relieved that someone was getting this lunatic off his back.

"As long as this is a side project for you, it is. Mr. Lum would tell us if he knew anything that would help his wife."

A look of total misery crumpled Lum's face. "I want to help my wife," he insisted, then he turned away from us, toward her room. I made space for him to pass. He did, shuffling as if he'd been beaten, sliding his hand along the wall for support.

After Lum was gone, I turned back to Ravi. "We going to be able to work together, Dr. Singh?"

"If you let me do my job."

"Which is not this. Your boss know you're here today?"

He didn't answer.

"This is my deal, bud," I said. "Not because I want it to be, but as you said, nobody will officially touch this with what we have now. San Francisco doesn't see anything here. The state won't give a damn about this until another half-dozen cases pop up."

"I run my own show."

"Of course you don't. You got some wiggle room, but you don't run your own show. I'm the only one who runs his own show."

"And you have no cred. Not now. Not a shred of it."

"I didn't say it was perfect." I thought for a moment, trying to see all the angles—me, Ravi, California and San Francisco public health departments. "You be careful with Monica. Don't let her get sucked into this any more than she already is. It could get very dicey."

"Monica's a big girl. She wants to be involved." He paused. "And she likes skin. Fuck it—I got a meeting." He stalked down the hall past me, then stopped. He turned. "They said you didn't play too well with others."

"Funny. They said the same thing about you."

He grinned. "This is going to be a blast, McCormick."

Weird thing is, I think he meant it.

50

ON THE WAY OUT OF the hospital, I turned the conversation with Mrs. Lum over in my head. One thing kept bubbling to the surface. A gestalt. A feeling. It was the same vibe I got down in Milpitas from Mr. Yang, with his dead wife, his knife, and his huddling kids. These people were terrified.

So your wife is bleeding out and you go to the hospital. You didn't go sooner, because you were scared of something. But if you're so scared, why hang around for the consultations with plastics, derm, oncology? Why not bolt as soon as your wife is stabilized? Despite the new laws protecting admitted patients from prying eyes, it wouldn't have been difficult for a motivated party to find out where the Lums were camping out. There were better places to get lost than at the General.

So why didn't they leave? Why did they think the General would be safe?

Because they wanted to have their cake and eat it, too.

I stopped abruptly, and a man on crutches stumbled into me. I threw an apology over my shoulder as I ran.

"Where's the billing department?" I asked at the information desk.

The elderly lady there dutifully pulled out a map, searched on it for what seemed like two weeks. "Don't get that question much," she explained, before reaching for the phone.

Information received, she directed me to the fourth floor of a building located in front of the main hospital.

A hospital's billing department has got to be one of the most depressing places on the planet. First off, there's the environment—all drab cubicles and computers and buzzing fluorescent lights. More depressing is that the billing department is ground zero for many of the problems facing health care at the moment. Listen carefully, and you can almost hear the foundations of the system groan.

I stopped at the desk, hit a tiny bell, and looked out over the stockyard of billing personnel. I imagined the conversations with Medicare or Medi-Cal or some private insurer, the battles just to get thirty cents on the dollar. I played out the calls to collection agencies who were set loose on some poor soul who got way in over his financial head with his chemo treatment. This office doled out misery, it received misery. Underneath it all is the vague feeling—screw "vague," the *acute* feeling—that this just cannot go on any longer. And yet it goes on.

An overweight woman with a pretty face answered the bell. I gave her the spiel, and she called a Mr. Diggs to assist me. Diggs was a skinny black man with a big smile and bigger glasses. Surprisingly, neither Diggs nor the receptionist looked miserable. I made a mental note to test the water here after I was finished with this mess.

Diggs asked how he could help.

Here goes, I thought. "I need access to the billing records of a patient." Then I gave him the whole CDC line, flashed the old ID. I prayed he wouldn't see the need to double-check with my nonexistent superiors.

Diggs really was in a good mood that day—perhaps Medicare had just increased reimbursement—and didn't hassle me. Instead, he led me through the warren of cubicles to his desk. "We don't see CDC much," he confided.

Neither do I, I thought.

"In fact, I don't think we ever see them. Something going on?"

"Unfortunately, I can't discuss."

"Sure, I know. Just asking. Patient name?"

"Beatrice Lum."

He batted a few keys on his computer. "Asian, huh? Avian flu stuff?"

"No, thank God."

"Good. You guys know what's happening with it?"

"I don't. Different division."

"Should I be stockpiling Tamiflu?"

"Is this the record?" I asked, avoiding his question. I mean, this guy didn't listen. *Different division,* Mr. Diggs. As in a division that's not affiliated with flu, CDC, or any organ of government, federal, state, or local. Still, I had sympathy for the man. There's a lot to be worried about these days and not a lot of answers.

"This is it," he announced.

I scanned the screen. Surgical fees, payment for the anesthesiologist, hospital fees, other sundries. This bill came to over forty thousand dollars.

"That's weird," Diggs said.

"What?"

He pointed to the bottom of the screen: the word "Paid" was there, with today's date. "Hold on a second." He tapped more keys. "Looks like this woman is paying for services just as soon as they're done. Cashier's check. I mean, I like to see this. But . . . "—he rubbed at his face, baffled—"no one does that."

"Check the patient's address."

Diggs went to the patient record, found the address.

"Can you get on the Internet here?"

"Sure."

"Let's double-check the address online."

Diggs cut and pasted the address into Google. "Weird," he repeated. "That address doesn't exist."

"Weird," I agreed, already backing away from Diggs and his computer. Because now I knew that the patient didn't exist either.

51

I RAN—DOWN THREE FLIGHTS in Building 20, across to the main hospital, up another four flights. By the time I arrived on the fifth floor, I was out of breath and disoriented by the hospital's layout. I collared a group of physicians and asked for 4D, the surgical ward. They told me. I ran.

I burst into Beatrice Lum's room. The curtain was drawn around Beatrice Lum, and I ripped it back.

The bed was empty. Two IVs dangled and dripped onto the floor.

I slid the curtain to the wall, for the first time looking at the patient in the window-side bed. She was elderly, dark-skinned, and shocked by my sudden appearance. "Did you see these people leave?" I asked her. "Did you hear them say anything?"

No trace of comprehension on her face. The name on the whiteboard near the entrance to the room read "Martinez."

"Estas personas están saliendo? Estas . . . es la . . ." I might as well have been speaking Farsi. Damn my laziness in Spanish class.

I ducked back into the hall, grabbed a nurse. "You have 15-2?"

She nodded.

"Where's the patient?"

"She's in the room."

"She's not."

The nurse walked quickly to the room, stuck in her head. "Maybe they went for a walk. She's ambulatory and we've been trying to get her out of bed."

"Her belongings are gone. Call Security."

"I'm sure they just went for a—"

"Without her IVs? Call Security!"

The nurse glowered at me, set down the pitcher of water she was carrying, and headed for the ward clerk. A minute later, I heard a broadcast over the PA system. *"Patient Beatrice Lum, please contact Security. Patient Beatrice Lum . . ."*

52

SO, THE LUMS WERE SO tweaked they did not want anyone to know they were at the hospital. They paid in cashier's checks to preserve anonymity. That worked—until Ravi's scorched-earth tactics and my probing of Mrs. Lum pushed them too far.

They were gone.

And what was scaring them was scaring me.

As I raced to my car, I kept checking over my shoulder to see if anyone was following me. The tall man in the oversized T-shirt? No. The burly guy in construction clothes? No. The delivery man? The gardener? The short one, the fat one? No, no, no.

The Asian guy with the tweed vest? Maybe. The Asian guy strolling along, talking on a cell phone? Maybe.

My guts were twisted by the hangover, the smoothie, a mounting paranoia, and the suspicion that I was becoming a racist fuck.

I tried to peer into the dark black water that seemed to be engulfing me and those I came in contact with. Daniel Zhang, the Lums, the Yangs, the Murphys . . .

Murph.

A few hours, I thought. A few hours more of Paul Murphy living and breathing on this planet and telling me what had disfigured these people. A few more hours in which I could have told him to bundle up his kids, flee to a place far from here. But I'd screwed up and come too late. Murph was dead and his wife and kids were dead. Now other people were dead and dying.

I got into the car, pulled out my phone, and dialed Ravi. "The Lums bolted," I told him.

"What are you talking about? They checked out?"

"No. They left AMA—" Against Medical Advice. "Yanked out the IVs and split."

"We'll track them down at home," he said.

"We won't. They gave a false name and address."

"Check Billing."

"Already did. They paid with a cashier's check."

"Un-be-freaking-lievable. Damn it. Damn *it.*" There was a pause. "Don't say it, McCormick."

"What?"

"Don't say 'I told you so.' "

"Much as I'd like to blame you for everything, Ravi, I

think you only accelerated things. It was only a matter of time before they left."

"Why?"

"Because they're scared stiff about being found by someone, and it's not us. And they're more terrified of them than they are of a bunch of tumors."

53

SO WE DIDN'T KNOW WHO and we didn't know the details of where, but we did know what—aggressive, weird fibrosarcoma. But a few cases had not and would not get public health into an uproar. For the time being, any queries had to be on the underneath. Which meant I had to call in more favors.

I dialed a number in Atlanta.

"Millicent Bao."

"Millie, it's Nathaniel McCormick."

"Oh, my goodness. Nate. Where are you?"

"California."

"Wow. Still there. So you're actually making it work with Brooke?" She sounded skeptical.

"Working at making it, more like. How's the brood?"

"More chaotic than the Middle East. Clive just turned one, and our eldest, the potty mouth, is trying to make sure his first word isn't 'mommy.' Ellen's started to become materialistic already, and . . ."

Millicent Bao was researcher in the National Center for HIV, STD, and TB Prevention at CDC. She'd spent her early years doing fieldwork in China, where the blond-haired, blue-eyed girl from West Texas met a dark-haired, dark-eyed Chinese grad student named Li-ming Bao. Love, marriage, five kids. I met Millie through Li-ming, who did epidemiology work in Africa, which was part of my CDC beat. In that last year, when I wasn't on a plane to visit Brooke, they took me in. You got five kids, what's one more, right?

Most important today, though, were Millicent Bao's very deep contacts in China.

"I need a favor," I said.

"How big?"

"Moderate."

"A one or two nights' babysitting favor?"

"I'm on the West Coast, Millie."

"But you'll be back."

"You hear what I'm asking, then you decide."

"Watch out," she warned. "I'm sensing no matter what it is, we'll want a week."

"I need you to check with Hong Kong public health, find out whether they've had a spike in cases of dermatofibrosarcoma protuberans."

"Uh, say again."

"Dermatofibrosarcoma protuberans. Soft tissue tumor. Rare."

"You doing cancer now?"

"Not really."

"Can I ask what this is for?"

"You can ask, but . . . Well, let's just say I don't think CDC is going to be interested in this yet. And don't let anyone know the request came from me. Definitely don't say anything to the ex-boss."

"All right. And what do I tell Hong Kong?"

"I don't know. Act like you don't speak the language that well."

"They speak English in Hong Kong, Nate."

"Tell them you only speak Laotian. Just tell them we have a low suspicion there's a cluster there, but we want to make sure. We can bump it to the next level if need be. Right now, though, we don't want anyone to think we're crying wolf."

She laughed. "'We.' No 'we' about it, pumpkin. You don't work here anymore, remember?" Her tone became serious. "Nate—is this something we should be worried about?"

"Not yet. Let me do the worrying for now."

"Two nights," she bartered. "Consecutive. On a weekend."

"You trust me that much?"

"No. But I haven't seen a movie in the theater for a year."

I gave Millie my cell number and disconnected.

So, the what was answered, progress was being made on the where. It was time to do something about the who.

54

"GANG TASK FORCE," THE FEMALE voice said.

I'd spent a few seconds deciding whether to call the number for General Works or the Gang Task Force. But it wasn't really a decision: Asian victim, Asian thugs. The scale tipped toward the GTF.

I read the receptionist the case number from the follow-up report the officer had given me after Daniel Zhang's assault.

"Just a moment," the receptionist said, and began to hum. "That case is assigned to Inspector Tang. I'll connect you."

Click, click. Ring, ring.

"Jack Tang," a voice said.

I introduced myself, mentioned that I was calling about the assault of Daniel Zhang the night before. Tang asked me to hold on. I could hear shuffling around the telephone, then the voice in my ear. "Who are you again?"

I told him.

"Right," he said. "The witness. Your friend never returned my follow-up calls."

"I'm not surprised."

"He didn't want EMS. Or to go to the hospital."

"Right. I have some questions—"

"Questions . . ."

"Kind of about who did this."

"That's exactly what we'd like to know, Mr. McCormick," Inspector Tang said.

"The officer last night—Officer Polaski—said something about gangs. He said things like that don't happen without a reason."

"And you're going to give me a reason?"

"No. I don't know any reason."

"Maybe your friend knows about a reason."

"Maybe. Look, I was just wondering if you guys were going to go through any files to find them."

"What files?"

"I don't know. Your *gang* files. Yakuza stuff. I don't know."

"You're telling me Zhang's attackers were Yakuza? What makes you think that, Mr. McCormick?"

"God, I don't know. I just want these thugs caught, okay?"

"Were they Japanese?"

"I don't know."

"If they were Yakuza, they would be Japanese."

"I'm not saying they're Yakuza."

From the report, he read, "'A large tattoo on left neck resembling the tail of a dragon.' That could be Yakuza."

"I don't know if they're Yakuza."

"There are no known Yakuza in the United States now."

"Then they're probably not Yakuza. Maybe they're Chinese. Daniel Zhang is Chinese."

"And Zhang has connections to organized crime?"

"Christ, I don't know."

"Look, Mr. McCormick—"

"I'm an MD—"

"I assure you that we'll do everything we can—"

"Do you have mug shots or something I could look at? Maybe one of the guys I saw—?" There was no response. "This is going nowhere," I said. "Forget I called."

"Wait, wait. Wait a second." I could almost hear him smiling into the phone. "Why don't you come down to the station, and we'll talk a little. You can look through mug shots, if you want."

Well, Inspector Tang, I wanted.

55

THE HUNK OF MUNICIPAL CONCRETE and glass called the Southern District Police Station rose impressively next to an elevated section of Interstate 80. Most of the building was blocky, small-windowed, Orwellian. But on the west, the concrete gave way to undulating glass, evoking ocean waves rippling along the highway.

The Gang Task Force was five floors up, located in a space crammed with cubicles and desks topped by computers. It could have been headquarters for a retail bank or an insurance company, except that most of the workers here packed heat. And handcuffs. And looked a hell of a lot tougher than your average loan officer.

The secretary pointed me to a cubicle at the far end of

the room. There, a man sat with his feet on his desk, laughing with another guy in a cubicle across the aisle.

Mid-thirties, styled hair, two days' stubble, sport jacket with an open shirt, Jack Tang could have been the swaggering lead cop from some hip Fox show. Chow Yun-Fat for the American set. Inspector Cool.

Tang pulled his sturdy-but-stylish shoes off the desk and stuck his hand out to shake mine. He didn't stand. "That was fast, Mr. McCormick."

"Speed limit all the way," I said. "And it's actually *Dr.* McCormick."

Normally, the Mr. McCormick thing doesn't bother me, but when I felt like I needed some respect, and when we'd already been over that territory before, I plugged the "doctor" thing. I always felt a little dirty when I did it.

"I know you're a doctor," he replied. "I got about a dozen doctors in my family, and they all get fussy about that, too."

"I'm not fussy."

"Of course you're not." He leaned back in his chair, indicated the one next to his desk. "You have anything else for me?" he asked as I sat.

"Only what I told you on the phone."

"Which is not much."

We didn't seem to be getting off to a good start, and I told him that.

"I'm this way with everybody," he assured me. "Just look at this from my perspective, okay? I'm Gang Task Force, right? Extortion, assaults, prostitution, gun violations—anything nonfatal that has to do with gangs."

"Sure."

"And I have a case file bigger than my car."

"Okay."

"And the patrol officer figured this assault might be gang related, so your case ends up on my desk."

"Reasonable."

"But the investigation can't go forward unless one of you two guys starts cooperating. At this point, you're not telling me anything that would lead me to believe this was gang related. Except that the men in question were of a particular race and that they drove a nice car. So what am I supposed to do with that?"

"A guy got beaten up by three men with guns."

He smiled, crossed his ankles, exhaled. Twenty years before, this guy would have been smoking like a chimney. "Your friend told Officer Polaski the whole thing was just a 'misunderstanding.'"

"It wasn't just a misunderstanding."

"What was it, then?"

"I'm not sure, but I have a feeling."

"A feeling?"

I told him I used to work for CDC, used to be a "medical detective." I figured it would give me a little credibility.

"'Medical detective.'" With another big exhalation, he leaned forward, as if he had to get to more important things: joking with his buddies, going over scripts for next week's show.

Still, something in the momentum of our meeting had changed. "You were here to look at pictures. So let's look at pictures." He put his hands on his knees and hoisted himself out of the chair, led me over to a woman who sat at the edge of the constellation of desks. "Dana, please show *Dr.* McCormick the mug shots we have for Asian gang members, affiliates, suspected members." He looked at me, then back at her. "And Dana—be thorough. Give the doc here everything we have." He disappeared to make a call, I assumed, to his agent about that NBC pilot.

Dana, a middle-aged black woman, led me to a computer. "You want any coffee, hon?" she asked.

"No thanks."

"You sure?" She laughed. "Asian guys in their twenties or thirties. Ooo-wee. You're going to be here awhile."

She logged me on to the workstation and brought up the cataloging program, hit a couple of keys to sort for race, age. A full screen of names came up.

"How many are here?" I asked.

"Oh, maybe six hundred in the system, the ones who've been booked and have mug shots. You come get me when you're finished with those. Then we'll get you the binders with the other ones."

"The other ones?"

"The ones who were detained but not booked. We get their pictures just to have them on file."

"How many of those?"

"A couple hundred more," she answered cheerfully.

So, *ooo-wee,* I was going to be there awhile. And the hangover worked through my brain like a bone saw. "Maybe I will take that coffee, after all."

56

THE FOLKS AT THE SAN Francisco Gang Task Force had been busy over the years. There were the mug shots, of course, and then the binders: photo after photo of sour-looking young men against nondescript backgrounds. The photos were labeled: "Benny Tan, aka, Legs, aka Bean." Many also had "known associate" or "? associate." The name of an organization followed. Joe Boys. Wah Ching. United Bamboo. Jackson Street Boys.

I put the cup to my lips and sucked the early afternoon tar that was on tap at the SFPD.

Two hours later, after all the quality time spent with two-dimensional, dangerous-looking people, I found almost nothing. On the computer, I brought up the one mug shot that interested me. Unlike the gent who'd slapped his paws on the hood of my car, who swung the bat into Daniel Zhang, this man's face was pocked with acne scars. He had no tattoo. And he was not smiling. But there was something about the eyes, I thought. Similar bone structure, perhaps. A caption underneath the picture read: *Michael Kwong, member Tun Bo On org.*

The second thing I'd found—a picture in the binder—may or may not have been the man with the baseball cap who'd stuck his gun into my face the night of Daniel Zhang's beating. The eyes drooped at the sides and the whites were bloodshot, as if this guy were, like me, on just the other side of a hangover.

"Mr. McCormick, how's it coming?"

"Señor Tang," I said, smiling. "It's coming along okay. I found two—"

I indicated the picture of the guy who could have been the man in the baseball cap. Tang glanced at it, ran his finger over the identifying information. "William Yun. Billy Yun. Not your guy."

"You sound pretty sure."

He hunched over my shoulder to the computer, opened a new window, typed "Yun" into the search field, and hit a key. The screen filled with text and, in its upper corner, a small picture of the man in the binder photo. "Mr. Yun is currently serving eight years at Folsom for attempted murder," Tang said.

"Okay," I said. "Not him. What about the other guy?"

Tang closed the window with Billy Yun's mug on it, and stared into the dead-looking eyes of a man named Michael Kwong. "Probably not."

"Probably?"

"Michael Kwong is no longer in the country."

"How do you know that?"

"If he's here, he's stupid."

"Can you elaborate?"

If my insistence bothered Tang, he gave no sign of it. He bent to the computer again. "There was a racketeering charge against him. About seven years ago, we indicted six guys, Kwong was one of them. He served two years at Pelican Bay before his conviction was overturned on a technicality. Only way to get rid of him was to deport him to Hong Kong."

"Who is he?"

He clicked back to the picture, ignored my question. "Besides, Michael Kwong was not muscle. I can't imagine him whacking some guy with a baseball bat."

"But who is he?"

Tang straightened. "There are five big crime syndicates—triads—in Hong Kong: 14K, Sun Yee On, Wo Sing Wo, Wo Hop To, Tun Bo On. Michael Kwong was with Tun Bo On, the smallest of the five. He was sent here, we believe, to expand their operations into California."

"So the—what are they called? Triads? They aren't normally active here?"

"The triads are Chinese grown and cultivated, and otherwise Asian oriented. The money's much bigger for them over there, but periodically, they make pushes into Canada and the States."

"And Michael Kwong was part of that?"

"We think. Tun Bo On was hammered pretty hard by Hong Kong and Taiwanese police back in the early nineties. They lost a lot of ground in Asia, and we think they expanded here in California and in Vancouver to increase revenue. It didn't go too well for them, though."

"No?"

"Nah. We nailed Kwong eleven months after he got off the boat. There were rumors that he was a big cheese in Hong Kong, but it turned out he was a low-level operator—a *dai lo,* street boss in HK. Two gambling halls under his belt, small potatoes. He comes here with big ideas, he affiliates with a local street gang, gets a little vice going, a little gambling, some drugs. We worked with the FBI and busted him under RICO. Murder-for-hire rap."

"So you guys think he's out of here."

"The triads sent a minor guy to test the waters. Kwong gets busted, they retreat." Tang clicked back to the image of Michael Kwong. "There hasn't been any triad activity in the States since then, but we've had some signs that the triads might be making a play for SF again. We've hammered the youth gangs and some tong members, so there's something of a power vacuum now. The triads could be trying to take advantage of the chaos."

"The Chinese triads."

"Right. Triads are only Chinese."

"And the tongs are also Chinese?"

"No. Homegrown. Chinese-American."

"And the youth gangs?"

"Same. U.S."

"So maybe this Kwong guy is working for them."

"Michael Kwong is triad. He's Chinese."

"Maybe he's a tong member."

"Then he's not Michael Kwong," the inspector said, frustration creeping into his voice. "Kwong is *triad.*"

"Jesus, I thought biochem was confusing." Frustration at not understanding—the same tight feeling I got when trying to figure out fatty acid oxidation in med school—was filling my head. Ten minutes ago, I thought that effing Chinese gangs were just effing Chinese gangs; now I had tongs, triads, and youth gangs. "All right. Enlighten me: who are the tongs?"

Tang looked at his watch. "I don't have time for the history lesson, Mr. McCormick. I've got someplace to be."

"Then I'll walk you to your car, Inspector. I think the history lesson might be important."

* * *

"We've had Chinese trouble in this city since the nineteenth century, right? Coolies come from the mainland to build the railroads. They're profoundly bummed about being in a racist country so far from home. The tongs pop up to help these guys. They start out as community organizations and merchants' associations. They help the new arrivals with places to gather, help them with jobs and so on. But these profoundly bummed guys are also profoundly bummed about having no women. So, the vice industry kicks up. The coolies numb themselves with opium, which was legal, by the way. They gamble for companionship and to pass the time. The tongs see the money to be made in prostitution, gambling, and opium. They fight over turf for the illegal trade, and, voilà, the Tong Wars of the nineteenth century." Tang scooped up his cop stuff—jacket, gun, cuffs, sunglasses, breath mints—then headed for the elevator. I stuck to his heels. "Don't you have some diseases or something to detect?"

"I would, but we won the war against disease."

"Yeah. And we stamped out crime yesterday. Anyhow, things quiet down and don't really get kicking again until immigration law changes in the sixties and normalization of relations with the mainland in the seventies. Then the gates open, new immigrants come, their kids come. The kids are disaffected and picked on; they coalesce into the youth gangs. There starts to be some violence, some turf battles."

"Tong Wars of the twentieth century," I said.

"No. The Tong Wars were fought by tongs—the old guys—who operated their gambling and prostitution as well as their legit businesses. No, these were youth gangs. They started out pretty innocent—selling firecrackers—

then took a page from the criminal gangs back in Asia and started shaking down merchants in the area for protection money. Initially, they had no connection to the tongs. But they were making more and more trouble, so the tongs decided to deal with the Huns rather than to fight them. Some of the tongs linked up with youth gangs. The tongs got street muscle; the gangs got places to hang out and some legitimacy."

"Not like the Mafia."

"Hell no. The American Chinese mafia is a myth. Think of the tongs and the youth gangs as two separate groups with different but intersecting interests: the young guys get places to hang out, places rented for them by tong members. They go from being a bunch of kids with small-time rackets to kids with small-time rackets and elder affiliation. The old guys get the irritating youth off their backs, and get the bonus of someone to protect gambling and vice establishments."

The elevator stopped on the basement floor. We stepped out into a bleak hallway. "You heard of the Golden Dragon Massacre?" Tang asked.

"No."

"In 1979, a youth gang called the Joe Boys opens fire in the Golden Dragon restaurant to kill some guys from a gang called the Wah Ching. No Wah Ching were hit, but five bystanders were killed. Eleven others were wounded. In '83, Wah Mee Club in Seattle, fourteen people hogtied and shot. Christmas Eve, '82, New York City, three murdered in a Chinatown bar in a turf war. A thirteen-year-old was gunned down. A gang called the Asian Boyz was linked to twelve murders in one year in the mid-nineties."

"That seems like ancient history."

"Allen Leung, a community leader and former head of Hop Sing Tong, was gunned down last year. Last week two Mexican illegals were beaten to death a couple blocks from Central Station. Asian gang involvement is suspected in both cases. That recent enough for you, Mr. McCormick?"

We were in a large garage now, and Tang made his way to one of the unmarked Chevys that sat, beetle-like, in a long line of other unmarked Chevys.

"These guys are violent and uncontrolled. SFPD got hip to things after Golden Dragon and created the Gang Task Force to deal with them. We've done a pretty good job crippling the youth gangs with RICO, and have actually managed to bring down a few tong members. The situation is in flux, though. Hop Sing, for example, is now legit. But in flux or not, I still don't see any connection to your friend Zhang. My gut says this is a waste of time." Tang put his hand to his lips.

"When did you quit?" I asked.

"Sorry?"

"Smoking."

Tang pulled his fingers from his lips. "Nice catch. The doctor in you or the disease detective?"

"The former smoker."

"Ha. You know what cigarette is in Chinese?"

"No."

"*Yan.* Also means 'to castrate.' "

"I can see the public health campaign already."

"Yeah." Tang laughed. We were standing in front of the car now. He reached for the door, opened it. "Look, Dr. McCormick, I love talking about this stuff. It's my life, right? And I'm happy you're interested, but I really got to go."

I sized up Inspector Tang. Perhaps because he took the time to talk to me when he didn't want to, perhaps because he was a former smoker, I'd begun to trust the guy. "It wasn't just a misunderstanding," I said.

Tang smiled. In that moment, I realized he'd played me—let me get comfortable, let me ask my dumb questions. His gut told him there was more, and his gut knew I would tell him. "Where's your car?" he asked.

"Parked in front."

"Get in. I'll give you a ride."

57

WE SAT IN THE OFFICIAL vehicle, hazards on, blocking traffic, and I gave him the whole sordid mess. About Murph and family, the guy with the dragon tattoo. About Daniel Zhang and Dorothy Zhang. About the men and women with the mauled faces. I didn't mention the hot weapon I'd flashed on Daniel Zhang's attackers.

"It seems as though there may be some intimidation going on," Tang said.

"*May be* some intimidation? Four people were killed. Two kids and a woman included. I watched a guy get the shit kicked out of him."

"I know, but this doesn't . . . I can't make any sense of this." He scratched at his stubble. "Let's break this down:

we have two things going on—your buddy in Woodside and your friend Zhang up here."

"Daniel Zhang is not my friend."

"The thing in Woodside still doesn't read like a street gang to me."

"What about the pictures? The sick people? They connect Daniel Zhang to Woodside through his sister."

"I can't say that they do or that they don't. Are you sure your buddy—what's his name?"

"Paul Murphy."

"Are you sure Paul Murphy wasn't involved in anything unpleasant?"

"Like what?"

"Gambling, drugs, women . . ."

My initial reaction was no, of course not. But after the first knee-jerk, my surety—strong and solid as granite—crumbled. What the hell did I really know about Paul Murphy? That we'd been buddies ten years ago? The closeness I'd been feeling toward him since he'd died in my arms was an illusion. I knew nothing about Paul Murphy, father, scientist, dead man.

"I don't know," I said. "I don't think so."

"And Daniel Zhang?"

"I already said. I only met him yesterday."

A car behind us laid on the horn, and Tang motioned the person around us. "Well, we're not going to get too far with this."

"So you're not interested?"

"Man, give me a break here. I wasn't interested and now I am, okay? Just because things don't add up here doesn't mean I don't think something's going on here. Something is going on, obviously."

"Obviously."

"You said your guy had a tattoo?"

"Yes."

"What did it look like?"

"It looked like the tail of a dragon or something. Red and black. On the left side of his neck." I traced a finger under my ear. "Here."

"Did it look like it came from behind? Like the rest of the piece might have been on his back?"

"I suppose. What does that mean?"

"Triad generally goes for a black dragon on the left biceps, white tiger on the right biceps. Some of them go for more, like, say, a big dragon down the back. They do it in the old style, hand poked, to show how much pain they can take." He watched the traffic for a moment, then said, as much to himself as to me, "Tattoo suggests gang."

"You said you didn't think it was a gang."

"I say a lot of things. That detective down in San Mateo, Sanchez, right? I'll give her a call and have a conversation."

"Good. Finally."

"But I'm not on the Paul Murphy case. Not my turf, man."

"Christ," I said. "You guys are worse than public health with the jurisdiction thing."

"My world's big enough as it is. I don't need to go rooting around down south for work."

I opened the door, nearly dinging the side of the Corolla. "Hey," Tang said, "I thought all you guys drove Mercedes."

"And I thought you guys didn't profile. We'll talk soon, Inspector."

58

AS I MADE MY WAY over the Golden Gate Bridge, red like a raw wound against the surging Pacific, I turned Paul Murphy over in my head, looked under that rock. Poked around the dark bits, the "gambling, drugs, women . . ."

Paul Murphy, gambler? No. Beer-soaked games of poker did not a gambler make.

Drug addict? The Pope was more likely to develop a raging crack habit than Paul Murphy, who had always been one of those "my body is my temple" types.

Women? Most of the pictures on Murph's drive were women, sure, but I couldn't see him risking hearth and home to sow his wild oats in such diseased territory. Still, there could be something there.

Back in school, Murph was what you'd call "a player," if being such could be cleansed of its oilier connotations. He never seemed to want for female companionship, and was always bolting from the lab to have dinner with "a friend," then returning to his bench relaxed and rejuvenated. For me, who seemed to be doing constant battle with the one woman I was dating at the time, the easy liquidity of his relationships was galling. He was never one to gab much about the girls, and I never got the sense that Murph felt they were conquests; it didn't seem to me that he moved through women to shore up a weak ego. Rather, he just seemed to like them, and I mean *all* of them. He was democratic in his tastes. A plain-Jane, firebrand poli-sci PhD had as much chance as a former homecoming queen. Some guys got their jollies from extreme sports, some from combat, some from making money. With Murph, I thought, unkindly, it was women. He became expansive around the ladies. At every party where he had a female in tow, he would introduce me and, *sotto voce,* say that whoever was "a really terrific girl. Really great." Then he'd be back at her side, beaming, that tree limb of an arm draped around her hips. How many times had he beamed? I wondered. How many hips at how many parties?

But the Casanova Murph had departed long ago, hadn't he? Married, two little Murphys, a "monster of a mortgage"? I'm no naïf when it comes to the secrets people keep. The forward, twisting stride of disease—AIDS, syphilis, herpes—relies all too often on deceit. But I could not label Paul Murphy like that. I could not call him an adulterer.

And yet a question kept nipping at my heels: *Why not?*

I am uncomfortable with this, I thought. Take a break from it. Focus on Daniel Zhang. Flip the stone. Find nothing.

Concentrate on the road. Concentrate on Highway 101, then 37 east to Napa Valley. Watch the traffic flow through the concrete vessels arborized around the city. Watch the traffic stagnate, clot, coagulate to a line of crimson brake lights. Curse.

To Dorothy Zhang then, turn her over, the woman you were going to see. Think of Daniel again, who had undoubtedly talked to his sister. Think of Daniel, who Jack Tang suspected was involved in something unpleasant.

Wonder if Dorothy and Daniel and a man with a tattoo who was not Michael Kwong would be waiting for you. Wonder if calls were made to triads, Joe Boys, Wah Chings, to other monsters.

My guts knotted and I felt as though I were about to throw up. It wasn't the hangover this time. It wasn't the coffee. I thought: *I am sick of this. I am sick of ignorance, sick of not knowing.*

Try to concentrate on the scenery. Look at the Bay to your right. Watch the gulls. Feel sick again.

For luxury seekers not fortunate enough to have visited Napa, well, don't get too worked up about it. It's not some quaint jewel in wine country, not Edgartown amongst the cabernet, not Savannah nestled in zinfandel. Napa's an old ag town originally born as a station stop for goods making their way south to San Francisco. Despite the cultural mystique of the place, the actual city has the struggling, pull-yourself-up-by-your-bootstraps feel of an old East Coast city—Reading, Pennsylvania, say. There's been a good stab at redevelopment, centering largely on a revitalized riverfront, with pricey new eateries, galleries, a new museum. But pull back the curtain a bit, and you see a working, sweating village: low-slung office buildings, bail bondsmen, burger joints, and taquerias boasting a grade of "A" from the local health department.

But Napa is not Napa is not Napa—that is, the town is not the Valley and not the vineyards. The bulk of tourist dollars bypass the city. The money finds its way to the wineries and tiny, precious, wallet-busting towns along Route 29, which cuts north-south through the Valley. Some of the best restaurants in the world are up here, in Yountville and St. Helena. I'd love to try one, but the five-hundred-dollar price tag for dinner for two was a bit of a buzz kill. I figured I could always trade the Corolla for an entrée, but I'd be left holding the bag for the appetizers, dessert, and tip.

Using the directions I'd gotten at Miles's place, I found my way to a quiet street at the north edge of urban Napa, to a small complex of town houses that looked as if they were designed on an architect's computer and dropped wholesale—trees, homes, kids on bikes—onto the ground.

I double-checked the address. Heart thudding with anxiety, I got out of the car.

The town house was a brown-shingled two-story faced by computer-generated shrubbery. I punched the button for the bell, bracing myself to go face-to-face with a Chinese beauty. Inside, a chime. The peephole darkened. A lock clicked. The door opened.

It was not Dorothy Zhang.

The guy wore dress pants with a white shirt, unbuttoned at the collar. He wore reading glasses and carried a newspaper draped across his arm. Middle-aged, middle height, Asian.

"May I help you?" he asked.

I said I hoped so and told him I was looking for Dorothy Zhang.

"I'm sorry," he said, seeming confused. "Who are you looking for?"

I repeated her name. Behind him, the television quietly babbled some news program.

"Well, she doesn't live here," the man said with an avuncular tone, avuncular smile. "I don't know who this woman is."

Over his shoulder, in the living room, I could see a boy, seven or eight. He watched us solemnly. "That must be Timothy," I said.

The man laughed. "No. That is not his name." I waited for him to offer the boy's name. He didn't.

I asked, "Where's his mother?"

He continued smiling pleasantly. "His mother is not here. May I ask your name?"

Since we were both lying here, I defaulted to a previous namesake. "Bert McBrooke. I'm a lawyer."

"And what would you want with a Dorothy Zhang, Mr. McBrooke?"

"I really can't say. You understand."

"Of course. I apologize for asking." The politeness of this exchange was so heavy, I felt like I was in Buckingham Palace, trading niceties with a duke.

"I'd like to talk to your— Is he your son?" I craned my neck to see the boy, who stepped out, then back, as if he had accidentally touched an electric fence.

"And I cannot possibly imagine the reason he would want to speak with you, Mr. McBrooke. Thank you for visiting us. Good day."

Before the door closed, I caught another glimpse of the boy, staring at me with unblinking eyes.

59

THE NEXT DAY, I DID the most difficult thing I'd ever done. Well, maybe I exaggerate, but it was tough.

I sold the Corolla.

The more I thought about it, the more I decided the car was a liability. This aging gray thing with its Georgia plates was a beacon for anyone who chose to follow it. So, with a heavy heart, I sold my baby into the murky used-car market.

The representative of this market was a dealer in Napa I found through diligent research, that is, by driving past his lot. This particular functionary in the experienced-car trade was a white man in his fifties, face blasted red by a summer spent hocking his wares on the open lot.

After sticking his nose into the innards of my speed machine, he dropped the hood and frowned at me. "Five hundred."

"Five hundred dollars?" I was incredulous.

"Yup."

"Come on. I was thinking a thousand. The blue book is a thousand fifty."

"Blue book for excellent condition." He began a slow walk around the Corolla. "You got rust—" He pointed under the driver's-side fender, to a cracking line of oxidized metal. "You got tears in the upholstery." True enough;

I'd torn the bejeezus out of the backseat hauling a mountain bike years ago. "You don't have a CD player."

"It plays cassettes. It has a sunroof."

He looked at me like I was a moron.

"Okay. Nine hundred," I said.

"Five twenty-five."

"Eight fifty."

"Five forty."

"Eight hundred."

"Five forty-five."

I could see where this was going. He had me by the short hairs, as my grandfather would say. "Five forty-six," I said firmly. "Cash."

He smiled. "Sounds good to me."

I'm sure it did. Asshole.

60

IN THE END, I NETTED five hundred forty-one dollars, since the bastard made me pay five bucks for a ride to the car rental agency. "Gas prices." He shrugged. The irony that my car netted me about ten days of San Francisco rent wasn't lost on me. That it brought me one-fourth what I paid for the laptop in my shoulder bag wasn't lost on me either. There were a hundred other inequities that weren't lost on me, but I had bigger things to worry about. For example, the stares I was getting at Glenfield Elementary School.

I'd arrived there midway through the school day, just as the kindergartners were being belched from the building. I'll say this for the parents of Napa Valley: they are vigilant. For them, a thirty-something white guy, sitting in a nondescript car, parked near the front doors of an elementary school, is about as inconspicuous as a nudist at a Rotary meeting. And just about as welcome. After the fourth mom hurried her tot by my midsized Saturn, I decided to spare the worried parents any more strife.

So I drove aimlessly around Napa, letting my mind drift, which was a mistake. A drifting mind, I found out, took me right between the Scylla of tattooed men and the Charybdis of Brooke Michaels. For a second, I considered calling Brooke to check in, but scrapped the idea. With all the other things going on, deciding not to call Dr. Michaels was a small and probably Pyrrhic victory. But it made me feel better.

I was still feeling pangs about the Corolla, but the anonymity of my new wheels was a comfort. As was the highly functional air-conditioning, the sound system that consisted of more than just one tweeter, and the driver's seat, which didn't poke an unruly spring into my ass. My laptop was in the backseat, along with my deodorant and toothbrush. I was ready for anything.

61

I DITCHED THE CAR A good distance from the school and walked. The kindergartners were at home now, their mothers no doubt shivering at the memory of the creepy guy in the blue Saturn. The grounds were deserted, leaving me to enjoy the stunning September day. There were tidily planted flower beds outside the school, a flagpole with Old Glory hanging limply from its summit. The tinny sounds of band practice drifted from some unseen music room.

It had been only a few months since I'd last stepped foot on the grounds of an elementary school. The occasion had been a whooping cough outbreak in a rich suburb of Atlanta where quite a few of the affluent, Internet-savvy, and misinformed parents had gotten it into their heads that vaccinations were more of a liability than a benefit. Pertussis wasn't even my bailiwick at CDC, but I wanted to see the disease close up, so I tagged along with the investigation. Two days with wheezing, grunting, miserable juveniles and their nitwit parents. My colleagues and I decided that nitwits who are so flipped about the dangers of vaccines that they don't take their kids for their shots should be forced to breathe through a straw for a week. Let the parents see how it feels. Then we can talk.

Security wasn't high at Glenfield—apparently the kids

there had not yet discovered the joys of packing heat to math class—but there was a man sitting behind a desk near the entrance. I showed him my ID and he directed me to the principal's office.

The admin suite was new and smartly appointed. Glenfield, I guessed, had a deeper tax base to draw on than Daniels Elementary, where I'd honed my early intellect. These guys had purchased their furniture sometime in the past few years, whereas the Daniels administrators had inherited theirs from the Greatest Generation or before.

The principal of Glenfield turned out to be one Ginny Plough: short, plump, and with that kind of boundless energy you'd expect from someone who grooved on kids. I told her I was a public health physician here to speak with Timothy Kim. Surprisingly, Ms. Plough asked to see my credentials. I pulled out the expired CDC ID badge. She squinted up at me, worried.

"Golly, I hope there's nothing wrong."

Golly?

"There isn't," I said. "I just want to talk to Tim for a few minutes."

"Should he be in school?"

"Of course," I said. "Really, it's nothing to worry about."

"Tim's all right, isn't he?"

"I'm sure he's fine."

"But you'll be sure to let us know . . . Timothy is new this year, and we have many children . . ."

I beamed a reassuring public health smile, and she picked up the phone and called her secretary.

Five minutes later, I sat alone in Principal Plough's office, thinking of all the songs I would have come up with for her had I been a third grader here. "Principal Plough was a sorry old cow . . ." That kind of thing. Kids are so mean.

There was a knock on the glass door and Principal Plough arrived, clasping the hand of a short Asian kid who looked about as thrilled to see me as he would a plate of Brussels sprouts. Whether it was the sight of me, or whether it was because he'd been hauled out of class to the principal's office, I couldn't tell.

But one thing I could tell: this was the same child who'd been staring at me the evening before.

Principal Plough deposited the boy on a chair next to mine and excused herself. "I'll be right outside if you need anything," she told the boy, then shot an uncertain glance at me before departing.

"Hi, Tim," I said.

He mumbled something.

"I'm a doctor from the government and I have some questions for you. Is that okay with you?"

He bobbled his head, which I took for a nod.

"Great. Thanks." First things first. "Did you see me last night at your house?"

He shrugged.

"Is that a yes?"

He shrugged again. Evidently, young Tim was confused about whether we'd crossed paths before.

"Do you live with your mom?"

He mumbled.

"I'm sorry. I didn't hear you."

"No."

Strike one, I thought.

"Who was the man I saw you with last night, Tim? Was that your dad?"

"My great-uncle."

"Your great-uncle. Did you always live with him?"

"No."

"Did you live with your mom?"

More mumbling. Christ, what's with kids and diction these days?

"I can't hear you."

"Yes." He said it firmly.

"And your mom's name is Dorothy Zhang?"

"Yeah."

"She used to work on TV."

"Yeah."

"Can you say anything besides 'yes' and 'no'?"

"I said 'my great-uncle' before," he reminded me, annoyed.

"Of course you did. I forgot."

Now, I suppose I should say something about me and children: I'd really like to like them. Truly, I would. Scratch that, I'd really like to be "good" with them, which I assume has something to do with liking them. Being good with kids goes a long way in this baby-obsessed society. Especially with women. Especially with women of a certain age. I have this image of myself—totally fabricated—with my shirt off, about ten additional pounds of chest muscle, clasping a chubby bambino in my arms. Even I get all doey-eyed thinking about it. I post something like that on an Internet dating site, I'd be beating them off with a stick.

As it was, kids made me about as comfortable as a severe case of jock itch. The odd things that came out of their mouths demanded responses. During that whooping cough outbreak in Atlanta, I kept misreading my audience. I would talk to a ten-year-old as if he were a toddler, then I'd overcorrect and speak to a seven-year-old like she was a professor in economics. I was totally unconscious of this, of course, but one of my supportive (female) colleagues pointed it out. Then she added, helpfully, "You really don't get along well with kids, do you?"

I'd get along better with them if they were twenty years older, I told her.

Tim Kim crossed his arms.

"Do you like gum?" I asked, and dug into my pocket for a pack I thought I put in there sometime during the last election. Maybe treats would help me worm my way into his good graces.

"We're not allowed to have gum."

"Right. This is school. I forgot." Good thing, too. I looked at the half-pack in my hand and saw that the foil had come off the sticks, which were now coated in pocket fur. I jammed the pack into the pants. "Tim, do you know where your mom is?"

"No."

Strike two.

"Is she okay? Does she feel okay?"

"Yeah."

Base hit. Tim Kim's eyes cut to the window behind me. I looked around to see Ginny Plough wiggling her digits at us. I wiggled back. My time, it appeared, was running out.

"Now that you live with your great-uncle, do you talk to your mom sometimes?" I persisted.

"Not now."

Interesting, I thought. Though my philosophy of parenting might be called reptilian—lay the eggs, then watch the little tykes emerge from the sand and embark on a peril-filled life—I had to admit I found Dorothy Zhang's abrupt abandonment of her child a little weird, so I asked him, "Why'd she go away?"

Tim shrugged. *No big deal.*

"Was she trying to protect you?"

Another shrug.

"Why didn't your uncle let me talk to you?"

Tim clamped his lips together; he was in full mutiny now.

I stuck up one finger, signaling another minute to the concerned principal. Ms. Plough nodded and turned away to administrate something.

"Tim." I reached into my pocket for my wallet, and took out the last CDC card I had left. The old 404 office and fax numbers were still on the card and I scratched them out, leaving only my cell. "You take this and tell your mom to call the number if you talk to her." He took the card and studied it intensely, like it contained the answer to some great mystery, like whether the Harry Potter franchise really is kaput. "This is important: don't show this to anyone else, Tim, and don't tell anyone but your mom you talked to me. Okay?"

"Okay," he said, without enthusiasm. "You said your name was Bert McBrooke."

My cover. Blown.

"I never said that."

"You did. Last night."

"No, no . . . I, uh, said I had to burp and I was broke. I

didn't have any money 'cause I spent it on sodas. Don't drink soda."

Please let this end . . . It didn't; Tim was still engrossed in my card.

"What's 'path-o-gens'?"

"Put that in your pocket. Don't show it to anyone but your mom," I said curtly, not making a friend. He obliged, though, and slid the card into his jeans, his eyes now fixed suspiciously on me. "A pathogen is a disease that makes you sick."

"Why don't you just say 'disease'?"

"Technically, a pathogen is an agent, usually an organism, that causes disease."

"Like bacteria?"

"Like bacteria. But I worked—I work—with viruses. Viruses are like bacteria."

My card did say "Special Pathogens," which was in the Division of Viral and Rickettsial Diseases, which was also on the card, so Mr. Smarty-Pants could have figured out the answer to his question from context. Seriously, though, it had taken mankind fifty thousand years to piece together the germ theory of disease, another thirty to discover viruses; Tim Kim was synthesizing this before my eyes.

"Viruses are smaller than bacteria," he informed me.

"Yes."

"So why don't they call them small bacteria?"

Like a man overboard, I looked frantically through the window to the office, hoping to see Ginny Plough. "Because viruses are different from bacteria in other ways."

"How?"

"Well, viruses don't have the ability to reproduce by themselves. Bacteria do. 'Reproduce' means to have babies."

"I know," he said impatiently. "Why can't viruses reproduce?"

Because that's the way it is, little man. "Because they evolved that way. Viruses need another cell to replicate."

"Why?"

I was calculating exactly how long it would take to strangle him. "Well, Tim, in the beginning—"

Just then, the heavens sent me a savior. Ginny Plough rapped on the door and stepped into the office. "Everything going all right in here, you two?" she inquired brightly.

"Sure is," I said. "We two were just finishing up a discussion of viruses and bacteria."

"Oh my," she said. "I can't stand things like that." She shuddered. "I walked out of that *Outbreak* movie after ten minutes."

I gave my best grand-old-disease-hunter laugh. Ha ha ha.

Ginny Plough led Tim from the office and traded him off to some hall-monitor type for return to, she informed me, science class. I hoped my little friend wouldn't pull out the card and treat his fellow students to a dissertation on "path-o-gens." Not only would my cover truly be blown, but I'd run the risk of being invited back to talk to the class.

"Dr. McCormick, please tell me if there's something I should worry about." Anxiety clouded Principal Plough's pretty, plump face. "We have four hundred children here—"

"Who are perfectly safe." I put a reassuring hand on her doughy shoulder. "There was some concern that Timothy had visited the Solomon Islands, where there's been an outbreak of typhus. But it's not him. It's another Tim Kim, down in Walnut Creek. We were just making sure."

"Oh . . . okay . . ."

I patted the shoulder. "There's absolutely nothing for you to worry about."

I wish I could say the same for me.

62

AS I WALKED OUT OF the school, past the big "Go Cottontails!" banner and the security guard, I contemplated infractions big and small. Big infractions included impersonating a CDC official. God forbid that Ginny Plough call up my former superiors to ask them exactly how much peril her four hundred pups were in from whatever disease. God forbid they find out I was using my old ID and cards. That kind of stuff could probably land me in jail.

Come to think of it, there were no small infractions at that point.

I walked west from the school grounds, toward the Napa River, toward downtown. Third Street took me over a bridge, past the courthouse, past the bail bondsmen. The irony of my surroundings wasn't lost on me.

So, Nate McCormick was fast becoming a small-time criminal. In keeping, I supposed, with my history. The fabrication of that old data back in med school, for example. Old habits, old dogs, so on and so forth.

I beat myself up on that for a while, then decided to beat myself up on the hash I was making of this investigation. Sure, I thought, *investigation.* Obsession, maybe. "Investigation" was giving it too much credit.

And just as I was about to go get arrested for something, my cell vibrated. Ravi.

"We found the Lums," he said.

"Great—"

"And the name's not Lum. It's Ming." His voice didn't sound quite as triumphant as I would have thought. In fact, he didn't sound like Ravi at all.

"Great work. Where are they?"

"They're home. In San Francisco." He heaved a breath. "They're dead, McCormick."

63

SHOT IN THE FACE. POINT-BLANK. I could see the powder burns on her face. Beatrice Lum's bandages were off now, and I didn't know if they'd been blown off by the gun or not.

I was kneeling on the pale blue carpet next to Mrs. Lum—Ming—looking down at the mass of glistening flesh—the unclean line of a lip partially devoured by tumor and surgery, the knob of oozing flesh next to her eye. The bullet's entrance wound under her left eye was the cleanest mark on her.

There was her mouth, open, agape, a black hole. Screaming.

"They took the tongues postmortem. That's why there's not much blood." It was Ravi, standing behind me.

I'd come straight from Napa. Ravi had arrived earlier, greased my way inside, bullying cops left and right to get me into the house.

"And the kids?" I asked.

"At school when it happened," Ravi said. "Daughter found them. Cops got here right after that."

"Jesus."

With a latex-gloved hand, I covered Mrs. Lum's face again with the sheet. The forensic investigator had given us permission to look at the bodies, but not to touch. The couple lay as they'd been found. An arm poked from underneath each sheet, reaching for the dead hand of the nearby spouse. Dead fingers intertwined. I remembered Mr. Lum sitting by his wife's hospital bed, gripping his wife's hand.

"Anything on the husband?" I asked Ravi.

"Shot in the face, tongue gone."

"You two the doctors?" The voice behind us was too sharp, too loud. I turned to see a stubby man with a bristle mustache. A badge dangled from his jacket pocket.

"Yes," I said.

Ravi and I backed away from the corpses slowly, like stepping away from a ticking bomb.

The Lums/Mings had been murdered in their living room in their house in the Sunset district, not far from Daniel Zhang's place. Family photos in silver frames sat atop a baby grand piano. There was a small drawing in an enormous frame above the mantel, with a typed note stuck into a corner of the glass. One of those old picture lights hung over the top of the piece; the lamp was turned on.

"You saw the Mings at SF General yesterday?" the cop with the mustache asked us.

"And you are?" I asked.

"Inspector Hindrick. Homicide." I introduced myself, peeled off the latex glove, and shook his hand. Hindrick and Ravi shook hands.

"Yes," Ravi confirmed. "We saw them yesterday."

"Any idea as to what might have happened here?" Hindrick flipped out a small notebook.

"No," Ravi said. "We talked about her disease, is all."

"Yeah. That. Poor lady."

"Yeah," Ravi said.

"They were in the hospital under a false name," I offered.

"Huh," Hindrick said. "Why?"

"Don't know," I said. "We only found out their real names today."

"What did they say their name was?"

"Lum. They paid for the medical services in cash. Cashier's check, actually."

"We'll chase that down." Hindrick wrote something in his notebook. "So, we're guessing they didn't want to be found at the hospital?"

I thought about that again. If the Lums/Mings were trying to hide out, they certainly didn't do a good job. They didn't care if people knew they were at home, they cared if people knew they were at the *hospital.* Which meant they cared if people knew Mrs. Ming was sick.

"I guess that's what we're guessing," I said.

Hindrick closed the notebook and aimlessly scanned the room. His eyes avoided the couple on the pale blue carpet. "Dunno, dunno," he said. "Dunno who, dunno why. Robbery maybe. Jewelry's gone from the bodies and from upstairs. Some electronics gone. They didn't touch the Chagall, though."

"The Chagall?"

"Drawing up there. It's real. At least so says that little paper."

Ravi stepped over to the drawing, read over the certificate of authenticity plastered right there on the front of it. "I'll be damned." He turned his head, cracked a tiny smile that said *tacky*.

Tacky, sure, but humanizing. It made me feel even worse about the mess on the floor in front of us. That drawing, with the ugly paper stuck into the too-big frame, seemed honest to me. *We've arrived,* it said. The people I knew from college and grad school, those trying like hell to claw their way into the upper middle class, would have put the Chagall in a small frame, prominently but not-too-prominently displayed. Then, in the first five minutes of conversation, they would direct you to it, let it drop the thing was genuine.

"Drugs, maybe," Hindrick said. "Medicine cabinet upstairs was raided."

I closed my eyes for a second, opened them. "She was taking Percocet and Vicodin for her pain."

No one said anything. "The prescribing doctor's name would have been there," I explained.

Hindrick nodded, acknowledged the lost lead. After a beat, he closed the notebook and produced a card each for

Ravi and me. "If you guys think of anything or find anything, you know, it would be a help."

Ravi did his part in the dance and handed over his own card. "You, too. We're worried this might be something public health needs to be worried about."

"Yeah? The wife's face?"

"Yes."

He let his eyes linger on the covered bodies, then said, as much to himself as to us, "The tongues. This wasn't a robbery."

My thought exactly.

64

THEY WERE A BEAUTIFUL FAMILY, the Mings, the Lums, whoever they were. I hunched over the pictures on the baby grand. Mrs. Ming, pretty in her wedding dress, pagoda in the background. Mr. Ming, beside his bride, looking a little shell-shocked, like he'd gotten better than he deserved. But you saw them grow through the years, as you traced your way around the silver frames. There was a chronology here, black-and-whites and faded color toward the back of the piano, sharp color at the front.

Mrs. Ming pregnant, her hair permed. Then the babies, the school play, the family vacation in Italy with the boy pretending he's holding up the Leaning Tower. The little girl with the cello, the same girl in a prom dress. The same girl who found her parents today. The shot of the whole family with an older couple on a busy street festooned with lighted signs sporting a mix of English and Chinese. The trip to Hong Kong? Then the final picture, back at the house, in front of the Chagall, just mom and dad. Mrs. Ming looked like a million bucks. Mr. Ming beamed.

"Doc?"

I turned. Hindrick again. "You want anything else with the bodies? The Medical Examiner's wagon is going to be here soon."

"I'm finished," I told him, then began to walk toward the front door. Hindrick stopped me in the hallway.

"You said they paid their hospital bills up front, right?"

"Yes."

"How much?"

"About forty thousand."

"That's a lot of cash for a guy who ran a couple gift shops. On top of that, you got the Chagall. You got a new Mercedes in the garage. A lot of cash for a merchant like him."

"Maybe the shops did very well."

"Maybe. And maybe these folks were in over their heads."

I processed for a moment. "You're thinking loan sharks?"

"Dunno." Hindrick sighed. "Not a lot of reason to cut out people's tongues. Unless, of course, you're trying to send a signal. This," he gestured toward the floor, "would send quite a signal to others who owe."

"If it's loan sharks, why didn't they take the Chagall? Try to get some of their investment back?"

"It'd be hard to fence. Black-market art doesn't like

double homicides. Besides—keeping with the theory here—they wrote these folks off. More valuable to the bad guys to make an example. Or, this is just a robbery. Some knucklehead who got carried away. One of those things."

Probably not one of those things. "You heard about those murders down on the Peninsula? The Murphy family?" I asked.

"Yeah. Four dead. The husband mutilated. Yeah."

"I was friends with the husband. I found them."

He raised his eyebrows. "I'm sorry, Doc."

"I don't know how many mutilations you get in the Bay Area, but it seems there might be a conn—"

"I was already planning to call San Mateo, if that's what you're asking."

"That's what I'm asking. And may I ask one more thing?"

"We're on a roll, aren't we?"

"Could you tell Jack Tang about this? I think he'll be interested."

Hindrick gave a half-smile. "You're in my head, Doc. Already called him. Inspector Tang was here an hour ago."

Having done my best to facilitate inter- and intra-agency communication, I stepped onto the front stoop. Night was closing in on day, and there was actually something of a sunset: an orange flake pinched between the ocean and the clouds.

Ravi was there, smoking. He glanced at me, reached into his jacket, produced a pack of Marlboro Reds.

"I keep them in my car, you know, for times like this," he said, and shook the pack at me.

I took a cigarette. It had been a year since one touched my lips, so my lungs weren't prepared for the smoke. I wanted to cough. I stifled it, exhaled, took another drag. The nicotine flowed into my brain, kneaded it like bread.

"The police think the Mings were involved with loan sharks," I said.

I watched Ravi light another cigarette off the glowing tip of his first. "At least they have a theory." He stubbed the first out on his shoe, stuffed it back in the pack. "I've never been to a crime scene before." His voice was quiet.

"You should count yourself lucky."

"I don't know, McCormick. It feels like we're right where we're supposed to be."

"At the scene of a double homicide?"

"In the thick of it. This ain't like hunting diseases, that's for sure."

"You are hunting diseases, Ravi. That's what this is all about."

Ravi drew on his smoke and was silent for a while, so that I wasn't sure he'd heard me. Then he said, "I know. I know what I'm doing." He turned to me. "What are you hunting, McCormick?"

Ravi was gone now, back across the Bay to catch the latest on *American Idol* or do whatever he did to forget a day like this. I stayed on the stoop, smoking my way through a second cigarette. My lungs felt as though they'd been worked over by sandpaper.

I watched the van from the Medical Examiner's pull up along the curb. I watched the ME's crew pull their grim necessities from the van—two body bags, a stretcher.

Sending a signal, I thought. Hindrick thought the signal was intended for other deadbeats, a screaming advertisement to pay up. But it was more than that. The Mings had lost their tongues. Murph had lost his tongue, eyes, and ears. The signal wasn't subtle and it wasn't vague.

The ME's men passed by me with a stretcher.

Ears, eyes, tongues.

Hear no evil, see no evil, speak no evil. In other words, keep your head down and shut up. Shut up or be dead.

I couldn't shake the feeling that I'd missed something, something more than symbolic mutilations. The guys from the Medical Examiner's were busy zipping Mrs. Ming into a black body bag and loading her on the stretcher. I stepped around them and went to the Chagall. The purchase was six months before, if the date on the certificate could be believed. Maybe Hindrick was right, and the Mings were recently flush. Maybe they were flush from borrowed cash. Maybe the vig was too much for them.

To the family photos on the piano. To Mrs. Ming staring straight at the camera looking very pretty, very young. A world different than the disfigured woman I'd seen in the hospital. Mr. Ming smiling at his wife, an arm reaching out to touch her cheek. Rarely had I seen a man look so proud.

And why not? He had a great piece of art. If Inspector Hindrick was to be believed, he had a new car. And he had a stunning wife.

A stunning wife . . .

I cast my eyes over the photos from the previous years. Age stamped creases into Beatrice Ming's face, it stretched tissue. From the bride to the pregnant woman to the woman in Pisa to the woman in Hong Kong, she looked older each time.

Then that last photo. It was as if ten years had been erased.

65

MY INTERVIEW TO GET INTO med school had been with some bigwig hematologist. A real ballbuster. He likes you, you get in, one of the students told me. He doesn't like you, well . . . Where else did you apply?

The interview was held in the prof's house, a massive thing with a garden that looked like it had been plucked from southern France. California was new to me—I'd been there for one day—and I was still getting used to the sunshine, the citrus trees. Penn State this was not.

It was with that sense of dislocation that I rang the doorbell. Somewhere in the back, a dog yipped. The door was opened, not by the great man himself, but by a slight woman in her sixties. We exchanged niceties, and she told me the doctor was upstairs in his study. It was all a wee bit formal and more than a wee bit intimidating.

The doctor sat behind a massive carved wooden desk, smoking a pipe. There was the welcome, some chat about Pennsylvania. Then, after I made some stupid comment about Big Ten versus Pac Ten football, he asked me abruptly, out of nowhere, "Did you happen to notice the color of my wife's eyes?"

And you know what? I had. "Hazel," I said. "More green than brown."

He asked me how next year's football team was shaping up.

On the way out of his study, he shook my hand. "You're a good noticer, Mr. McCormick," he said.

My acceptance letter came three weeks later.

These are the thoughts I thought in a stiff bed in a motel near the airport, a place my grandfather would have called a "fleabag joint." I hadn't found any fleas yet, but the place was cheap as dirt and I wouldn't be surprised if I woke up the next morning scratching like a barnyard dog. It did have cable, though, and a "Hi-speed" Internet connection, and a coin box on the bed for Magic Fingers.

So, I notice things. A good talent, I guess, for being a doctor, but it only gets you so far. You notice, for example, that a woman is not aging like she should, that there's a little jog—or a big jog—in that normal progression. You notice that the reversal seems to occur after she goes to Hong Kong and before her face explodes in tumors.

You think of distribution of the tumors, along the NLF, those "smile lines" that run from the side of the nose to the corners of the mouth. The tumors around the eyes. These were favored sites for so-called "injectables," the cosmetic products that dermatologists and plastic surgeons pumped into the faces of the aged and aging.

You notice that, but you have no idea what it means, how it ties into a raging case of dermatofibrosarcoma protuberans or being murdered in your home. Did Mr. Ming take out a mother of a loan from some shady types, buy a

Chagall, buy a luxury car and jewelry, get his wife one of those massive cosmetic reworkings that the movie stars get? Did he use that same money to pay up front for medical expenses in an effort to keep their identity hidden from . . . from whom? From a guy with a tattoo? Did he then get rubbed out, as they say, and robbed because he couldn't make good?

It didn't make any sense.

What did make sense was that somewhere around the time she visited Hong Kong, Beatrice Ming had gotten something done and she'd looked great. Then something happened, and her face erupted. How and whether these things were related, I didn't know. But I did know someone who could help me: a man I'd first met when he was a skinny, intense kid in his second year of medical school. Bill Yount. And if the slow Hi-speed Internet in my motel room was worth a damn, he'd set up a slick dermatology practice in San Francisco.

I had just scribbled the address of Yount's clinic on a scrap of paper when I heard a car door slam outside. My body went rigid. Quickly, I closed the laptop, killed the light, wished I still had the Smith & Wesson. I sat there in the curtained darkness, staring at the door, wondering how long the two locks on it would hold.

Footsteps outside. Amber light from the parking lot leaked around the curtain. The light winked as someone passed in front of the window.

For a moment, I heard only my breathing and my heartbeat. Then, footsteps again, growing fainter.

I got up from the bed and went to the window. The curtain was about as pliable as cardboard and I moved it to the side. Nothing except for a family of three piling exhausted from a beat-up SUV.

Lying on the bed again, I tried to calm myself down. I failed.

Time, I guessed, to go for broke. I found two quarters and dropped them into the coin slot, to see if Magic Fingers would tickle away the tension. The bed started to jiggle and vibrate and make a total freaking racket. It didn't undo the knots of anxiety, but did tie me up nicely with nausea.

So, I spent the next fifteen minutes sitting in a chair in my boxer shorts, one eye on the door, the other on a convulsing thirty-year-old bed.

66

NEXT MORNING, I AWOKE JUST after dawn. "Awoke" implies that I slept, and I'm not sure I did. Every car door slamming, every step outside, had me bolting up in bed, holding my breath, listening to the quiet *nachtmusik* of the motel.

I went for a run, tried to burn off some of the adrenaline. But running along streets near the airport did nothing to relax me, so I returned to the motel and ran the stairs, up and down two stories, for about twenty minutes. Some derelict businessman and a teenager in a miniskirt gave me a wide berth as they made their way down to the parking lot. I heard the guy mutter, "Asshole." Nothing like encounters with random hostility to start your day off right.

I showered, shaved, and packed up, got ready to quit this sty, with its crap Internet and its crummy locks. Yanking the charger from the cell, I noticed I'd missed a call. Blocked number. No message.

Maybe it was Ravi. Maybe that tattooed bastard. Maybe it was the Murphys and the Mings, ringing me from on high, calling to let me know what a bang-up job I was doing with this justice thing.

I put in a call to Millie Bao at CDC.

"I think something's happening in Hong Kong," I said to her. "They need to be looking for DFSP with fibrosarcoma admixed."

"It's after ten p.m. their time, Nate," she pointed out.

"Then they had a whole day."

"It's not a reportable condition. Which means they don't have the info in a database anywhere. Which means they have to do a little legwork. Which means I have to call in a favor to get them to do it."

"Empowering, isn't it? Getting other people to do your work." Not a flicker of acknowledgment from Millicent. "Not in the kidding mood?" I asked her.

"Ellen got sick last night. Barfed all over her sister, the one who gets squeamish looking at oatmeal, and who, of course, barfed, too. No, not in the kidding mood, Nate."

"That's a lot of barfing."

"Don't think you're getting off the babysitting hook. One day if I don't find anything. Three, if I do. I'll call you when I hear anything."

I shouldered my bags, eager to quit this freaky, paranoia-inducing place for good. I planned to set up camp outside

Premiere Aesthetic Associates, PC, Bill Yount's dermatology practice.

Loaded down, I walked through the wakening motel. People were around now, packing up cars, moving toward the motel office. I opened the trunk of the Saturn, dropped my bags inside. When I closed it, something caught my eye: through the glass, I could see something white on the windshield.

My first thought was: *ticket?*

But as I rounded the car, I saw that the white thing was too thick to be a ticket. It was a clump of take-out napkins wrapped around something—half-eaten doughnut?—that raised the wiper from the windshield by a few inches.

I plucked the small bundle from underneath the wiper. From the texture, I knew it was not a doughnut. Hot dog maybe. Sausage.

There was a trash bin next to the motel office. As I walked the package over to it, I noticed a spreading stain in the white napkin. It wasn't the greasy stain you'd expect from a hot dog or a half-eaten sausage. It was too red.

Slowly, I peeled open the napkins.

It was a human tongue.

61

"WHAT IS THIS TELLING YOU, Mr. McCormick?"

I was sitting in the Bryant Street Police Station, fifth floor, looking at Jack Tang. Between us sat a paper cup from the Buena Costa Motel office. The tongue was inside it. At my feet sat my luggage.

"I think it's pretty clear," I said.

"I'm glad you see that."

"Kind of hard not to."

"Why do you think you got this message? Why do you think you weren't assaulted? Or worse?"

"Because I'm on the outside. They don't want to touch me. Either that or they didn't know where my room was."

"They knew where your room was." He took a sip of the dark SFPD tar, grimaced. "Terrible," he said. "How many more warnings do you think you're going to get before things get extremely bad for you?"

"I don't know. Between five and eight?" I forced a smile; Tang didn't.

"I like you, Mr. McCormick. You're kind of a jackass, but, hey, I can forgive that. I owe you one for bringing me into the loop here. But you are swimming into dangerous waters. I don't want you or your friends to get hurt."

"I don't have any friends."

"Funny guy." He took the cup with the tongue in it and

leaned back in his chair, holding it in front of him, regarding the white paper cylinder with the lump of flesh inside. Aristotle contemplating the bust of Homer. Or Homer contemplating the bust of Aristotle. I needed to bone up on my Rembrandt. Or my Caravaggio.

"We found a large transfer of funds into the Mings' bank account eleven months ago," Tang said. "Upwards of seven hundred thousand dollars. I was on the phone with Hong Kong last night to trace the origin of the funds."

"How did you find out about the money?"

"Some very sophisticated policing. It was written in their checkbook."

"Oh."

"We haven't yet nailed down the details, but it looks like the windfall that might not have been such a windfall."

"What do you mean?"

"I mean that maybe the seven hundred grand was borrowed."

I thought of telling Tang about my theory that Mrs. Ming looked *too good,* but stopped myself. I realized my view of events was being clouded by my training. Things biological, for me, are always the central elements. But perhaps I wasn't seeing things clearly.

"Hindrick and I also talked to Bonita Sanchez, down in San Mateo," Tang continued. "There've been large deposits in Paul Murphy's bank accounts over the past few months. Sixty thousand here, forty thousand there. You know anything about that?"

I was shocked. "No. I don't."

"Your friend never told you about money troubles? Gambling, drugs?"

"I told Detective Sanchez that. I told *you* that. And if you're suggesting he had to go to a loan shark for money, I don't buy it. He had a great job, a nice house. He could have gotten money the way normal rich people do. He could've gone to a bank."

Tang shrugged. "Maybe he wanted to keep the loans from his wife. Maybe that nice house was too much for him. Who knows?"

Right, I thought. Who knows? Whatever it was, though, Paul was doing it for the right reasons. The right reasons, right?

"What about the people I told you about. Paul's pictures?"

"Look, there's a lot of sick shit in the world. Maybe your buddy had a fetish thing going on."

I scowled.

"Sorry," he said. "He's your friend. But look, if we had a thousand guys working on this, we could chase it down. We don't. Public health is looking into the sick people, right?"

"Sure, but—"

"There you go. They do what they do, we do what we do. And as for you . . ."—he waggled the paper cup toward me—"you need to get out of here. Take a girl and head down to Santa Barbara. Go taste some wine. Just get out of here. Six people are dead, and I don't want to see it be seven." He stood. "I gotta break some news to you: your car's going to be out of commission for at least the next twenty-four hours. The forensics guys will want it for at least that long."

"Great." I frowned. "Of course. You guys have any loaners?"

"Stopped our car loaner program last week." He picked up the cup with the tongue inside. "I got to get this bagged and tagged. Sorry about your car. There's a rental shop a few blocks away."

He turned to leave. Then he turned back.

"Go to Santa Barbara," he said. "Go there today."

I thought of the Mings, who were dead because they talked to me. I thought of the Murphys, who might be dead because Murph talked to me. I thought of the poor bastards whose tumors were wrapping around nerves, bursting through flesh. "We'll see," I said.

He stepped to me, leaned into me, his face only a few inches from mine. "Do not do this, Dr. McCormick. Do not be involved now. You will get hurt. I can guarantee you that."

Three different cars in two days. This time, out of homage to my old wheels, I chose a Corolla.

While still in the lot, I dialed the hyperkinetic Sikh across the Bay.

"You need to watch yourself," I said. I told him about the body part on my windshield.

"Jesus," he said. He was quiet for a moment. "We found another one, McCormick. The fibrosarc strikes again."

"Another woman?"

"Man. Monica put the word out to her old dermatology contacts, found out about a case two months ago at Kaiser Oakland. Caused some buzz there, even became a grand rounds presentation. Worst case of our kind of fibrosarcoma they'd ever seen."

Grand rounds were the weekly educational meetings held by the various departments in a hospital.

"Grand rounds," I said. "So they got a biopsy and pictures."

"Both, but the patient fell off the map. Didn't even show up for the pathology results. Dropped his Kaiser coverage right after the first visit. We're doing our best to track him down now."

"Is he a match to those pictures I gave you?"

"We think he matches one of the guys. Yeah."

I brought my hand to my head, rubbed the temples. "More than a couple of cases. Shit."

"Yeah."

"These people are sick, Ravi. They need to get into treatment. And they're not going to do it when . . . Have the Ming murders hit the news? I haven't had the chance—"

"Yes."

"Press mention the mutilation?"

"Sure did."

"Damn. No mention of fibrosarcoma though, right?"

"That, too."

"How the hell did they know about that?" I played back the previous day. "Oh, no, man. You did not—"

"Some reporters got to me when I was leaving the Mings' place last night. I thought if I put the word out, more people might come forward."

"Shit, Ravi. Shit—"

"You'll be happy to know that people here are real pissed I talked to the media. They got me on a short leash—"

I couldn't care less about the fallout at Ravi's workplace, the length of his leash. "This is going to drive everybody underground. The people who have this *know*. They don't want to get shot in the face for talking to us."

"I thought the cops think it's all tied to loan-sharking."

"They do think that, or they might think that. It's not what *we* think. Damn it." I told Ravi about the photographs displayed on the Mings' piano. I told him I thought she'd had some cosmetic procedure done either in Hong Kong or around that time.

"You can't just jump to conclusions about cosmetic procedures because of one picture on a piano—"

"I—"

"And you can't say that the Mings were offed because the wife had fibrosarcoma. Think about it: too complicated and too wild. Who gets killed *because* they have cancer? Come on, bucko, the cops' explanation is *way* better than that."

"And Murph and his photos? These people with cancer vanishing from the radar? What's that?"

"I can't explain it," he said.

"Of course you can't. Because you don't see that the fibrosarc and the missing people and the murders are the same thing."

"Try telling the police this," he said.

"I've tried. There're too many pieces missing."

"Stop worrying about missing pieces and start worrying about a goddamned tongue under your windshield wiper, McCormick. Worry about *that*."

"I am." I looked at my watch. "Go find the guy from Kaiser. Get him connected and start treatment. We can't have people hiding out and rotting away. Oh, man, maybe your fuckup with the press will help us. Maybe someone will come forward." Ravi made no response. "You gonna hang in with me, Ravi? Quick now: I need a yes before I get off the phone."

"Okay, McCormick. Sure."

You will get hurt, Tang had promised.

I sat in the idling car at the entrance to the rental lot.

I thought about where I'd been identified, where paths had crossed. I thought about how a tongue had found its way to my motel. I thought about the Mings.

The Mings.

I'd let my guard down at their house, consumed as I was with having noticed things. I hadn't even bothered to glance behind me as I traced my way through the city to the Buena Costa Motel. And that morning, consumed as I was with the discovery on my windshield, I hadn't bothered again.

Which meant I could have been followed to the police station, followed to the rental car lot.

I began to sweat.

After a quick look left and right, I jammed the accelerator and blasted into the street.

South through the city, then back north. I ran a red light. I turned the wrong way into a one-way alley. I ran another red light, desperate to avoid bad guys who wanted to do me in and cops who wanted to ticket me.

After fifteen minutes of this kind of driving—a quarter hour with my eyes as much on the rearview as on the road in front of me—I turned onto California Street.

68

CALIFORNIA STREET RAN FROM ONE end of San Francisco to the other, from downtown to Lincoln Park. Near the end of its course, near the Presidio, it bisected a neighborhood called Pacific Heights. Pac Heights, where the rich nested. Like Beverly Hills, but foggier, with a bay view and a 94115 zip code. All this is to say that there are worse places in the world to locate a dermatology practice. And it was on California Street, smack in the middle of Pac Heights, that I found Premiere Aesthetic Associates, PC.

I parked curbside, sat in the car, hands on the wheel, watching the block.

From the corner of my eye, I saw a vehicle pull next to mine and stop. I figured the guy was waiting for the light to change, but he just hung there in the middle of the block. I felt myself go rigid. Again, I wished I still had the goddamn gun.

Slowly, I looked to my left.

A man in a blue Jaguar flipped his hand at me. White guy. Sixties. Unarmed. I caught the universal signal: *You leaving?* I shook my head, and the Jaguar motored on.

Get a grip, McCormick.

I exited the car.

Yount's practice had done well, it seemed, metastasizing through the first floors of at least two adjacent buildings.

"William Yount, MD" shimmered in gold on the glass doorway of a gray stone building with deep inset windows. "Premiere Aesthetic Associates" was also written in gold. This contrasted with Premiere Aesthetic Associates Day Spa, which occupied the storefront next door. Big picture window, with gargantuan plants taking over inside. From the street, I could see the blond wood and brushed-metal furnishings inside. I could see the displays of chic beauty products and the tasteful blowups of perfect female forms on the walls. There was something predatory about this place, as if my own flawed, worried face reflected back at me in the glass was a disease, and a quick trip to Premiere Aesthetic offered the only cure.

I walked to the corner entrance and pushed into Bill Yount's reception area. Three people waited on plush antique chairs, perusing *Vogue* and *Elle* and other anxiety-producing fare. Bill had preserved much of the original character of the building: carved wooden lintels, a dark wooden floor with a large Oriental rug thrown across it. It looked more like a private surgery plucked *in toto* from Harley Street—that ancient center of British medicine in London—than a twenty-first-century derm's office in a far-flung region of the colonies. It jarred me, then, to see the very modern android sitting behind the carved receptionist's desk.

The woman's filler-injected lips pulled to a smile. "May I help you?"

I walked close to her, lowered my voice. "I'm here to see Dr. Yount. I'm an old friend of his from medical school."

The smile didn't budge on this poster child of cosmetic medicine. In addition to the bee-stung lips—wasp stung? hornet stung?—she'd had a face-lift so severe it gave her the look of someone stuck in a wind tunnel. The plastic sheen of her skin suggested dermabrasion. That her raised eyebrows generated nary a brow line told me she'd been Botoxed. And at least two sectors of her anatomy had been implanted and were straining at the low-cut blouse. It was a battle to keep myself from staring.

"Do you have an appointment?" she asked pleasantly.

"No. Like I said, I'm an old friend—"

"Dr. Yount is very busy. Would you like to make an appointment?" She began tapping on the keyboard to her sleek, flat-screened computer.

"I—"

"Best we can do is three months from now. Or we could give you an appointment with one of Dr. Yount's associates, in which case—"

I put my palms on the desk. "We're not connecting here. I am *not* a patient. I am a *friend* of Bill's from—"

Just then, the heavy door to the receptionist's right opened violently. A short, bespectacled man strode two steps into the room. His blond, thinning hair was unkempt. With his sparse beard, sagging cheeks, and creased face, he looked a decade older than his thirty-something years. Obviously, the man didn't practice his trade on himself. He didn't wear a white coat, sporting instead checkered golf pants and a lime green golf shirt.

Bill Yount stopped cold when he saw me.

The receptionist opened her puffed mouth. "Dr. Yount—"

"Wait," he said, eyeballing me, shaking a finger like a schoolteacher. "I know you."

I nodded. "Bill, it's N—"

"No, I can get this. Ned Ertel. Academy meeting, Chicago, two years ago. December."

"No."

"Derm surgery conference, Philadelphia? Braxton? Neal Braxton. You gave a dynamite talk on flap repairs—"

"Bill—"

"Wait. No. I'm Bill." He laughed, the three patients in the room laughed, the receptionist laughed. Don Rickles of the dermatology set. I could see why he was fully booked.

"Bill," I said. "Nate McCormick. We were at med school together. I was two years behind you."

Yount's mouth bloomed to a big smile, revealing perfect white teeth. "Nate," he said, crossing to me and slapping me on the back. "Nate, Nate, Nate. How're you doing?"

"I'm doing—"

"That's terrific. Terrific. Good to see you. Just book an appointment with Tina—hey, Tina, give the doctor here a slot next week—" He looked at the three waiting women, who most likely didn't enjoy such speedy service. "Professional courtesy, ladies." He turned back to me. "I'll see you—"

"Bill, I don't need an appointment. I need to talk to you."

"Talk? Talk? That's new. Here, step into my office." Yount looped an arm around me and we pushed through the door onto the street.

Once we were safely on the sidewalk, Yount said, "What's the hubbub, bub?"

"I need to know about injectables. Fillers, Botox, all—"

"What about injectables?"

"All about them."

Behind the glasses, his eyes narrowed. "You're not thinking about starting a cosmetics practice? You were—what?—surgery?"

"Internal medicine. And no, this is just interest."

Yount glanced at his thick gold watch. "Now's not the best time, since I got—" He stopped himself, and he flashed the teeth. "Since I just got stood up. Tell you what. You do something for me, I'll tell you all you need to know about injectables."

"What do I need to do?"

Yount smiled. "You play golf?"

That's how I found myself, thirty minutes later, swinging a couple of warm-up irons with Yount, a bowling pin–shaped venture capitalist named Tobler, and a squat surgeon named Lee. There was no end to the scorn heaped on the missing fourth—a patent lawyer in the city called, variously, "Dickhead," "Nutless Wonder," and "Ted." When they achieved a quorum, these guys called themselves "the Duffer Quartet."

"We all suck," Yount explained.

Yount had been kind enough to loan me his wife's clubs—"she's used them exactly zero times," he said—which happened to be three inches too short for me. Her golf shoes were five sizes too small, so I played in my utilitarian, box-toe oxfords.

"Looks great." Yount was watching me hunch over the stubby driver. "Have a beer." He thrust a Budweiser into my hand.

I took a sip. "About the injectables, Bill . . ."

"After the first hole. I need total concentration until then."

The Duffer Quartet, unmotivated novices all, hit the links at the Lincoln Park Golf Course in the city every Wednesday afternoon. It wasn't about actually playing a sport, Yount said, more about escaping the humdrum of work and family. The Quartet eschewed golf lessons and had picked up the game only a few months before. I could see why they chose Lincoln Park.

The course covered the high ground near the Palace of the Legion of Honor, and looked out over the Pacific and the Golden Gate Bridge. Stunning, really. But the course itself? Not stunning. Pockmarked greens, debris-strewn bunkers, fairways so overgrown with grass and weeds with tiny white flowers you were as likely to lose a ball on a perfect drive down the middle as on a line drive into the rough. A perfect place for golf stooges to relax and hack divots.

At the first hole, I found myself scanning the grounds, looking for armed Chinese men emerging from the foliage. There was nothing, then something.

In a clutch of trees and bushes between two fairways, I saw the leaves shiver. I focused on them, felt my legs tense as I readied myself to run.

But it was just a septuagenarian in a green windbreaker rummaging for a ball. He stepped out, a golf club in one hand, dropped the ball on the grass, and swung.

"You all right there, Nate?" Yount asked.

To get my mind off the grinding, permeating threat I felt, I made a stab at normal conversation. I brought Bill Yount up to speed on what I'd done in the past twelve years—med school, Peace Corps, med school, residency, CDC. He brought me up to speed, as well—med school, derm residency, fellowship, quick entry into the world of cosmetics. "Should've done derm," he told me.

"I should have done a lot of things," I replied.

We teed off.

The Duffer Quartet—now the Duffer Trio—did, as

Yount had warned, suck. Truly. Each of them hooted and hollered as their Titleists sank into the ground ten yards ahead of us or sliced dangerously into the next fairway.

After they'd taken their shots, I stepped to the tee box and swung the mini-driver a few times.

"Make us proud, Nate," Lee said.

"Not too proud," Tobler said.

"Let the man focus," Yount said.

For the first time in ten years, I addressed a golf ball. I chose my line, then circled to the left for the swing. *Lay off the arms,* I told myself. *Easy swing.* Surprisingly, the club felt natural in my hands. I took a last practice swing before settling into my stance. *Head up, relax into your stance like you're sitting on a bar stool, forget you haven't played in years.*

I pulled my arms across my body, pivoted my hips, let my arms follow.

Under most circumstances, the shot would be considered average. But relative to my competition, it was one hundred percent Tiger. The ball sailed straight up the fairway, bounced, and came to rest a decent eight-iron shot from the green.

"Holy shit," Tobler breathed.

"A ringer," Lee said.

"You sonofabitch," Yount said.

Eight-iron, chip, two-putt. A bogey on the first hole.

As we rode the carts to the second hole, Yount looked at me. "So, injectables . . ."

"Yes," I said.

"A man who plays golf like that gets all his questions answered. Can I ask the interest?"

"Work."

"Fair enough." Yount stopped the cart. "Is your work

something I should know about? I mean, we're not talking Ebola contamination or anything, right? I use this stuff all the time."

"No Ebola."

Lee and Tobler pulled out their drivers for the short par four. Yount and I followed suit. As we did, he began to talk quietly.

"A little history of the injectables. Botox, I assume you know. Botulinum toxin paralyzes muscles and reduces the wrinkles caused by the bunching of those muscles."

"I know Botox."

"How much do you know about skin and wrinkles?"

"About as much as you know about Ebola."

"Okay. The beginning, then." He did a little half-swing with the driver. "For starters, wrinkles result from the loss of three skin components—elastin, collagen, and hyaluronic acid. The drug companies have done a pretty good job with the latter two. Injectable collagen has been around since the seventies, though the original stuff came from cows, didn't last very long, and generated allergic reactions in some patients. A couple of years ago, human bioengineered collagen came on the market. No allergic reactions, but it still only lasted a few months." Yount paused while Lee smacked his ball into a clutch of tall grass. "A few years back, we get hyaluronic acid, or Restylane. She holds together collagen and elastin and pulls water molecules into the space where she's injected. But hyaluronic acid is problematic. Injecting her hurts and causes inflammation and results are good only for a few months."

"Beauty's a bitch," I said.

The Quartet played ready golf, and Tobler was ready next. His ball skated off the club's toe and tunneled through the bushes to our right. "I'm taking a mulligan," he said.

"What's big now," Yount told me, "is the new fillers. Sculptra, poly-L-lactic acid. Radiesse, calcium hydroxylapatite. And Artecoll, polymethylmethacrylate."

Tobler nailed his second shot, and Yount approached the tee. He hunched over his club, used too much arm, and sent the ball skidding along the fairway. I followed with a shot that landed fifteen feet from the green.

"A ringer," Lee said again.

After finishing out the hole, me with a double bogey, the other three with even less respectable scores, we climbed back into the carts. This section of golf course skirted the beaux arts Legion of Honor, which was, in fact, an art museum, a three-quarter-size concrete replica of a similarly named building in Paris, complete with Corinthian columns and friezes. I wondered what the French would think of this setup. Art museum in the middle of a golf course? Sculpture an errant five-iron from hole two? *C'est fou.*

As we dropped from the building, a break in the trees afforded a view of the Pacific all the way to the Farallon Islands.

Unconsciously almost, I looked around for any threat. *Stop it,* I scolded myself.

"The last two you mentioned—the Radiesse and Artecoll," I said. "They're used in bone repair."

"Yes. Well, the substances themselves came from orthopedics. For the skin, there's a different carrier."

"They all work the same way?"

"More or less. You want mechanisms?"

"Give me mechanisms-lite."

"Okay. Basically, the endpoint of all three of the new

fillers is to bring fibroblasts into the treatment sites. The fibroblasts lay down collagen and, voilà, you end up looking like your picture from the senior prom."

"Any word on tumors being caused by this stuff?"

Yount gave me a sideways glance as he stopped the cart. "No. No reports of cancer for any of them. We get granulomas sometimes"—granulomas are the body's reaction to foreign material, fibrous collections that create bumps in the skin—"or deposits of the material in tissue. But no tumors."

We arrived at the third hole, a par three. Lee punched a good shot toward and over the green. Tobler whooped and slapped him five, then stuck his tee into the ground.

"Anything else that's out there you know of that could cause cancer?" I asked.

Yount thought. "There's been some work done with autologous fibroblast transplants, but the science isn't there yet. It's all research stage."

Autologous fibroblast transplantation is a process whereby fibroblasts—the building blocks of skin—are harvested from a patient, grown in culture, then reintroduced into the body.

"And," Yount continued, "I really can't see the transplants causing cancer. The cells would either take hold or they wouldn't. And the trouble the researchers are having is that the cells are *not* taking hold and *not* growing in the body. The response just isn't that robust. I haven't heard anything about tumors." He unsheathed a six-iron. "This is my favorite hole. I actually parred it once."

Parred it once, but not twice. Yount's ball ricocheted off a tree back toward the tee box. It lodged in an old divot fifteen feet in front of us. "Damn," he said.

After we finished the hole—I'd actually parred it, and basked for a moment, at least, in the envy of my fellows—Yount turned to me. "Nate, have to say your questions are making me nervous. This is my livelihood. So if you know something about these things, I'd hope you'd clue me in."

I told him about the cases of fibrosarcoma, about the women's images.

Looking grave, he removed his driver from the bag. "I haven't heard anything. No reports of illegitimate treatments causing problems, definitely no reports of legitimate treatments doing this."

Lee and Tobler began heckling Yount to take his shot, but he ignored them. "I'll keep my eye out. And you let me know if there's anything I need to worry about."

I told him I would.

He gazed out over the fairway for hole four. "You got to find out what's going on, Nate. Not just for me, I mean it's just a job, after all. But what you described to me . . ."—he shook his head—"nobody should have to suffer that."

Fire and tobacco and a double bogey on the fifth hole. Tobler, the venture capitalist, reached into his bag and produced four squat, dark Maduros. With the beer, my admirable skill on the links, and now the good cigars, I felt some of the coils in my body unwind. As the pungent smoke curled and dispersed, I decided that I liked these men. I liked that they liked me. I enjoyed their admiration, even for something as inconsequential and dubious as my golf ability. There was even talk about booting the lawyer Ted from the foursome permanently.

I took a drag on the cigar and blew a cloud. Had I

followed a different path, this could have been my life: playing hooky with buddies on a weekday afternoon, chatting about practice management and marital strife. Somehow, though, as good as the cigar tasted, as good as the conversation flowed, and as good as the clubs felt in my hands, I couldn't shake the sense that these were moments in someone else's life.

I pulled off the driver's head cover at the ninth hole, Lee telling me he'd give me twenty bucks for a par on this one. Before I could accept the bet, I felt the cell vibrate in my pocket.

I told Yount to go ahead, and answered the call.

"Dr. McCormick?" It was a woman's voice, slightly muffled.

I said it was.

"This is Dorothy Zhang. I believe you were trying to get in touch with me."

69

I WAS TO MEET DOROTHY Zhang in Berkeley, at an address she'd given me. I was not to tell the police. If I see the police, she'd warned, you will not see me. But I trust you not to bring them.

"Why do you trust me?" I'd asked.

You were Paul's friend, she'd answered simply.

Dredging up some memory of Berkeley's geography, I

got off on Ashby Avenue. The bad guys knew my car—I was pretty sure of that—but I didn't have time to switch vehicles. Next best thing, I figured, was to lose them in the middle of a college campus in full academic swing.

Ashby took me up to Telegraph, a stone's throw from People's Park, haven for homelessness and drug addiction, and subject of enough sociology and public health theses to fill a library. Part of the city's charm—the People's Republic of Berkeley, for those who remember its halcyon rebellious days—was its embrace of those not even on the first rung of the socioeconomic ladder. Restaurants would leave leftover food in the park; the bourgeoisie from the Berkeley Hills would leave leftover clothes. Sort of like giving to Goodwill, minus the tax write-offs.

On Telegraph, I passed some of the more exotic members of the species. A kid with a tattoo—a thornbush crawling up his cheeks and across his forehead—sauntered in front of my car. A goth couple, swathed in black and adorned with various skeletal accessories, walked hand in hand, stopping to take in the display at Amoeba Music. Well, I thought, if Dorothy Zhang comes at me with a bazooka, I could sprint down to Telegraph, don a rasta hat, pierce my eyelid, and just fade into the crowd.

After covering every square inch of asphalt around the Berkeley campus, after nearly mowing down a few coeds who were dumb enough to cross the street while I concentrated on signage, I finally found the address I'd been hunting. It was a light green building, maybe ten units total, on a small street near the campus. No idea why Dorothy Zhang would be here and not with her baby-Einstein kid Tim in Napa. No idea why she'd dump him on a guy who denied the kid's name. Unless she was masterminding murder and mayhem across the Bay Area. You don't want your offspring to see something like that.

I parked across from the apartment, shot looks up and down the block before I got up the courage to pull my sport coat from the backseat and step out.

Clean, with two floors of apartments surrounding a small courtyard, Dorothy Zhang's building looked more like a motel than a permanent residence. Not charming, but not a hovel. I stepped along the open walkway on the second floor to the far end of the complex. Number 8.

Standing to the side of the peephole, I knocked.

No one answered, and I knocked again. Again, nothing.

I tried the doorknob, turning it easily. The door swung open.

I stepped inside.

70

"MS. ZHANG?"

The sparsely furnished studio apartment—futon, wooden table, one chair—was wrecked. The futon mattress had been sliced open. Clothes had been ripped and tossed. The carpeting was torn from the baseboards and pulled up in places, as if the floor itself had been flayed.

A video camera lay on the floor, its inner workings bursting forth like intestines.

I walked past a closet, where the few clothes from inside had been spread over the floor. Its ceiling had been punched in. In the bathroom, pill bottles were emptied into the sink. Shampoo and conditioner spattered the shower floor.

I checked out the pill bottles. Vicodin, OxyContin. The pills were dissolving on the basin's damp porcelain.

The kitchen had fared no better. The refrigerator and freezer were wide open, the contents—peanut butter, couscous, ice cream—smeared on the counter. Beside them, Chinese food cartons spilled their gelatinous insides into the melting ice cream.

There was a back door, leading to a back staircase. The lock was shattered.

I was struck, at that moment, not just by the ransacking, but by how spartan the place was, under the broken furniture and scattered foodstuffs. Not a touch of personality here. Except . . .

On the kitchen linoleum, there was a photograph: sky-blue background, little boy whose hair had been wet with water to tame it for the shot.

Timothy Kim.

I reached down to grab the picture when I felt my phone vibrate; I answered it.

"Get out," a female voice snarled. *"Now."*

"Who—"

But a sound cut my words. It was the door at the front of the apartment. Then hushed voices.

I ran like hell for the back door.

71

I BOLTED DOWN THE BACK staircase to the patch of grass that passed as a yard. There was a shout above me, a fence in front of me. I clambered over five feet of wood and dropped into the next yard, snapping the necks of some birds-of-paradise. Without looking back, I tore across the yard, to a shorter fence, scrambled over it.

I could hear voices, excited now.

I cut left through the yard, to an alleyway. Over another fence, through another domestic haven, to a street. And then I ran, ran, ran. Four years of high school cross-country finally turned out to be worth something.

When I hit the campus, I got as far into it as I could. Eventually, I stopped and slumped over, hands on my knees. I was heaving pretty good now, sucking air deep into my lungs. Bile flooded my mouth and I spit onto the grass.

If you're going to try to get lost, a campus is a pretty good place to do it. Especially a university as stuffed to the gills as Berkeley is. I scanned the grounds, but didn't see anybody hell-bent on putting a bullet into my brain. Still, I was feeling too exposed here, so I walked quickly to the nearest building—some Earth Sciences hall—and slumped down on a bench inside. Classes had changed a few minutes before, and the halls were full of youth and vigor.

But my youth and vigor peaked during those cross-country days, and it took two more minutes for the pounding in my ears to stop. When it did, I began to process the Dorothy Zhang grist.

I'd very nearly found her, and she'd vanished. Again.

The cell vibrated.

"Dr. McCormick?" Same female voice.

"Ms. Zhang," I said.

I hunched over the phone like I was protecting something, which, when you get right down to it, I guess I was.

"Where are you?" I asked.

"Where are *you*?"

"At Berkeley. On campus. I was in your apartment."

"And that's precisely why I told you to get out."

It was hard to miss the edge in her voice.

"We need to meet," I said.

She laughed.

"What?" I asked.

"Who else did you tell about the address? Who did you tell where I *was*?" she spat.

"No one."

"I've been at that apartment for over a month, Dr. McCormick. Two hours ago, I tell you where I am and . . ." She didn't finish the sentence.

"I told absolutely no one about you. Not the police. No one." I felt Dorothy Zhang slipping from my grasp. "I didn't tell anybody. I don't— These people have been after me, too. There was a couple killed last night and they removed their goddamned tongues and left me one as a message. Call the San Francisco police, ask them."

She was silent.

"I know about the sick people," I told her. "I found the

pictures Paul Murphy had. Paul wanted to show them to me." I felt myself getting heated. "You need to tell me what's going on."

She didn't answer that. Instead, she asked me, "Do you know where the Greek Theater is?"

My memory of the campus had rusted over the years. I had to ask directions three times. Each of the students I stopped wore flip-flops. Each had a breezy air about her, a sun-fueled California cheeriness. What a stranger I was, what a strange land.

I hoofed it across campus, past an open swath of grass with kids sunning, studying, talking Kant and Jessica Simpson. Enjoy life, kids, I thought. Worry about grades and who hooked up with whom while you can. The world gets dark, dark, dark after you grab that diploma.

I cut between the Hearst Mining Building and the so-called Mining Circle, a reflecting pool with a few furry bushes rising from its center. At the business school, I wove my way to the Greek Theater.

A few cars gathered dust on an asphalt lot shaded by eucalyptus. One—an ugly Chevy Malibu parked at the top of the sloping lot—was occupied. As I approached it, the driver pushed open the passenger-side door. It was a woman in a big white hat, large dark sunglasses on her face. She wore stylish blue jeans, a tight olive turtleneck sweater. A faint scent of perfume wafted from the car.

But there was something wrong—

"Get in, Dr. McCormick," she said.

—with her face. Even under the glasses, I could see marble-sized knots of flesh on her upper cheeks and on her temples. A tumor lifted the left side of her lip. A scar ran to her right lip, across the right cheek. I let my eyes rest, perhaps a little too long, on a formerly beautiful face, now destroyed. Dorothy Zhang's face.

"I'm glad you—"

I never finished the sentence.

I felt wetness on my face. The next thing I knew, I was clawing at eyes that felt as though they'd been burned from my head.

72

SNOT AND TEARS POURED FROM places I didn't even know produced snot and tears. A hand, not my own, reached into my jacket and pawed around. I hardly noticed it, though, since my blood vessels had dilated and breathing had become difficult.

Between gags, I managed "What . . . are you . . . doing?"

"Just making sure," she answered, and I felt the hand move away.

"Making sure of what? I don't have anything."

She didn't answer.

"Can I at least get a tissue or something?"

She said, "I don't have any," so I pulled my shirttail from my pants and wiped my eyes and nose, which still flowed like the Ganges.

"Paul gave you the pictures?" she asked.

"He didn't have the chance. He was killed before he could."

"How did you get them?"

"I broke into his house. I found them there."

"You found them and the police didn't?"

"I'm a better noticer than they are."

"Noticer," she repeated skeptically. "Did Paul tell you to contact me?"

"No. Your name was on a file in the jump drive where I found the pictures." I blew my nose into the shirt. Inelegant, but effective. "You have it, don't you?"

"What?"

"The fibrosarcoma."

"I have it, Dr. McCormick."

"Do you know how you got it?"

"Of course."

By this time, my shirttail was soaking wet with secretions. Still, I could not see.

"Here," Zhang said, and I felt something soft land in my lap: a clutch of tissues. Again, I blew my nose.

"You said you didn't have any."

"You can't trust anyone, can you?" She sighed, but I thought I detected a hint of amusement in it. "Tell me why I should trust you."

"Check out my résumé. I don't usually go in for attacking newscasters."

"I did check it out."

"And Paul? What did he say about me?"

"Paul said you were one of the good guys."

"Okay, then. I'm a good guy. You just maced one of the good guys."

I dug the heels of my hands into my eyes. Christ, I

thought, this really is unpleasant. Then I remembered the fate of the others who'd gotten tangled in this mess. All in all, I had it pretty good by comparison.

"We can't talk here," she said.

"Okay," I said meekly.

"But I have to be careful. I'm sorry, but I have to drive."

"Then drive. I certainly can't—"

"I'm sorry," she said again.

"For what? Oh, no—"

Another jet of spray hit me in the face.

73

THE CAR STOPPED; THE FIERY heat in my face, the liquid dump from my eyes and mucous membranes, did not. Apart from light and dark, I still couldn't see much. I heard the driver's-side door open, then close. The door at my elbow opened.

Pepper spray, oleoresin capsaicin. The cayenne pepper derivative is an inflammatory agent, not an irritant, which is why it opened the pipes in my face so wide. But to say it's not an irritant doesn't mean there's no pain. The fucker hurt.

"You didn't have to hit me twice," I whined. "That stuff lasts for thirty minutes."

"I didn't read the directions," she said. "Here, I have

your arm." Fingers wrapped around my biceps, hoisted me out of the vehicle. "Fresh air should help."

Fresh air, for those who haven't had the opportunity to get a snootful of pepper spray, does not help.

"You're not going to push me off a cliff or something?" I asked.

"No." Dorothy Zhang led me by the elbow across what felt like broken bones.

"On second thought, do push me off a cliff. Put me out of my misery."

"Here," she said, handing me a bottle. "Wash out your eyes with this."

"Water won't help. You have any hand lotion? Anything greasy?"

Her hand dropped from my arm, and I think she had reached inside her purse. A moment later, she said, "Here." She pushed a tube into my hand. "Hand lotion."

I squeezed what was left of the tube into my hand and rubbed it over my face. I wiped my face on my shirt.

"Now the water," I said.

By the time I was done with my ablutions, the fire in my face dampened, and my vision cleared somewhat. I could just make out her form—tall and thin—with the floppy white hat slanted over her face. She looked like a tulip.

Water ran down my front. I used my shirt again. Blew my nose.

I thought I heard a giggle.

"I'm glad this is so much fun for you," I said.

"It's just—" She tried to get out more words but stopped herself because she was laughing. *Laughing.* "You just look . . . You don't look happy."

"My entire front is soaked with personal effluvia, as well as a couple ounces of hand lotion and half a liter of water. Wonder how happy you'd be under the circumstances," I grumbled. "Where are we?" I could see that I was standing on the edge of a white expanse, with masses of color smudged across. Beyond, I could see green and brown. Above me, blue.

"Strawberry Canyon," Dorothy said, naming the semi-wilderness a short distance east of the Berkeley campus.

"Why here?"

"It's quiet," she said.

And a great place to get rid of a half-blind, pesky doctor, I thought.

Her arm threaded through mine and she led me to what must have been the trailhead. Arm in arm, we began our odd journey upward along an old fire trail canopied by spreading oaks.

"I used to come up here a lot," she told me. "When I was a student. We used to go running here."

As if on cue, I heard the thump-thump of feet on the trail and glimpsed a blur of white, blue, and pink bounding toward us. I saw Dorothy tilt her chin, shielding the view of her face with that big hat.

I tensed as the footsteps passed. Dorothy seemed to notice. "It's just a couple joggers."

We walked in silence for a few moments. "I had a lot of first dates here, too," she said. "Hiking dates. Better than coffee. If it doesn't go anywhere, you still get your workout in."

Her touch was strong and tender. Her voice, too. I guessed it wasn't just her knockout looks that had kept the viewing public coming back for more, night after night.

"I had a first date up here."

"How'd it go?"

"Great, until the girl pulled out the pepper spray and blasted me."

"I had to do that, Dr. McCormick."

"Nate."

"Nate. I couldn't take chances until I trusted you. Those people show up at my place right after I tell you where I am . . ."

"But you trust me now?"

"I'll trust anyone who's stupid enough to try to be funny while they're crying their eyes out."

So, first dates and Strawberry Canyon. Who'd a thunk Dorothy Zhang and I had anything in common besides our names in a dead man's data storage?

As a swinging single in that first year of medical school, I'd been set up on a blind date with a Renaissance Studies grad student at Berkeley. We bonded over the phone enough for a first get-together, then decided on a low-pressure hike up through the canyon. The orchestrator of the event was a friend from Penn State who was at Berkeley for engineering. Why he thought an MD-PhD student and a PhD in Renaissance Studies would mix any better than ammonia and bleach, I still can't figure. But there I was, over a decade before, sweating up that same hill.

The conversation with the Renaissance PhD withered after we'd moved through the easy topics: where are you from, how was undergrad, and boy the weather is nice. It completely died after she told me I looked just like her old boyfriend. Somehow, the woman took my silence as dumbstruck love. When she called to set up another date, I pleaded stomach trouble and overwork. When she called a second time to check on the dyspepsia and workload, I came up with a lie about a girl back home. After that, I let all her calls go to the answering machine and never called back. Nate McCormick, paragon of chivalry.

I don't know why, but I told Dorothy the story. Maybe I wanted to show her I didn't bear any grudges after the pepper-spray incident. Maybe her arm in mine was making me feel too comfortable.

Dorothy's hand tightened on my arm and her head dipped again. Two humanoid shapes were approaching us.

The couple murmured cheery hellos as they passed.

"Why don't you tell me what you've been up to for the past few weeks?" Dorothy asked. "Since Paul died."

"After you tell me what I'm dealing with."

"Don't get greedy, Dr. McCormick. You don't want me to not trust you again."

"You still have the spray?"

"Poised and ready to strike one for jilted Renaissance PhDs everywhere."

I smiled, surprised that this woman—the woman I'd been seeking for so long, the beautiful TV celebrity, the mauled fugitive, my only solid link to a murdered friend, the woman who'd caused me such physical pain—was charming my socks off.

Thus charmed, I began to talk.

14

"I FEEL LIKE I'M IN the dark," I said, having just finished my long spiel. "All of these things are happening, but I can't put it together. I can't point to anything."

By that time, my vision was pretty much back to normal. The view to the west was impressive. In the foreground, Berkeley was a pastiche of green and gray, the campus and town interwoven with oaks and eucalyptus like patches on a quilt. The big tower in the middle of campus—the Campanile—jutted up like a middle finger, a not-so-subtle fuck-you to reactionary forces everywhere.

Berkeley. Christ.

Then there was the Bay, dotted with sailboats, and sliced this way and that by enormous tankers. And San Francisco itself, the downtown. Not a lot of glass there. Mostly white or dun-colored stone solidly rising skyward like fossilized teeth in the jaw of some prehistoric reptile. From up there, everything seemed so still, so stable, so *peaceful.*

I looked at Dorothy. In profile, I could see under the large sunglasses to a few bumps at the corners of her eyes. The hat brim shaded her face, but not the scarred knot of flesh at her lip, which, at rest, pulled her mouth into a snarl. I found it difficult to look at her, difficult to turn away. Like the proverbial train wreck.

She caught me staring at her, and shifted away to face the view.

"So, what's going on?" I asked her. "What am I missing?"

"I can only tell you what happened to me."

"That's more than I have now."

"I suppose," she agreed softly. "Okay, me. What I've been doing for the past . . . Oh, God . . . the past year." Her fingers nudged the sunglasses higher. "Thirteen months ago, I heard about this new cosmetic treatment. Better than Botox. Better than Restylane. Much, much better. I was working as an anchor at the time, and had done my duty with Botox. Such a pain. Literally. Needles every few months. And the results were good, but not great. You still get the slackness of the skin, the drooping. You still age. Anyway, this is to say that I'd been somewhat familiar with cosmetic medicine so, when I heard of this new treatment, I was intrigued."

"Where'd you hear about it?"

"My mother, actually. Her sister had it done. Her sister had friends and those friends had friends and they'd all had it done, according to my mom. Everyone was thrilled with the results. My aunt, she looked great. I mean, here was this woman in her late fifties who looked like she was forty."

"Oh, man. Why did you do it?"

I don't think she'd been expecting that question. The sunglasses turned toward me, then away.

"Because my priorities were screwed up," she answered after a moment. "Because in my business how you look is worth a helluva lot more than what's going on between your ears. Because there's a goddamned website that rates

TV newswomen and I was high in the rankings and I *loved* it, and because I had just dropped behind that KRNO bitch Kristin McField and I *hated* that."

We walked for a bit before she continued, "I was an average-looking kid. I lie: I was kind of ugly. My head was too big for my body, my face was chunky. But things began to change when I hit puberty. I didn't really notice the changes, but I did notice when other people noticed. Doors that had been closed to me for my whole life began to open. School plays, slumber parties, dates. It only became more obvious during college. If I'd been the same awkward thing I'd been in sixth grade, no one would have suggested broadcast journalism to me. If no one had suggested broadcast journalism . . . You get the picture."

"The mysterious power of beauty."

"It's not mysterious if you pay attention. Anyway, I knew that my career, my prospects with men, even some of my mother's love, owed a lot to my face. So *I* owed a lot to my face. I never wanted to be that ugly kid again."

The last sentence contained, perhaps, more savagery than she'd intended, because she hastily changed the subject. "Anyway, Auntie Joan gave me a name of the guy who represented the man who did her cosmetic work, and after going through a few intermediaries, I finally saw the pictures."

"The pictures?"

"The Before and Afters. This man—Jasper, he said his name was—brought along a binder of photos. The women looked fabulous. There were a couple of men, too, and they looked great. Amazing, like someone had just erased lines and rolled back the years. A decade younger at least."

"Did this Jasper guy talk about the risks?"

"He didn't, and I didn't ask. I did not *want* to know the risks then. All I saw is what it did for these people and what it could do for me."

I shook my head.

"Do not judge me, Dr. McCormick. That's already been done. And I'm paying the price, okay?"

"Okay."

She turned toward the west, toward a fat yellow sun that was dropping like a bomb onto the city.

"Jasper told me that the procedure involved injections into the skin, just like Botox. That the results were very long-lasting. That the doctor who performed the injections had done some of the original research on the substance at university."

"Which university?"

"The University of Illinois in Chicago, I think. Why?"

There was a flutter in the back of my mind, a tickle. I concentrated on that for a moment, then zeroed in: Tom Bukowski, the founder of Tetra Biologics, now deceased, had his lab at the UIC before setting up shop in California. "What was the doctor's name?"

"Wei-jan Fang. Anyway, Jasper showed me pictures, assured me it was perfectly safe. He said the effects lasted for years, and he had all these testimonials. He said that the treatment was being used all over China and there had been no major complications. He said the injections were legal over there, that they just hadn't reached the States yet."

"*Is* it available in China?"

"He said it was."

"You didn't check?"

"My aunt had it done. Her friends had it done. They looked *great.* It *seemed* safe."

"I'd just assume that if you were going to get something like this—"

"Not everyone is a damned physician who does fifteen years of research on everything."

Everywhere I stepped, I seemed to tramp on a nerve. "How much did it cost?" I asked. That seemed like a safer question.

"Twelve thousand dollars. Cash."

I tried to whistle, but there was still too much goop in my mouth. The sound fluttered pathetically. "This happened a year ago?"

"Nine months."

"Where did you get it done?"

"The Richmond, on Geary Street. There was a nail care shop in front, which, I think, was just that—a front—since there was never anyone getting their nails done there. The back was just like a doctor's office. Just as clean, just as professional looking. There were four other women in the waiting room. All Chinese, except for one I thought looked Vietnamese."

"What was the name of the nail place?"

"What does it matter? I heard they moved to a place called Spectacular Nails a few months ago."

"Where was it?" I persisted.

"Clement and Thirty-sixth."

"What exactly did they tell you they were injecting?"

"They called the product 'Beautiful Essence.' Great name, huh?"

"Sounds like aromatherapy. What did they tell you Beautiful Essence was supposed to do?"

"Regrow tissue that had been lost."

"Regrow tissue? How?"

"They refused to discuss that. They called it a trade secret."

I thought about that, about "regrowing tissue." This can be done in a few different ways: implanting stem cells that take root and proliferate, adding substances to make cells already in the body grow, or turning off the cellular mechanisms that stop growth. But engineering tissue growth isn't easy. The body has checks and balances against uncontrolled growth, better known as cancer. Like Bill Yount told me, the early work on fibroblast stem cells had been disappointing.

For me, the most likely culprit would be the fillers, which Yount had said were substances that bring cells to the injection site. The technology is old and widely available. I didn't have too much trouble imagining a poisoned batch of fillers cooked up in some lab in China.

But whatever it was, it had sprayed cancer into Dorothy Zhang's face like buckshot.

"Did you at least ask about side effects?" I heard the impatience in my voice. So, it seemed, did she.

"They said there would be swelling. And that I should stay out of the sun for a couple of days."

"That's it?"

"That's it." She raised her head and looked off into space for a moment, zipping through the atmosphere, visiting distant planets. "The procedure itself was easy. There were more injections than with Botox. I think they said they gave me over fifty separate injections—around my eyes, my mouth, on my forehead. Wei-jan Fang himself administered the injections. I should have left as soon as I saw him." She said it bitterly.

"Why?"

"I'd never seen someone looking so stressed out. He came into the room looking like a fugitive—"

"Maybe because he was a fugitive? Because what he was injecting was illegal?" Again, I sounded harsher than I intended.

More than ten million cosmetic procedures were performed in this country last year. Four million Botox injections. A million chemical peels. Three hundred thousand boob jobs. Liposuction. Eyelid surgery. Sclerotherapy. Face-lifts. Of course, there's the fringe stuff, too. For the girls: buttock implants, vaginal rejuvenation. For the guys: calf and pectoral implants. All in all, ten million chances for a better life, or at least a tighter jawline or a J.Lo rear.

In addition to all that, you got the black market. No one really keeps track of the illegal stuff, but every once in a while, a body floats to the surface. Liposuction in a basement in Massachusetts, a blob of fat travels to the lungs, a young woman dies. Four people paralyzed after their doctor (who'd already lost his license) injects them with a non-FDA-approved form of botulinum toxin. There are the gray areas—the ob-gyn legally injecting Restylane after a weekend workshop—and the black areas—anyone injecting a substance not approved by the FDA for use in humans. What Dorothy Zhang was describing to me sounded pretty black—a clinic moving around, nondisclosure about what was being injected, refusal to talk about risks. A thousand-to-one chance that injecting Beautiful Essence into someone's face was about as legal as injecting diesel.

"Twelve thousand a pop, huh?" I asked.

"And forty minutes."

"A ton of money." My public health antennae began to quiver anxiously. "And a lot of people. What do you think: ten patients a day? More?"

"More, I think."

"How's your aunt?"

"Fine, as far as I know."

"And her friends?"

"I haven't spoken with anyone in the family for months, except my brother. I think they're fine."

"It's not everyone then . . . the fibrosarcoma."

"No. Only the unlucky few." Her voice wobbled, and she swiped at a rivulet of saliva that had escaped from her mouth. "After the injections, Dr. Fang said I should see results in the next week or so, and then 'positive changes'—that's how he put it, 'positive changes'—would continue over the next few months as the tissue began to fill in. He told me to set up an appointment for a checkup in two weeks. After that, I'd need bimonthly checks."

"And the results?"

"All the hype was true. Everything went just as Dr. Fang said it would. My face looked even better after a month. I began formulating the story I'd run when the drug hit the U.S. market. You know—a before-and-after piece, the kind of thing that drives up your ratings. I was stupid enough to think about talking to Dr. Fang about an exclusive. I was so stupid, Nate, so pathetically naive . . . Four more months passed before I saw the first bump."

"Where?"

"Free Beautiful Essence treatments if you guess right."

"Your lip. Right lip."

She gave me the barest smile; it lasted only an instant.

15

"IT STARTED WITH A TINY bump, so small I could barely feel it with my fingertips. I showed it to Dr. Fang when I saw him in follow-up. He got a little worked up about it, asking me when it started, if there were any other spots. He took a little tissue, to analyze it, he said. His reaction made me nervous, so I told him I planned to go to my regular dermatologist to get it checked out. That's when he flipped out. He told me they'd take care of it in the clinic, not to worry, blah, blah, blah."

"You didn't listen to him."

"Hell no, I didn't. I scheduled an appointment with my doctor for the following day."

"You got a next-day appointment with a dermatologist?"

"One of the perks of being on TV. Anyway, my dermatologist biopsied it. He called it dermatofibrosarcoma protuberans."

"Nice pronunciation."

"I've had plenty of time to practice it. I freaked out, of course. I mean—cancer?" She got quiet again. "Dr. Fang called me the day after I got the biopsy results, to make sure I hadn't seen another doctor."

"What did you tell him?"

"I told him to take his MD and shove it up his ass. And

I told him that I was going to seek further treatment at UCSF. He said doing that would be a mistake, that he wanted to protect me from people who would hurt me, hurt my family. He said he knew that I knew what he was talking about."

"Did you know?"

She said nothing.

"Come on," I prodded. "Your brother said the same thing. Talking about 'these people' and 'you don't know who you're messing with'—"

"I *do* know who I'm messing with. So does Daniel."

"Who the hell are they?"

"Remember I said my mother's sister had the procedure done?"

"Yeah."

"Well, Auntie Joan is married to Uncle Tony."

"Fascinating."

"Uncle Tony is 'those people.'" She touched the corner of her glasses again. "I didn't even know he was involved until Dr. Fang mentioned it. We always knew that Uncle Tony had some things on the side, but we didn't know what. Anyway, after that, I was scared. I'd been off work for a month by then. I went up to Napa, took Tim with me, tried to disappear. I mean, my face was a mess and who could I complain to about it? I knew what I'd done was illegal. I was being threatened. I was scared. But my face was getting worse—I was scared. I ended up going to a Mohs surgeon, who cut out the tumor."

Mohs micrographic surgery is a tissue-sparing procedure for removing skin cancer. The surgeon narrowly excises the tumor, then looks at it under the microscope to see if he got it all. If not, he cuts again, looks at the scope again.

He repeats the process until no cancer is visible at the margins.

"He got it all?" I asked.

"He said so. Great, right? Clear margins. Maybe with makeup, I could even go back to TV."

She tried to smile, but the scarred right lip, the tumor-infested left, pulled to a snarl, couldn't pull it off.

"When did the other tumors develop?" I asked.

"A few weeks after the first one was removed."

"But you didn't go back to the surgeon? To remove them?"

"No."

"Why?"

"They found out about the first surgery. 'Those people,'" she said bitterly. "So they took my boy. They took Tim."

16

THE SUN HAD DROPPED ANOTHER inch in the sky, the shadows cast by the trees were lengthening, and Dorothy Zhang said she was beginning to hurt.

"I didn't have time to get the painkillers," she explained as we made our way down through the canyon to the car.

"They're in the sink at your apartment," I told her. In a grand-old-doctor sort of way, I added, "The tumor wraps around and invades the nerves. That's where the pain comes from."

"I don't care where the pain comes from," she snapped.

There are times, I admit, when I forget there's a reason not everyone in the world went to medical school. What doctors think is fascinating—causes, mechanisms, pathogenicity—is, for most people, beside the point. They hurt, they want relief.

At that point, though, I was not what Dorothy needed. I had a DEA number, but had not gone through the bureaucratic labyrinth to get licensed in California. Being able to write prescriptions for my nonexistent patients hadn't seemed like a priority. Now, however, it would have been nice to write a script or two. It would have been nice to relieve someone's pain.

"We can't go to your apartment," I said. I thought of Brooke for a moment, then of Ravi Singh. "I have a friend who can write prescriptions. What's most effective?"

"OxyContin worked best."

"I'll call him."

I rummaged for the cell phone, but she put her hand on my arm. "No. It's okay."

"I thought you said—"

"It hurts. But the drugs make me fuzzy and I can't . . . I need to be able to think."

"You need to deal with the pain," I insisted. I felt the overwhelming need to protect this woman, to offer her relief in whatever way I could. Maybe it was that whole Nate-only-likes-sick-people thing; maybe it was something else. "I'm here now, right? We'll work tog—"

"You don't understand." She removed her hand from

my arm, and started again down the hill. "I think they're very scared."

"Good. That's good."

"No, Nate, it's not."

Since I could now see, and since Dorothy was adjusting to a world without narcotics, I drove her car. She kept touching her face, massaging it lightly here and there. She hadn't taken her sunglasses off until long after the day's bright light had faded. Half a dozen small tumors spread out from the corners of her eyes.

For the first time, I noticed her fingers—long, fine, the skin beautifully maintained. Her nails were painted pink; I caught another whiff of perfume. Strange, I thought, that we grab on to these insignificant things to keep ourselves grounded. Long ago, I cared for a patient who had the bad luck of getting squamous cell carcinoma on her forehead. Normally, this was a very curable form of cancer, but hers had tracked along a branch of the trigeminal nerve and had gotten into her brain. The surgeon who tried to remove the cancer—who chased it across her forehead and along the nerve—finally gave up. Or, at least he gave up trying to cure her. Even though the woman had a life expectancy of less than a year, she insisted the surgeon give her a cosmetic reworking. And so she endured yet another surgery—flaps, skin grafts—just to look presentable in her final months of life.

So, little things matter. Pink nail polish matters.

"Let me call my friend," I told Dorothy. "There's no reason—"

"No," she said, and turned away from me.

We found a cheap motel on University Avenue in Berkeley. Dorothy went to the room while I walked a few doors down to grab some Chinese takeout. When I returned, I saw that Dorothy had laid out a couple of towels on one of the beds; a roll of toilet paper perched next to the towels. Her hat and sunglasses were off, and I could see hints of the beautiful face—the cheekbones, the almond eyes—under the roiling flesh.

"Don't spill," she said, "or you're going to be toweling off with hoisin sauce."

We sat cross-legged with the food between us. The boxes canted dangerously on the lumpy bed; not only was I worried about toweling off with hoisin, I was worried about sleeping in it. I readjusted the moo shu.

"We should get your car," Dorothy said.

"It's outside your place. Probably not wise to get it just yet."

"Probably not."

Expertly, Dorothy maneuvered a sizable bite of beef and broccoli into her mouth with the chopsticks. As she chewed, soy sauce and broth rolled down her chin on the left, where the tumor prevented her lips from closing. She ripped off a piece of toilet paper and daubed. The crumpled toilet paper then went to the floor, to a growing mound of white dappled with brown and tan. We had worked our way through the restaurant's napkins in the first five minutes of the meal.

Another stream of saliva escaped her mouth. Frustrated, she grabbed again at the TP.

"This is so disgusting," she said. "I can usually control it, but—"

"Hey," I said. "It's fine."

"It's not fine. It definitely is *not* fine." She threw her chopsticks on the towel. "I can't even eat with somebody. I can't even *eat*." She rested her elbows on her knees, gripped her hair in her hands. I reached out a hand to touch her, but she flinched away from me.

"You need to go back to surgery," I said. She shook her head. "The Moh's surgery worked, right? No recurrence?" She didn't answer. "We need to find everyone who has this, get them to the surgeon. It can be taken care of."

"I can't. They can't."

I felt my frustration spike. Simple solution, right? You have a disease, there's a cure. Just get it done. It's like watching a guy with two bypasses, on twelve different heart meds, and a train wreck of an echocardiogram continue to smoke two packs a day.

"Dorothy, this is *killing* you, and there's no reason for it. I know about the Mings, I know people are scared, but come on, if everybody came forward at once . . ."

She looked up at me. The harsh yellow light on her tumors inked shadows across her face. "And what if not everyone comes forward? What if it's only you, and you're out there in the open and your kid doesn't come home from school one day? Nobody's going to do *anything*, Nate. Why can't you see that?"

"We have the pictures," I insisted. "Paul's photos."

"I had the photos, too, Nate. I had names. That's why my apartment was wrecked. You know how much good they did me and how stupid the bastards were who came to my apartment? The names were all *fake*. I followed up on each one of them and every one was a lie. Come on, Nate, what do you think the pictures were *for*? The ones Paul had? What do you think they were *for*?"

"You wanted to do what I'm saying," I said weakly. "You wanted everyone to come forward."

"It was a stupid and naive plan that Paul and I had to expose this whole thing. I was going to do a huge story on them, take the whole scam to the police or *Sixty Minutes*. But it never worked out. We didn't even really know who was doing this—"

"Your uncle—"

"Okay, my uncle's involved, but how? It's not like I can give him a call and say, 'Hey, Uncle Tony, what's going on?' It's gone too far for that—they don't trust me and I certainly don't trust them. And now that Paul's . . . Now that he's gone, I can't do anything. I can't go poking around. I'm a freak, Nate. Just looking at me scares people off."

"Paul was killed because of this?"

"Of course he was!" she said furiously. "What kind of people do you think we are? We tried to do what you're suggesting. I sat outside the clinic, waited for anyone in a big hat and sunglasses or anyone who kept her face to the ground, anyone who looked like me. When I found them and they saw I had the fibrosarcoma, they were willing to talk. Good little reporter that I am, I built rapport quickly. Some of them let me take their pictures, as long as I swore to them they would be safe. If I pestered enough, some even gave me their name. But they were scared out of their minds; Dr. Fang had given his warnings about their safety, about their families' safety. When the names they gave me started turning out to be false, Paul and I didn't know what to do. That's why he contacted you."

"The Mings," I said, feeling sick. "I spoke with them."

"And now you know why they were murdered." Dorothy said it bluntly. "And everyone who has what I have knows exactly why they were murdered."

I placed my chopsticks on the towel, hoisin sauce staining the white fabric brown. I pictured Beatrice Ming, her gaping black hole of a mouth. I thought about Ravi and me stumbling into a world Beatrice and her husband were trying so hard to protect, and destroying it. I understood now why they'd left the hospital. I wished they'd left sooner. I wished I had never seen them.

"What's the deal with you and Paul?"

"Does that really matter?"

"You tell me."

She sat up straight and, for a moment, I thought she was about to answer. Instead, she grabbed a fortune cookie, broke it in half. I took my cookie. Dorothy tossed the broken pieces to the towel and read the little slip of paper inside. She didn't speak immediately, so I read mine aloud: *"You may have some interest in travel, the arts, or business.* Wonderful," I said, and ate the cookie. "That's the dullest fortune I've ever read. What's yours say? *You may possibly be reading a fortune from a fortune cookie?"*

Dorothy crumpled her fortune, threw it onto the towel. "Are you done?" she demanded.

I said I was.

"Then let's clean this up."

We began to break down, separate, and consolidate the remains of our picnic. "How well did you know Paul?" Dorothy asked.

"I hadn't seen him in ten years. I hadn't even talked to him. How well did you know him?"

Dorothy got off the bed, walked to the sink, which was set in a slab of wood and formica at the end of the room opposite the door. She began washing her hands. The remnants of her fortune cookie lay like a cracked snail on the white towel; the little piece of paper was there amongst the wreckage. I put the broken cookie into my mouth and read the fortune. *Beware false friends,* it said.

Dorothy shut off the water and dried her hands. She turned, leaned back against the sink. She crossed her arms in front of her, as if she were protecting something. "Then you didn't know Paul was having trouble with his wife."

The wife. Diane, was it? The woman I let die. That phrase of Dorothy's—"having trouble with his wife"—brought Diane back to me. I imagined the fights, the tense silences suffused with Mahler floating from the cheap radio in the kitchen. In that moment, she seemed very alive and I began to fill in the blanks on a woman I'd never really met: readying the two kids for school, crawling into bed next to Murph, the PTA meeting the night she was killed. Diane.

Then the blood covering her body. The last breath.

"Paul and I met at a charity event in the city," Dorothy said. "An educational foundation the TV station and Paul's company both supported. His wife wasn't there because of something to do with the kids. My husband wasn't there because I no longer had a husband. Paul and I just started talking—"

"Ah, Christ—" I did not really want to think this about Murph, about the husband whose wife now lay in a grave beside him. I did not want to think this about the Boy Scout.

A look of real displeasure dropped like a veil over her mutilated face. "One thing led to another."

"When did it start?"

"Nine months ago."

"When did it end?"

Her face had gone slack, as if something were shutting down. "When he died. They took my boy and then they took the man I loved."

This was the time to be sympathetic, to walk over and comfort this woman who'd lost her kid, her man, her career, her identity. Her *face,* for God's sake. But I couldn't bring myself to do it.

"So," I said, my words acid, "you had an affair with a guy who had a wife and two kids. Go on."

Dorothy shook her head and turned back toward the sink. "I'm taking a shower."

"Oh, come on—"

Her voice blazed. "Let me tell you something, Nate: people have affairs. Don't be a sanctimonious jerk about it."

"And that makes it all okay, then, right?"

"Paul was unhappy. He was no longer in love with his wife. She wasn't in love with him. She was in love with the kids, with being a mother, with that nice house in Woodside. But she was not in love with him."

"And she's dead because Murph was fucking around with some woman whose vanity was so strong she couldn't bear to look her age." Even then, I knew I was being unnecessarily cruel.

"He was trying to help me punish the people who did this—to me, to all those others."

"Good for him."

She stepped from the sink to the bathroom and slammed the door. Hard.

How quickly these things happen, I thought. How quickly I walk into emotional minefields with my chest puffed out and my head swimming with whatever zealotry I'd adopted that day. That day, in that motel, my zealotry was trained on adulterers.

No, that's not quite it.

I was furious at myself for being duped, for squandering my grief and sympathy and juvenile revenge fantasies on a Boy Scout who forgot the oath to keep himself morally straight. Now I'm sure as hell not morally straight, but when did I ever claim to be a Boy Scout?

I cleaned up the rest of the meal noisily, feeling like a teenager awash in emotions he can't understand. After dropping the last white box into the trash can, I went to the bathroom door. From inside, I could hear crying.

I knocked. I waited for a moment, then spoke.

"Paul was my best friend in medical school," I said. "You already know that. But we had a falling-out, which you probably also know. Paul was a little judgmental, and I couldn't forgive him for that. So, I guess I'm saying I'm a little confused. This guy I spent all these years thinking was holier-than-thou, or at least holier-than-me, was having an affair that ended up getting his family killed."

There was no answer.

"Look—I know life gets complicated. I'm not good at seeing things as complicated, which . . . which complicates things, actually. I'm trying not to blame anyone here. I'm trying not to blame Murph for getting three people who loved him killed. I'm trying not to blame you and all these other people for chasing the Fountain of Youth and getting burned because of it. Half of me's splitting apart with sympathy for all of you. And half keeps saying you got what you deserve." I forced a laugh. "How's that for a public health doc? Blame the victim and all that."

I listened; at least the crying had faded. "Paul stayed with you through the fibrosarcoma?" I asked the door.

After a long moment, the response came. "Through the first tumor and surgery and the other tumors and Tim being taken from me. Yes—Paul stayed with me."

"He was a good man," I said.

"Mostly good."

I heard the lock pop, and the door opened a crack. Her eyes were wet, the boiling flesh around them plumped from weeping. Her face at that moment was grotesque and beautiful.

"How is your pain?" I asked.

"Stop being a doctor. Don't get so obsessed with my pain." She shook her head. "It's bad, but I'll live."

In that moment, I knew we were both thinking of those who didn't live—Murph, his wife, the two kids, Cynthia Yang, the Mings . . . How many more? I wondered. How many deaths?

We stood in the doorway for a few beats. My body was six inches from hers; I could almost feel her heat. I felt her fingers touch my left hand, watched her raise it to my face. "Your scars," she said, and traced the heaped, glassy flesh with a pink fingernail.

Then she opened my hand and brought it to her face. Palm against cheek, fingers splayed from her temple to the corner of her eye. I could feel the hard knobs of tissue.

"We need to get you to the surgeon," I said.

"We can't. Not yet."

"Because we need to get your son."

"Yes. Yes, we need to get Tim. I won't do anything else until we do."

11

I COULD HEAR DOROTHY PRETENDING to sleep in the next bed, shifting back and forth between the sheets. Pain doesn't rest.

After a while, I got out of my bed and found my shirt. I left the motel room with my cell phone.

"Jesus, McCormick, you know what time it is?" Ravi's voice was thick with sleep and irritation.

"One-twelve a.m., Pacific time. I need a favor."

"Drop dead."

"An easy favor. I need a script for OxyContin."

"Oh, man. You kidding me? You woke me up to—"

"Ravi, I need it now."

He paused. "You can't write for it?"

"Not in California. Not yet."

"It's triplicate," he moaned.

Certain drugs—the narcotics, the drugs liable to be abused—have to be written on special triplicate pads. One copy to the patient, one to the doctor's records, and one to the government.

"Who's this for?" Ravi wanted to know.

"A friend. But make the script out to me. If you get any heat, tell them it's for my hand." The silence on the other end of the line told me what Ravi thought of that. "It's for a friend. Trust me. I need it."

There was some harrumphing, the rustling of movement. For a moment, I thought he was going to hang up on me, but there was more movement. "Okay, Rush Limbaugh, I've got my pad. Come and get your damn prescription."

Ravi's place was only a ten-minute drive from the motel. He met me outside in slippers and a terry-cloth bathrobe that lacked a belt. One hand clutched the robe closed in front of him; the other held a piece of paper.

"You're asking me to commit fraud," he said, shaking the paper at me. "You tell me who this is for, I give you the script."

"Don't be an asshole," I said.

"Don't make me be an asshole."

I looked up and down the quiet block. Not that anyone was around, but still . . . "I can't tell you, Ravi."

He looked at the script in his hand, looked at me. "You're not even going to scratch my back, are you? What's the problem, you don't trust me?"

No, *actually,* I thought, *I don't trust you.* By talking to the press, Ravi had put himself out on a limb with the fibrosarcoma thing. His bosses were pissed; he'd embarrassed them; they figured he was full of shit. If Ravi wanted anything at this point, it was to deliver them some fresh meat. Dorothy Zhang would be the perfect offering, but putting her in the headlines would be worse than calling the police. Much worse.

"Your bosses interested yet?" I asked.

He gave me a lopsided grin, knowing I was changing the subject. "Mildly. We found the Kaiser guy today. Face blown apart like a battlefield."

"What did he tell you?"

"Slammed the door on me when I told him where I was from."

"What did the powers that be say?"

"They were like, 'Hey, that's interesting. You making any progress with the flu plans? You going to help out with the salmonella outbreak in Mendocino?' Everybody here is up to their elbows in shit. Who cares about a few isolated cases of sarcoma when you got the pandemic brewing and people crapping their guts out from bad chicken?"

"They weren't upset that the Kaiser guy didn't talk?"

"They thought it was weird, but what can we do? Nobody wants to label this a public health situation yet. We can't compel the guy to talk. And we don't have a scrap of evidence that his not talking is endangering anyone else."

So, the public health writing was on the wall: I tell Ravi about the clinic, about Dorothy Zhang's biological meltdown. That tips the scales enough to interest the public health commanders. There might be a raid on the clinic, there might not be. But I didn't trust public health to move quickly or quietly enough. Dorothy would be served up, that much was clear. Her kid? Well, we could just hope that Tim stayed alive until the bureaucracy could get in gear and find him.

If Dorothy believed the life of her son depended on not

involving the police, she'd certainly think it depended on not involving public health, since the good doctors there wouldn't be able to raise the cavalry and go in and save her son. Still, I needed to arrange the chessboard so that public health would be ready. Ready for what, I wasn't yet sure.

"You got to trust me on this," I told Ravi. "These are not isolated cases."

"I think that. You think that. No one else does."

"What about the pictures Murphy had?"

"No one's sure it's a cluster. We don't even know where they're from, man. Those pics could just be some sicko's fascination with tumors."

"That's what your bosses are saying?"

"That's what they're saying."

"They're wrong. And we just need to make sure your ass is covered when they find out just how wrong they are."

78

AT THE TWENTY-FOUR-HOUR pharmacy, the pharmacist gave me a long, pharisaical glance down the nose. No surprise there, considering the state of my shirt and post-pepper-sprayed eyes. Just another yuppie junkie coming in for his fix, I guess.

"It's for my hand," I said, waving my scarred left paw at him as proof.

"Sure," the pharmacist said. I wouldn't be surprised if

the guy flagged the prescription and Ravi got a call in the morning.

The motel room was dark. When I stepped inside, I heard nothing and hoped that Dorothy had finally fallen asleep. I sat on my bed, the one closest to the window, removed my shoes, and began peeling off my shirt. A voice—wide awake—came from the other bed. "Where were you?"

"Clubbing," I said. "After a long day, I like to go out and shake the booty." I got up and stood by her bed, shook the pill bottle lightly, then set it on the pillow. "You don't need to use these," I said. "Just in case."

"You got me some Ecstasy at your club. How sweet."

"OC, baby. Killers. The good stuff."

"You didn't go back to my apartment?" she said, instantly wary.

"I'm not that stupid."

"I'm not so sure. You went to your friend?"

"Yes."

I heard her lift the bottle from the pillow. "You didn't need to do this."

"I know."

There was nothing but breathing for a few moments, and I moved back toward my bed, removed my shirt and pants. I crawled under the sheet and lay there, awake. Five minutes passed before I heard the pills rattle again, then: "I've come to like the dark."

This wasn't what I expected to hear.

"But it is so lonely," she said. "I'm so tired of being lonely."

"You know," I said, "this mattress is way too soft. Like sleeping on oatmeal."

"This one's much better," she said. "Like sleeping on guacamole."

In my boxers now, I moved slowly from my bed to Dorothy's. I slid under the covers, into a bed soft as guacamole. In the inky dark, I could barely make out the rippled, ruined flesh of her face.

She moved close to me, snaked an arm over my chest, a leg across mine. She pulled me tight into her, pushed the curve of her cheek to my shoulder. The movement felt desperate, like I was the only man on the planet and she was the only woman and if we pulled apart we would die.

Her head moved, and I felt her breath on my face. My body stiffened.

"What is it?" she whispered.

"I'm sorry," I said.

"Sorry for what?"

I rolled away from her. What was I sorry for? Was it Brooke? An unwillingness to betray her when the détente between us was so new? Or was it repulsion at the thought of Dorothy's mangled lips touching my skin? Was I a card-carrying member of the culture I took so much pleasure in denigrating, the culture of *US Magazine* and *America's Next Top Model* and stupid *PerezHilton.com?* Or even worse, was I a hypocrite? A man who believes he's able to see past the face and skin to the person *underneath,* but for whom that bitch Beauty really is queen?

I pulled Dorothy's arm over me, laced my fingers into hers, hoping the small gesture would assuage my guilt. I felt her body hesitate for a second, then mold to my back. In the dimness, I focused on her small hand, the pink nail polish. I knew I would not be able to turn to her.

Disgusted with myself, I closed my eyes.

19

I WAS AWAKENED NOT BY an alarm or by sunlight, but by movement in the bed. There was a scramble, the quiet purr of a cell phone vibrating.

Dorothy was out of the bed, pawing in the darkness.

"Yes?" she said. I could hear the tension in her voice.

Nothing for a moment, then Dorothy said something in Chinese. Again, silence. Then a few words in Chinese.

"I have to go," she said. This was to me, not to the phone.

I flipped on the light: 4:48 a.m. Dorothy was in panties and a bra; the luminous skin of her body was a shock after seeing the ruined landscape of her face.

"Where?" I asked.

"Don't ask questions I'm not going to answer."

"Who was that?"

She didn't reply. She pulled on jeans, pulled on her blouse.

"I'm coming with you," I said.

"You're not. Where are my car keys?"

I grabbed my pants from the floor. "I'm coming with you," I repeated.

"I need to do this myself."

"Do what?"

"You can walk to your car from here. Give me the keys." She put out her hand.

"My car is still in front of your place. I can't take the chance. What is this about? Tim?"

She nodded.

"I know a cop named Tang, he's a good—"

"No!" she snarled. "Why do you think Paul is dead, Nate? Because he wanted to go outside, because he contacted *you.* You do not go to the outside with these people. People *die* when you do that."

"You were going to go outside with the pictures."

"I was going to do it when Paul and I had enough so that we could bring everything down at once. Can't you see that? You can't just wound them. They get scared when they're wounded. Paul moved too quickly. He told me he was going to contact you, but I didn't think it would be so soon. He scared them. And people died because they were scared. I *will not* let you get my son hurt."

"You need to go to the police with what you know. Let them—"

"Don't be an idiot! They have my son, Nate. They know where each and every person who has this sarcoma is. Can you guarantee me that the police will swoop in and grab Tim and protect him? Can you guarantee that *your* public health friends will protect all of those who are sick? No. There's no time for warrants and investigations and questioning. *They have my son.* Can't you see that?"

I thought about the little kid with the "path-o-gens" obsession, about where he was now, about the threat he was under. And I thought about why he was under that threat. Though Dorothy didn't say it, this started when I visited the apartment in Napa. Or earlier, when I talked to Murph. It started with me.

I felt I'd become toxic. And I'd do my damndest to change that.

"I'll drive," I told her, and headed for the door.

80

WE HAD CROSSED THE BAY Bridge and were pushing our way into San Francisco, the city just beginning to blink and stir from slumber. Only delivery vans and sleek cars piloted by financial guys—the ones keyed to the market in New York—rocketed through empty streets.

"Promise me you'll stay in the car," she said.

"I can't do that." I accelerated through a yellow light.

Suddenly, she undid her seatbelt, fumbling for the handle on the door. I felt the pressure in the car change as the door opened.

"Okay, okay!" I shouted. "Close the door. You win. I'll stay in the car."

She slammed the door.

I waited till I heard the seatbelt click before I said, "Who called, Dorothy? Who did you talk to? Your uncle?"

"It doesn't matter. I don't want my son to get killed. Turn left here."

I glanced at her. "You need to trust—"

"Park here," she interrupted. It was a no-parking zone just beyond the green-topped arch that beckoned tourists to make the climb up Grant Avenue and into the commercial heart of Chinatown. "Keep the engine running."

"Where—"

She was already out on the sidewalk. The white hat was back on, so were the sunglasses. If you didn't look too closely, and if you didn't know it was before dawn, you would think she was just another shopper out for the day.

She climbed the steps alongside the arch and disappeared from view.

I cursed myself for being manipulated by her, cursed myself for white-knuckling the steering wheel and forcing myself to stay put in the car.

Then I thought of those thin strong arms pulling me a few hours before. I pushed the thought from my mind.

Fifteen minutes passed. Twenty. The interior of the Malibu, with its soft fabric seats, its rental-car smell, suddenly felt too close. I got out, walked over to the arch. Grant Avenue slowly came to life—metal roll-up doors were being raised, patches of sidewalk were being swept and hosed. Chinatown stretched and yawned, ready to bring the world another offering of cheap fans and plastic toys and paper lanterns.

Behind me, someone yelled.

I swung around, heart thudding.

It was a jerk in a delivery truck, gesturing furiously at the car, barking away in a language that, in San Francisco at least, passed as English. Choosing not to engage with him, I waved, then backed the car to the other side of Grant.

Out of the vehicle again to take up my post in the shadows at the bottom of the hill.

And that's when I saw him. Tiny, bobbing down the hill as if he walked on springs instead of legs. From that distance, the kid seemed to have no bones in his body.

Tim. He had a backpack, and as he came closer, I could see the tiny set jaw, the eyes locking on me.

I ran toward him, calling his name. He saw me, recognized me, but didn't—couldn't?—move faster, just kept a steady, bobbing pace. "Where's your mother?" I asked.

The muscles in his jaw bulged. His eyes blazed.

"Tim, where is she?" I bent to him, grabbed both his arms, shook him a little. "Where? Where's your mom?"

His lips tightened.

"Where—"

And I stopped myself because I knew what had happened. "No, no," I said, straightening. "No, no, no."

Dorothy Zhang had just traded herself for her boy. And I'd stood by while she'd let them take her hostage. Uncle Tony—whoever the hell he was—had reduced his risks by one.

I knelt back down, tried to force calm into my voice. "Tim, are you hurt?"

"What do you care?"

"This isn't a joke. Are you okay?"

"Yeah."

"Where's your mother?"

In answer, he raised his hand, which held a black piece of cloth.

A hood. The bastards had hooded an eight-year-old. I

felt a spark of anger—that revenge thing kicking at my gut—and took the cloth away from him, wanting to strangle someone with it.

"Let's go." I grabbed the boy's hand and began pulling him up Grant Avenue, his legs moving double-time to keep up with me. I stopped at the corner of Grant and California, next to an old church. "Did you come from here? Where did you take off the hood?"

He pointed down the block, to a section that had not yet come to life. "Show me," I said. We walked twenty yards and stopped in front of a steel rolling door between two other steel rolling doors, each one spattered with graffiti.

"Here," Tim said.

"Did you come out of a building? Did you get out of a car?"

"Car."

Shit.

There was an old man sweeping the sidewalk near the far end of the block. I seized Tim's hand and tugged him toward the sweeper.

"Excuse me," I called, and began hammering the old guy with questions about a car, a woman, the boy next to me. The man shook his head in tiny motions and, as the volume of my voice escalated, I realized he had no idea what I was saying.

"Come on, Tim," I said, and began to walk. Dutifully, the kid fell in next to me. I got the sense he was holding it together a lot better than I was.

"You're supposed to call the hospital," he told me.

The sentence was such a non sequitur, I was thrown. "What? Which hospital?"

"You're supposed to ask for Dr. Michaels."

"What's Brooke—?"

But I didn't finish the sentence. I didn't even finish the thought before I was yanking at Tim's hand and fumbling in my pocket for the cell.

81

I DROVE FAST, STRAIGHT TO the university hospital—no zigzags this time, no detours through mall parking lots. The speedometer in Dorothy Zhang's car was pinned, and my fingers were choking the steering wheel. Anxiety ripped through me as vehicles wiped past in a blur. I half hoped that some unfortunate cop would pull me over so I could do something stupid—scream, fight—*something* to vomit up the impotent rage I was feeling.

Tim was silent in the seat next to me. His small hand gripped the door handle and his eyes stayed locked on the scenery blowing past him.

On the phone, the hospital functionary had told me Brooke was in the ICU, on the neurosurgery service. He wouldn't tell me anything else.

In the hospital, I tugged Tim by his arm through the corridors. In the ICU, I didn't bother with the nurses, didn't bother to respond to their *Can I help you, sirs*. A big whiteboard was mounted behind the nurses' station, names written in dry-erase marker. Halfway down, *Michaels* was printed tidily in green, followed by the name of the nurse caring for her.

"Where's bed five?" I asked the ward clerk.

"Visiting hours aren't until—"

"Tim, stay here." To the ward clerk, I snapped, "Watch him for me."

I left Tim, walked quickly along glass-fronted rooms housing the poor souls teetering between death and life. Behind me, I heard commotion as the staff tried to decide what to do with the sweaty, distraught white man and the small Asian boy he'd just dumped on the ward clerk.

Room 5. The nurse—tiny, Filipina, charting madly at a small desk next to the room—looked up and said something I didn't hear.

At the sight of Brooke, words came out of my mouth—"Oh, God," I think—but I was hardly aware of them.

You can see a thousand patients in the ICU, you can see a thousand of the sick and dying, a thousand bodies mauled by violence and disease, but years of such sights can never prepare you to see the woman you love nested amongst tubes and lines and all the artificial and ugly decorations that sustain her life.

Brooke's lips were chapped and fissured, open around the plastic tube that led into her throat. Her blond hair was shaved from the left side of her head, a bandage loosely adhering to the skin there. Around her left eye, the flesh was discolored and swollen.

I looked at the monitor: vital signs were within normal limits. I began to examine her for other injuries.

"Sir, you can't"—the Filipina nurse was behind me—"do that. You need to step—"

"I'm a goddamned doctor. This is my fiancée," I snarled. "Get the resident."

She glared at me. "Get the resident now!" I roared.

She disappeared, leaving me to continue the exam.

No injuries on the extremities, no injuries evident on the torso. Her face, though . . .

"Brooke," I said. Then, louder, "Brooke!" There was no response. I saw that one of the drips flowing into her was propofol—a sedative—which would have made her unable to respond. I reached toward the drip to dial down the propofol. It would be ten minutes before it wore off enough that I could give her a thorough neurological exam—

"Hey!"

A young guy in a white coat came through the door. He was short and pudgy, with two days' growth of beard. He looked as though he hadn't slept since his residency started.

"I turned off the propofol so I could examine her," I told him. "I'm a doctor," I added lamely.

"I don't care if you're Jesus Christ or His mother. You can't do that. Step away from the bed."

Others gathered outside the room: nurses, another resident. Everyone was watching me like they expected me to brandish a machete at any second. No one liked that I was monkeying around with the patient.

"You need to step out of this room," the resident said. He fingered the propofol, dialed it back up.

"What's her GCS score?"

"Outside."

Brooke lay there, the monitor beeped, the drips dripped. I nodded. "Okay. Outside."

In the hallway, I asked, "What'd you get for her GCS

score?" The GCS, or Glasgow Coma Scale, is the scoring system used to assess traumatic brain injury.

"You're a doctor? Her fiancé?" the resident asked.

"Yes to both," I said, feeling a little dirtier each time the fiancé thing came up.

"All right. But you do *not* fool around with her, got it? You do that again, I'm throwing you out of here." He sighed. "We've been doing one-hour neuro checks. GCS is eight to nine, which is what we'd expect."

"What you'd expect for what?"

He looked wary again. "The police didn't contact you?"

"If the police contacted me, I wouldn't be asking, would I? All I know is that she has a head injury."

Bored by years of delivering the worst news, the resident's tone was insouciant as he told me what I assumed I would hear, what I dreaded hearing. "She was assaulted. Outside her home, I think. They got her with a bat or a club or something."

The helplessness returned, washing over me like an icy wave. But there was something else there, too. Something darker and much worse: the knowledge that I had caused this as surely as if I'd swung the bat or club or something at her myself.

82

I PUSHED PAST THE RESIDENT, through the small throng of health care androids. I almost overlooked Tim, still with the ward clerk. "I'll be back," I managed to say. "Watch him."

Tears filled my eyes. Choking on my own grief and rage, I walked half-blind through the hospital. Heads turned. I heard someone say, "Are you all right?" But I couldn't answer. I began to run. Fast through the corridors of the hospital, down the steps, to the main hallway. I dodged people in wheelchairs, men with canes, doctors with their crisp white coats. Even in this world of cancer and disease, not one of them knew the depth of the world's blackness.

Out of the hospital, past the benches where nurses sat in pretty scrubs decorated with bears and balloons, past the eruption of color in the flower beds. When I was past them all, when I was in the plaza outside the hospital, when I was sure anyone who was interested could see me, I strode right into the fountain and only then did I stop.

"Here I am! Here!" I spun in a slow circle, arms wide. "Come on! Here he is! Nathaniel McCormick! Nathaniel fucking McCormick! Your man! I'm *here*!"

I screamed until my voice cracked, until I felt my vocal cords split.

I hardly felt the water wicking into my shoes and pants. I hardly saw the security guards as they approached me, stepped cautiously into the water with me, as they reached out to restrain this man who was screaming, crying, sloshing around in the fountain. I barely noticed the little boy who'd followed me through the hospital corridors and who now stood at the water's edge, his black eyes staring.

The world tilted and bucked like a boat in a hurricane. "Nathaniel fucking McCormick! Come and get *me*!" I screamed.

83

AFTER THE STUNT IN THE fountain, the ICU team wasn't especially keen to have me back in the fold. It was only through the intervention of the attending physician that I got back into the unit at all.

I waited for the attending in a small, ugly conference room near the ICU—beaten chairs, ravaged whiteboard—staring at the wall, my mind flying from Brooke to Dorothy to Murph's photos to the kid who sat slumped silently in the chair next to mine. I had trouble imagining Tim's emotional landscape at that point: his mother gone, a trip to the ICU, his *ad hoc* protector having some kind of psychotic break and splashing around with the ducks. What does that do to a kid?

It breaks a kid; it drives him to extreme lengths. In this

case, extreme lengths was Social Studies. Tim pulled the text from his full backpack—he seemed to be carrying an entire classroom in there—and flipped through it for ten minutes. When he exhausted that subject, he pulled out another book, a novel by the looks of it.

Though I wanted to be back in the ICU with Brooke, there were reasons to keep myself planted. The Filipina nurse was probably on orders to have me shot if I showed up there again without escort. Stomping around in a fountain is not the best way to demonstrate your stability. That, and bursting in before visiting hours. That's a felony in some parts of the country.

"What are you reading?" I asked, trying to get my mind off things.

"The Hobbit," Tim said.

"That's pretty advanced stuff for a third grader."

"I already read it twice."

"Twice? Wow."

"Actually, I read it once by myself," he corrected himself. "My mom read it to me once."

"Who's your favorite character?" I asked, trying to keep him away from the mother topic.

"Thorin," he said, not missing a beat. "He's the head dwarf."

"I always thought head dwarves are cool."

"Thorin is a hero."

"What about Bilbo?"

"He's a bit cowardly." Tim said it matter-of-factly, like it was a universally acknowledged truth.

A bit cowardly? "He does his best."

"He's still a bit cowardly."

Well, let's see how well you do facing down a dragon,

kiddo. "It's about his journey," I said. "He starts off a little shaky, but he becomes brave."

"Thorin *starts* off brave," he pointed out.

"But isn't it better if you're afraid and still do brave things?" Was I really defending the honor of a hobbit against the judgment of an eight-year-old? This, as much as anything else, told me I was not yet ready to sire a McCormick brood. But I soldiered on, because arguing with a kid about hobbits and dwarves was a lot more pleasant than thinking about . . . well, everything else. "Who saves the day?"

"Bard the Bowman."

"But who finds out about the soft spot on Smaug's belly?"

"Bilbo," he acknowledged reluctantly.

Take that, Einstein. Eight-year-olds of the world beware: do not try to best Dr. Nathaniel McCormick in an argument. About viruses or hobbits. "You want me to read it to you?"

"No thanks," he said decisively.

Ouch.

I reached over to Tim's shoulder, grabbed it lightly. "We're going to find your mom," I told him. "We're going to get the people who did this." I didn't elaborate on what "this" was. Probably because I didn't know.

The door to the conference room opened. I'd never been so happy—scratch that, I'd never been happy at all—to see Jenna Nathanson. But I was thrilled to see my old classmate that day. Even in her OR booties and dirty white coat, I was thrilled to see her.

"Oh, Nate." Her whiny voice didn't seem irritating to me then. It was soothing. "I'm soooo sorry. Your fiancée?"

"No. I said that because . . . we were living together, but not engaged." I remembered the Brides R Us webpage on Jenna's computer.

"Well, you had to do what you had to do. Who's this?" She gestured to my young sidekick, who refused to look up from his book. Probably on the hunt for damaging info on Bilbo.

"That's Tim. I'm watching him for a friend."

"Hi, Tim," Jenna said, sticking out her hand for a shake. "I'm Dr. Nathanson."

Tim studied the hand for a moment, then shook it.

Jenna sat. "First, let me say that everything should be fine. Brooke's sedated, as you saw—"

"*Should* be fine?"

"She had quite a . . . uh, she took quite a blow to her left temporal region and had a good-sized epidural hematoma in there. But we got in fast last night, did a quick burr hole, then opened the calvarium and drained the blood. We did an epidural tack-up to the craniotomy edge—"

"Jenna—"

"Yes?"

"I don't care about the details. What was she like when she came in?"

You can get away with talking to a neurosurgeon like this if you're a doc and have nothing to lose.

Jenna let it slide. "She had some focal neurologic signs when they brought her in, but I don't think that will be a problem. We got to it before there was any real herniation. She's young, thank God."

"Yeah. Thank God. How long will she be in the ICU?"

"A few days at most."

"Permanent damage?"

"None that we see yet. It's early, but I think she'll be okay. We'll get a CT later today to check for any more bleeding. Neuro checks so far have been good."

"Did you talk to the police?"

"No, Nate. We don't have time for things like that. You know that." She sighed; her soupy brown eyes softened. "I guess you didn't talk to them, either."

"Not yet. I came here right away."

She looked to Tim. "What are you reading?"

"The Hobbit," he said.

"What's that?" she asked.

Christ, I thought, we do live on different planets.

"Can I see her?" I asked, before Tim could launch into a dissertation on Middle Earth and the problems there.

"Sure," Jenna said. "No more splashing around in the fountain, though, okay? And no more screwing around with her drips."

"Scout's honor." But I couldn't even bring myself to do the dumb three-fingered salute.

Jenna leaned forward, put her hand on mine. "She's going to be fine, Nate. Really."

She stood. I told Tim to stay in the room and read. He responded by keeping his eyes glued to the book.

As we made our way to the warren of the ICU, I said to Jenna, "Congratulations, by the way."

"On what?"

"Your wedding." She looked at me as though she didn't understand. "The vineyard," I said. "When you left the library, you had that wedding page open on your computer. I closed the window for you."

"Oh, that." She tried to smile, but couldn't really force it. "I'm not getting married. That's where I'd do it, though.

You know, if something worked out. It's the perfect place, isn't it?"

I looked at this woman, and suddenly realized she was in some ways as broken and wounded as Brooke Michaels. Or me, for that matter. "Yeah," I agreed. "It's the perfect place."

84

I APOLOGIZED TO THE NURSE at Brooke's bed, who shrugged and took a long look at my legs. Word had gotten around, I guessed, about the loose cannon with the wet feet.

Brooke just lay there, bruised and battered and with a hole in her skull drilled by Jenna Nathanson.

"Brooke, it's Nate."

She didn't answer me, of course, so I just sat there having a one-sided conversation. "This is my fault," I said. Like countless others who'd sat at this bedside before, I told her over and over she'd be okay. Her only response to me was the *click-hiss* of the ventilator.

After ten minutes, I left the room. I went to the nurses' station and called the local police. The assault had occurred outside of Brooke's house, at about nine p.m., the detective on the case said. She was discovered by a neighbor out walking his four dogs.

"You don't have anything," I said.

"We're doing what we can," the detective said curtly. He asked me a few questions that I couldn't answer, and we ended the call, both of us unsatisfied.

Unlike the local police, I did have a lead. Telling the cops, I figured, would have complicated things. Brooke Michaels's assault was not going to be helped by another set of police worrying around the edges.

Perhaps a wise person would have quit then, would have heeded the warning. Brooke was in an ICU, a safe place, sure, but not that safe—the hospital hadn't protected the Mings. I wouldn't put it past Dragon Boy or Uncle Tony to don a white coat, saunter into Brooke's room, and play hell with her meds or ventilator.

So, I should have quit then. I should have raised the white flag, hung it out in the hospital cafeteria, left Dorothy Zhang to rot, let the pain continue to sear through her face, let the tumor continue to grow, let her be locked up, tortured, whatever they were going to do to her, let an unknown number of people with sarcoma eating through their tissue skulk untreated behind closed doors.

In the end, I decided not to heed the warnings. I decided to give whoever was behind this a lot more to think about than a snowed Brooke Michaels lying in her ICU bed.

"Tim, let's go."

The Hobbit lay open in front of him, but he hadn't been reading. His eyes were red but not wet. He wiped his sleeve across his face the moment he saw me.

"Where's my mom?"

"We're going to find her now."

"Where *is* she?"

I expected his lips to quiver, but they did not. I could see the willpower at work, could see that the kid wasn't going to let himself crumble. "We're going to find her." I hoped I sounded resolute, strong.

"You said that already." Lately, everyone seemed to enjoy pointing out my failings.

I took the book from him, kept the page with his pink construction-paper bookmark, and put it in his backpack. "I'll carry this for you," I said, slinging the pack over my shoulder. God, the thing was heavy. "Come on, buddy."

He didn't move, just sat there. I reached for his hand; he didn't take it. "Tim?"

Desperate times call for desperate measures. When I reached down and scooped him up, he offered no resistance. He was lighter than I thought; probably weighed about as much as his books.

It was like that—a backpack over one shoulder, a kid who had no faith in me on the other—that I left the hospital.

85

I DIDN'T KNOW WHETHER THE bad guys were watching us, and, at that point, didn't care. There was no way I'd get out of the lot without being seen. Besides, by the time we got to the hospital lobby, my arm was aching with the unaccustomed weight of the boy, and I just wanted to get to the goddamned car. My respect for suburban moms skyrocketed.

"What's wrong with the lady in the bed?" Tim asked.

"She got hurt."

"She got hit on the head."

"That's right." *So why did you ask me what's wrong with her?*

"Is she your wife?"

"Not really."

"She's your girlfriend."

"You got it."

"She's going to be okay. The doctor said."

"Yeah. Doctors never lie."

My arm was really killing me now. Strange, but I didn't want to put the kid down. Tim asked, "Did the people who hurt your girlfriend take my mom?"

"I don't know, Tim. I think they might have."

"I hope they don't hurt my mom, too."

I hiked him up, readjusting his weight. "They won't," I said, trying not to scare him.

"You don't know that for sure," he reminded me, with what I was finding out to be his customary zeal for the truth.

I didn't respond, which, somehow, seemed to be the best response.

The kid then did an amazing thing. He read my mind. "I hate Uncle Tony," he said.

Leaving the parking garage, I took a detour through a mall near the hospital.

I told Tim to look out the back window and see if anyone was following us.

"I can't turn around," he said.

"Take off your seatbelt," I suggested.

"Mom says I always have to wear a seatbelt. It's the law."

"This is break-the-rules day. You can take your seatbelt off for a second."

He thought about that, then clicked off the belt.

"That one," he said, pointing. I looked in the rearview. A red sedan was creeping along behind us. I turned down a row of parked cars. The sedan continued straight.

"That one," Tim said again. A green SUV had fallen in behind us, turned off thirty seconds later.

"Just the cars that follow us for more than a little while," I instructed him. "Not *everyone* who's behind us."

A black SUV swiveled in about thirty feet back, and Tim really seemed to be getting into it. "I think that one—" The SUV slotted into a parking space.

"Okay, break-the-rules day is over. Turn around and put your seatbelt on." The kid looked hurt. "You did a terrific job," I said, insincerely.

On the way to 280, I took a half-dozen more turns through the lot, ran a stop sign, and blew through a red light. The deep scowl on the kid's face suggested he'd noticed my transgressions.

Put the thing in perspective, and it all seems so goddamned silly. *Giving a tail the slip?* Right, McCormick. Go slip your tail, grab your gun, polish off your Scotch and your smoke, and solve the crime. But you don't think about that when the cops-and-robbers crap becomes real. You don't think about that when your erstwhile girlfriend—

the woman you're supposed to love more than yourself—just had a few tablespoons of clotted blood removed from the surface of her brain.

I pressed the accelerator and swung onto the highway. Then, because I was in over my head, I made a call.

"Brooke's in the ICU," I told Ravi.

"You're shitting me." A sensitive healer's response if I've ever heard one.

"She was assaulted last night."

"Oh, shit . . ."

"Went to neurosurg to evacuate an epidural hematoma. They said she'll be fine."

"Jesus, McCormick. What the hell did you get yourself into?"

I swung the car recklessly to the left lane, pushed it to eighty-five.

"I need your help, Ravi."

He gave me a breathy "Dude . . ."

"But this needs to be quiet, okay? Because—"

"McCormick—"

"—because Brooke's kind of exposed now and there's another person who's in danger—"

"McCormick!" Ravi barked. "Do you know the situation here?"

"Yes, I know the situation: your bosses aren't supporting us on this, blah blah. But what I'm about to tell you, you can take it to your bosses, you'll just have to sit on it for a little while—"

"No, no, McCormick. The situation *here*. *Now*. Did you

impersonate a CDC official with some schoolteacher up in Napa?"

"Uh . . ." I thought back to Ginny Plough, the principal at Tim's school.

"Stellar job, McCormick. Woman called CDC yesterday because that kid you went there to see didn't show up at school. They told her you didn't work there anymore. And guess what? She flipped. *They* flipped."

"Shit."

"They're freaked that you used your old IDs and now this schoolteacher's got it in people's minds you're some kind of perv. They're saying the kid's been abducted and that you came to his house a few days ago asking for him, lying that you were some sort of lawyer or something."

"This is not so good," I said.

"You're damned right it's not so good," he yelped. "*And* my bosses know we've been working together, so they're riding my ass about it. I got your stink all over me. The hell did you think you were doing?"

"I needed to talk to the kid."

"Ah. Jesus Christ, McCormick—now you're going to tell me you snatched him."

"Uh, Ravi?"

"What?"

"I do have Tim Kim with me. The kid."

In my peripheral vision, I saw Tim's head swivel toward me. On the phone, there was a pause. Then: "Oh, no, no, no. You *do not* have him with you."

"But I didn't pull him from school. The uncle did. It's a long story—"

"I'm sure it is. And I'm sure counsel at CDC will want to hear every bit of it."

"Did anyone bring the police into this?" My mouth was dry. "I mean, about this 'abduction'?"

"Of course they did. He's a *kid,* goddamn it."

"There's no AMBER Alert or anything, is there?"

"Not yet. The word here is it doesn't meet their criteria—they're not sure who took him and they're not sure how much danger the kid is in. But now I know you have him, I'll issue my own fucking AMBER Alert, you goddamn—"

"Calm down." I slid the car to the right, to a slower lane of traffic. Last thing I needed was to get pulled over for doing ninety, then nabbed for abducting the kid.

"You're supposed to call CDC stat," Ravi said. "I'm supposed to tell you that if I talk to you again, which I haven't done, okay? I haven't spoken with you."

I tried to think of a way to explain the Tim Kim situation, but failed. I decided to go from the beginning. "I know what's doing this."

"I don't *care* what's doing this. No more cases of fibrosarc have popped up. With this whole thing with the kid, everybody's backing away from it anyway. They're backing away from you and whatever you're doing. It's poison. *You're* poison."

"I'm trying to stop a—"

"To stop what, dude? A cluster of cancer that no one thinks is a cluster? Next thing we know you'll be saying you've found plague at a day-care center and you're holding the kids hostage to—"

"It's centered on a cosmetics clinic in SF. Don't know what the causative agent is, but we have location for all this—"

"All this? *There are no new cases,* McCormick. *None.*

Nada. The guy at Kaiser, that Yang person Brooke found, the Ming woman. That's it. Three cases do not add up to a freakin' nightmare." He paused for breath. "We don't even have the Kaiser guy anymore. The unlucky bastard got munched by a car late last night—"

"What?"

"Hit by a car in Oakland. Dead at the scene."

"Details."

"It was a hit-and-run. I called his house yesterday and his wife told me. I called Highland Hospital, they confirmed it. His blood alcohol level was .29. He stumbled into the street, bombed out of his skull. We probably drove the poor guy to drink—"

"Shut up a second. Who else knew you were talking to him?"

"Lots of folks. This wasn't clandestine, McCormick. Not a lot of black ops here at the Department of Health. And unlike you, I try to go by the book—"

"Well, don't go by the damn book anymore. There's someone feeding information from state. The Mings? This guy from Kaiser? Who else but me and you guys knew we were talking to them?"

"San Francisco Public Health knew about the Mings."

"But not about the last guy. Come on, man. Work with me here."

He was swearing again. For a moment, I thought he was going to hang up on me.

"Everyone we knew about is dead, Ravi. And there's another case."

"And you were going to tell me this when?" His tone was shrill, but it had lost some of its venom. Maybe because of the realization there was a traitor in his midst or perhaps because I'd again raised the stakes. Ravi wanted fame so bad the poor bastard could taste it.

I looked over at Tim, wished I could stuff his ears with some plugs. "I found a woman called Dorothy Zhang. Newscaster who disappeared months ago."

Silence on the phone and in the car, but I knew my audiences were interested now. I covered the mouthpiece of the phone and whispered to Tim, "Your mom's going to be fine." The way he stared at me said I had all the credibility of a things-are-going-swell-in-Iraq pol.

As for Ravi, the hook was set: high profile, one more case leading this to a tipping point, career advancement, the chance, if this worked out, to bust someone in his own backyard . . .

"Dorothy Zhang gave those pictures to Paul Murphy," I said, speaking quietly. "The people in the pics are all here in the Bay Area. They're lying low because they don't want to end up like the Mings. It *is* a cluster, Ravi. I'm sure of it."

"What's being injected?"

"Like I said, I don't know. Some cosmetic filler, sounds like."

"Who's doing it?"

"That's why I'm calling you."

"Oh, don't call me. Call the cops."

"Right. And what do I tell them? This is Nate McCormick, ex-CDC, suspected child abductor—"

Tim turned away, toward the window. I snapped on the radio, to some static-filled classic rock station, and kept the phone pressed tight to my ear. "*I'll* call them," Ravi said.

"And what are *you* going to say?" I asked. " 'Hey, guys, there's this clinic in the Richmond that's doing some black-market crap that's resulting in sarcoma and, oh, yeah, we don't know where all the cases are because the patients are scared out of their wits and hiding and, oh, yeah, some of them have been murdered in some pretty yucky ways. Oh, and there's a little complication that we might have of a mole somewhere here in the health department. And, by the way, the bad guys have taken that newscaster who vanished and could we please find her soon because the bad guys are going to be real pissed we talked to you and they're going to—" Too late, I stopped, aware that Tim's eyes were boring into me.

Ravi stayed quiet for a second. "They have this Zhang woman?"

"Yes. It's why I have her son. She traded herself for the kid." I yanked the line again, trying to get Ravi into my boat. "I thought this is what you wanted. Guts and glory and all."

Ravi swore, Ravi equivocated, Ravi gave me a cover-his-ass response. "I'll get things together on this end."

"No," I said. "You're not listening. No police. No public health."

"I'll work around things on this end. I won't say anything to anybody—"

"Then what good are you going to be sitting in your office? I need you in the field, with me. Not planted behind your desk not talking to anyone. Meet me in the Richmond. Corner of Thirty-sixth and Clement. There's a clinic where all this is happening—"

"I can't, man. I'll back you up from here—"

"There's no 'backing me up' from there. The field, Ravi. You remember the field. Excitement, adrenaline, all that." A note of begging crept into my voice. "I need some cred on this. I can't use the damned CDC bit anymore, can I?"

"McCormick, why are you doing this to me?"

"And I need someone else. I don't want to go in alone. I don't know what I'm going to find."

There was a silence. For a moment, I thought I'd won him over. But as is often the case with me trying to figure people out, I was wrong. "No go, McCormick. This is a little too hot for Ravi."

"Fuck you, then," I snarled.

I hit End on the phone, cutting the line, letting Ravi run back into his exciting career. I glared at Tim, who hastily shifted his gaze back to the side window. I snapped off the radio.

"Don't say that word, Tim. It's a bad word." I came up fast on a station wagon, switched into the next lane just as the wagon switched, forcing me to hit the brakes. Under my breath, I whispered, "Fuck."

86

THE SHOP DOROTHY HAD MENTIONED as the last location for the clinic, Spectacular Nails, was kitty-cornered across the street from me, sandwiched between a tiny Chinese grocer—tangerines, durian, and persimmons piled in open bins along the sidewalk—and a tiny restaurant with fogged front windows half obscuring the duck carcasses dangling there. Right next to me, the neon sign for a place called Razr Nails glowed garishly even in the daylight.

I didn't want to leave the kid alone in the car, but I couldn't take him with me. I couldn't drop him off with a friend, since my friends were either dead, in the hospital, or they were Ravi Singh, who would agree to take the boy about as readily as he'd agree to eat a plutonium sandwich. For now, I was stuck. And the kid was stuck with me.

"You have your book," I said to him. "Break that thing out and read. Stay in the car."

"Where are you going?"

"I have to talk to some people."

"Who?"

"Some people who might know where your mom is."

"Shouldn't I come?"

"No. Where are you in the book? What's happening?"

"I'm at the part with the trolls. Where they're arguing about eating all the dwarves and Bilbo and—"

"That's a good part. Finish it out. I'll be back in three minutes."

As I exited the car, I peered into the weirdly named Razr Nails. I took a few deep breaths, a moment to dream up a game plan, a moment to wish that I were not going into this alone.

In Razr's ruthlessly lit space, a dozen women sat at manicure tables or with their feet in bubbling water baths, chatting, reading magazines. Careful, ladies, I thought. A few years before, there was an outbreak of mycobacterium in folks who'd gotten pedicures in the San Jose area. It seemed the salons in question didn't really bother washing out the footbaths between patrons, which left the water swimming with the ironically named *Mycobacterium fortuitum.* A few unfortunate pedicure devotees shaved their legs before a visit to the salon, allowing the enterprising bug to set up shop in the tiny nicks and cuts. Days later, painful, small sores would pop up. Weeks later, the sores blossomed into large, tender boils.

Good thing I was bent on going solo into a criminal cosmetics joint and not getting a pedicure. Safer that way.

I took a few more breaths, glanced back at the car. Tim sat watching. I opened my palms into book halves and mimed like I was reading. I never was any good at charades, and the kid had no idea what I was doing. He stared at me without blinking.

One last look up the street, one last chance to see Ravi tearing up the asphalt. Throngs of old ladies pushing shopping carts, but no ballistic Sikh.

Alone, I picked my way across the street.

Spectacular Nails had the same general layout as Razr Nails. Five footbaths, five manicure tables, enough fluorescent wattage to light a stadium. But whereas Razr buzzed with life and gossip, Spectacular was desolate. Not a single soul inside yammered on about life, love, the most effective clear polish.

I entered, met by the sounds of some laid-back, flowery music flowing from a boom box behind the welcome counter. That was it for greeting; no person stepped forward to welcome me.

I stood and waited. Evidently, it was self-serve all the way at Spectacular Nails. Spectacular. I walked toward a narrow hallway extending from the back of the salon.

Halfway there, I was intercepted by a five-foot-tall woman with fake nails and fake boobs.

"I can help you?" she wanted to know.

"I need to talk to Wei-jan Fang."

She looked at me, baffled. "Wei-jan Fang," I repeated. "Dr. Fang."

"There no doctor here. This nail salon."

I pointed to the closed door. "Is there a medical clinic back there? I need some medical treatment."

She shook her head vigorously.

This is why I needed Ravi. To flash the badge, to bring down the full weight of public health. "Ma'am, I need to see what's back there."

"You do not go back there."

Screw it, I decided, I'd already dug my grave. I yanked out the CDC creds, waving the plastic ID around to confuse her.

"Health Inspector," I snapped, moving toward the hallway.

She scrambled after me, a look of horror on her face. "Where you go?"

"Inspections." I opened the first door in the hallway. A bathroom. The toilet was running.

"No health there," she said. The woman was on my heels like a rabid Chihuahua. "No health there, up here." She jammed her hand toward the front of the shop.

"There's health everywhere, ma'am."

I tried the knob on the second door. Locked. "Closet," she said.

"Open it."

Keys jingling in shaky hands, she obeyed. A closet.

Only one door left. I stepped to it. Again, locked.

"Unlock the door, please."

"No health here," she insisted. "I not have key."

"Sure you do," I said cheerfully.

I heard the electronic ring signaling someone entering the salon. I swung around. A balding Asian man stopped when he spotted us.

"We *closed,*" the woman shrilled.

"Unlock the door," I repeated.

The man looked confused for a moment, then beat it out of the shop.

"I not have key!"

I was hot on the trail, I could feel it. Man coming to a nail salon? The nervous woman? Well, well, Dr. Fang, prepare to meet Dr. McCormick.

"I'm sorry," I told her. I took a step back, put my shoulder down, and rammed.

The cheap door popped through its lock, flying open like a cardboard set piece, startling the hell out of me. Momentum carried me into a dim, carpeted reception area, which gave way to a hallway flanked on either side by two closed doors. To my right, a few cheap plastic chairs surrounded a cheap plastic table.

In two of the chairs sat two women—girls really—in skimpy lingerie. They leapt to their feet.

There were no nurses buzzing around. No doctor's office smell. Definitely not an illicit clinic. It was, however, an illicit something else.

The girls looked like caged animals in a thunderstorm, their eyes roaming wildly from my face to the door to the woman screeching behind me. Two cigarettes burned in an ashtray on the table.

"Hello," I improvised brilliantly.

One of the other doors opened, then shut instantly. I glanced back at the proprietor, who was now muttering something in a language choked with diphthongs.

"Come here," I said to her, as I walked back into the nail salon. "Where is the clinic?"

"I no think about clinic."

I pulled out my cell phone. "Now listen to me very carefully. Unless you help me out here, I will call the police. You understand me? You help me out here?"

She gaped at me, bewildered. "You want *girl*?"

"No. I don't want a girl. There was a medical clinic here, a while ago. The doctor did medicine back there." I stabbed a finger toward the smashed door. "The doctor works on ladies' faces."

"Ladies' faces?" she echoed.

"Come here." I stepped to a mirror and pushed the woman in front of me so she was looking at herself. Then I put my hands on the sides of her face. She jumped at my touch. "He makes ladies look younger." I pulled back her skin, a quick and dirty face-lift.

The proprietor was shaking her head against my hands. "Dr. Fang," I told her.

She tensed, and I knew I'd managed to get through the cultural barrier. I took my hands away. "Where is Dr. Fang?"

"You no call police."

"I won't call the police if you tell me where he is."

She was quivering now. "Down street," she insisted, her voice cracking. "Pretty Hands. Dr. Fang there." She gripped my jacket. "You no tell Dr. Fang," she bargained, then switched back to a language I didn't understand.

She was pleading with me now, her desperation turning her voice breathy and shrill. I removed her hands from my lapels, gave her my best disapproving gimlet-eyed stare. Odds were this place would be vacant by the end of the day and by tomorrow the girls in back would be turning tricks somewhere else.

I turned, walked past the rainbow hues of polish, through the gauntlet of manicure benches and pedicure chairs, a thousand watts of fluorescent light beating down on me from above, my reflection bouncing at me from a dozen mirrors.

87

THE CAR WAS STILL THERE, and Tim was still in it. But he wasn't reading. He was in the driver's seat, hunched up close to the window, watching me. As I walked nearer, he scrambled hastily into the passenger's seat and grabbed his book.

"Trolls are the worst," he said.

The kid was a rotten actor, but telling him that wouldn't speed up the bonding process. "Just stay in the car, okay? You don't have to read if you don't want to." I struggled to think of something that would occupy him. "You want a snack? Some candy?" Kids like candy, right?

"Is my mom in there?"

"No."

"Who was in there?"

I didn't intend to be the one to fill Tim in on the more commercial aspects of the birds and bees. That's what the Internet is for. "You want some candy or not?"

"You're not supposed to have candy until after dinner."

"It's break-the-rules day again."

He watched me skeptically.

"Chocolate bar good?"

"I like licorice better."

I stepped into a corner store, forked over the cash for a couple packs of licorice and a few Slim Jims. On the way to the car, I wolfed down two of the Slim Jims.

"Eat this stuff slowly, all right, Tim?" Like, slow enough that you don't start getting curious about what I'm doing. "It'll make you sick if you eat it too fast."

"I won't get sick."

"I'm a doctor. You will get sick. Upchuck everywhere."

He giggled. It was the first time I'd heard him laugh. "I won't upchuck," he said, savoring the word. Kids are weird.

"You will. I'm serious. Red, blue, green upchuck, all over the car."

If his smile was any indication, Tim really seemed to like that image. I said, "Just stay in here—"

At that moment in the Dr. Nate/Tim bonding, a car stopped next to me. Someone said, "You're under arrest, Dr. McCormick."

My heart flipped, and I twisted around to see a late-model Acura with tinted windows. The passenger-side window was down. "I'm hauling you in!" the driver shouted at me.

"You're blocking traffic, Dr. Singh," I told him.

"Yeah, yeah. I'm going on a bust. I don't have time to park." I kept the smile, but began to wonder whether it was a good idea to have Ravi along after all. *I'm going on a bust.* The guy vacillated between the man in the gray flannel suit and Gunga Din.

"Who's that?" Tim wanted to know.

"That's Dr. Singh. Don't . . . don't learn anything from him, okay?"

"Okay." Tim had dispatched with one of the Slim Jims and was halfway through the licorice.

"And slow down on that thing," I said.

"I won't upchuck."

Little man just wouldn't let the upchuck thing rest. "Read about viruses or bacteria or trolls or something, okay?"

Ravi parked, then strolled up. I made introductions.

"I'm trying not to upchuck," Tim promptly informed him.

"You sick?" Ravi asked.

"No. *He* said I would upchuck if I ate this too—"

Time to put an end to this medical exchange. "Tim, I need to talk to Dr. Singh for a second."

I filled Ravi in on the scanty details of the clinic, Beautiful Essence, on Dorothy Zhang and Paul Murphy and the botched exposé Dorothy had planned.

"All this for freaking *Botox,*" he said to no one in particular. "So what the hell are we going to find?"

"No clue. Let's go. It's down the block."

"It's right there." Ravi pointed across to Spectacular

Nails. Then, of course, I had to explain to him about my crack intervention there with a down-market house of ill repute.

This delighted him no end. "You get any play?"

"Yeah. Twenty girls, me, and five minutes." Ha ha ha.

The laughter faded. "Yeah. So. What's the plan?" Ravi asked.

"We're just going to ask some questions. Act like we're medical device salesmen—at least until we get to Fang."

"I thought you wanted me along because I'm official."

"Only be official if we need it. We want to scare them into talking to us, but not scare them *scare* them, you know what I mean?"

"Doesn't sound like much of a plan."

"You have a better idea?"

"Yeah. Call your friend the cop. Have him take care of this."

"We don't want the police." Ravi's sudden case of cold feet irritated me, mostly because it was giving me cold feet. "Stay in the car if you want. Talk to the kid about malaria."

He scratched at his jaw. "Oh, man . . ." In the end, Ravi decided against trolls and malaria. "Okay, McCormick. Let's do this."

I smiled, clapped him on the shoulder, and we crossed the street. I swung around and gave the thumbs-up to Tim, who refused to give me a thumbs-up back. The kid wouldn't recognize a hero if he bit him.

We walked in tandem: thin nervous white guy, thick nervous brown guy. Cue the music.

"What's the doctor's name again?" Ravi asked me.

"Wei-jan Fang," I said. "Dr. Fang."

Ravi smiled. "Awesome. *Dr. Fang.* Awesome."

88

"I'M SORRY. WE'RE CLOSED TODAY." The woman who greeted us from behind the reception desk looked as if she had just been yanked off the assembly line at a plastics factory—plucked eyebrows, heavy makeup, gargantuan smile.

"Wei-jan Fang," Ravi said.

She blinked. "Excuse me?"

Behind her stretched a space remarkably similar to the brothel I'd invaded thirty minutes earlier: long narrow room, manicure tables and pedicure chairs lining the walls. I nudged Ravi, whose eyes were locked on the door—a peephole set into its middle—at the back. He nodded almost imperceptibly.

"We're here to see Dr. Fang," Ravi told the receptionist.

"I'm sorry," she said. "I don't know that name."

"We're with the Sygistics Company," I said. "Dr. Fang had ordered some hyfrecators and was having some difficulty—"

"Gentlemen, I apologize, but you must have the wrong establishment."

"That's odd," I said, "we spoke with Dr. Fang this mor—"

Ravi pulled out his ID and waggled it an inch from

the woman's synthetic smile. "California Department of Health."

I wanted to lop off his arm and staple shut his mouth. *Too soon, too soon,* I almost screamed.

The woman's eyes flickered and I saw a hand slide under her desk. "I'm sorry, gentlemen—"

By then, I was already halfway across the room, moving toward the door with the peephole. "She hit the alarm," I yelled.

The door was locked, so I stepped back a few paces and rammed it with my shoulder. Unlike the piece of paper I'd burst through up the street, this damn thing was solid as granite. Pain blasted through my left side.

The woman shouted that the cops would be here any second.

"Move!" Ravi bellowed, and put his 220 pounds in motion. He thudded against the door, bounced off like a bag of flour, swore.

There was a fire extinguisher attached to the wall. I yanked it from its mooring, hauled it back, and drove it at the doorknob. It bent the metal, but did not loosen the lock. I hit it again. And again. Still the door held.

"Let me," Ravi said, shouldering me aside. The receptionist was screaming now, calling Ravi a "hooligan." He grabbed the extinguisher and began pounding it furiously against the knob.

The woman's screaming stopped abruptly. I turned and saw she was gone.

I should have known they would be ready for us. I should have known they would have procedures in place. As the *bang, bang* of the extinguisher crashing into door filled the space, I could almost feel everyone slipping from the building.

Wood splintered, metal bent. Cursing, Ravi hit the door again. The knob popped off and clattered to the floor.

"Okay?" he huffed, dropping the extinguisher.

"Okay."

His body slammed into the door. Wood ripped and the thing blew open like a shutter.

There was no one behind it.

I picked up the fire extinguisher—a dry-chemical type—and unhooked the nozzle. Not exactly a Smith & Wesson, but a face full of monoammonium phosphate would slow anyone down.

The door opened into a well-appointed waiting room. The walls were white, decorated with prints from museum exhibits. The carpet was gray. Glossy beauty magazines were arrayed on a dark wood coffee table surrounded by four empty chairs. A cutout in the wall yielded a view of a receptionist's area. I crossed to it, stuck my head inside. A cup of pens and a phone sat on the desk. A laptop's power cord stretched across it, attached to nothing.

Clearly, Wei-jan Fang had upgraded since camping out at his previous digs.

As I placed the extinguisher on the floor, I heard Ravi yell "Nate!"

There were six doors off the hallway, three to my right, two to the left, and one at the end, which was just then swinging shut. I darted through the door, kept my foot jammed behind it to keep it from closing and locking us out.

To my left, I could see Ravinder Singh running like a loaf of wet bread up the alley. He stopped at the end, and though I couldn't hear him, I could read lips well enough to know a stream of blue language flowed from his mouth.

When Ravi got back to me, he was breathing heavily. "I saw . . . I saw two people running that way—" He pointed to where he'd come from. "They disappeared." He leaned over his knees. "Shit." He spat. "Shit!"

The first door I tried opened into a small canteen/storage area. A coffeepot, water cooler, sink, table, and a low green metal cabinet were the only accoutrements. No personal touches, as I've seen in countless other doctors' offices across the world. No staff pictures, no birthday cards, no thank-yous from patients. It had all the personality of an unfinished shed.

"Charming," Ravi said from the doorway.

I crossed to the green cabinet, opened it. Six plastic five-gallon cans with "flammable" emblazoned across the front. I uncapped one of the cans.

"Gasoline," I said.

"Why the hell—?"

"Maybe a black market filling station is next on the list for these guys." I recapped the can and closed the cabinet.

Ravi entered the room across the hall, while I continued to a door adjacent to the canteen, which revealed a space tiny enough to be a closet. A three-foot square freezer—temperature controlled at minus 85 degrees Centigrade—filled a corner of the room. On a table sat an open rack of ten-milliliter plastic tubes and a small, high-speed orbital shaker. An incubator the size of a microwave was tucked on the floor under the table. Between the freezer and the wall were a number of broken-down cardboard boxes. A trash can—stuffed with paper towels, other garbage—was pushed against the opposite wall. Next to it was a squat, insulated barrel. Liquid nitrogen. Maybe Wei-jan Fang had added wart removal to his Beautiful Essence treatments.

The freezer had a padlock on it. Locked.

I walked back into the hallway.

"Procedure room," I heard Ravi say from across the corridor. And, indeed, it was. There was a pale green examination chair in the center of the space, under a jointed examination light. Two wheeled cabinets. Hand sanitizer, but no sink. Nothing was attached to the walls; again, not what you'd expect in a physician's office. Except for the light, everything was temporary. Mobile. Upon closer inspection, even the exam light was jerry-rigged. It had been bolted to the ceiling, but its wiring ran externally to the wall and down to an outlet.

"Exam gloves, syringes, gauze, chucks, blah, blah, blah." Ravi slammed a cabinet drawer. "Nothing."

"I found a freezer in the other room, an incubator, some Falcon tubes. Liquid nitrogen."

He cocked an eyebrow. "What was in the freezer?"

"Locked."

"Then there's gotta be a key." Ravi began tearing through the drawers, casting all manner of medical accoutrements to the floor. "No key," he grumped. "What the hell are they mixing up in there?"

"Beautiful Essence, I guess. The incubator, though . . ."

"They need it to warm something."

"Yeah."

I went back into the closet-like lab, checked the temperature setting on the incubator: 37 degrees Centigrade. Body temperature.

Across the hall, I heard another door open. Ravi called, "Whoa, they were getting ready to do it." I followed his voice.

Yet another procedure room. Same cart, same furniture. In this room, however, an instrument table had been pulled up to the exam chair. An empty syringe and a vial of topical anesthetic lay neatly arranged on top, along with an opened packet of gauze. A couple pieces of blue, crumpled paper had been cast on the floor. Ravi was busy ripping the place apart, and I let him rip.

Even with the room's innards exposed, it had a spartan feel. "Got to admire their efficiency," I said. "All their records on a laptop, which they can take with them. Everything else stripped."

"Except what's in the locked freezer."

"Yeah. The incubator was at 37 degrees."

"So? They were warming something to inject it."

"I know. But why not let it go to room temp? Why body temp?"

Ravi shrugged. He pulled one of the drawers from the cabinet and let it drop to the floor. He spread the contents with his foot. "No freezer key."

Outside the procedure room, we split, Ravi to the receptionist's alcove, me to the last of the closed doors. As the Sikh rolled like a tank down the hall, I tried the doorknob, expecting to see another exam chair, another exam light, another shotgun space for filling people with toxins.

And I wasn't disappointed: exam chair, lights, rolling

stack of plastic drawers. In every way identical to the two rooms we'd already seen. In every way identical, except for the man sitting in the examination chair, a small pistol in his hand.

"You must be Dr. McCormick," he said.

89

THE MAN IN THE CHAIR was Asian, about forty years old. Dark crescents hung beneath his red-rimmed eyes; his hair fell in a limp, thin tangle over his brow. In general, he had the air of someone who'd just come off a three-day bender or was just emerging from heroin withdrawal. He wore a white coat—no name on it—and he hadn't bothered to remove his latex gloves. Spots of blood dotted the gloves.

"Dr. Fang," I said, as Ravi joined us.

The man with the gun nodded. "Who's that?" he asked. He thrust his chin toward Ravi.

"Ravinder Singh," I told him. "A doctor with the California Department of Health."

"So the sleeping dragon of public health has finally woken up, huh?"

I didn't much give a damn about dragons or public health at the moment. "Where's everyone else?" I asked.

"Look around you. They're gone, Dr. McCormick. Gone, gone, gone. You're left with just me." Wearily, Fang pushed himself out of the chair. Ravi and I stepped back.

"Relax," Dr. Fang said. He looked down at the gun in his hand. "This is what's got you worried?" He dropped the gun into the pocket of his white coat. "There. All better. Now, if you'll excuse me for a second, Doctors, I need to grab something. No need to worry: I'm not leaving. I could have done that when you were taking your time getting in here."

He pushed by us, walked up the hall, and disappeared into the small canteen.

"We should call the cops," Ravi said.

"We can't."

"Why? This is way beyond—"

"The kid's mother, okay? They have her. Why do you think he's so cocky?"

Fang reappeared. He held three small paper cups and a bottle of Scotch. He sat in the exam chair, neatly lined the three cups up on the instrument table. "You two miss me?" he asked. His lips spasmed into an insincere smile. Then he filled the cups to the brim with the liquor. "Drink up, gentlemen. A toast." Fang held aloft one of the cups.

"I'm okay," I said.

"Me, too," Ravi said.

"Pity." Fang shook his head. "All right, then, I toast myself. To a brilliant yet unheralded scientist. And to a doctor who's come to the end of the road." He drained the small cup. "You guys sure? This stuff is a hundred and twenty bucks a bottle. No? Another toast, then." He placed the empty cup on the table, took another. "To Yahlin Mao, my first patient." He lifted the cup. "The beautiful Yahlin Mao. Down the hatch." He drank.

"One more," Fang insisted. "To all those who had faith in me from the beginning. To my mother!" He laughed softly, then drank.

"Oh, that is good," he murmured. He held his hand in front of his face, looked at it. "Steady as a rock." He said it proudly.

"Where's Dorothy Zhang?"

Fang focused on me with a little difficulty. "You're here for her?" He sounded surprised.

"Where is she?"

"That's what all this is about? Come on. You boys want more than that."

"Okay," I agreed, "we want more than that. Where is she?"

"Got me. I didn't even know they had her."

"Who has her?"

Fang smiled, showing us a mouthful of crooked teeth. "The same people who are going to be here . . ."—he looked at his watch— "in maybe fifteen minutes."

"Dorothy Zhang is an afterthought now," Fang told us.

"What do you mean?" I asked. "What's going to happen to her?"

Something glimmered in the glazed eyes. "She got to you, didn't she?"

I rolled a stool in front of Fang's chair and sat. "You're here because you want to talk. We're here because we want to talk."

"Sure, but first I want to talk about *me.* You guys really don't have a clue who you're dealing with, do you?"

"I have some idea."

"Then, you know I have some problems, right? You know I'm as good as dead," he said flatly. "Unless I get your help."

"What do you need?" I asked, wary.

"I need protection," Fang said, his eyes bright now. "I need you to call the FBI or the cops or whoever you're working with and get me and my family some protection."

"We can't just—"

"You're the CDC guy. He's the state guy. Make it happen."

"It doesn't work like that."

"Make it work like that," he said. He poured a cup, spilled fluid over the lip.

"What is Beautiful Essence?" I asked.

"Beautiful Essence . . ." He let the ugly phrase roll in his mouth. ". . . that's my baby."

"*What* is it?"

"They're coming, Dr. McCormick. No time for—"

"Where does it come from? Who supplies you with it?"

"Dunno. I'm just a poor little guy who can't get the government to help—"

"Who attacked Brooke Michaels?" He gave no response. "Who killed Paul Murphy?"

His eyes cut to me, then away, and I knew he knew the name. "Who killed Paul Murphy?" I repeated. I felt fury rising and I imagined myself grabbing the lapels of his white coat, beating the bastard into a mash of contusions and lacerations. I was furious for what he had done to Dorothy, for squirting poison into her skin. For doing it over and over and over to anyone foolish enough to walk through his door. I jerked away, slammed the bottle of whiskey with my hand, knocking it to the floor.

Fang looked down at the shattered glass, grinned. "Doc, you owe me a hundred bucks of Scotch."

I stepped away before I did something really stupid. Like slamming a fist into his skull, popping a vessel in his dura and giving him a hematoma, doing to him what they did to Brooke.

"We get a deal together, I'll lead you to the promised land, Dr. McCormick," Fang said. He reached into his white coat and produced a key.

"We're not making any deals." Ravi was twitchy, opening and closing his big hands, staring hard at the man in the chair.

Fang cocked his head, a drunk smile twisting his lips. "Then I guess we're not talking." He dropped the key back into his pocket and pushed himself out of the chair.

In a single motion, Ravi was in front of him, shoving him back down. "We're talking," he said. "No more games, you son of a bitch—"

Fang found this funny. "You like the rough stuff, huh, Dr. Singh? You wait around here, you're going to see a lot of rough stuff, a lot—"

The sound of Ravi's palm striking Fang's face took me by surprise. "What the hell are you doing?" I yelped.

"We don't have time for this!" he shouted. "We have, what, Nate? A few minutes left? We got almost a dozen people out there with their faces exploding. Your *girlfriend* is in the ICU and—" He cut himself off and swung back to Fang. "Who's sick?"

"Ouch," Fang said, rubbing his face, forcing himself to laugh. "That's good. That was a good one."

"Who's sick?"

"You want to hit me again? Come on, Doctor, see if you have it in you."

"Ravi—" I put out my hand.

But his fist was already moving through the air. It cracked loudly in the middle of Fang's pasty face.

"Stop it!" I shouted. I grabbed him.

"Yes!" Fang shouted. "Again, Dr. *Singh*!"

The Sikh struggled against me for a second, then relaxed. I let go of his arm.

"Hit me!" Fang yelled.

Ravi shook his hand ruefully, then shook his head. "You crazy asshole," he told the panting man in the chair.

I rolled the stool over to Fang and sat. Twin streams of blood trailed from his nostrils.

"I think he broke my nose," Fang said.

I reached to his face, touched the swelling nose. He winced. The blood had slowed, but still oozed. I grabbed some gauze from the instrument tray and handed it to him.

"We'll get you to the ED," I said.

"No," he said.

I watched him for a moment, watched him wipe his lip, then push the gauze into his nostrils.

"What is Beautiful Essence?" I asked. "Does it have anything to do with the company Paul Murphy worked for—a company called Tetra Biologics?"

Wei-jan Fang's eyes hardened; his voice was thick from

the cotton-stuffed nose. "I can't talk about that unless we have a *deal.*"

I was about to lie regarding the protection—screw the asshole—but I never got the chance.

Somewhere in the front of the building, an electronic bell chimed.

90

WEI-JAN FANG'S BLOODIED FACE TWISTED. "Get out of here," he whispered.

I jumped from the stool and dropped back to the doorway, cut a quick look down the hallway. I couldn't see into the salon.

Fang had pushed himself out of the chair and wobbled toward me. "Get out," he repeated, covering me with boozy breath. He tried to push past me.

"Stay *here,*" I said.

"They're going to kill you. You get that?" He shoved me against the wall and stumbled down the hall.

"The key!" I said.

Fang waved me off and pushed through the back door to the alley. Next thing I knew, Ravi was blowing past me, moving quickly after the doctor.

I grabbed the Sikh's arm. "Wait," I said.

Ravi stopped running. "What? We gotta get out of here, McCormick. Are you nuts?"

"There was one chime."

"So?"

"So they wouldn't have sent only one guy, right? And no one's coming into the clinic. It's probably a customer who came and left when she saw no one was here."

"McCormick—"

"We need what's in that freezer."

Ravi didn't move.

"Call the cops," I said.

"I thought—"

But I was already gone. I jogged down the hallway to the door we'd broken through. I put my eye to the peephole and saw a fish-eye picture of the nail salon. The view wasn't perfect—the sight lines gave me only half the salon—but I saw no one.

"If they came in and left, why only one chime?" It was Ravi, whispering at my back.

"I thought I told you to call the police. We must have missed the other chime. I don't know, man. No one's there."

Ravi pressed his face to the door, his eye to the peephole. I scooped up the fire extinguisher and walked toward the makeshift lab.

I maneuvered the freezer away from the wall to give myself room to swing. Then I hoisted the fire extinguisher to my shoulder and cracked it downward into the small padlock. There red metal bit into the fixture, but the lock held.

Ravi was behind me now, standing in the entrance to the room, cutting his eyes back and forth from me to the nail salon's door. "There's no time," he hissed.

Again, I hoisted the extinguisher. Again I slammed. Still, the lock didn't break.

"McCormick—"

I pulled the extinguisher back, glanced at Ravi. His eyes were fixed on something in the hallway.

"—they're here," he said. "The door—"

Without warning, Ravi ripped the fire extinguisher from my hands. I watched him gallop for the door, the metal cylinder in his hands like a red battering ram.

The door inched, then swung open.

91

RAVI SHIFTED HIS MOMENTUM AND slammed into the wall next to the door. The fire extinguisher popped from his hands and clanged to the floor.

For a moment, there was silence. Then I yelled, "What the hell are you doing here?"

"You said it was break-the-rules-day," Tim Kim whined. His voice was only a little unsteady, and I wasn't sure he'd grasped just how close he'd come to being flattened by a raging Sikh.

Ravi rubbed his shoulder. "Goddamn," he said. "God-*damn*."

"I wanted to find you," Tim said. "I had to pee. I went to the bathroom." He stuck a finger back toward an opened door in the nail salon.

I ran a hand through my hair. "You okay?" I asked Tim.

"Uh-huh."

"Come here, Tim. Ravi—are you hurt?"

"Broken clavicle. Dislocated shoulder. Other than that, I'm friggin' perfect." He was glowering at the kid.

"Take him out the back," I said. "Tim, you go with Ravi."

"I want to stay with you," Tim said.

"You can't stay with me. I need to do something first."

How long did Fang say before the bad guys came? Fifteen minutes? How many of those minutes had passed?

"Get Tim back to your car," I said to Ravi. "I'll call you when I'm done."

"I'm staying with you!" Tim insisted. His face was pink now, crumpled with anxiety. I didn't blame the kid for not wanting to climb into a car with the guy who'd nearly crushed him and, now, looked as if he wished he had.

"Ravi, take him *out.*"

Ravi reached down for Tim's arm, but the kid scampered away. Another one of those precious minutes was dissolving while My Two Dads fumbled through Basic Childcare.

"Okay, okay. Tim, fine, you can stay with me. Ravi, get out of here. Call the police."

"I thought we didn't want the police—"

"Now I want them. If someone's coming, I want them."

I didn't have to say that I'd rather be locked in a cell getting my one phone call than have my tongue cut out. Ravi got it. "Call from a pay phone so they don't ID the call," I shouted after him. To Tim, I said, "You stay in the hall, hear me? Break-the-rules-day is *over.*"

He nodded. From his wide-eyed face, I couldn't tell if he was scared out of his wits or thinking this was some fun game. Scared, hopefully. They tell me kids keenly sense what the adults around are feeling and take cues from them. And I was scared out of my mind.

I dragged the fire extinguisher back into the closet with the locked freezer. "Tim, stay out there." I heard nothing, but wanted to make sure he hadn't run off. "You hear me, young man?" I sounded like my father.

"Yeah," came the small voice.

How many minutes left? Five? Fewer?

I wailed on the lock a few times, but its moorings on the lock held.

"Tim, you still there?"

"Yeah."

"*Stay* there."

I uncapped the top to the insulated tub of liquid nitrogen. There was no ladle, so I picked up the entire thing and brought it to the freezer. Slowly, I drizzled the cold liquid—about minus 200 degrees Celsius or minus 320 degrees Fahrenheit—over the small padlock, and the liquid immediately boiled to a gas when it hit the metal and the floor. After ten seconds, I was sure the lock was near minus 200.

"Tim, you stay right where you are. There's gas in here."

The tensile strength of steel is about 500 millipascals if memory from physics class served me. Supercooling the metal makes it brittle, greatly reducing its tensile strength. Using liquid nitrogen is one way thieves break through those "theft-resistant" bike locks.

Quickly, I put down the tub and picked up the fire extinguisher again. Raising it above my head, I brought it crashing down on the lock. With a *clink,* the metal finally split.

I took one of the broken cardboard boxes and fanned it a few times over the floor to disperse the gas. Then, with the room relatively free of nitrogen, I dropped to one knee in front of the freezer. I pulled at the door. Cold air flowed out like breath.

It was empty.

"Goddamn," I breathed.

To the trash can on the opposite side of the room. I began pulling material from it, tossing it on the floor, hoping the clinic workers were conscientious about keeping their sharps out of the general trash.

"Wow. You beat up that refrigerator." Tim was in the doorway.

"It was giving me backtalk. Hey, what's that in your hand?"

Tim regarded the piece of plastic and metal held tightly in his fingers. "It's a knife," he reported.

"It's a scalpel. Put it down. It's dangerous."

At the bottom of the can, a number of things had sifted through the paper and other light material: pipette tips, small plastic tubes with green screw tops, slightly larger plastic tubes with orange screw tops. Labels had once been affixed to the tubes with the orange caps, but had since been removed.

I glanced at Tim, saw that he still held the scalpel. "What did I say? Put your knife down."

"But I *need* it."

"You don't need it."

"Bilbo had Sting. His sword. *You're* the one who likes Bilbo."

I didn't have time for this, but I also didn't need to be worrying about an armed eight-year-old. "You don't need it," I told him. "Bilbo didn't really need it. His best weapon was his wits. Use your wits. They're much better than a scalpel."

This argument—dubious as it was—seemed to suffice, and Tim set the scalpel on the floor.

I plunged my arms deeper into the trash can, pulled out all the tubes I could get my hands on. A few fell on the floor.

"You're losing them," Tim observed.

"Don't worry about it. You hear anything outside?"

"No."

"No sirens?"

"I hear sirens." He was on his knees, chasing the tubes I'd spilled.

"That's *something,* isn't it?" I snapped. Did I have to spell everything out for the kid? "Let's go."

A siren wailed somewhere in the distance.

"Let's go," I said again. Tim was peering into a Styrofoam box. "Leave that."

"I found things," he said.

"Come on," I said, in a softer voice. Maybe a kinder, gentler cajoling would work. It didn't. I reached down to grab the kid's arm and wrench him out of here. "What are you looking at?"

He held up his hands. In his left was a crumpled piece of paper. In his right was a plastic tube with an attached flip-top. The tube was unlike the ones I'd pulled from the trash. It contained a pink, indistinct mass.

I took the tube. It was cool to the touch.

Tim held the paper to me. A bill of lading. He pointed to the recipient's name: Dragon East Importers.

"That's Uncle Tony," he informed me, smoothing out the paper carefully.

I snatched it and scanned.

"Dragon East Importers" was neatly handwritten in the "To:" line. The name and the logo of the shipping company, Cellegix Solutions, occupied the upper left-hand corner, along with an address and phone number. There was a lot number for the item shipped, but no description.

The sirens were getting louder. A couple blocks away at most.

I shoved the bill into my pocket along with the tubes I'd collected and the one Tim had found. I grabbed the boy's hand.

And then I froze.

The electronic chime sounded. Then it sounded again.

This time, there was no doubt that more than one person had entered.

92

I YANKED TIM FROM THE closet. His body felt light and doll-like. He squeaked in protest. "Not now," I snarled.

Down the hall, I heard the door to the clinic slam open. Nasal shouts in a language I couldn't understand. Tim squirmed wildly against my arm as I dragged him through the back door.

The alleyway. To the left, a large SUV lumbered toward us. To the right, a black sedan had jammed into reverse, tires squealing, making tiny jerks and adjustments as the driver tried to keep the nose of the vehicle from swinging him into a spin.

I tightened my hold on Tim and ran toward the sedan.

The driver slapped the brakes. "Get in!" Ravi shouted.

I threw Tim into the front seat and stole a look behind us. Two men had appeared in the alley.

"Go, go!" I screamed.

Ravi did, the Acura heaving forward. Tim was in a ball in the footwell; I kneeled on the seat above him.

Behind us, the two men hopped into the SUV. The sirens were very close now, their whine coming from the other side of the block, coming from behind us.

The SUV lurched. A siren's blare ricocheted off the buildings flanking the alley. I glanced forward, saw the cross street rushing toward us. Then, something I'd never heard before except in movies and on TV: an explosion. A big one.

"Jesus!" Ravi yelled. As we spun out onto the street, I wheeled, saw black smoke belch into the alley.

"What happened?" Ravi pushed the car faster.

"They blew up the clinic." The SUV turned behind us, following. "Damn it. Faster, Ravi!" I shouted. Below me, Tim had his arms over his head, and I tried to do my best to avoid stomping him.

Ravi raced through a red light, then another. The SUV blew the lights easily, getting closer with each one. Behind it, I caught a glimpse of flashing lights. "Turn!" I shouted.

Ravi turned down an alley and gunned the engine, laid on the horn as we flew past guys unloading produce from a truck. I looked out the back window, saw the SUV shoot past the alley entrance, the SFPD in hot pursuit.

93

I HELPED TIM INTO THE backseat, though he didn't much need it, hopping like a monkey over the leather upholstery. In the distance, sirens had taken up a chorus.

"Put on your seatbelt, Tim," I said, in some lame attempt to regain the moral, child-protection high ground. Thankfully, the kid didn't call me on it.

"Did you see it blow up?" he wanted to know as he buckled himself in.

"No," I said.

"It was loud, huh?"

"Yes."

"It was almost like you could feel it in your stomach. Even when I was down there, I could feel it."

"It was loud, that's for sure."

Ravi drove slowly now, but everything else was happening fast, fast, fast.

"I almost crushed the kid," Ravi muttered, irritated. We were driving next to Golden Gate Park. A fire engine raced in the other direction, its yammering and squawking pressing down on us, then fading.

"He's all right."

"Freaking ankle-biters," he said. I twisted around to see Tim scowling.

"You got to let it go now. The kid had to use the bathroom. It was break-the-rules day."

Ravi shook his head. "Thirty gallons of gasoline—a fucking *bomb,* man. And I beat the shit out of some guy, nearly crushed a kid. What a day."

"Watch the language," I said, tilting my head toward the backseat.

"That's the least of his worries."

It was an annoying observation, but unfortunately true.

"Not so stealthy, were we, McCormick?"

"No," I agreed, half listening to him, half figuring out what to do next. Dragon East and Cellegix Solutions. Uncle Tony. And the thawing, sweating tubes of whatever crap was now in my pockets. Ten disfigured people. Eleven, counting Dorothy.

Ravi laughed, seemed to be rediscovering some of the bluster he left back in Spectacular Nails. "Hyfrecator salesmen? That's fantastic."

"Yeah," I said. I took out the bill of lading. Dragon East. Cellegix.

"You think they're scared now?" Ravi asked, unconcerned with what I'd pulled from my pocket, his brain still preoccupied with the previous hour.

"Yes. Unfortunately."

"Why unfortunately?" Ravi asked. "They'll shut down operations. No more sarcoma."

"They can open another clinic tomorrow. Or you're right and they're going to close shop for good. Either way, it's not great for us."

"Why not?"

I glanced into the backseat, saw Tim Kim watching me. "Because there are too many loose ends they need to cut," I said.

94

I HAD RAVI CIRCLE BACK toward the Richmond so I could retrieve Dorothy's car. We parked a good distance away from it—five blocks or so—on a side street. Then I pulled out the plastic tubes again. The three different tubes—green-topped, orange-topped, the flip-top Tim had found—rolled in my hands like a heroin fiend's bounty.

"From the freezer?" Ravi asked.

"From the trash. And one that was dropped when they cleaned out the freezer. Tim found it."

I concentrated on what Tim had found. Inside the tube was a gelatinous substance. It surrounded what looked like a little pink jellyfish.

"It's tissue," I said. The liquid nitrogen in the shotgun lab made sense now. They were taking biopsies—those tiny snips of tissue—and flash-freezing them. "It's a biopsy."

"Biopsy? Where's it coming from?" Ravi asked.

"Coming from the clinic. Going where, I don't know."

You get a biopsy for one purpose only: to analyze it, to see what's going on.

"We'll want histology on this," I said, dropping the tube in the console between us.

"What're those?" Tim's seatbelt was off and he was scrunched forward between the two front seats, pointing at the green- and orange-topped tubes in my hand.

"That's what we took from the trash," I said.

"Can I see?"

"*May* I see. Sure." I handed him one green and one orange. He stared at them like they were diamonds. "What's histology?" he demanded.

"It's the morphology of the . . . It's the way cells look under the microscope." To Ravi, I said, "Get immunohistochemistry on the biopsy, too, if you can."

"Immunohistochemistry for what?"

"Try CD34. I bet—"

"What's immnochemistry?" Tim wanted to know.

Christ, Bio 101 again. "Immunohistochemistry is a way to find types of cells in tissue. Ravi, try CD34 to look for DFSP—"

"How?" Tim interrupted.

"How what?"

"How do you find the cells?"

Ravi was scowling. He had less patience for this than I did. But, as they say in med school, there's always time for a teaching point. "We use antibodies to find proteins that are unique to different cells in the body. The antibodies are like puzzle pieces. They only fit certain proteins, which means they only fit certain cells."

I waited for another question, but Tim was still chewing that over.

"Why would they have biopsies in the clinic?" Ravi asked.

"Dorothy said they took tissue. I'd guess they're culling it from everybody."

"It doesn't make sense that they would keep the tissue."

"No, it doesn't. Unless they're—I don't know—monitoring what's going on."

"That's a little much to ask of a bunch of criminals, isn't it?"

I was having the same trouble as Ravi, making a case that Uncle Tony and his bunch cared much about the biology of what they were doing to these patients. Cellegix, perhaps. But the bill of lading showed the shipment *from* Cellegix *to* Dragon East, not the other way around. Cellegix sent something; it didn't receive it.

"What about these?" Ravi gestured at the other tubes, the ones with green and orange tops.

"I'd be willing to bet a year's salary one of them is Beautiful Essence."

"You got no salary, you unemployed bum." Ravi held

the green-topped tube to the light. "Fountain of Youth, huh? No idea what it is?"

"None."

"Needle in a haystack. I hate that." Ravi uncapped the tube, sniffed at it. "I'll see what we can scrape from the inside of these things, then shotgun it with a protein microarray, see if we—"

Tim piped up, "What's—"

"A microarray is a way to look for a lot of different proteins at once," I said. "A bunch of antibodies that capture proteins are put on a little chip—Ravi, how big's your microarray?"

"Five thousand, I think."

"Tim, you have five thousand different antibodies that are like jigsaw pieces and they're stuck on a tiny chip. You take your substance—like the stuff in these tubes—and tag all of it with a fluorescent marker. You dump all of that on the chip. If something in the substance you're interested in finds its corresponding jigsaw piece on the chip, it gets stuck there and lights up. Then you know what it is. You understand that?"

"No," Tim said.

"I'll draw you a picture," I said.

"Okay."

"After you're in college." I turned back to Ravi. "Get to the lab, man. Find the needle in the haystack."

Tim and I walked along the street toward his mother's car. The boy fell into step with me, intent on lengthening his strides to match mine. "You put protein on a chip?" he asked, his eyes on his feet.

"A silicon chip. It's very complicated."

We got through half a block before Young Einstein opened his mouth again. "What's a fluorescent marker?"

"Something that lights up. Like a glow stick. Quiet now, I have to do something important."

I pulled the bill of lading and my cell from my pocket. Cellegix Solutions sported a 617 area code. Boston. I checked my watch. Four p.m. East Coast time.

When the switchboard answered, I asked to be put through to sales. Ten seconds later, I found myself talking to LaTonya.

"I'm wondering if you have an item in stock," I said. I gave her the lot number from the bill.

LaTonya came back on the phone and cheerily let me know they did, in fact, have the item in stock. "We have aliquots of fifty thousand and one hundred thousand cells."

"Cells?"

"That's what you're interested in, right? The fibroblast stem cells?"

"Yes," I said. "That's exactly what I'm interested in."

I cut the call.

95

"WHOA," TIM SAID, AS WE arrived at the car. The street in front of Spectacular Nails was choked with police cars, ambulances, fire trucks, and, already, TV news vans. It was good to see he had some interest in normal eight-year-old-boy things, and not just in microarrays and other perverse stuff.

Maybe he had too much interest. He broke from my side and started speed-walking toward the commotion.

"Tim," I said, but he was already weaving his way ahead of me along the sidewalk. Truth was, I wanted to see, too. I followed him.

The crowd thickened, and I caught up to Tim, bent to take his hand. His fingers were cold and wet. Television crews had staked out their territory, positioned themselves so the reporters could be shot with a dramatic backdrop of boiling black smoke and churning men in uniform. Barricades had been set up, a few uniformed cops standing behind them, splitting their attention between the curious masses and the emergency response.

"Anybody hurt?" I asked, sidling up to a policeman who had to be half my size.

The cop looked at me warily, then at Tim, and in that moment, I realized I may have just made a crucial mistake. I'd forgotten that I'd "abducted" Tim Kim. How does the child abduction thing work again? How does word spread through the police force?

I knew I should have gone to law school.

"I'm a doctor," I said, by way of explaining away any resemblance I might have to a child molester.

The cop seemed unsatisfied, but he answered. "Windows blew out. Guy in the shop next door was hurt, a few pedestrians got cut, far as they figure it. We don't know about the situation inside—" He broke off to listen to the radio squawk on his shoulder. "Not sure if it was a gas line or something—bomb or whatever." He shook his head. "I mean, if terrorists are blowing up nail salons now . . . Bastards."

"*Damn* bastards," I agreed heartily, gripping Tim's hand before the kid could start an Honest Abe thing and begin explaining what really happened.

I started to back slowly from the cop. Hurrying away from the scene of the explosion with a boy the cops in four counties were looking for didn't seem like such a great plan.

From the corner of my eye, I saw someone standing at the barricade. Peripheral vision isn't good at details, but I could tell the person was staring at me.

"Mr. McCormick," Jack Tang said. Scenes of handcuffs, struggle, me explaining how I'd gotten the kid, jail, fending off advances from a burly cellmate called Tiny, all tumbled through my brain.

"Mr. Tang," I said, trying to keep it friendly.

Instead of shooting me, Tang gestured at my little buddy. "Who's this?"

"Uh, this is Teddy, I'm watching him for a friend."

Tim protested. "My name's—"

"Teddy." I squeezed his hand, hard. "What's up, Inspector?"

"Wanted to ask you the same."

Christ, here it comes. I guessed the freaking AMBER Alert had gone out.

"Look, I can explain," I said. "It's not what you think."

"Great. Enlighten me."

I swallowed hard. "Yesterday, I went out to Berkeley—"

Tim squirmed, and I realized my fingers were crushing his. "Can I go watch the fire trucks?"

"I don't think that's such a good idea, Teddy," I said.

"Not every day a kid gets to see something like this," Tang said. "You remember how much you used to love fire trucks, Uncle Nate?" He smiled at me.

And I smiled back.

"Just stay where I can see you, Teddy. Don't go across the barriers," I said, responsibility flowing from me like, well, water from a fire hose. "And don't cross the street." I watched Tim go, then turned back to Tang. "Why don't you just ask me what you want to know?"

"No problem, Doc. The San Mateo folks looked at your friend Murphy's financial picture. I told you about the big transfers. We didn't know how big, though. One transfer of a hundred sixty thousand dollars about four months ago, another of over three hundred less than a month ago. Tax records show the guy's salary was about two hundred K, wife didn't work. He had interest in the company, but that was never cashed out."

"Jesus," I said.

"The monies came from a numbered account offshore, as did the other transfers, the smaller ones. But we don't know if it was held by Paul Murphy and he was milking it when he needed it, or whether it was held by someone else, who just made payments to him out of it."

"No inheritance?"

"None for him or his wife."

"Where did the money go?"

"That's the funny thing. Two payments to his parents in Iowa, total over two hundred thousand. A couple other payments to other individuals."

"His *parents*?"

"Yeah. San Mateo's tracking them down. Parents seem to be unreachable now."

"Jesus." Wrestling with this new information about Paul, I asked, "So what do you want to know from me?"

"Since you were his buddy, I want to know if you know anything about why he had nearly a million dollars in his bank account."

"No idea."

"He had enormous cash flow coming in and you didn't notice anything different?"

"We hadn't . . . Like I said, I hadn't seen the guy for years. You said the Mings had big expenditures. They had money. Maybe they were giving some to Murph. Maybe that's how this was connected."

"*That* was from inheritance. Mrs. Ming's father died about a year ago. The old man was loaded." He looked out over the mayhem. "This is not making sense, but I think you're right, Mr. McCormick. I think they're connected. Maybe it's not that the Mings were funding Mr. Murphy, but connected somehow."

The urge to divulge all, to bring this guy into the fold, was almost overwhelming. To unshoulder my burden, let Tang and the tax authorities and whomever else take the weight. I mean, what the hell had Murph gotten himself into? And what did I owe him, anyway? My mouth opened, but then I looked over at Tim, up on his tiptoes, clinging to the blue police barrier. I thought of his mother's body pressed against mine. And I realized I couldn't chance putting her in more jeopardy.

"What happened here?" I asked Tang. "You think it was a gang thing?"

"Gangs, terrorists, gas line." He shrugged. "You don't have a cigarette, do you?"

"No."

He shook his head. "This is really going to fuck up my day." He gave me a hard look. "So, why are *you* here?"

"Teddy wanted to check out the pet store on Geary. The kid's nuts about hamsters."

"You're playing babysitter?"

"I got all this time on my hands ever since you guys told me to back off for my own protection."

From his look, I couldn't tell if he believed me. "You were saying you went to Berkeley . . ."

"To pick up Teddy."

"Sure." Tang sounded doubtful.

There was a shout at the police line as some onlooker tried to squeeze through the barricade. Lots of Chinese was being spoken. Tang looked back to me. "Well, have fun at the pet store. Let me know if you remember anything about your friend's bank account."

I told him I would, and I watched as he pushed to the barricade, flashed his badge, and placed himself between a big white cop and a red-faced, shouting Asian man. Tang did a little translating, and the man calmed down. Tang made a move to leave, but stopped himself. Instead, he headed toward Tim. My heart sank. He bent and said something to the boy, who looked back at me, then said something in return. Tang shot a glance my way, held it for a second. Then the barrier was pulled aside, and Jack Tang disappeared into a sweating mass of humanity and machinery to tend to his fucked-up day. Tim stayed where he was, watching.

At the barricade, I reached down to Tim. "Want a boost so you can see better?" He nodded, and I hoisted the boy onto my shoulders.

"Whoa," he said, taking in the sights. "They have all these hoses going like crazy. And there's this guy with blood on his head."

"What did that policeman say to you?"

"He asked if we were going to the pet store."

"What did you say back?"

"I told him I hope so. Are we going to the pet store?"

"Soon," I said. I patted his knee.

With one arm firmly hooked over Tim's leg, I took out my phone. It was awkward, but I wanted to preserve whatever physical contact with the kid I could.

I dialed the hospital down south, was put through to the paging office. "Jenna Nathanson," I said.

96

ON THE WALK TO THE pet store, Tim couldn't quite shake the post–bomb blast excitement. "We were *there*. We almost got *blown* to *bits*."

I put the boy down and held out my hand. He didn't take it. "I can walk by myself," he said. He appeared to be equally jazzed with having almost been blown to bits, and with the prospect of seeing rodents.

On the sidewalk outside the store, I could smell the musty odor of animals, their food, and their by-products. I was about to step inside when my phone vibrated.

"Go poke around," I told Tim. "But be careful of the kid-eating tarantulas." I didn't know if there were any spiders in the place, but I had a theory that looking for them should keep overly curious kids occupied. Tim vanished into the store. I answered the phone.

"This is Dr. Nathanson," a slightly peevish voice said. "I was paged."

"Jenna, it's Nate McCormick. How is she?"

"Uh, hi, Nate," she said, probably scanning through her mental patient list as to who "she" was. "Brooke's doing well. We may be able to extubate her tomorrow."

"Listen—I need a huge favor. I need you to transfer Brooke to another ICU. Santa Clara Valley or Sequoia or wherever is easiest."

"She's in serious condition, Nate," Jenna reminded me primly.

"I know that. I can't really get into this, but she's in danger. The people who beat her up will be back."

"And you've told the police about this?"

"Of course," I lied. "They told me to get her a transfer. And, Jenna—don't tell anyone who doesn't need to know where she's going."

"This isn't done."

"I know that. But it's to protect her, you understand that?"

"Who's going to pay for this?"

"Her insurance. Me. Have Billing call me if there's a problem. Just do it, Jenna. You don't want something bad to happen to her on your watch."

She thought about that. "I'll see what I can do."

"Don't see. Just do it and do it fast." I added, "Please."

I hung up the phone, hoping that I had generated some get-up-and-go in the neurosurgeon with a bunch of talk pulled straight from ancient pop culture. *Just do it.* Christ.

Tim hadn't reached the darker recesses of the pet store, the place where the tarantulas nested, but was stuck a few feet inside the door, waylaid by a large wire cage. His finger was in the cage, and a puppy—a yellow Lab, by the look of him—licked at it furiously.

"You done?" I asked. "I have to go over there and use their computer." I pointed to a café that advertised a few Web-ready computers.

"Can't I stay here?"

"No. We have to stay together, you and me. Come on. I'll get you a latte."

Tim gave me a weird look. Right. The kid's eight. "I'll get you a soda."

"I think I'll just stay here," he decided.

"You can play on the Web over there. You can look at—I don't know—look at puppies on the Internet. Play video games. I'll pay for it."

"I want to stay here," he repeated. So this is what it means to be a parent—constant negotiations, the constant sense of being outmaneuvered.

The puppies, the kid, the wildly flicking tongue. Hell, when it gets right down to it, *I'd* rather stay here. "Don't move, then," I told him. "I'll only be ten minutes."

As I made my way across the street, I tried to piece together what we had.

The Mings, a charred clinic, a bunch of people chewed by fibrosarcoma but too terrified to seek treatment. Murph, who'd been getting massive infusions of cash from somewhere and paid for it with his life; I couldn't even begin to make sense of that. Not yet, anyway.

We had samples of what was probably Beautiful Essence. As long as the substance didn't denature in the heat of Ravi Singh's pocket, it would be a start. But it would take too long to track from a molecule to a manufacturer to a distributor to Wei-jan Fang. Too long for Dorothy Zhang, anyway. Too long to ensnare any bad guys who were already closing shop with massive Molotov cocktails, guns, intimidation, and mutilation. And too damn long to explain why Murph was dead and why he'd forked over two hundred grand to his parents.

"Damn it, Paul," I said aloud.

We had the tissue, the biopsies. The analysis of these would be faster, but still too slow. And the results of any tests on them might not change what we did. Generally in medicine, you only order a diagnostic test when it promises to have some bearing on treatment. If we waved our analytical wand over the tissue and it showed dermatofibrosarcoma protuberans, what would really change? Not much, I decided. But I hadn't really thought that through when I sent Ravi off to the lab. It would keep him busy, though. And you never know what things like that might yield.

Most importantly, I had a name and I had a cell type. Dragon East and fibroblasts. Now I needed to get to a computer.

I forked over a couple bucks for a coffee and a half hour of time on one of the small boxes they had at Jazzin' Java.

First thing I keyed into Google was "Dragon East Importers." Nothing. Not a website, nary a link. I shifted the quotes to "Dragon East" and "Importers" and got a Google-spray of bullshit: "—tail of the **dragon, east** through the valley . . ." and "**Dragon: East** Coast Champs . . . Mumbai Treasures, **Importers** of fine . . ." That sort of thing.

Sifting through this kind of crap wasn't my strength. In the lab, sloshing antibodies over tissue, that's where Nate McCormick was meant to be. Or out beating the streets, wearing out his shoes, chasing down viruses. He was not meant to be in Jazzin' Java, pursuing who-knows-who through websites and bills of lading. My abortive search on Dragon East proved that.

So, I returned to science. I ran a search on fibroblast stem cell transplants and jotted down some of the names of researchers working with the cells. If Dr. Fang had been playing in this field, I supposed it wouldn't hurt to contact them . . .

Still, I felt, I was missing something. To wit: Beautiful Essence was *not* stem cells—those super-powerful progenitors that could differentiate into any cell in the body. Sure, it involved stem cells, but that drew only half the picture. The incubator in the shotgun lab at Fang's clinic suggested incubation, and not just the warming of cells. Something had been mixed with the fibroblasts and allowed to cook for a while before being injected. But what was being mixed with the cells? Run-of-the-mill cell culture media? Something else?

I stared at the computer screen, grew tired of looking at the burning pixels, and turned to look out the window. I saw myself reflected in it, let my eyes drift over the ghostly contours of my face. It hadn't been gnawed by cancer; it hadn't been hacked by knives. The wounds I'd suffered thus far had been emotional ones, not physical. Something to be grateful for.

And I let my mind drift to Murph, whose wounds had been plaguing me since this began. He knew about the sick people, of course, through his affair with Dorothy. What else could he have known? And where would the knowledge have come from?

Tissue is the issue, I told myself.

Tissue, fibroblasts, tissue regeneration, cosmetic application. Then, I thought: tissue regeneration, wounds, wound healing.

Tetra Biologics.

I turned quickly to the computer.

One of the hallmarks of science, at least science in the

last century and a half, is that it is open. You don't hold on to your discoveries anymore. You show them to the world, allow others to read what you've done and build on that. In other words, you wave your own flag. The bulk of the modern scientist's compensation comes from that: recognition and honor. As such, all of the foundational work for everything that was going on in Tetra would be public, detailed in the literature.

I started at the beginning, with a PubMed search on Tom Bukowski, founder of Tetra Biologics. Forty-seven articles popped up. I zeroed in first on the mid-nineties papers, when the professor still called the University of Illinois at Chicago his home. Bukowski, it seemed, had interest in a protein called fibroblast growth factor-1 or FGF-1, which, per its name, stimulated fibroblast cells to grow. The titles of the papers were arcane—"Fibroblast growth factor-1 stimulates collagen scaffold in mouse models," for example, and "Recombinant fibroblast growth factor-1 and tissue growth *in vivo*"—but intriguing. Seemed too coincidental that we were dealing with a cancer of fibroblasts and Bukowski had been working on fibroblast growth factor. Still, the connections were tenuous.

Until they weren't.

When my eyes fixed on the title of the paper, I felt the way a prospector might when he glimpsed the first glint of gold. "Fibroblast growth factor-1 and fibroblast stem cells: a controlled approach to tissue regeneration." Only two authors. The second was Tom Bukowski. The first was Peter Yee.

And both of them had been killed by an explosion on a boat.

Excited now, I followed the trail, searching through the

rest of Bukowski's and Peter Yee's articles. I broadened the search to Jonathan Bly, the scientist who headed up the Regenetine project at Tetra, the guy with the handshake of a dead man. I found another nugget: "Fibroblast growth factor-1 causes dysregulation and mutagenesis in fibroblast stem cells." Put more simply, FGF-1 can cause cancer.

Christ, I thought, *it's coming together.*

Fibroblast stem cells in a clinic in the Richmond. FGF-1 at Tetra. Tissue regeneration, wound healing. The same goddamned thing. All at once, the puzzle began to assemble.

Tetra's blockbuster product wouldn't be a blockbuster because of wound healing; I'd been correct to think that the market was too small for a billion-dollar molecule. Tetra's blockbuster drug wasn't even a drug at all—it was what the industry calls a biological. And that biological, Regenetine, blended with fibroblast stem cells, was poised to find its way into every cosmetic dermatologist's and plastic surgeon's office in the country.

So why all the secrecy? Why the obfuscation about Regenetine? Why not parade the fact that it was a fibroblast growth factor? Why not just fess up and say the promise of the treatment was that it would erase ten years from your face?

Because they didn't want anyone to do what I was doing. They didn't want anyone to connect the dots between an illicit clinic, fibrosarcoma, and the promising new product from a company slated to become the next big thing in biotech, the next Genentech, the next billion-dollar gold mine.

Immediately, I called Ravi Singh. "Make sure fibroblast growth factor-1 is on the protein arrays," I said.

"I'm still in traffic, man. Bay Bridge is way backed up. People getting out of the city, I guess. That explosion is all over the news."

"Don't even bother with the microarrays. Just run an ELISA."

"You found something?" Now I had Ravi's interest. Bless his glory-seeking little heart.

"They're adding it to the fibroblast stem cells," I said. "They're using FGF-1 as fertilizer for the fibroblasts."

"What the hell does that mean?"

"Beautiful Essence," I said, savoring this victory. "We've nailed Beautiful Essence."

97

I DON'T KNOW WHETHER OR not you can trust the dead, or whether it really even matters. I guess it mattered, though, since the decedent in question was the guy who sucked me into all this in the first place. Paul Murphy.

The Boy Scout was in deep with Tetra and with the bad guys behind Beautiful Essence, deeper than Dorothy Zhang suggested when she'd told me she and her beau were putting together a misguided, naive exposé of what was happening. Though Murph's involvement had killed him, I hoped it wasn't also paying him. Dying like he did is bad enough. Dying like that because you're shilling for someone is unforgivable.

In any case, the noose was tightening around Murph and around Tetra. Beautiful Essence was FGF-1. The connection between the two was strong—too strong to be coincidental—but the reasons for it were unclear.

Just as I crossed the entrance to the pet store, my phone vibrated. It was Millie Bao at CDC.

"Nate, what's going on?"

"I'm leaving the trade, Dr. Bao," I said, looking into the recesses of the store for Tim. "Got a big idea. Pet supplies on the Internet. Think I'll call it Pets.com. I'll make billions."

"I'm serious here," she said. "What's this I hear about you impersonating an EIS officer?"

"Oh, that. That was just a joke."

"Well, the folks here don't think it's so funny. They're pissed, Nate, especially Dr. Lancaster. He started swearing again."

Dr. Lancaster, my former boss at CDC, was famous for his almost-swearing: f-this and GD-that. I'd actually provoked him into profanity the year before. That time, he nearly fired me. No firing possible this time. Prosecution, imprisonment, maybe.

"Lancaster flipped when he heard you abducted a child, Nate."

"I didn't abduct any child."

"Good," she said, "because I couldn't stand the thought of you in jail. And I really need that babysitting time you owe me. The health of my marriage depends on it."

"So, you found something."

"Maybe, possibly something. My friend in Hong Kong said they've found a slight uptick in reported cases of dermatofibrosarcoma protuberans. Weird thing is that most of the people they have on file were diagnosed postmortem."

"The patients *died* from DFSP?"

"No. That's the weird thing. They were killed by other means."

"Killed?"

"Accidents, violence. There wasn't enough to establish a pattern, but my friend said his suspicions are up."

"My suspicions are up," I said. "There are at least four confirmed cases here; two who died violently: a woman with the fibrosarcoma was murdered, a man who had it and was killed in a hit-and-run."

Millie was silent.

I said, "It's there, Millie. It's in Hong Kong."

"Prove it," she said.

"Give me a day to confirm something. Then you can throw a giant bone to your Hong Kong pals. If I'm right, they'll babysit for you for the next year."

"You're worried, aren't you?" Millie knows me well.

"Yes," I confessed. Worried that each passing minute was another in which a needle could be slid into the skin in San Francisco, in Hong Kong, and God only knew where else. Twelve billion dollars—twelve *billion*—spent on cosmetic procedures in the past year in the U.S. alone. The lure of beauty was irresistible, immutable, and, in this case, lethal. Not even the warning signs of underground clinics and shady physicians would scuttle the quest for the perfect face. That much was already clear. Beauty's call was too seductive.

"Tomorrow, Millie. Meantime, tell Hong Kong public health to start looking for a connection between the cases and any new cosmetic procedures. Injections, especially.

The name here is Beautiful Essence. Millie—tell them to be discreet."

She laughed. "Discreet. I didn't know that word was in your vocabulary."

I ended the call.

So, probably a dozen cases of the fibrosarcoma in the Bay Area, an unknown number in Hong Kong. This is not the kind of thing a public health guy liked much. We like our outbreaks—our clusters—to be localized, not sprayed across the world. It's why we hate flu so much, why we hate AIDS and SARS. It's all a question of numbers and geography and spread. It's all a question of *control.* And when something's stretched across the ocean, you got sucker's odds of controlling it.

Tim was no longer at the puppy cages. At the front of the store, I saw an older white woman in a rubber apron brushing scum from the inside of a fish tank. She looked matronly, like she'd be able to detect kid-presence with some sixth sense. I liked the look of her, and asked her if she'd seen a small Asian kid wandering around.

"I wondered who left him," she said. "I don't know who's so irresponsible to leave a child that age alone."

"He's very responsible," I answered, not, actually, liking her anymore.

"It's good that *he* is, at least," she said as she pulled the dripping brush from the tank. "You leave him alone in the car on a hot day, too?"

"Um . . ."

"Lord, that poor boy—"

"Where is that poor boy? Do you know?"

She sighed. "Over near the arthropod tanks."

The tarantula terrarium was the perfect height for Tim to gaze into, and he stood with his nose a couple centimeters from the glass. I squatted down, put myself on his level. To me, the black furry things looked like moldy pieces of pumpernickel roll.

"I just got a talking-to for leaving you here by yourself."

He kept his eyes on the tarantulas. "You're not supposed to leave kids alone."

No one—absolutely no one—cuts me a break. "Who says? I was left alone a lot," I said defensively.

This was the perfect time for Tim to say something like "And look how you turned out." Thankfully, he hadn't yet mastered the art of the cutting retort.

"They're not man-eaters," Tim said, concentrating on a spider in the tank's corner. "The pet store man said. They eat insects and some eat mice, but not people."

"Every time you see one of these things on TV, they have a man's foot hanging out of their mouths," I said.

"No they don't."

"In the movies they do." I flicked the glass with my fingernail.

"Don't do that," Tim said. "They don't like it." He pressed his fingers to the glass. "I'm hungry."

"Okay, we'll get something to—"

"And I'd like to see my mother now."

The kid had a lot of needs. "I would, too. We'll find her."

"Where is she?"

"I don't know that yet. We're trying to figure that out."

"Uncle Tony took her."

"Maybe. Hey, you remember in *The Hobbit* when Bilbo and his friends got attacked by those spiders? What did they say to scare them off? 'Attercop'?"

"Don't say that. Spiders *hate* that."

"Attercop," I whispered loudly to the spiders. "Attercop."

"Stop it!" he shouted, real anger in his voice. Customers turned. The matron at the fish tank glared.

"Okay," I said. "Sorry." I began to flail. "You want to talk about microarrays some more?"

"I want to see my mother."

"Let's go," I said to Tim. He didn't move. "Let's go, Tim."

I touched his shoulder, and he twisted away from me. "Tim . . ."

"I want to see my mother!" he yelled.

"And I'm trying to find her. Give me—"

"I don't care what you're doing. They're going to *hurt* her!"

"You calm down, young man." The sentence felt strange in my mouth—the words stiff and tacky—but sounded familiar. This time, when I grabbed his hand, he tried to tug it away, but I didn't let him. "We're leaving. Right now, Timothy." That was it: now I sounded just like my mother. Appalling.

"No!" he shouted. "I want my mom!" I yanked him firmly away from the terrarium. "I want my *mother*! Let me go!" And so we went, my hand clamped on his, past the aquariums, past the kittens and puppies in their cages, past the worried onlookers. "Let *go*!"

"He got scared of the spiders," I explained to the worried spectators.

"I was *not* scared! I want my MOTHER!" The last word came as a shriek, and I started to worry some do-gooder might intercede before I reached the door. Tantrums stop at three, right? "NO!" Tim screeched.

I wondered how a guy like myself is supposed to deal with these situations. Where the hell is the manual?

Finally, the sidewalk. A few patrons and store employees gazed at us out of the darkness of the shop as if from their own cages. From the looks of them, I couldn't tell if they had sympathy for me or were about to call Child Protective Services.

I knelt in front of Tim, who continued to yell—*Let go of me! I want to see my mom!*—and took both his shoulders in my hands.

"Stop it," I hissed. "Don't be such a baby."

He stopped yelling, but he didn't stop fuming. He breathed fast through his nose, his jaw was clenched. His eyes were dry and narrowed.

And I have no doubt that Timothy Kim, eight-year-old boy, would have enjoyed nothing more at that moment than watching me be eaten alive by giant tarantulas.

98

I GOT TIM BACK TO the car, wondering how difficult it would be to find a nanny in this neighborhood. He sulked quietly on the seat next to me, not even touching the hot dog I'd bought for him. Candy and hot dogs, I thought. Stellar nutritional fare from a public health doc.

I asked Tim again if he wanted to talk about microarrays. He didn't bother to answer me. The silence was good, though, giving me a chance to think. The aimless rolling of the car over San Francisco asphalt was soothing in a way. The light odor of Dorothy's car, the scent of her somewhere in there, was soothing to me, at least. But maybe that's what calmed the kid down, too. The smell of his mother.

Since my research into Dragon East had been a bust, I decided to call a guy who could, I hoped, plumb a lot deeper than I could.

"Dr. McCormick, didn't know if I'd hear from you again." No "dude" this time. No "man." No talk of revolution. This professional Miles Pikar was new to me. "How'd it go with finding what you needed?"

"I found him. Thanks for the Napa information."

"Great. Went well?"

"Went okay. But I need to ask you another favor."

"Hold on." I heard Miles say something I couldn't make out, then something like "close the door."

"Had to secure the area, dude. One of my project managers was in here. He got *Black Nexus 4* last night and he couldn't stop playing. Says the character development's better than the movies. You a gamer?"

"No."

"You got to try it, man. Putting Hollywood and the publishing industry out of business. It's the new juggernaut. Try it."

"Maybe—"

"I'm one hundred percent serious here." There was a brief pause, and I could almost hear the lightbulb buzzing to life. "We got to get together and talk about possibilities, dude. The pandemic angle, the flu thing. Tracking down a virus before it blows up all over the world. You could educate folks about—"

"Maybe next week, Miles. I got that favor—"

"Righto. Shoot."

Miles seemed not the least bit perturbed that I'd squelched discussion about a pandemic video game. The guy's relationships with ideas—video games, databases, revolution—was impressive both in its depth and in its detachment from them.

"A big favor," I said.

"You're starting to worry me. Just ask, and I'll let you know if I can do it."

"There's a company called Dragon East Importers. I need to know about them."

"Need to know what?"

"I'm not really sure. The basic stuff: what they are, what they do, who owns it."

"Not a problem. You can do this yourself, you know. Hop onto the Net."

"I did that already. I didn't find anything. I was hoping you could go a little deeper."

"How can I go a little deeper, dude?"

"I don't know. You're the database guy. You have friends, right?"

"I might or might not have friends, the existence or nonexistence of whom I will neither confirm nor deny." He laughed. I didn't. "What's this about?"

"Same thing. That disease I told you about. And those murders in Woodside. It's about both of them. You hear about that explosion in the Richmond?"

"Yeah. All over the news. Amazing no one was killed."

"It's about that, too."

"Oh, shit, dude. You need to be talking to the FBI or something, not to Miles Pikar."

"I'm talking to Miles Pikar because I *can't* talk to the FBI or the cops or anyone else. There are some considerations here."

He laughed again. "Considerations? Man, you going solo on this? The public health doctor? What about considerations for anybody else getting hurt if you *don't* go to the cops?"

"People are going to get hurt if I do go to them. The story's only half put together, and right now I need the bad guys to think everything's okay."

"Bomb going off in the city sure seems like everything's okay." There was silence on the phone. "Okay," he finally said, "you're talking to me. You're talking to Miles Pikar." He exhaled. "Dragon East, meet the dragonslayer."

99

I DIDN'T WANT TO TAKE the sullen kid with me, but didn't really have a choice. Taking him to an arcade and leaving him there would have been bad parenting, right? But leaving him in the car in the parking lot of a biotech company? Dr. Spock stuff.

"You did a great job," I said. "Finding that piece of paper. That helps a lot, Tim."

He didn't respond.

"We're going to get your mom, kid. Don't worry."

"*You* can't find her."

"What do you mean?"

He didn't tell me. I changed the subject, tried to put him in a better frame of mind. "What's the favorite thing you ever did with your mother?"

Tim was quiet for so long, I thought he'd ignored my question. But then he said, "If I was good, she would get a pizza and we would eat it on Thursday nights. She'd let me stay up late to watch TV."

"I bet you got to eat pizza every Thursday, didn't you?"

"Yup. Once, we went for a pizza to a place where Uncle Paul knew the man there—"

"Uncle Paul?" The kid called Murphy *Uncle Paul*?

"Yeah. And the man showed me how they spin it before they put all the stuff on it."

"Wow."

"And he let me put our pizza into the oven and I touched the oven with my hand and burned it."

"That doesn't sound fun."

"It hurt a lot. But I didn't cry. Uncle Paul said that I was the bravest kid he ever saw. He's really big. A lot bigger than you."

"I know," I said, a little melancholy now. "Uncle Paul was big."

"And then we ate the pizza and got another one and Uncle Paul said we were a great family. He said he wanted us all to be together soon."

My heart began to break.

"What did your mom say?"

"She said I shouldn't get my hopes up. But I knew

Uncle Paul wanted to be with us. He said I was the best son anyone could have. He really likes Mom a lot. He was supposed to come live with us but then Mom got sick."

"You didn't see him again?"

"Yeah. He said he was coming to live with us. But then I had to go live with Uncle Tony."

I wanted to ask Tim about his father, but couldn't bring myself to do it. I couldn't bear to hear that his dad was planning real soon to show him the big lake right next to Chicago.

The kid's story dredged up something deep, something I'd spent half my life trying not to disturb. All those promises not kept. My father promising, year after year, we'd go on a big vacation together—Disney World, deep-sea fishing trips, Phillies games. The promises, after his divorce from my mother, that we'd see each other every weekend, which quickly became two weekends a month, then one weekend a month, then holidays. The promises that he loved my brother and me just as much as he loved his new family, his new kids. But his new kids got to go to Disney World. We never did.

It's the tiny cuts that hurt the most.

I hadn't spoken to my father since I was kicked out of med school. He found out the day it happened, from a frantic call from my mother. He called me, made a stab at sympathy that lasted about five seconds, then gave me hell for what I'd done to my mother. Dad, defender of the woman he'd dumped fifteen years before to go shack up with a nurse twelve years his junior. Gloria was a taut blonde who'd drifted into my father's OR one day, then drifted into his bed. Mother to my father's other children, the kids he always wanted. Dad, the surgeon, who made sure my half- and step-siblings got whatever remote-controlled whatever, who made sure my mother had to go to court to fight him for every penny she needed to feed and clothe my brother and me. Dad, for whom Christmas was a vehicle to assuage his guilt. The extravagant, empty presents. The go-cart that neither my brother nor I could use because Mom lived in an apartment in town.

"I can't believe I raised a son who would do this," he said in that call from Pennsylvania to California all those years ago. *Raised a son?* All I could manage was a terse "Fuck you," which I'm sure confirmed for him that he'd done the right thing in neglecting this tainted, rotten offspring of his.

Just like me, the little boy with the fond memories of pizza had been set up. Paul Murphy wasn't planning on living with you, kid. Even if he hadn't wound up with his face mutilated and his throat cut, he wasn't going to live with you. A guy with two children, a wife, and a big house in Woodside wasn't going to say fuck all and come shack up with his deformed mistress and her kid, no matter how brave that kid was.

You liar, Paul Murphy, I thought. *You lying bastard.*

"Where are we going?" Tim asked.

"I have to talk to someone. There's a company . . ."

But the end of the sentence didn't form. Both Murph and my father were nattering away in my head. *Lying bastard?* they said to me. *Take a look in the mirror, Nate.*

"What company?" Tim asked.

My lies are little ones, I protested to the phantoms in my brain, *for a higher purpose. Higher purpose?* they mocked. *Like fudging that data?*

Okay, I told them. *Not that.*

"It's a company called Tetra Biologics," I said to Tim.

Murph and dear old Dad wouldn't let up. *Higher purpose? Like telling this kid his mother's going to be okay?*

She is going to be okay, I replied.

She's not. And you know that.

"Cool. That's where Uncle Paul works." Tim was peeping up over the dashboard, looking expectantly at the road ahead. "Maybe he knows where Mom is. Can we see him?"

I took in the face with the excited almond-shaped eyes, the hopeful half-smile, and realized this boy hadn't had much to smile about lately.

"Uncle Paul's got a lot to do," I said, the lie ripping to shreds any honor I had left.

100

"THAT WAS FAST," I SAID.

"I'm nothing if not fast," Miles Pikar replied. "Dragon East Imports, my friend, is a small company in the City by the Bay, which—"

"I know that," I said.

"—which does not do a lot of importing, it seems."

"So, what do they do?"

"Nothing, man," Miles said. "Its listed value is about three hundred bucks. Got no assets except for a phone and a fax machine."

"Damn it."

"But, it does have an owner, Sino Sun Holdings—"

"Great—"

"Which is a shell corporation based here."

"Not great," I said. "Are the officers listed?"

"Of course. Three of them. All deceased." I thought I heard keys tapping.

"They're straw men," I said.

"Sure are. Dead men don't do a lot for the bottom line."

"So, the only connection we have is these three people. Can you run the names to find out if these guys are listed as officers for other companies? If they used them once, then—"

Miles sighed heavily.

"Look," I said, "I need to know who was running the clinic. I need some sort of proof."

"Maybe it's time to talk to some of your government pals."

"I don't have many government pals left."

"Guilt somebody. Someone might be interested."

"I can't go to anybody. That's why I called you."

"Why not?"

I looked at Tim, made decisions and revisions. After a beat, I told Miles about Dorothy Zhang, choosing my words carefully. I could tell that the kid—now munching pensively and delicately on his hot dog—was tuned to me like a shortwave. I told Miles about Brooke.

"Whoa, man," Miles said. "Heavy. Sounds like you need the cops more than me."

"I don't need the police. I don't want the . . . the bad people to do anything. You think if the police get involved they're just going to let . . ."—again I looked at

Tim—"they're just going to let DZ go? And lay off Brooke?"

Silence on the phone, then Miles said, "I gotta think about this, man. I gotta think."

The click on the other end of the line was rushed, hasty, and hit me like a slap.

Frustrated, I threw the phone into the console.

"He's not going to help you find my mother," Tim informed me.

"It doesn't matter. We'll find her." I hoped I sounded at least half convincing. As an afterthought, I said, "Don't be a coward, Tim. Try never to be a coward."

A few minutes' drive from Tetra, I asked Tim whether he wanted a soda. Kids love soda.

"You said soda was bad for you," he informed me.

"When did I say that?"

"When I saw you in school. You said it made you burp and go broke."

The kid's brain was like Velcro. I made a note to watch what I said. "I was kidding. Do you want any or not? Offer going once, going twice . . ."

"Yes, but I have to pee."

I didn't see how those two things were exclusive of each other. "We can do both, Tim. That's the single greatest thing about America: you can get a soda and pee at the same place."

My sarcasm quieted him and gave me yet another thing about which to feel guilty.

We stopped at a convenience store. I bought two Cokes, and Tim disappeared into the back to use the can. Outside,

I dug around in my pockets for a card I hoped was still there. It was, and I dialed the number. Alex Rodriguez said she was surprised to hear from me.

"I need to meet you now," I told her.

"I don't know if this is the best—"

"It's about Paul and—" I stopped myself. "We need to meet, Alex."

"But not now. How about tomorrow? I have meetings all afternoon. My schedule is packed."

"Clear it."

"Excuse me?"

"Clear your schedule. Tetra is involved."

"In what—" She didn't finish the sentence. "When can you be here?" she asked instead.

"Seven minutes."

101

I SWUNG THE CAR INTO THE Tetra parking lot, and pulled to the far end, away from the colony of vehicles close to the building's entrance. It was hot in South San Francisco, much hotter than in the city proper. The dizzying number of microclimates in the Bay Area always stumped me, a guy from Pennsylvania who was used to hearing it would be 92 in York, 93 in Harrisburg, and 92 in Lancaster. That day, it was more like 71 in San Francisco, 91 at Tetra. "Nature's air conditioner," as the folks in SF called the fog, was great for Caucasian guys like me with an overactive metabolism. The problem was that Nature's air conditioner had just about the range and coverage of a window unit.

Anyway, I was not dressed for Mojave temperatures. And I was not dressed for success. The patina of dried water, tears, sweat, and mucus had formed a palimpsest on my shirt, which meant I'd have to keep the jacket on. At least the big white monster of a building in front of me would have real, man-made central air.

"Come on, Tim." I opened the door and reached for his hand.

I wasn't happy about towing the kid behind me, but if the events of the day taught me anything, it was that you can't abandon an eight-year-old in a vehicle in ninety-plus degree heat.

We walked across the parking lot. Tim's sweaty hand kept slipping from my grip when our steps fell out of sync. It was like holding on to a squid.

"Uncle Paul took me up to his laboratory before—"

"Tim—"

"—and showed me liquid nitrogen and we froze a grape and smashed it on the floor. It was like a marble. It was so cool."

He looked up at me. Why was the kid making me do this? "Uncle Paul isn't here today," I said.

"Where is he?"

"He's . . . on vacation."

"With his other family?"

"Yeah," I said, loathing myself. "With his other family."

* * *

From all the way across the lobby, I could tell that Alex Rodriguez wasn't thrilled to see me. And when her eyes locked on the yard monkey next to me, her face pulled to an actual scowl.

She drew close to us, and I stood. "This is Tim," I told her.

"Uh, nice to meet you," Alex said. She stuck out her hand and Tim, taking the cue, shook it. From the stiff formality of her movements, I could tell Alex was about as comfortable with minors as I was.

She glanced at the security guard behind his desk, returned her gaze to me. "Let's talk outside." Somewhere in the subtext was the message that Tim was not invited. Alex, though, wasn't satisfied with subtext. "It'll be cooler in here for Tim."

I put my hand on the kid's head. "She's right, it is cooler inside. You stay here, okay, kiddo?" I took a few steps, then turned back. "You going to be all right? You want your book?"

"I'm all right," he said.

Maybe some dormant paternal gene awakened then, because I kept stealing looks back at Tim as I followed Alex across the marble, through the glass doors.

"You're babysitting?" she asked once we were outside. She wasn't wearing a lab coat, just normal, meeting-type garb: thin, tight summer-wool pants, a blue button-down shirt open to just above the cleavage. Very put-together.

"You could say that."

"Not only do you yank me out of my meetings, but you bring a child—"

"I didn't have a choice. You can't leave a kid in the car in this kind of heat. Anyway, he's well behaved."

Her face froze for a moment, a moment in which it seemed she was trying to read me. Then she broke the stare. "Okay, Nate. Why don't you tell me what's going on?"

"Why don't you tell *me,* Alex?"

She cocked her head sideways, eyes slanted toward me, giving the sense she felt she was conversing with a nut. "I . . . I really don't know what you're talking about. You said this had to do with Paul. And Tetra."

"The disease in the photos I showed you is dermatofibrosarcoma protuberans. You heard of it?"

"No. I'm not an MD—"

"It's a cancer of fibroblasts."

I searched her eyes for any flicker, but saw nothing. I continued, "One of the women in the photos I showed you is dead. Last name Ming. She was shot in the face along with her husband. Her tongue cut out."

"I read about that—"

"Another man we found died in a hit-and-run."

"You're saying Paul *knew* about these people?"

"Yes. He had photos of both of them. And he had photos of eight others who are not coming forward because they're terrified of ending up like Paul and the Mings. These people are in pain, Alex. The condition might be treatable if it's dealt with early."

"What do you expect me to do about it? Paul and I were just friends—"

"I found the substance that's doing this, an injectable with a street name of Beautiful Essence. It was being used in an illegal clinic in the Richmond. Best I can figure, they're taking Beautiful Essence, mixing it with fibroblast stem cells, and injecting the combination." I tried again to read her face. Again, nothing. "The clinic was blown up today—"

"Oh, my God," she murmured.

"You heard about this?"

"It's all over the news." Her face was ashen. "I thought it was a terrorist attack."

"Why would terrorists blow up a nail salon?"

"The news said . . . You're saying that Paul was involved with this?"

"Yes, Paul was up to his chin with this. He knew about it and I think he wanted to stop it, which is why he had those pictures. He was going to expose the whole thing, Alex." I paused, deciding to withhold, for the moment, any mention of Murph's financial windfalls.

"But that has nothing to do with me," she said.

"Tetra's involved. That's how Paul got involved."

A flagstone path led to a bench atop a small mulch-covered knoll. Alex walked up the path. "What are you talking about?" she asked.

"Regenetine."

"Regenetine has nothing to do with this."

"It's recombinant fibroblast growth factor-1, right?"

"Yes . . . How did you know that? That's confidential."

"It's all over the literature. Tom Bukowski and Peter Yee initially published on it at the University of Illinois. Jonathan Bly published on it here. You're taking fibroblast stem cells and amping them with FGF. That's the process, isn't it? You make the fibroblast cells grow by adding the growth factor."

She sat on the bench. I sat next to her, facing away from Tetra, toward a complex of squat buildings shimmering like polished steel between us and the Bay. Emblazoned in colors on the upper corners of the structures were the names of the inhabitant companies: Hieroglyph, Tenzer, BCI Communications. The buildings surrounded a three-sided courtyard, with gaps where the points of a triangle would be. Inside, I could see a fountain and well-watered ornamental vegetation. No animal life, though. No human trailing a hand through the rippling pool, no seagull hacking apart a french fry.

"What happened between Bukowski and Yee?" I asked Alex.

"They were killed in a boating accident about two years—"

"I know that. I want to know what happened *between* them. Why was Peter Yee never part of Tetra? If Regenetine was such a blockbuster, why would the guy who headed up the original research not want to take part in the bonanza?"

"I don't know."

"Come on, Alex. There had to be rumors."

"There were rumors, sure. There'd been some kind of falling-out between Bukowski and Yee. Yee was a postdoc in Bukowski's lab at UIC. Something happened. The boat trip was them trying to patch things up. That's what the rumors say, anyway."

"Why the falling-out?"

"I don't know. I got here after they died." She looked at me. "You really can't believe Regenetine has something to do with these sick people."

I took out the bill Tim had found. "This was in the clinic that was blown up, the one where Beautiful Essence was injected. It's for a shipment of fibroblast stem cells. We also have samples of what we think is fibroblast growth factor. We're analyzing them now."

I handed her the paper, scrutinized her face for any reaction. There was none.

"Do I have to spell it out?" I asked. "Stem cells and FGF at the clinic? Stem cells and FGF at Tetra? Come on, Alex—"

"Regenetine is for wound healing. It's not cosmetics." She said it firmly.

"Spare me. You guys aren't going to make billions from wound healing. You're going to make it from cosmetics."

"That's true," she answered evenly. "Wound healing would be first, and then we'd exploit the cosmetics treatments. The CEO wanted to extend the patent by first getting approval for wound healing. Tetra was going to push off-label use for cosmetics—get some traction there—and then apply for a patent on the cosmetic use."

"How much work has been done on the cosmetic angle?"

"We're setting up Phase 2 trials now."

"Phase 2?" In the long road to FDA drug approval—sometimes upwards of ten years—Phase 2 was when efficacy was evaluated. Phase 1 was safety. Both involved tests on humans. "All the safety data is in?"

"Yes. It's all been cleared. It's very safe."

"Has it always been very safe?"

"I don't know. It's not my project."

"And no security breaches at the company? No possibility of an early batch of Regenetine sneaking off?"

"Of course not. Security is extremely tight."

We sat in silence as sweat slid from my hairline down

my cheeks. Only the faintest hint of perspiration glossed Alex's forehead. I was a Pennsylvania boy, after all, and she from sweltering central California.

"This is too much, Nate. You come to me, tell me the company I work for is embroiled in this fibrosarcoma thing *and* with Paul's murder? That's impossible."

I took back the bill of lading. "Look, the folks who ran that clinic were using the same process you're developing here. If Beautiful Essence resembles anything like Regenetine—if it's FGF—Tetra's on the hook."

"And you call that evidence? I mean, you're not a cop or anything. This will just be your word against . . . I mean, aren't there laws about evidence?"

"I don't know about the laws of evidence. All I have is a piece of paper and the samples we're analyzing. But you're right, any good lawyer would tear this to shreds. I don't even know if the police would be interested."

"So why are you doing this?"

I did not answer her. Instead, I gazed across the searing landscape to the sun-burnt hills separating us from San Francisco, looked over my shoulder to the futuristic structures encroaching on the old machine shops and light manufacturing. Apart from the signs that injected the occasional red or blue, the colors were muted and dead, as if life had been drained from here. As if both the past and the future of South San Francisco was not humanity's, but machines'.

I wiped my arm across my forehead, and it came away wet. "Alex, I need your help here. I need to see the Phase 1 report. I need to talk to the man who did the research on Regenetine. I need to see Jonathan Bly."

"Nate, I can't do that."

"Then, I may just need to go to the police."

Without looking at me, she inhaled deeply, held the breath for a moment. Then she exhaled. "Do you always go for the scorched-earth tactics, Nate?"

102

FIFTEEN MINUTES LATER, ALEX WAS telling her administrative assistant to watch over Tim. The assistant—a tall, muscled white guy named Ty—was good-humored about it, actually more than good-humored. Perhaps it afforded him a little break from the drudgery of returning phone calls, sending faxes and e-mails, and otherwise being the paper and electron shuffler for his bosses.

Tim gripped *The Hobbit,* which we'd retrieved from the car, in both hands.

"You want some juice?" Ty asked the kid.

Tim looked at me.

"That's a great idea," I said, surprised he'd sought my okay. "Ty's going to take good care of you. I'll be back in a few minutes."

"C'mon, Tim," Ty coaxed. "We got a bunch of different kinds of juice. Grape, cranberry, orange. You look like a grape man to me."

I decided Ty either had rug rats of his own or was the oldest in a family of fifteen.

"Sure," Tim said.

As we broke from Ty and Tim, who were beelining toward the canteen, Alex said, "I can't believe I'm doing this."

"You're doing the right thing."

"I'm doing the right thing. But maybe for the wrong reasons."

"The wrong reasons?"

"For that son-of-a-bitch Paul Murphy." Her tone was too sharp—it was a little tell—and I decided to go fishing.

"Your son-of-a-bitch just-a-friend Paul? You were just work buddies, right?"

"That's my business."

"Once people started dying, it stopped being your business, Alex. He had kids, Alex. Five and two."

She stopped. Her eyes blazed at me. "We had a fling, Nate. Is that what you want to hear?"

"I just—"

"Six weeks. That's it. And one month after that, he was killed."

Murph, I thought, *Murph, Murph, Murph. Who the hell are you?*

"Paul never said anything to you? Nothing about the sick people?"

The elevator doors opened, and we were nearly bowled over by Dan Missoula, he of Harvard and the monster handshake. He looked up from a sheaf of papers he was reading, met my eyes, then said to Alex, "What's he doing here?"

"Not now, Dan."

Missoula stuck his foot against the elevator door, keeping it open. "Alex, this is *not* appropriate—"

"Not now." She pushed past him into the hallway. Though Dan Missoula was technically Alex's boss, there was no hint of deference in her voice.

As we made a turn in the hallway, I looked back. Dan Missoula stood there, holding open the elevator doors, his eyes drilling into me.

We arrived at the Regenetine suite, and walked into the lab. There was a quiet hum of activity in the place: white-coated, goggled worker bees with pipettes in their hands hunched over multi-well plates, orbital shakers gyrating slowly with trays of liquid on top.

"I don't need to see the lab, Alex. I need to see the report and to talk to Jonathan Bly."

She kept her eyes on the people and equipment. "You can't see Jon," she answered.

"Why not?"

"He's on vacation or something."

"Or something?"

"I don't know, Nate. I was told he was on vacation."

"Great time for the lead scientist to take a vacation, huh? Right before you go to the FDA again? Did he go on a boating trip or something?"

"That's not funny, Nate. Jonathan probably hasn't had a break for over a year. People burn out."

Right, I thought. There's a time and a place for burning out. For Jonathan Bly, head of the Regenetine project, this was neither: the boss does not take a vacation during what had to be one of the most crucial times for the biological. Companies generally don't fuck around with the drug approval process. "There's nothing I need to see here."

We entered a small conference room. There was a binder on the table. "I spoke with Dustin Alberts—"

"Your CEO?"

"The one and only. He okayed this." She pointed to the binder. "The Phase 1 report," Alex said. "Knock yourself out."

Irritated, I said, "I am here, Alex, because I am trying to figure out who killed Paul and his family. I am here because there are at least nine people out there who are dying because they got some bullshit cocktail shot into their faces."

"You have no idea the position you're putting me in."

"Whatever position you're in isn't nearly as bad as that of the people who got shot up with Beautiful Essence." I took my seat at the table, reached for the binder. Alex left the room.

In the end, I needed less than five minutes. The report—what had been provided to the FDA to prove that Regenetine was safe—was crammed with table after table of data. But I wasn't interested in that. I looked to the end, to the summary, then to the FDA response. As Alex said, Regenetine was safe. No fibrosarcoma. Nothing more than redness and erythema at the injection sites and one case of superficial infection.

I leaned back in the chair. Here I was, enjoying almost unprecedented access to the inner workings of a freaked-out biotech. I had no doubt Alex's boss—Dustin Alberts, the Big Man himself—had done the calculus and figured letting me poke around would be preferable to the public relations shit storm that would occur if anyone even got a whiff of a connection to a strange form of fibrosarcoma.

Maybe everything *was* copacetic. Something stank, sure, but it was possible Tetra was an unwitting accomplice.

Alex appeared in the doorway. "Find anything?"

"No."

"So you're done now? Or you want to check the bathrooms to see if we stuffed any corpses into the toilets?"

"You're going to be fine."

"I don't *know* if I'm going to be fine. I'm vouching for you, Nate. If you go screaming to the press about what we're doing here, or go to our competitors, Tetra will sue me to the last stitch of clothing I have."

Not that that would be the end of the world, I thought. I asked, "Do you have Phase 2 data for the cosmetic application of Regenetine?" Phase 2, the stage in clinical trials where the efficacy of a drug or biological is established.

"The clinical trial is blinded," she replied. Blinded trials are those in which neither the participants nor the researchers administering the treatment know whether a placebo or the real drug is being injected. "The data's still coming in," she said.

"Do you have pictures?"

"Pretreatment and at two months."

"I want to see them."

"It's blinded. We don't know who got the treatment and who didn't."

"I still want to see them."

Alex glared, then said, "I'll be back in a minute." She left the room and returned, well, about a minute later. "Follow me," she ordered.

She led me out of the conference room and lab. On the same floor, we arrived at a small room so crowded with computers there was little room left for the humans. Inside, a man sat hunkered behind broad flat-screened monitors. He looked up when we entered, mumbled hello.

"Jerry," Alex said, "can you bring up the Regenetine images, the series 1 images from Phase 2 for the antiaging?"

Jerry, a Polynesian-looking guy with spiky hair and sharply angular glasses, stared at her. He didn't move.

"Just do it," she told him. "Mr. Alberts authorized it."

"Who's *he*?" Jerry asked, eyeballing me.

"It doesn't matter," Alex said.

"I'm not comfortable with this," he said stubbornly.

Alex glowered at him, then picked up a phone. "This is Alex Rodriguez again. Is Dustin available?"

Dustin? My, my, we seem to be on super personal terms with the CEO. Then again, it was a relatively small company, and Alex had been with them for a while. Still, I got a hint of why Alex could give the brush-off to Dan Missoula. This woman knew where the power lay, she knew how to forge alliances. If she'd been born a millennium earlier, she'd have been making treaties with the king, marrying off a daughter, running her own fiefdom.

She shoved the phone at Jerry, who took it as if he were being handed a live viper. "Uh, hi, Mr. Alberts, this is Jerry Tagaloa down in Bioinformatics and— Yes. Okay. Okay, sorry to bother you, I just wanted to make sure."

He hung up and, not meeting Alex's eyes, swiveled back to his computer.

On the big screen, an image popped up: a white woman, in her fifties, crow's-feet around the eyes, furrows in the brow, fine wrinkles throughout. Her nasolabial folds looked like they'd been dug from the nose to the corners of the mouth with an awl.

"Before," Alex told me. Jerry brought up another picture and placed the two side by side on the screen. "After."

The difference was striking. The woman's nasolabial

folds had been smoothed out, the crow's-feet nearly erased. The furrows looked like they'd been filled in with putty. Though the study was blinded, it was obvious this woman had been in the treatment group. And the damned treatment worked. Boy, did it work.

Regenetine was going to be a blockbuster. A lot of people were going to get rich.

"Jerry, bring up the whole series," Alex told him.

He obeyed. The screen exploded with small before-and-after pictures. I could see that some of the study subjects—both men and women—showed a noticeable improvement. Some did not.

"Not going to be hard to tell the treatment group from controls," I said.

"Probably not," Alex agreed icily. "You had enough?"

"Almost," I said, and walked into the hallway. When we were out of earshot of the suspicious Jerry, I turned to Alex. "You have no bad feelings about Regenetine?"

"It's not my project—"

"Doesn't matter. Do you have any reservations about it?"

"No," she said firmly.

"Did Paul have contact with the Regenetine group?"

"None that I know of."

I thought hard. I felt as though I were back in residency, confronted with some baffling patient, ordering test after test and coming up with nothing. You know something's wrong—the patient has a fever, her blood tests are a little screwy—but everything diagnostic comes up negative. So you begin to scramble. You order tests for every virus under the sun, you order a repeat of that X-ray. You cross your fingers that you find your answer before you have to throw in the towel, before you punt and tell your patient the last thing she wants to hear: *We just don't know what's wrong.*

"I need to talk to Bly," I told Alex.

She scowled at me. "I told you, Jonathan's not here."

"HR won't know where he is?"

"You think he told HR where he was going?"

"If he's the director of research, yeah, I expect he did."

She was silent.

"Paul Murphy and Tom Bukowski are both dead, Alex. Peter Yee is dead. And you're telling me no one knows where Jonathan Bly is. How—"

I shut up. Two white-coated women appeared at the end of the hallway, walking toward us. Alex said hello to them and they passed us, resumed a conversation about someone's bat mitzvah and the exorbitant cost of flowers.

"I'm going to have to call the police on this," I said, lying to increase the pressure.

"Don't," she said. "Let me think for a second." She cut her eyes to the floor for a moment, then looked back at me. "Don't call the police. Give me today, I'll find Jonathan." She pulled out a business card and wrote something on it. "This is my cell. Call me before you do anything."

I agreed.

"And, really, don't call the police. If something is wrong—*if,* Nate—calling in the police will just alert people here that they're being looked at."

"They already know they're being looked at. I'm here. They know I'm here. Even your damned CEO knows I'm here."

"But you didn't find anything, did you?"

I smiled at her when I saw what she was driving at. "No. I didn't find anything."

103

I DON'T KNOW WHAT I expected when I returned to Alex's suite. Maybe Ty bouncing a giggling Tim on his knee. Maybe Ty reading from *The Hobbit,* doing funny dwarf voices, Tim guffawing and eating it up, escaping for a time from the darkness that engulfed his little life.

But what I saw was not the *Romper Room* scene I'd hoped for. What I saw was Tim sitting in a chair, his elbows on his knees, head in his hands. Ty had pulled his office chair around to face him, and spoke in low tones. He raised his face to me.

"No one told him about Dr. Murphy," Ty said. "So, I . . . I didn't know," he faltered.

"That's okay," I said quietly, not meaning it.

I felt Alex move away from me. I heard the door to her office close.

Slowly, I walked to Tim. "You lied to me!"

"I know," I said. "And lying is a very bad thing and I'm really sorry I lied to you. Let's—"

"I'm not going with you!"

"Tim . . ."

"Why did you lie? You can't lie. You *can't.*"

"I told you I'm sorry."

"We were going to be a family! And now we're not. And my mom's going to die, too, isn't she? She's going to *die*!"

Unable to think of anything substantive to say, I offered more grape juice.

"I don't want juice!" he screamed.

I extended my hand toward him, trying to be gentle, avuncular, contrite, whatever would get through to him and give him comfort. He wanted none of it.

"Get away from me!"

Before I could figure out another lame attempt to mollify him, he hopped off the chair, shoved me back, and ran.

The boy ran the wrong way. Wrong way, because the hall dead-ended in the direction he was going. He saw this, too, and wheeled around. His eyes met mine and I have no doubt that this furious, grief-stricken child would have come at me swinging if he'd had a few more pounds on him. As it was, he didn't have a few more pounds and he didn't swing. He did have legs, though, and he ran past me. I ducked back into the office, grabbed his book, and ran after him.

Tim punched through a door marked Exit. I chased him down the five flights of stairs, across the lobby, to the parking lot, through the vehicles shimmering like scarabs in the late afternoon sun. He was running without direction, as if pushing himself to exhaustion would exorcise the too-powerful emotions. As I trailed behind him, I couldn't help but think of myself at the hospital, screaming as I waded through the fountain. I couldn't help but sympathize.

Eventually, Tim could keep it going no longer. He slumped to the asphalt at the tail end of a green SUV. He sat rigidly, staring straight ahead, refusing to acknowledge me. I sat cross-legged in front of him, saying nothing.

We held that pose for ten minutes. A few people passed us, leaving work for the day. I smiled; they either forced a smile or asked me if everything was all right. I assured them all it was fine.

"I shouldn't have lied to you," I told Tim.

He didn't reply.

"It was wrong of me. But I wanted to protect you. I knew you would be upset. You have a lot to deal with, for anyone, really, a kid or an adult. Your mom and . . . I just didn't think you'd want to know about Uncle Paul." The words seemed to evaporate in the heated air.

Tim brushed off his pants and got to his feet. He was a good kid—a very good kid—and it was killing me that he was going through this. It killed me that he'd been forced to put his trust in someone who kept breaking faith with him.

And because this kid was with me, because I'd lied to him, I thought about a change in tactics. I balanced risks and benefits; I balanced getting someone found versus the risk of getting them killed. I made my choice.

"Want to take a little hike?" I asked.

As we retraced the steps I'd taken with Alex just an hour before, I punched numbers into the cell.

Evidently, Jack Tang had finished picking through the burnt-out shell of Spectacular Nails, since I was able to reach him at the Bryant Street station. He barely got through his salutation when I blurted out, "They have Dorothy Zhang."

The unflappable detective was . . . flapped, I guess you could say. "The newscaster? Who does?" he asked irritably. I guessed the explosion at the nail salon had, indeed, fucked up his day.

I told Tang everything I'd been holding back from him: the clinic, my being there, Beautiful Essence and the stem cells, Regenetine and the stem cells, Dragon East. Tang drank the information silently. When I mentioned Uncle Tony, Tang stopped me.

"Uncle Tony, you said."

"Yes. You know him?" I asked.

"Sure. Tony is the name of a big cheese in the Chinese community here. Real name's Garheng Ho. He's one of the elders in a tong called the South Chinese Merchants' Association. Businessman with a couple shops on Grant Avenue. Go on. Finish your story."

As I finished, Tim and I made our way past the bench where Alex and I had stopped. He was leading me now, along a path through the mulch and into a parking lot for the next building. A hundred yards in front of us, the black granite fountain was framed perfectly by the corners of the two silver buildings, backgrounded perfectly by the mirrored face of the third. The fountain itself sputtered six inches of water that fell and spread out over its broad, flat surface before falling to a trough below. Tim headed for its clean lines, maintaining a distance close enough to hear my words. His steps were careful and unhurried.

It's going to be okay, I wanted to say to the boy. *We got Bard the Bowman with us now. I did my best, but it wasn't enough. I know when to ask for help, kid.*

It's going to be okay.

"What do you want me to do about it?" Tang asked.

For a moment, I could not speak; this was not what Tang was supposed to say.

"I don't know," I said. "You're the police. Go find Dorothy Zhang."

Tim stopped and turned.

"I'll put the word out," Tang said.

"Good." I expected him to offer something else, but he didn't. I helped him. "Go after Dragon East. Go after the owners of Dragon East. I'll give you something else: it's a front company. It's owned by another company called Sino Sun."

Tim began walking again, into the lonely courtyard, toward the lonely fountain.

"We know that," Tang said. "I have someone working that up for me."

"Good."

"My next question is: how do you know that?"

I didn't think it appropriate to involve Miles Pikar with the police. "I have someone working that up for me," I evaded. "But that's not important. The important thing is that Tony—Garheng—is involved somehow."

"You know that for sure?"

Sure I was sure, but I didn't really want to tell him an eight-year-old was the source of the information, or that he was with me, leaning into the trough of the black stone fountain, fishing something out of the clear water.

"It's your job to figure out how he was involved, right?" I asked, hearing the annoyance in my voice. "I'm telling you this much: he's involved. Go out there and get him."

"We can't just 'go get him,' Doc."

"Why not? He's a kidnapper. He kidnapped Dorothy Zhang. Don't you people freak out with kidnapping?"

"Look, Dr. McCormick, you've given me some valuable information. I am going to talk to Mr. Ho, I will talk to the people at Tetra—"

"What about Ms. Zhang? Kidnapping, remember?"

"According to your story, Mrs. Zhang went willingly with someone you *presume* to be Mr. Ho. She never actually told you that's who she was going to meet, correct?"

"*Ms.* Zhang. She didn't tell me, no."

"And you have no indication other than some gut feeling that she didn't go with him willingly. Correct?"

I saw that what Tim had fished from the fountain was a collection of pennies. He tossed them, one by one, back into the water: *I wish, I wish, I wish.*

"Correct."

"And," Tang continued, "if we're going to talk about missing persons, I don't even want to get into the possibility that you have something to do with an eight-year-old who might or might not be missing—"

"Arrest me, then."

"I would if you were here. Then I'd shoot you for all the trouble you're giving me. The boy still with you?"

I sighed. "Yes, he is."

Tang's tone changed, and if you could hear a man smiling, I heard it. "I'm not going to arrest you or shoot you, okay? The Tim Kim missing persons report had some problems with it, basically that they couldn't get in touch with the family and were going only on the word of the principal at his school."

"So you want me to bring him in?"

Suddenly, Tim spun from the water, three pennies sitting wet and glistening on the black stone.

"Sure. Bring him in. We'll contact Child Protective

Services; they'll stick him in some facility for a few days or weeks until someone picks him up or they find foster care—"

"Forget it." To Tim, I said, "You're staying with me."

"I want to see my mom," he said. I could hardly hear him over the splashing water.

"The police are going to help us find her, sport."

"You can't lie," he said.

"I'm not lying." Speaking into the phone, I said, "Inspector Tang, would you mind telling Tim here that we're going to find his mother?"

"Look, I can't guarantee—"

"Here's Tim," I said.

I pushed the phone to the boy.

"Yeah," he said, his eyes on me. "That explosion *was* big." Then, "I just want her to be okay. *He* can't find her," he said. "She went with Uncle Tony." Then, "Okay." He handed the phone over to me, then went back to tossing the pennies, retrieving them from the water.

"I don't appreciate you making me say that to the kid," Tang told me. "I don't want to get his hopes—"

"And I don't appreciate the foot-dragging. Remember the Mings, Inspector? We don't have any time—"

"There's no *we* here," he said. Now he was irritated. "There's just the SFPD. So, Inspector Dr. McCormick, since you have it all figured out, why don't you tell me how to do my job?"

"Go find this Tony, bring him in. Question him and . . . and arrest him. I don't know."

"And if he's threatened *Ms.* Zhang, what exactly do you think he'll say to us? If he has something to do with this clinic blowing up or the Mings' deaths, what's he going to say?" He didn't wait for an answer. "He's going to insist on getting a lawyer. And let's not even consider the kind of shit I'll catch for hassling a prominent member of the community when all this proves to be crap."

Yet another reason to opt for vigilante justice. If you can hack it, if you can stand the thought of going to jail for your efforts.

"You've been watching way too much TV, Doc. We can't break down doors, torture the shit out of people, and get the information we need before the commercial." His tone softened. "Like I told you, I'll talk to Garheng Ho, we're tracing Dragon East. And I'll speak with the Tetra people about any dealings with Mr. Ho. I will build a case if a case can be built, but it will not happen today." He waited a beat. "You're not happy with this."

"I'm ecstatic. Can't you hear my giddy laughter?"

For his part, Tang did laugh. "Get yourself some rest, Doc. Take the kid to see a movie. And don't screw around with this anymore. You could be right. And if you're right, you're in danger. Both of you. And worse, you could fuck up my case. You understand me here?"

Yeah, Inspector Tang, I understand you.

I ended the call. It was hot here, entirely too hot. The combination of highly polished architecture and solar migration had, at that point of the day, focused much of the sun's energy on this courtyard. I didn't blame the denizens of Hieroglyph and Tenzer for staying cool in their reflective, air-conditioned buildings.

"Come on, Tim," I said. "Let's go."

As he flung the rest of his pennies into the fountain and

scrutinized the ripples, my cell vibrated. I punched the Talk button.

"It's Alex," the voice on the phone said.

"Alex—"

"Jonathan Bly wants to meet with you."

104

"I'M SORRY," TIM SAID.

We were driving west toward Pacifica, a small town along the coast just south of San Francisco, to see Jonathan Bly, the wayward scientist from Tetra. I'd gotten his number from Alex, called him, and set up the meeting.

"Sorry for what?"

"I yelled at you."

"Yeah, well . . . I should have told you the truth about Uncle Paul."

The sun was in its late-afternoon fireball stage—huge, orange, flaring—and gave us an eyeful as we dropped to Route 1. It was much cooler here, thank God, than it had been a dozen miles east.

"You were trying to protect me," Tim reminded me.

"Yeah, I was," I agreed. "I'm happy you noticed." My smile—rock solid a second before—began to quiver. Taking the boy to a rendezvous with Jonathan Bly was not, I knew, doing a great job of protecting him. But I had nowhere else to take him. Once again, I toggled through my options. Ravi? In a lab across the Bay, and one of the last people Tim would want as a babysitter. Millie Bao? In Atlanta. Jenna Nathanson? Some random teenager at the mall?

Child care is such a bitch these days.

"We're going to find my mom, aren't we?" he asked.

My smile completely fell away. "You heard Inspector Tang. You bet we're going to find her."

Tim considered this, then turned to his window, dragged his finger across the glass. "Why is the sun so big at the end of the day when it's smaller in the middle of the day?"

"You have to ask a physicist about that."

"A physicist?"

"Yeah. Physics. The physicists are a weird bunch, though. They have pointy heads and can't hold a conversation. Not like the biologists. Biologists are cool."

"Are you a biologist?"

"Kind of."

"Well, I think biologists are cool then, too."

Tim Kim's charm offensive was working wonders. We were finally bonding. Really, how hard could this child-rearing thing be?

"You hungry?" I asked. We had an hour or so before I was to meet Bly.

"I think I'm pretty starved, Uncle Nate."

Uncle Nate.

"You like Taco Bell?"

"Oh, *yeah,*" my charge said.

Pacifica, California, famous for its surfers and its fog and, oddly, for a south-of-the-border fast-food joint located squarely on the beach. The sun was giving its last show over the Pacific; gulls and teenagers cackled and squawked on the broad deck outside the Taco Bell. Tim had his chalupa, I had mine. Sun, sea, hormones, rampant commercialism . . . I couldn't help but feel good about a perfect moment in a Californian paradox.

But perfect moments don't last. The chalupas disappeared; the sun vanished. Darkness ushered in darkness. My mind began to drift to unpleasant things.

"Who are you calling?" Tim asked when I pulled out the cell phone.

"Remember the lady we saw in the hospital?" He nodded. "I just want to make sure she's feeling better."

The ward clerk answered the phone, took my name, and found the resident on duty. The hospital had my name as a contact and so the resident was willing to part with information.

"Transfer orders are in," the resident told me. "Ms. Michaels went to Sequoia a few hours ago."

I got the number from him.

"What's the insurance situation?" I asked. Nothing's scarier than health care bills these days. Fibrosarcoma afoot in the population? Missing TV celebrity? Ha. Try five grand for a transfer between hospitals. *That's* terror.

"Dr. Nathanson came up with some justification. I don't know if there will be a fight with the insurance company over the transfer or not."

I made a note to do something very nice for Jenna. I could always set her up with Ravi, but that had as much chance to be punishment as gift.

I called Sequoia Hospital—"Who are you calling now?" Tim wanted to know—and confirmed that Brooke had arrived. She was doing well, they said. May even extubate her tomorrow, they said.

"You make too many phone calls," Tim observed as I dialed the next number.

"There are a lot of things going on."

"Can I go over there?" He pointed to the railing. I told him not to fall off as I punched the Talk button.

"You have sent me on a wildest of wild-goose chases, my friend, but I'm about to snare the crafty fowl." Miles Pikar's voice cracked over the cell.

"Good—"

"But I'm not quite there."

"How close?"

"Don't know. Best guess is not that long. We got some pretty wily dudes on our hands. Shell corporations, on- and off-shore. Dummy front companies. You'd of thought these guys worked at Enron. One more thing. It seems that one of the companies holds a big interest in . . . Guess."

"Ah, Jesus, you're going to tell me it's Tetra, aren't you?"

"You are a man of wisdom and prescience, Dr. Nate."

I took a mental breather, tried to assimilate this. "Miles, see if you can tie any of this to a man called Garheng Ho and something called the South Chinese Merchants' Association. It's a tong in San Francisco."

"Tong?"

"A Chinese-American gang . . . or, not really a gang. It's complicated. Look, I'll try to get back to you later tonight. If I don't, give Jack Tang at the San Francisco Police Department a call—"

"Whoa. Whoa. I'm doing this for you, dude. Not for the cops."

I wanted to protest, but decided against it. I didn't want to be responsible for any flack he caught for helping me out. Besides, I was exhausted, loaded down with greasy chalupa, and worried about too many people. "Okay, Miles," I said, "whatever you want."

"That's it? You letting me off the hook that easily?"

"You don't owe anything to me," I said halfheartedly. "It's my mess. Besides, the police are working on this. They already know Dragon East is a shell."

He laughed. "How long do you think it will take the cops to piece this together? To trap the beast, you have to understand the beast, Doctor, you have to *be* the beast."

I began to see where this was going; I began to see my role in this little waltz. "Don't be a beast, Miles. Go run your company."

"Look, dude, I'm already the beast," he said, sounding a little deflated. "You know, I started Paladin fifteen years ago. Security stuff for the little man, originally, before we branched into database work. Now, we have contracts with DoD Intelligence, the NSA, some big, privacy-snooping companies. I compromise myself every day I walk in to work. I build things that would have made the Stasi proud. Why? Because we got shareholders and we got customers."

"Everybody does, I guess."

"You know what a paladin is?"

"Kind of."

"He's a knight. A paragon of virtue and chivalry. We ain't knights anymore, dude. We play footsie with the devil now."

"Even so, this isn't your problem."

"Whether it is or not, I don't have to compromise on it.

I talk a good game, but it's been a long time since I put my values where my mouth is."

"So what do you want me to say?"

"I want you to twist my arm to do this. Guilt me. Remind me I'm a corporate hack who's lost his values. Then I got something to hide behind when Angel gives me grief or if the shit really hits the fan."

I smiled. "All right, you valueless, soulless corporate hack. I'm giving you the chance to redeem your soul and you spit in my face. You hear that?"

"What?"

"That's the sound of shoulder popping while I twist your arm."

South of town, the motel where I was supposed to meet Bly rose like a Styrofoam cooler sandwiched between another motel and the now-dark coastal scrub of a protected stretch of beach. It looked no different than the Holiday Inns you see scattered like refuse around the country, except that this one faced the Pacific instead of a strip mall. Bly's choice wasn't bad: if you're on a budget and have to hide out, this seemed like a decent place to do it.

I parked Dorothy's car in a dark public lot as far as I could from the brightly lit entrance of the motel. The Holiday Inn's sodium lights were fifty yards away, and cast long, sharp shadows around us. Combined with the low vehicular census, they gave the place a lonely, eerie feel.

I cut the engine and took the keys from the ignition. I sat for a second, thinking about Tim and next steps, finally deciding to go for a little partnership parenting, lead him to his own correct decision.

"We both know you shouldn't leave kids alone in cars, right?" I asked.

He nodded.

"But we both know that I want to protect you, too, right? That's something adults do for kids, they protect them."

"I know."

"So, we have a decision to make. It might not be safe where I'm going—"

"No, no. You can't—"

"I mean, it might not be safe for *kids*. I'll be fine." This was getting a little more complicated than I'd planned. "What would you do in my position, Tim?"

He didn't have to contemplate his response. "I'd take the kid with me," he said immediately.

Wrong answer.

"But maybe," I persisted, "maybe it would be better if the kid stayed in the car than for him to go into a place where it might be dangerous for kids."

"I want to go with you. I'll be good. I promise I will."

I sighed. "You have to stay here. No more debate."

Tim began fooling with the power window—up and down, up and down. Sea air washed into the car, smelling of brine. "You *can't* leave a kid in the car. It's against the law."

"I have to leave *this* kid in *this* car. Only for a little while." Up and down, up and down. "You're going to break the window," I said.

"No I won't."

"Stay in the car, Tim. Put the seat back and lie down so no one can see you."

He didn't move—except for the index finger that kept toggling on the power window switch—so I got out of the car, rounded to the passenger's side. I opened the door and lowered the seat. He continued to sit bolt upright.

I walked across the polished, dun-colored floor of the lobby, nodding to the young woman on the phone behind the desk. I took the elevator to the second floor. I was nervous, but didn't really see the reason for it. Jonathan Bly wanted my help as much as I wanted his. In fact, when I called him he'd said, "You have to help me. I'm in deep."

I tried to make him tell me how deep and in what, but he refused. "Not over the phone," he'd insisted, and hung up.

So, here I was. I knocked on the door, watched the peephole darken, listened to the voice that came from the other side of the door, asking who it was. I told him.

I heard a lock being undone, then the door opened a crack. The slide lock was still engaged. "You're alone?" he asked, his face only a slice behind the door.

"Yes."

"How do I know it's you?"

I sighed, then pulled out the CDC badge and thrust it at the crack. His eyeball roved up and down, matching the picture on the ID to my face.

The door closed, then opened wide. "Come in," he said.

Bly looked awful, as if his tall, wiry body had been run through a dozen rounds of chemo. His skin was yellowish, his red eyes sunken. The little hair he still possessed tufted uncombed from random places on his head. He looked worse than I did after a night on call. I wondered how long he'd been here: sweating, worrying, not sleeping. I asked him.

"Three days," he said.

Seventy-two hours in this suite—a large room with a sitting area broken away from the bed. The place was about as welcoming as a third-rate frat at Penn State—synthetic fabrics everywhere, pizza boxes strewn about, opened containers of Chinese food stacked next to the sink. The funk of human habitation—that and something else—stung my nose.

Bly sauntered across the room to an open window. On the window sash, a cigarette smoldered on top of a plastic cup. He brought it to his lips, and I could see his hand tremble. "I refuse maid service," he said, perhaps explaining the mess in the room, the smell. He sucked deeply on the cigarette and blew out the window. "Jesus, I haven't smoked since high school."

Since I didn't really care about Bly's health habits, and as I didn't have time to waste on small talk, I asked, "Why am I here?"

"You were Paul Murphy's boy."

"Paul Murphy's *boy*?"

"His boy. His fall guy."

"What the hell are you talking about? Paul came to me for help."

Bly lit another cigarette from the first, and dropped the first into the cup. Water covered the bottom, and the cigarette hit it with a *hiss*. "Yeah," he agreed sarcastically. "He came to you for help. Just what kind of help did he come to you for, Dr. McCormick?"

"He found out something about Regenetine and Tetra.

He found some connection between what you guys were doing with FGF and the stem cells and an analog called Beautiful Essence, which—"

"Beautiful Essence. Stupid fucking name."

"—which was being distributed through a clinic in San Francisco, and which was resulting in people getting tumors. Maybe Paul knew that an earlier, dirtier version of Regenetine had been stolen from Tetra and was on the black market." Yet even as I whitewashed Paul Murphy, my doubts about him grew. There was the money that had found its way into Murph's account; there was Jonathan Bly calling me Murph's *boy.* Murph's fall guy.

Bly continued to smoke, not saying anything. The whole situation began to feel very wrong, the disheveled room too small. I wondered how long the power window would occupy Tim. "I'm leaving," I said, and turned toward the door.

"Wait." He took a beat, then began bargaining. "I tell you what's going on, you help me."

This tactic took me by surprise. I remembered Wei-jan Fang's stab at negotiation in the clinic, his desperate attempts to get "protection." Now Bly was making a similar play. Both of them, rats jumping from a sinking ship. This told me that whatever secrets enveloped Tetra and Beautiful Essence were fraying quickly.

"Help you how?"

"Help me get out of the country if I need to, help me get some immunity from prosecution, depending on what happens."

I laughed. I mean, come on, who did this guy think I was? "I can't do that."

"*Help,* Dr. McCormick, *help.* I know you're not a prosecutor, but you can help me. You can put in a good word."

"All right. Whatever. I'll help you the best I can." I stepped back into the middle of the room, cleared a pizza box from the loveseat. "Talk," I said.

105

"REGENETINE IS SAFE," BLY TOLD me. "The process of using the growth factor to stimulate fibroblast growth is safe. The ratio we had for Regenetine and the stem cells is safe. There are no problems with the biological or the process. But we had an earlier version . . ."

"And that earlier version was not safe," I said.

He coughed. "It was still FGF-1, but we hadn't modified the molecule. It was too powerful. It caused the stem cells to proliferate like crazy."

"How could you not pick that up?"

"Because we didn't have the results from the longitudinal studies in animals yet. The long-term studies showed it was mutagenic."

Mutagenicity is the property of some substances to cause mutations in cells.

"I saw your paper on PubMed," I said.

"It was a good paper," he said absently.

"And this earlier version—the one that caused the mutations—is Beautiful Essence?" I asked.

"Yeah. As far as I know. Anyway, I started getting word about how to tweak our FGF-1. I followed my orders and I tweaked and, lo and behold, no problems. Whatever they were telling me worked. The mutations stopped."

"Who was telling you to make the changes?"

"It came from the CEO, of all people. Dustin Alberts."

"How did Alberts know what changes to make? He's not a scientist."

"Well, that's the thing. He kept telling me not to ask any questions. So I kept plugging away, keeping Regenetine on track. But I guess I have that curiosity-kills-the-cat thing, so I started poking around. I found a bunch of tissue samples. Human tissue, marked 'Affected' or 'Non-affected.' "

"Where were the tissue samples from?" But I already knew the answer.

"From the Fang clinic."

Dorothy had told me they'd taken biopsies of her tumor. I thought back to the small plastic tube of tissue Tim had found at Fang's clinic. "Fang's patients—they were guinea pigs. To work out the problems with the first product. That's why Alberts knew to tell you how to change the protein."

"Yes."

"Who was analyzing the tissue? Who told Alberts what to tell you?"

Bly looked at me with a half-smile on his face, as if he were waiting for me to acknowledge a joke. When I didn't, the smile broadened. "You really don't know, do you?"

It took me a second to track this, then I realized. "Oh, God . . ."

"Not God, even though he probably thought he was."

Bly was grinning now. The bastard was enjoying this. He'd probably spent his three days here waiting for a moment like this. "Yes, Dr. McCormick. Your good pal Paul Murphy."

My gut felt hollow. "Why would he do it?"

"Oh, he had his reasons. Paul always had his reasons, right? You live in Paul's head and you could justify almost anything. You know that old joke? The one about the kid who murders his parents?"

Bly's cigarette was gone, and he lit another. If he kept going like that, he'd have bigger things to worry about than immunity from prosecution, things like emphysema and cancer. "There's this kid who murders his parents, then gets up before the judge and asks for leniency because he's an orphan. That's Paul. I've been thinking about that joke a lot. Hilarious, right?"

"What were Paul's reasons?"

"You know about his company? The one that crashed and burned?"

"No."

"His biotech venture out of grad school?"

"No," I repeated, anger simmering in my voice.

"Paul figured he'd found the Holy Grail—the answer to cancer. Problem was, his answer was wrong. He couldn't get venture or angel funding, so he went to family and friends. He blew through a couple hundred grand from these not-rich people before he had to close shop. Paul felt terrible. He *really* wanted to pay it back."

"So?" I asked weakly.

"So, the bosses at Tetra tapped him for the extracurriculars with the tissue. Paul did the analysis for Tetra, got some cash on the side. But *some* cash wasn't enough. You know how these things go."

"No. I don't."

"He went down that slippery slope." He coughed—an annoying raspy thing that dissolved into uncontrolled hacking. "They needed someone to get the Chinese guys and their clinic out of the picture. They chose Paul."

"Who needed?"

"Alberts, Tetra's CEO. He was the only one who knew about Fang's clinic. He got Paul to think on it. He gave him lots of money to think. And Murphy thought and, eventually, he found a niece of one of the Chinese guys—"

"Oh, no," I whispered. "God*damn it.*"

"Yeah, it stinks, right? Paul finds this niece, who also happens to be real attractive, and tries to pump her for information on what they're doing. She doesn't know much, but she gets sick, and she gets pissed off. Paul and she hatch a plan to bring down the Chinese. This all has to be very quiet because there's a big wall between Tetra and the Chinese guys. The only connection was the tissue and the Chinese investment in Tetra. With Regenetine coming on line, Alberts was fuming that the Chinese would get a piece of the pie. Alberts thought the Chinese were parasites."

"Paul seduced Dorothy Zhang as part of this? Deliberately?"

Bly smirked.

"And what about me? How did I fit in?"

"Paul said you weren't the most . . . um, *moral* guy on the planet. If you didn't play along, he said you'd go for the money they were going to offer you. You get your money, you call in all your CDC friends and shut down the Chinese, you channel whatever investigation away from Tetra so that everyone there can say, 'What Chinese? What's going on here? We had no idea about the Chinese or people with tumors all over them.' "

"What if I couldn't be bought?"

"Paul didn't see it as a problem. As long as he could influence you to channel the investigation, Tetra would be okay. And if things went really wrong, Alberts could give the word and the Chinese would take care of you. That's how your buddy put it: *take care of you.*"

My thoughts swirled as if I had just popped into an epileptic seizure. The money in Paul's accounts, the half-information he'd deliberately fed me, his affair with Dorothy. A sad, sick, impotent rage filled me. There I was, having spent days brooding on revenge for Paul Murphy, only to find out that the friend I was so desperate to avenge had duped me. And to get revenge on *him,* a dead man, was forever beyond my reach.

The irony made me sick. "Why are you involved in this?" I asked Bly.

"I was involved from the minute I found the tissue in Paul's lab and asked him about it. Slippery slope."

"Why didn't you go to the FDA?"

"And tell them what? That I found some human tissue at the lab that wasn't supposed to be there?"

"Yes."

"And then what? Lose my job? Lose all my stock? Become one of those whistle-blowers who can't get hired as a grocery clerk because he's tainted goods?" Bly raised a bony hand to rub his stubble. "I should have gone to the

FDA. God, I wish I had. But I didn't. And then it was too late."

We sat there, me on the bed, Bly on his windowsill. The ocean spoke quietly in the background.

"Everything changed when Paul was killed," Bly said. "The wall between Tetra and the Chinese crumbled. Everyone got busy looking out for themselves."

"And now you want to look out for yourself."

"You bet your life I do. You saw what they did to Paul."

Silence filled the room. Even the sound of the ocean seemed to slip away.

"I'll call the police," I said, finally. "You stay here or go somewhere else, if you want. Just lay low, and I'll get in touch with you when—"

At the door, there was a gentle rapping.

106

BLY, AS CRACKED AS HE was at that point, didn't flip, as I would have expected. In fact, his reaction was all wrong, way too calm. He stubbed out his cigarette, walked to the door, and, without looking through the peephole, undid the deadbolt and the slide lock. I was standing now, my body tight.

A woman pushed into the room. "Hello, Nathaniel," she said.

"Alex."

"It's okay," Bly told me. "She's okay."

Alex gave me a wan smile, walked across to the open window, and removed her shoulder bag. "Nice view," she remarked, and turned from the window. "I need a drink."

"I got water," Bly offered. His voice had taken on an entirely different quality, softer somehow, more pliable. He smoothed his hair.

"A drink, Jon. Drink means *alcohol.*" She sat in a chair, stretched, her body tensing and relaxing like a cat's. "I need it but I don't need it. Tomorrow, when all this is done."

"What are you doing here?" I asked, but Alex ignored my question. Instead, she turned to Bly, who was filling a glass with tap water.

"You told him?" she asked. He nodded.

"You knew about this?" I asked her. If she knew what Bly had just told me, it meant that she'd been lying to me from the beginning. *They're all in on this,* I said to myself, *all of them.* I looked at the door, at the window, wondered which would be the best means of escape.

Again, she ignored my question. "Did you ask him?" she said to Bly.

"Ask me what?"

"Not yet," Bly said. He handed the glass to Alex.

"Ask me *what*?" Both their heads turned. Finally, I thought, someone realizes I'm here.

"We have problems," Alex said. "As I'm sure Jonathan told you. We need your help," she said.

Neurons buzzed and fried as I tried to make sense of what I was hearing. *Need my help?* The only thing I was sure of at that point was that I'd be damned if I'd help them. "Oh, no," I said. "No way."

"Nate, listen to me. This is a horrible situation. Truly awful. We're trying to make the best of it."

"You're *involved,* Alex."

"Yes, I'm involved. And I wish I weren't. But your friend Paul pulled me into this—"

"Ah, Christ. Paul again?"

"Yes, Paul. He was desperate for help. And then when we—" She cut herself off. "I tried to help him."

I stabbed a finger at Bly. "He said I was Paul's fall guy. He said I was being set up."

Alex flashed a look at Bly, who was leaning against the wall, arms crossed so tight he looked like he was hugging himself. "We weren't going to let anything happen to you. *I* wasn't going to let anything happen."

I sat on the bed again, overwhelmed and confused. "Why didn't you go to the police as soon as you heard about this?"

"I was being *threatened* as soon as I heard about it. We all were." She hunched forward on the chair, opened her big brown eyes even wider. "Jon and I have everything assembled on our end. All you need to do is talk to the police and public health people and anyone else you spoke with. You tell them that this was an arrangement between Paul Murphy and Wei-jan Fang."

"Why would I do that?" I asked.

"Because it would give us time. We just need for this to blow over, then we can think. We can go to the police later."

"And what happens to Tetra? What happens to Garheng Ho? Everyone just gets away with it?"

"No one's going to get away with anything. You're buying us time so we can deal with this on our own terms. Jon and I think this is as horrifying as you do. But there is no other choice right now."

"There's always another choice," I said. "What happens to the people with the fibrosarcoma?"

"We can help them later, when this is all cleared up. They're not going anywhere. But there are more pressing issues now."

"What iss—" But before the sentence was out of my mouth, I realized what she was talking about. "Dorothy."

"Yes. Her."

I felt fury begin to rise; I felt my face getting hot. "Where is she?"

"I don't know, Nate."

"What are they going to do to her?"

"I don't know. But we all know what they did to Paul." She looked at me with what seemed like sympathy. "They're trying to force your hand, Nate, just like they're forcing Jon's and mine. We have to play along right now. When this is over—"

"It's never going to be over," I spat.

"—when this is over, we'll have time to bring everything together. Then we'll take them down." Alex stood from the chair, crossed to the bed, and sat next to me. "Talk to your friends in the police and public health. I know you might be uncomfortable about implicating Paul—"

"That's not what's making me uncomfortable, Alex."

"Okay, then. Good. Anyway, he won't care what you do. And Wei-jan Fang—my God, he's the guiltiest of all. Look at the big picture here, Nate: you'd be doing the right thing by helping us. And then we can do the right thing again and make sure no one gets away with anything. We do that *after* we're safe."

Bly, who'd been silent for the exchange, finally spoke. "You have to do it."

I could not believe what I was being asked to do. I could not believe I was being asked to help those—even for a short while—who'd slaughtered the Murphys, the Mings. Who'd assaulted Brooke. Who'd taken Dorothy.

And I could not believe that—if I helped them—any of us would be safe.

"I can't do it," I said.

"Nate . . ." Alex said, reaching for my hand.

"I can't."

"You can trust us," Bly said.

"Quiet, Jon." Alex's cool fingers wrapped around mine. "Nate, I'm juggling a thousand balls here. Things are moving very fast. There's not much time."

"I know," I said, sliding my hand out of hers. "That's why I have to call the police. We need their help to find Dorothy. We do that, and Garheng Ho and whoever else doesn't have any leverage, right? We need to talk to the cops—all of us—get things rolling."

"No. There's not much time because—"

Just then, I heard a phone trill some pop tune that seemed so incongruous in the circumstances. "Goddamn," Alex said. She stood up from the bed. She rifled through her purse and removed a cell phone, glanced at the number. Before she clicked the Talk button, she turned back to me. "Nate, *please,*" she implored.

Unable to make sense of anything now, unable to form words, I just shook my head.

She groaned and pressed the phone to her ear. "Yes." Then she said, "No." She hung up, dropped the phone back into her purse, and stared at me. "Why did you bring the boy, Nate?"

I slammed against the side of the car, breathing fast from the run through the motel and across the lot, breathing fast from a rising panic.

Tim wasn't inside.

"Shit," I said. "Shit, shit, shit."

I scanned the deserted lot, my eyes darting from the minivan to the old junker tucked in the farthest corner. All shadows and amber light. No sign of the boy.

A game, I thought. Please let this be some hide-and-seek.

I yelled Tim's name.

Someone—not Tim—moved into shadow from the pool of light near the motel entrance. With a loose, unhurried gait, he glided over the black asphalt. It was the stride of someone in control. As he got closer, I could make out the features—the dark hair, the broad face, the smooth skin. A darkness, the tail of a dragon, marred the side of his neck.

107

"THIS IS KWONG," THE TATTOOED man said into a cell phone. There were a few more words in Chinese, a silence, then a click as he snapped the cell phone shut.

I was in the back of a black sedan; Tim was in the passenger's seat. Kwong—Michael Kwong, who was not supposed to be in this country, who did and did not look like the picture I'd seen in the police station all those days before—was driving.

Tim turned back to me, his dark eyes like two holes in his head. "I stayed in the car," he said. His voice was accusing.

"I know," I said. The words barely escaped from my throat.

"You wanted me to stay in the car and I stayed—"

Kwong said something sharp in Chinese, cutting Tim off. The boy turned away to stare out the window.

Whatever was going to happen to me I deserved. I deserved it for putting this kid in harm's way.

The sloping bridges of Interstate 280 came into view; tiny dots of light skimmed the floating roadway. Kwong eased the car onto the highway, and we joined the northward flow of mankind, whose greatest worry was whether there would be a parking space available or whether the dog had been left alone too long. I imagined the music playing in the sleek cars that passed us; I imagined the soft lilt of conversation inside. I felt so separate from these people, so alone.

"Where are you taking us?" I asked, but Kwong made no reply.

I began to feel very afraid.

And I decided I would help them with whatever they needed. Of course I would.

Tim began to play with the power windows—his favorite car game that night. On the second cycle, Kwong fingered a button on the console. A few click-clicks pierced the silence while Tim tried the locked window, then gave up. That's one way to deal with it, I thought.

I vacillated, first this way, then that, my mind jockeying between two paths, both dead ends. Help Mr. Ho and Michael Kwong and protect the kid and his mother, who were surely being used as leverage against me? Refuse to help? I wondered if it even made a difference.

In a minute, I found, there is, indeed, time for decisions and revisions which a minute can reverse.

Through this back-and-forth, one thing kept rising, like bile, like bilgewater: I am no hero, never was. Murph was right about me all along. Brooke, too. Not the most moral guy, a bad friend, a poor partner. A competent doctor, maybe, but a disaster of a caregiver. Maybe it was time I just accepted that this was who I am, accept those dark things curled like worms in my DNA.

"What are you going to do with him?" I asked. "What are you going to do with Dorothy?"

At the mention of his mother's name, Tim turned to me and stared.

108

SEEING THE HULK OF TETRA Biologics against a dark asphalt sea, I was again reminded of a ship: the *Titanic,* the *Lusitania,* those mighty vessels whose sterns tipped to the sky before being sucked into the inky, cold sea. And though Tetra hadn't yet collected the tragedies of its nautical forbears, there was time yet for that. I felt a chill run through me.

Kwong took the car around to the rear of Tetra, where the asphalt sloped downward to a loading dock. The car glided down the incline and stopped nose first at a concrete ledge, above which were two large automatic doors. No worries about the vehicle being spotted, since it had effectively disappeared for anybody not looking directly into the loading dock. But that was probably a nonissue, anyway; no one unconnected to this thing was there, I was sure. There were no late-night worker bees running experiments. The cleaning staff had been given the evening off, no doubt, a gift from the gods at Tetra. The reason would be a hazardous waste spill maybe, a lie about necessary building maintenance. Maybe it was Rosh Hashanah that year—I never could figure out the roving Jewish holidays—and CEO Dustin Alberts had told everyone to take off to blow a shofar or two.

Anyway, the place was deserted.

"Get out," Michael Kwong said.

Tim undid his seatbelt and hopped out of the car. He was frightened, I could tell, but not panicky. Perhaps he knew something I didn't. Perhaps he was even comfortable with these people whom he knew. More likely, though, his eight-year-old brain couldn't take in what sorts of things these men did in the course of their jobs.

Kwong tapped on my window with the barrel of his pistol. "Out," he said.

Gun trained on me, I exited the car and Kwong indicated a man-sized metal door set next to the larger doors. As I walked up the concrete steps toward the door, I thought briefly of running. The thought of a bullet tearing through my brain stopped me.

"It's going to be all right, Tim," I said.

"I hope—"

"Shut up," Kwong said, cutting off the boy.

At the door, Kwong slid a card through a black box next to the door. There was a click, and he opened the door. "Go in," he said. I went in first, followed by Kwong and Tim.

We entered into a cavernous loading bay: concrete floor, stacks of wooden pallets, boxes of laboratory supplies held together with thick plastic wrap. Large containers of liquid nitrogen and oxygen were chained to the wall like gray metal prisoners. Only one bank of fluorescent lights flickered above us, giving the room a ghostly, dead feel.

I heard the door behind me close, and turned to make sure Tim was holding up. I didn't see him, however. I saw only a blur before I felt an excruciating pain on my neck and everything cut to black.

109

THE FIRST THING I REALIZED: I was not dead.

I tried to open my eyes, but squeezed them shut when pain crashed through the back of my skull. I tried again to open them, slowly this time.

The loading dock came into view, hazy at first. The pain made turning my head a real bitch, but I managed to get a few degrees to the right and left. I was alone. And I could not move.

My feet were lashed to the legs of a chair. I couldn't lean forward to see what they used to tie me, since my hands were bound behind me and fastened to the seat. From the sharp line of pain in my wrists, though, I assumed they used cable ties. I pulled, felt the plastic bite into my flesh.

All in all, this was not a very promising situation. But I was alive, and I was confused. Why was I not dead? Why, if they weren't going to kill me, was I tied to the chair? The obvious threat they posed to those I cared about was enough to get me here without struggle. So why did they go over the top, braining me and tying me up?

I tried to rock my legs back and forth, maybe get a little play going in the cable ties, but it was useless. They'd used three ties per leg, I could now feel, which essentially fused the lowest parts of my body to the chair. Underneath the chair, they'd spread a sheet of clear plastic.

To catch the blood? Definitely not a promising situation.

I sat and I thought. If nothing else, I'd at least gotten the ego boost of having put together a large part of this mess. Tetra and the South Chinese Merchants' Association tong. Partners in crime. Who'd have thunk it, except one renegade doc with no job, a few pennies in his bank account, and a disintegrated romance? And now that renegade doc was as good as dead. But, damn it, he was right. Huge consolation.

Considering my physical predicament at that moment, I couldn't help but think about Paul Murphy and what had happened to him.

God, I thought, *I hope they don't cut out my tongue.*

I won't talk, guys, I promise.

To get my mind off imperiled body parts, I thought about fun things, like what the hell had transpired to put me in this loading bay, in this chair, with a headache gnawing at the back of my skull. First, Murph—drowning in debt—gets tapped to help analyze the tissue samples retrieved from Wei-jan Fang's illegal clinic. As Regenetine gets closer to launch, and as everyone starts getting dollar signs in their eyes, Dustin Alberts wants to "get the Chinese off their backs." Again, Murph is tapped. Who better to protect your little conspiracy than a six-foot-two ex-linebacker with a squeaky clean reputation, severe money problems, and a guilt complex? Murph—ladies' man, Boy Scout—taps Dorothy Zhang, because she's the niece of Uncle Tony. She doesn't have much information (too bad) but she gets sick (poor thing) and she gets upset (we can use *that*!). Maybe Murph plants it in her head that she could help bring down the clinic, maybe the seed is already there.

She is, after all, an ambitious reporter, which probably made her easy to manipulate. She gets pictures of people suffering the same fate as she is, which provides Murph enough—but not too much—to interest a wayward, mid-level, jobless public health official. Because he's wayward and jobless and not the most ethical guy in the world, Nate McCormick will be easy to put on a leash. It will be easy to control and shape his investigation into Beautiful Essence and Wei-jan Fang. But the best laid plans of mice and Boy Scouts . . .

Somehow—a careless word from Dustin Alberts? a threat?—the Chinese find out about Murph's gambit. Millions are at stake. Murder and mutilation and all other sorts of hell break loose. At that point, wayward Nate McCormick is safe because he doesn't know much. He's safe because he's still a civilian. But wayward Nate McCormick, as Brooke Michaels said, never could leave well enough alone. So he rejects all things wayward, and makes it his job to find out what happened to the Boy Scout and his slaughtered kin. He finds the images of people with their faces gnawed apart by tumor. He's finally found a mission. He's happy, damn him. As the rest of his life falls apart, he's absolutely thrilled.

There was more to the picture, though, tendrils extending much farther back than Murph's call to Nate or even Murph's acceptance to do a little tissue analysis for Tetra's chiefs. The Chinese were on Tetra's back. Why? Did it start back before the inception of Tetra, in a lab at the University of Illinois?

I thought about Tom Bukowski and his postdoc, Peter Yee. I thought about them being killed in a boating accident. "Accident." Right.

My mind continued to drift, again back to Murph. How had the Boy Scout justified this? Paul loses big money in a botched business venture, he wants to pay it back. Moral, right? The right thing to do. He wants to keep the house in Woodside, keep the nice cars. Not as moral, but what the hell? Wife likes the house. To pay back Mom and Dad, to keep the wife in her castle, all he has to do is close down an illegal clinic that just happens to be pumping cancer into people. That's good, no? Sarcoma is bad; what sort of Boy Scout wouldn't try to stop it? And so what if he gets a greased palm in the process? He'll just ask his old pal Nate McCormick to run interference with the Chinese, set public health loose on them. Nate, if he plays along, will get something, too. Everybody wins. The really bad guys go to jail, Mom and Dad get their nest egg replenished, even Nate gets a little spending cash, maybe to replace that rusting heap he's driving. Oh, and if things go wrong, if Nate doesn't play along, the Chinese can take care of him. But what does that matter? McCormick fudged data in his PhD; he should have been hauled in front of the firing squad ten years ago.

How long had Paul Murphy sat with these ideas? How much justification did he work his way through until he was able to pick up the phone and call me? How much time before these ideas simply felt *natural* to him? Before he got used to it, and became a beast?

There was a sick inevitability to this: whether or not Murph had been murdered, I would be in the same position—legs bound, looking forward to awful things. Murph probably knew all along I would need to be "taken care of." From the instant I answered his phone call, I was destined for this. I should have showed up here the first day, offered myself for sacrifice, saved myself a lot of trouble.

A door to the loading bay—on the side opposite the outside doors—swung open.

Two men walked into the room. One was my tattooed pal, looking mighty dashing in his black suit, cream-colored shirt, gelled hair. The other man was older. He too wore a black suit—well tailored, conservative—but sported a tie loosened at the neck. It was the same man who'd answered the door in Napa the first time I visited Tim. Uncle Tony.

Underneath a No Smoking sign, he pulled out a cigarette and blazed up. Kwong stood silently next to him.

"You've made life somewhat difficult for us, Dr. McCormick," Tony said.

"I'm just repaying the favor, Garheng. Or Tony. Or Mr. Ho. What do you want me to call you?"

Tony found a chair near a pallet stacked with boxes of pipette tips, and dragged it over. He sat facing me.

Goody, I thought, we're going to have a real face-to-face now. Maybe a counseling session. Talk therapy led by Uncle Tony.

"Who have you told and what have you told?" he asked.

"Oh, well, there's a lot of things I've told to a lot of people. I once told a guy in high school I could bench-press two hundred pounds. I couldn't, though. One ninety was all I could get. How much can you bench, Tone?"

He stared at me, then shot a look over his shoulder to Kwong. Unfortunately, the look didn't mean "Boy, isn't Dr. McCormick hilarious?" It meant "Kick his ass."

Kwong was happy to obey. Crossing to me, he drew back his arm and hit me with a closed fist across the face.

Pain lanced through my jaw and my bruised neck. My head snapped to the side. I spat a gob of bloody saliva on the floor.

"Who have you talked to, Dr. McCormick?" Tony asked quietly.

"His name was Ed Scarborough," I sputtered. "He sat next to me in band. It was a *long* time ago—"

Tony's henchman hit me again. More pain. More blood.

"You like this, Dr. McCormick?"

I was quickly learning the man didn't appreciate my wit. "Not much," I confessed.

He laughed, and pulled out a cell phone. *My* cell phone, I realized. "Some of these numbers we recognize, some we do not. Who are they, Doctor?"

"My broker. My masseuse, who's very good, by the way. You should call her. You look a little tense—"

"I'm growing weary of your jokes."

Didn't the guy know that I dealt with stress by cracking jokes? Come on, Tony, I'm *coping* here. I spat another gob of blood on the floor.

"What do you think will happen to those you care about?"

"I don't care about anyone."

"Is that true?" He nodded toward Kwong. "You do not care for my great-nephew? You do not care for my niece? So be it. But I have trouble believing that you do not care for Dr. Michaels."

My mouth remained shut. Inside, though, I screamed at the man. Brooke? They'd pulled Brooke back into this?

"You have been speaking to Inspector Tang and Dr. Ravinder Singh." Tony studied the tip of his cigarette. "We know all about that, Dr. McCormick. And we will find who else you've been speaking to. When we do, you will call these people. You will tell them that you have discovered evidence that directly links Paul Murphy and Jonathan Bly to Wei-jan Fang and his most unfortunate clinic."

"Yeah. All that evidence I discovered."

"We will provide that to you and you will provide it to the authorities. You will be paid handsomely for your efforts, and you and Dr. Michaels can go live your American Dream."

I would be lying if I didn't find the offer seductive: help these guys out, buy that big pad in Santa Barbara, spend my days sipping margaritas and watching the sun dip into the Pacific? Or, fight this, risk having something happen to Brooke, to Tim, to Dorothy. Guarantee that something ugly would happen to me. An easy choice, right?

Only if you believed Uncle Tony.

"What will happen to the people with the fibrosarcoma?" I asked. "The ones you've been scaring into keeping quiet."

Tony nodded. "You are a true humanitarian, Dr. McCormick. Do not worry about them. We will ensure they receive the proper treatment." He dropped his cigarette on the floor and ground it under his foot. "Although one could argue that they—in their vanity—brought it upon themselves."

"Exactly," I agreed cheerfully. "Like your wife. Joan, that's her name, right? She had the treatments done?"

"My wife is a vain woman." He shrugged in a what-can-you-do way, and I could tell he was not entirely displeased with his wife's vanity. What I wouldn't give to have Auntie Joan wake up one morning with a bugger of a tumor gnawing through her lip.

"Where's Dorothy?"

"She's safe."

"And Tim?"

"Quite safe. I sympathize with you. You have been betrayed. You were betrayed by the same man who betrayed us. You were even betrayed by a little boy."

"Bullshit."

"Tim told us about your last meeting with Ravinder Singh. The boy told us Dr. Singh had taken items that belonged to us back to his offices. He told us you spoke with Inspector Tang, who we know well." I didn't see how this rose to the level of *betrayal,* but to each his own. Tony continued, "You cannot trust a child. You should know that."

"I'll make a note of that."

"You owe nothing to Paul Murphy, you realize that. We are simply attempting to redress the wrongs he committed. No one enjoys what has happened here."

"That's good to know."

"So, I ask you again, who have you spoken to?" Tony was hitting me from every angle: threatening, cajoling, trying to establish common goals. He was throwing everything against the wall to see what would stick. He was also throwing it against the wall to keep me off balance, to keep me confused. All in all, he was pretty good, pretty smart. But I'd been in enough investigations, I'd seen enough hidden agendas, to know where this was ultimately going.

"And I'll tell you again, in different words this time: Fuck you, Tony."

Then, just as I was about to rip through the cable ties, just as I was about to unleash a flurry of kung fu and use my brain waves to burn Tony to a crisp, Kwong strode up to me. In his hands, he carried a length of two-by-four. I didn't think he was going to whittle me a toy pagoda.

Tony said something to Kwong in Chinese, then stood. He dragged the chair back a few feet to give his man room. Kwong smiled at me, flapped the wood in his hand like a Mafia heavy. He positioned himself in front of me, drew back, and swung. The sound of the wood slamming into my left knee was like a Louisville Slugger knocking one over the wall.

The knee exploded in pain. I felt the rending and destruction of tissue, felt the electric surge of pain. The impact traveled up my leg, jamming the femur into my hip joint. In spite of my best efforts, I cried out. Then Kwong hit me across the face with the two-by-four. I felt a bone crack, felt my brains scramble.

"It is unfortunate," Tony said, "that you and Dr. Fang had such a difficult meeting. It is unfortunate he had to do this to you."

At first, I didn't understand what he was saying. But then it made sense. Tony was giving me the line I was to use: Fang had tied me up. Fang had beaten me. That would be my story. The only glimmer of hope I had is that they were still unsure about whether they were going to let me live or not. If they'd decided to kill me, it wouldn't have been a two-by-four across the mouth. It would have been something worse. A knife in the eye, for example. I could explain away bruises and broken bones. I couldn't explain blindness.

But they would decide soon. They would play the angles. They would look at my recent past and would realize they couldn't trust me to keep quiet. It was only a matter of time.

Or maybe they'd already decided. And maybe they just weren't telling me yet.

Tony held up my phone. "We will find out who you called," he told me. "We will be back. And then you will help us."

He and Kwong disappeared through the door, leaving me alone with my thoughts and the blossoming pain in my body.

110

THE AGONY IN MY FACE and my knee had lost its edge. It had become instead a persistent throb, still intense, but allowing me to clear my head a bit. As I did, I began to see the impossibility of my situation. The cable ties might be cut, I might be afforded a reprieve to call Jack Tang, Ravi Singh. They would pull Miles Pikar's number from my phone. I would call him. I would lie and tell him everything was fine. I would tell him about the evidence I discovered about Wei-jan Fang.

Goddamn you, Paul Murphy. Damn the day I met you.

I have always had this belief that rage—absolute fury—would enable me to move mountains. That I would be able to break through walls, bend metal, all that. It was a foolish thought, planted, perhaps, by childhood TV, by the show *That's Incredible,* in which men were able to lift cars off pinned family members. I was not even trying to lift a car. I was trying to break three millimeters of goddamned plastic.

I pulled at my restraints until I felt the cable ties bite into the flesh of my wrist, until I felt blood roll into my palms and slick my fingers.

When the struggle proved fruitless, I tried to calm myself. *Assess,* I thought, and began to probe the inside of my mouth with my tongue. Three loose teeth. A lot of blood, making my mouth taste like metal. I thought my left cheekbone was fractured, but couldn't be sure. I tensed the quadriceps in my left thigh, and felt pain sear through my knee. I didn't think the kneecap was broken, but it hurt. God, did it hurt.

No atheists in foxholes, I thought. Though I wasn't in a foxhole, I said a few prayers—bargains, actually, with the Big Guy. *God, if you let me get out of this, if you let Brooke be okay, if you let Dorothy and Tim be okay, I promise I won't fuck up like this again. I promise to get a good job and a 401(k), and a sensible car. I promise, I promise.*

The door opened.

Wei-jan Fang's face was still black-and-blue from his encounter with Ravi, but I was sure it looked a hell of a lot better than mine. He stood, taking me in.

"They got you good," he observed.

Ya think?

There was a sink in the loading dock. Fang crossed to it, ripped out a few paper towels, wet them. Then he walked to me, pulled the chair close.

He began to wipe the side of my face.

"Check the zygoma," I said.

Fang paused. "This will hurt," he warned, then he prodded my cheekbone with his fingers; I could feel the bone grind and crackle. It hurt.

"Broken," he said.

"My knee? Left one."

His hand went to my knee and pushed into the bone, moved the patella back and forth. No cracking, which meant that the kneecap wasn't shattered, which meant I would be able to walk if I ever got up from this chair. "That's okay, I think," he said. "Hurts, though?" I nodded, which hurt, too. He finished wiping my face and tossed the crimson-stained towels to the floor.

"You should have taken my deal." His breath smelled sweetly of alcohol.

"If I could do it over again . . ."

"Yeah, well . . ." He stood. "Who else have you told about . . ."—he waved his hand around in the air—"our little arrangement?"

I said nothing.

He sat in the chair again, rested his fingertips lightly on my left knee. "Please don't," I said.

"Dr. Singh, Inspector Tang. Who else?"

"No one."

"What does Inspector Tang know?"

"He knows enough."

"Enough for what?"

"Enough that he can help us," I said. "They're setting you up, you realize that. You are going to take the fall for all of this."

Fang took his hand from my knee. "I know."

"You know?" I asked.

"Yes."

"Then help me. Get me out of here."

"I can't do that."

"Then call the police. Call Tang. They want me to tell everyone that you and Paul Murphy were working together. That the buck stopped with you."

"I know. I helped them put the story together."

I didn't comprehend.

"You should have taken the deal, Dr. McCormick. You should have helped me when you could."

"Help me *now,*" I pleaded. "It's not too late."

Fang gave me a sympathetic smile. He shifted in the seat and pulled something from his back pocket. A wallet. He opened it and showed me a picture inside: a pretty woman in jeans and a leather jacket holding what looked to be a five-year-old girl. Fang was in the picture, too, hand on the child, kissing the woman. "That's my wife and my little girl." He stared at the picture for a moment. He put the wallet back in his pocket. "I'm sorry, Dr. McCormick."

Things began to make sense. "They have your family?" I asked.

"I'm going to go to jail for a long time," he said. "But that way my wife and daughter will be safe." Fang stood. "This was me, you know that? They said you pieced together a lot of what was going on, but did you know this was mine?" He raised his hands. "Beautiful Essence, Regenetine, Tetra Biologics. Have you ever had anything stolen from you, Dr. McCormick?"

I seemed to remember having my lunch money taken once, but I don't think that was his point.

"Do you know how hard it was to come up with the perfect ratio? To change the FGF so that it fastened to stem cells in the test tube but didn't disperse through the body? Then to figure out its market? Do you know how hard it is then to have your life's work stolen from you?"

"Tom Bukowski and Peter Yee," I said. "They ripped off your idea."

Fang was silent.

It was coming together. Peter Yee and Bukowski had stolen Fang's work, or at least that's what Fang thought. Perhaps Fang worked with Yee in Bukowski's lab all those years ago. Maybe the falling-out between Yee and Bukowski had something to do with that, with the two scientists fighting over the spoils of Wei-jan Fang's work.

"You killed them," I said. "For stealing Beautiful Essence. Regenetine." I took his silence for agreement. My left eye was swollen, but I managed a good fuck-you stare. "Then you're getting what you deserve, Dr. Fang."

"Tom Bukowski got what he deserved."

"And Peter Yee? Or was his death just collateral damage?"

"Peter Yee is alive and not so well, Doctor."

"Yee is dead," I said. "He died when the boat blew up."

Fang smiled faintly. "Peter Yee, Dr. McCormick, is standing in front of you."

111

"YOU WORKED IN A LAB, you know what it's like." Fang was pacing now. "I sweated for years in Tom's lab at UIC. I published like mad. I figured out the peptide tail to stick the FGF to the cells; I perfected the process for making the altered FGF. I figured out that if you add it to stem cells in the test tube, instead of injecting it straight into tissue, you would get a more robust and controlled response. I perfected a process that would be worth a billion dollars on the cosmetics market.

"I trusted Tom. He was my principal investigator, last author on all my papers, my mentor, my damned *friend.* So I told him my idea. Within a month, he had filed a patent, without telling me. Six months later, he brought me into his office and offered me a staff position at a little company he was putting together to exploit the potential of *my* idea."

"Tetra," I said.

"Tetra. I was supposed to be happy being made a staff scientist in a company to which my work gave life. Tom got together with Dustin Alberts. I became . . . bitter."

I thought back to my days in the lab, to the infighting, the easy, ruthless, careless theft of ideas. If an exploited class exists amongst the educated elite, it is the grad student, the postdoc. And if you're unlucky enough to nest in the aerie of a rotten principal investigator, you are going to be devoured, you are going to be exploited, stolen from, abused. I felt some sympathy for Fang.

"Tom didn't know that I wouldn't roll over," Fang said. "He didn't know that I had a cousin in China who was 'connected,' as they say."

"Michael Kwong? Kwong was with a triad?"

"You love your research, don't you?" He grinned at me. "Anyway, Mikey put me in touch with labs in Hong Kong, and I set up a shop over there. Then I came back here and opened up another operation."

"And the shop in Hong Kong is still active?" I thought of the recent cases of fibrosarcoma in China that Millie Bao had mentioned.

"Of course. So much money to be made, right? Anyway, I wanted to get back to the good ol' USA. Kwong connects me with Garheng Ho, who sets me up. Tetra's still screwing around with preclinical work, so when Tom finds out I'm back in town, making money hand over fist with Beautiful Essence, he freaks. I was way ahead of them."

"You were also illegal."

"Of course I was. Tom decided to use that. He and his pal Alberts tell us they're turning us in to the police if we don't shut down. Problem was, they didn't know who they were threatening."

It started to come together. "Tom Bukowski gets murdered. And Alberts agreed to stay off your back," I said. "And he let Garheng Ho—Uncle Tony—invest in Tetra."

"You're doing great, Doctor. Keep going: what's the upside for Tetra? See if you can get it."

"Tetra gets capital from the Chinese." I thought for a second more, to the tissue in the freezer at Fang's clinic, to something Jonathan Bly had said. "And they get data. They get data on how the FGF analog works in humans from the tissue you were taking."

"Bingo. Prize to the doctor in the chair."

It was a brilliant scheme. Truly. Tony and the Chinese had a protected market worth millions for Beautiful Essence, at least until Regenetine came out. When that was released, they would reap a fortune from an IPO. Or, if Tetra stayed private, from the proceeds of the biological.

"They know how to make money," I said.

"Yeah. *Qian.* It's all about *qian* for these guys, all these guys. Alberts, Garheng, Kwong. But for me, it was never about money. I'm telling you this because I think you can understand this." The look on his face was almost desperate. He truly wanted me to understand: to understand his anger, to understand his need for revenge. He wanted the same thing I wanted from Paul Murphy ten years before: a little sympathy, a little respect.

"It was all working out. Then those bastards at Tetra got greedy. We had to call Kwong in."

"How did he get here? There was a watch out for him."

"He got here because I gave Cousin Kwong a new face back in HK. A little nip and tuck, a little FGF-fibroblast concoction. Looks good, don't you think? Fifteen years younger. I took care of the acne scars, too." Fang's face, proud for a second, darkened. "I created my monster, didn't I?"

I thought of monsters. "The fibrosarcoma . . ."

"About half a percent of the people who get the treatment get the DFSP. I can't—" But Fang didn't finish the sentence. Instead, he said, "My idea, Dr. McCormick. My *idea.* But that's not the worst of it. They made me do these things. All those people, all those tumors. They knew what was going on and they still made me do it. Such a beautiful idea and they poisoned it."

I saw my opportunity. "Get back at them," I urged him. "You can have your revenge."

Fang shook his head.

"Let me go," I said. "We'll call the police—"

"Stop with the *police.*"

"Then, we don't go to the police. We . . . we take them here. How many of them—"

"Shut up."

"—How many of them are there?" My mind was scrambling for fantastic plans of escape and revenge. "You have a gun?"

Fang shook his head.

"There's *no choice,* then. You have a cell phone? Call the cops. Call them now."

Fang glanced at the door, then back to me. He sighed. "You don't get it, do you? Either I go to jail or I die. You're dead. One hundred percent dead. Accept it."

"You think your family's going to be safe when you're rotting away in prison? You trust these guys who've already screwed you over? You're a liability, your family is a liability." That seemed to hit a nerve. He winced. *At last,* I thought, *I got through to the guy.*

"My family . . ." he said.

He reached into his jacket. I thought he was about to pull out his cell, end this mess. Instead, he produced a small black pouch. He unzipped it. Inside was a syringe and a vial. "Potassium chloride. For you. If you live through what they're going to do to you."

I guess I hadn't gotten through to him.

If you have to go, getting a vein full of potassium chloride isn't the worst way. It will burn going in, but once the cation reaches your heart, it sets up a nice arrhythmia, and you die of cardiac arrest. A minute or two at most. Much better than having your body sliced apart or battered to a pulp.

My heart began to pound and I felt my burst of hope spiral. *What they're going to do to you.* I thought of Murph's wife, his kids. Of the feel of a blade sawing through my tongue. Of metal puncturing my eyeball. Fang was offering me a way out.

"Don't," I pleaded.

"You get out easy this way. No knives. No pain." He pulled the syringe from the case. "I'll tell them you died from the blow to your head."

He took a needle, put it on the barrel of the syringe, and uncapped it. He tore the metal tab off the top of the vial of potassium chloride.

I thought of blades and blood and screams, and Fang's offer began to seem more attractive. The best option in a field of shitty options.

"Let me do this for you, Dr. McCormick." Fang pushed the needle through the rubber stopper of the vial and took up a big dose of the liquid. "Please."

But he never got the chance to help me out the easy way.

Two men stepped through the door of the loading dock. With them was Dorothy Zhang.

112

HER FACE WAS SWOLLEN, FROM the cancer, of course, and from crying. There was a tiny flutter, a brief uplifting of my spirits, when I saw her. At least she was not hurt. At least that.

A tiny sound escaped her mouth, the sound a child makes when she's startled. She broke from the men and walked toward me, spitting something at them in Chinese. I recognized them. One wore the same baseball cap I'd seen him in outside Daniel Zhang's apartment. The other had the same spiky blond hair. Slowly, the blond guy closed the door.

As Dorothy approached, Fang stepped back, slid the black case into his pocket. Dorothy shot him a hard look, then knelt in front of me.

"You're all right," I said. I tried to smile, felt the pain ricochet through my face.

Her hand went to my cheek, her touch unexpectedly light and comforting. In that moment, all I wanted to do was close my eyes, rest my head in that hand, and forget about everything except for the feeling of her skin on mine. "You're not," she said softly, her face contorting, bunching the knots of flesh around her eye, on her lip. "They promised they wouldn't hurt you."

"I'm pretty sure they don't keep their promises."

She wheeled around to the two men who'd brought her, barked in Chinese. Her words fell before them like dead birds out of the air.

"They asked for your help?" she asked, turning back to me.

"Yes."

"Well, *help* them, Nate. Please, help them. I'll make sure they let you go."

"They're never going to let me go."

"Nate, I'll—"

"They are never going to let me go, Dorothy."

"They have Tim," she said. "You need to help them."

I looked at the two men between Dorothy and the door, at Fang standing miserably next to a pallet stacked with boxes. Why had they brought her here to pick Tim up? Why not take him to her?

Because it was easy to clean blood off the concrete floor. Because, if you're going to do your dirty work, why not keep it in one place?

"Kiss me," I told Dorothy.

Fleetingly she looked surprised. In her hesitation, I thought she was remembering the night in the motel room, remembering my pulling away. It was her chance to rebuff me. Instead, she leaned forward. Her hair brushed my cheek, her lips touched mine. I felt the knotty flesh push into my skin.

"Now run," I whispered.

She pulled her head back from me slightly, her eye caught mine, and I could see that she finally understood why she had been brought here. It wasn't to retrieve her son; she was to be used to make me do what needed to be done.

And neither of us was going to live through this.

She straightened, composed herself. "Timothy," she said to me. Then she turned to the thugs. "I left something in the car," she said. "I'll be back in a minute."

The thugs looked at one another, and—thank God—I saw indecision on their faces. *Go,* I thought. *Go.*

She walked past the guy with the cap. She drew close to the guy with the blond hair, glances going back and forth between the two men. Not the sharpest tools in the shed, these two.

But sharp enough. The blond reached a hand toward her and locked it on her arm. "We wait," he said.

Dorothy spoke sharply to him in Chinese. But he held tight.

"Let her go." The voice came from across the loading dock. Tony stood in the open door with the tattooed Michael Kwong.

To Dorothy, Tony said something in Chinese. She stood there, abashed and afraid. Slowly, she moved meekly to her uncle, walking like a little girl, and stopped in front of him. And, as you would with a little girl, Tony kissed her on the forehead. I couldn't help but think of Gethsemane, the betrayal in the garden.

"Who is Miles Pikar, Dr. McCormick?"

I said nothing.

Tony spoke in Chinese again, this time to the man on his left. Kwong stepped to Dorothy, grabbed her roughly, yanked her arm behind her back. She cried out. Kwong's arm went around Dorothy's chest, immobilizing her.

"You were such a beautiful woman." Tony raised a hand to her ruined face, let his fingers fall lightly on her skin. "Who is Miles Pikar?" he asked me again, still looking at his niece, still fingering her flesh.

"Imaginary friend," I said. "I got him a cell phone last Christmas, and he's been blowing through minutes ever since."

Dorothy said something in Chinese. It was angry and fearful at the same time. The only word I could make out in Tony's response was "Timothy."

"No," she whimpered.

"I'm waiting, Dr. McCormick." He spoke in Chinese again, and I watched as Dorothy's knees buckled and she slumped against Kwong. A soft, high-pitched whine escaped from her throat.

Whatever Tony was saying to her, it had to do with her son.

"Tell him, Nate," she begged. "Please . . . just tell him."

I said nothing.

The stream of words from Tony continued as I watched the woman break and fracture in front of me.

"Tell him!" she sobbed.

I knew this was coming. I knew the boy would be used. I knew his mother would be used. But I didn't expect it all to happen at once. I couldn't see a way through this double-teaming of miseries. I needed more time to think.

"He's a friend," I said.

"Yes?"

"We play video games together. Had a date to play *Black Nexus 4* tonight. Great . . . character develop . . ." The look of horror and fury on Dorothy's face caused my voice to fail.

Tony frowned. His hand fell from Dorothy's mutilated cheek and he said something softly to her, something that sounded like an apology. Then he turned away, removing a handkerchief from his pocket to wipe his fingers where they had touched her face.

"We will expect your full cooperation, Dr. McCormick," he said. "We have all night." He swept his gaze from me to Fang, then crossed to the door and held it open for Kwong, who shoved Dorothy through it. He said something in Chinese, and I heard Dorothy whimper. The door closed.

"What did he say?" I asked, my eyes locking on Wei-jan Fang. "What did he say!"

Fang lolled his head toward me. " 'Knives.' He said, " 'Get the knives.' "

113

I BELLOWED; I HOWLED. I pulled against the cable ties, burying them farther into my wrists.

"Stop!" Wei-jan Fang shouted. "Just stop. Shut up."

The blood in my mouth was nothing compared to the blood now on my hands.

Scripts were being written for me—for Ravi, for Jack Tang, for Dorothy and Tim. The only power I had left to me—the only way I could rewrite those scripts—was to say no. But I couldn't say no forever.

Knives, Tony had said.

The futility of the situation was overwhelming. I should

have taken it like a man, I supposed, looked fate in the eye, mouthed a calm "I regret I have but one life to lose" or something. But I couldn't.

"They're going to kill us!" I yelled. "They're going to kill *us,* damn it!"

The blond guy smirked; I wanted to cut the lips from his face.

"You think they're going to let you off the hook here, Wei-jan? Why would they do that?" I persisted. "You're going to do what they need you to do, and then you're *dead.* Just like me and everyone else. You realize that? What have you told your wife? That you were running a little medical clinic? You think they don't know that *she* knows, too? You think when you're *in jail,* they'll trust her to keep her mouth shut? You think they don't know what she'll do?"

Fang's eyes were now as dead as the Mings', as dead as the Murphys'. He'd thrown up a wall in the past few minutes, and I was never going to break through. His fear was bone-deep. Yet, I continued, "They played out all the scenarios, Wei-jan. They're not going to take any chances. They have *never* taken any chances. You know that even better than I do."

Fang's impassivity infuriated me. Not only was he killing himself, perhaps his family, through his inaction, he was killing me, killing Dorothy. And Tim. *Tim.* Knives were being unsheathed.

Fang patted his jacket. "I need a smoke," he said to no one in particular. He pulled a pack from his jacket, slid a coffin nail from the cardboard box.

The baseball cap stepped between Fang and the door.

"We're supposed to stay here." He sounded like a surfer. Pure California all the way.

"I'm going outside for a damned smoke," Fang told us, lipping the cigarette. "Unless you idiots can't watch a guy in a chair by yourselves."

I saw irritation cross the thug's face.

The blond guy, the cool one, said, "Smoke here."

"I can't, you moron." He pointed to the tanks along the wall. "You know what happens if that oxygen catches fire? That nitrogen?"

Well, oxygen can make things burn faster, but it won't blow up. Nitrogen isn't flammable. For a moment, I was confused about why Fang needed to be outside. Then I got it: to make a call. To get us help.

"There are butts on the floor," the observant man with the blond hair said.

"That was Tony," Fang said.

"He smoked here, you smoke here."

"Tony is an idiot," Fang said. He pointed to the large No Smoking sign over the door.

The blond guy contemplated, then repeated, "Smoke here."

Fang shrugged. "Don't blame me if we go up in flames." The baseball cap produced a lighter, flicked it. Fang sighed, then bent over. He pulled the smoke into his lungs, blew a cloud.

And the phone would stay in Wei-jan Fang's pocket.

I watched the doctor take a few puffs, then wander over to the side of the loading dock, near a collection of metal cans. The two thugs watched him, then lost interest. They began talking about baseball, about the Giants' rout of the Padres the night before.

Fang took a seat on a stack of boxes next to the cans. He caught my eye, glanced quickly at the cans, nodded once.

From all those years in the lab, I recognized the colors and shapes of the containers. Even without being able to read the lettering, I knew what was in them. Still, I didn't know what Fang was trying to say.

He inhaled deeply, then took the cigarette from his mouth. His hand drifted toward the cans.

It was then that I realized what Fang was doing. And I realized what I had to do.

I watched the cigarette arc to Fang's lips, watched the coal on the end glow brightly.

Now.

I toppled my chair onto the concrete and plastic. I yelled. Lying there, I flailed. I cracked my head against the floor, the *pop* echoing through my skull. I cracked my head again. My ears began to ring. I tasted blood in my mouth again.

I began to sing the first thing that came into my mind—unfortunately, the theme song from *Sesame Street.* "Sunny days, sweeping the clouds away . . ."

"What the hell?" the guy with the cap said, and ran over to me. He grabbed at my shoulders, and I thrashed. I banged my head against the floor, trying to hit it hard enough to be convincing but not hard enough to do any real damage. Pain tore through my skull and broken face with each knock on the concrete.

"Give me a hand here!" the guy shouted. "He's trying to kill himself."

Hands encircled my head from the back and held it firm; powerful hands clamped onto my arms. I sang the rest of the first verse of "Sesame Street," the interior of my skull buzzing as though filled with bees.

Then I heard Fang yell, saw orange licking from the floor, as ethanol from one of the cans sheeted fire across the concrete.

114

"SHIT!" FANG SHOUTED.

Hands dropped from my shoulders, and as I sagged back down to the floor, I watched Fang sprint to a fire extinguisher on the wall. The blond thug trotted over to the flames, and began to kick the burning liquid away from a pallet of cardboard boxes.

I continued singing. "Sunny days . . ."

The baseball cap gripped my head tight. "Shut up!" From the corner of my eye, I could still make out the drama playing out across the room.

The blond man's foot was flaming now, covered in ethanol. "What the fuck did you do, man?" he screamed, stamping his foot on the floor.

The flames slid under the pallet of boxes.

Fang was back at the conflagration, the extinguisher in his hands. He pointed the nozzle at the blond man's foot, then swiftly raised it and let loose a blast of powder into the thug's face. The guy grunted, dug his palms into his eyes. With surprising speed, Fang dropped the extinguisher. He stepped to the man and jammed his hands under the jacket.

My head had begun to clear; the buzzing died.

The baseball cap loosened his grip on my head. Before he broke contact, I twisted and sank my teeth into the soft flesh of his palm.

He screamed.

Though pain lanced from my loose teeth, I did not let go. The baseball cap wrenched his hand back and forth, then dug his fingers into the broken left side of my face. Pain flared, and he ripped his hand from my mouth. Again, I could taste the metallic tang of blood, but this time it was not mine.

He scrambled to his feet, cursing and waving his injured hand. I heard a shout. "Cut him loose!" Fang yelled.

I could see the flames rising higher behind him. The pallet of boxes had begun to catch. In his hands Fang held a pistol. The blond man—covered in yellow powder—was still rubbing at his eyes. His foot was no longer on fire.

Above me, the baseball cap cradled his left hand in his right; I saw blood trailing through his fingers. "You're so dead, man," he told me.

"Cut him loose," Fang repeated.

The fire was licking at the cardboard boxes, which I could now see were filled with plastic pipette tips. If the fire grew—if the flames reached the other cans of ethanol, if they reached the oxygen tanks—I wouldn't have to worry about what I was or wasn't going to do for Uncle Tony. The whole place would erupt.

Fang couldn't hold the gun and use the fire extinguisher, and he couldn't risk having the blond wrench it away from him and blast him with dry chemicals.

"The tanks!" I shouted to Fang. "Shoot the nitrogen tanks!"

Fang seemed confused for a moment. Then he swung the nose of the gun toward the metal tanks lining the wall closest to the flames. He fired four bullets in quick succession. In the seconds of quiet that followed, I could hear the hiss of the frigid liquid nitrogen as it sprayed from the tanks, the hiss as it hit the concrete floor and boiled away to gas.

"Now cut him loose!" Fang screeched.

With his good hand, the baseball cap reached into his jacket and produced a butterfly knife. He opened it with a flick of the wrist.

The knife slid between my wrists; they popped apart. I brought my hands to my front. A single gash ran around the outside of each wrist, and blood had dried like a partial glove over my palms and fingers. Pain cascaded into my hands as circulation flowed.

"His legs," Fang commanded.

As the nitrogen cascaded across the floor, it began to choke the fire from its oxygen. The flames grew no higher.

The moron with the cap shook his head as he cut the ties and my legs bumped forward. That little movement—the tiny extension in my legs—was agony.

The guy with the cap was backing across the room, away from me. "You are such a goner, dude," he told Fang. "Your kid—"

"Shut up," Fang said, and cut a look at the fire, which had begun to sputter and die.

The blond guy had moved away from Fang, toward the stacked boxes. I tried to stand, but stumbled. I continued to flex my joints, trying to will some life back into the muscles.

"Your little daughter's going to bleed," the baseball cap warned, circling wide. The two goons were on opposite sides of the room. Not good.

"Shut up. Stand still." Fang looked at me. "Help me tie them."

I pushed myself up from the chair and nearly toppled over. "His gun," I said, nodding my head toward the baseball cap.

"Oh," Fang said. To the guy with the cap, he said, "Get over here. Now."

"Your girl's going to—"

And then it happened. The blond guy—the cool one—feinted behind the stack of boxes. Fang swung the weapon toward him and fired.

I fell to the floor.

Fang swung the gun toward the thug with the cap and fired twice, but by that time he had rolled out of sight, behind a large piece of boxed lab equipment. Best I could, I scrambled along the floor to where the baseball cap had disappeared.

Fang was maneuvering toward where I crouched, as if I could be any help to him at that moment. I caught a glimpse of the baseball cap, now with an automatic pistol in his hand. Fang was directly between the two thugs, both of them crouching behind their barricades. He continued backing up, having forgotten, I guess, about the man behind him.

My legs worked well enough to scrabble low around the pallets. I saw him, the baseball cap, squatting behind a large stack of boxed plastic Falcon tubes, searching for a clear shot into Fang's back.

Willing every bit of juice to my muscles, I jumped.

He tumbled.

"Doctor!" Fang yelled.

I clawed for the weapon in the baseball cap's hand. He was strong, younger than I was, better at this kind of struggle. He hadn't just spent an hour with little blood circulating to his limbs. Despite my bite marks in his hand, I knew I'd never be able to overpower him. Somewhere deep in my cortex, there were a couple of neurons that weren't totally burned by fear and anger and exhaustion. Those neurons fired.

I heard the blast from the fire extinguisher, then a shot. Fang cried out.

Three more shots exploded through the room.

I rolled the man on top of me, which surprised him, I think, because the move put me in such a compromised position. All his efforts were now bent on keeping me from pointing the gun toward him. So, I didn't. I swung the pistol at the row of liquid nitrogen tanks along the wall. I managed to squeeze off four bullets before I felt a kick to the side of my face. I nearly fainted from the pain, and went slack.

"Jerk," I heard the blond guy say, and he kicked me again.

The hiss from the liquid nitrogen tanks had grown louder. I noticed the fire had gone completely out. I needed to get off the ground. I pushed myself to all fours, fell flat.

"You fucking let him have a smoke," the baseball cap told the blond, disgusted.

Strong hands hauled me to my feet. They pushed me to where Fang lay, trails of blood coming from his head and torso, his body covered in yellow dust. The blond set the chair upright. "Sit down." I did.

"Fucker bit me," the baseball cap complained. He wiped his bloodied hand on his pants, regarded it, wiped it again.

"That stuff put the fire out." The blond seemed distracted by the liquid nitrogen squirting from the tanks, cascading along concrete that was far above its vaporization point.

"You didn't have science in school?" the baseball cap sneered. "Nitrogen doesn't burn. Oxygen burns."

The blond guy shrugged. "High school was like four years ago." He watched the liquid. "You think we should get out of here?"

"Nah," his buddy replied. "There's nitrogen all over the air. It's, like, normal."

The liquid had cooled the floor enough that it wasn't vaporizing as quickly and so could sheet farther across the loading dock. It slid to Fang's body, and I watched the pool of blood freeze to a dusky red. Fang's flesh—where it touched the floor—quickly froze. The medial side of his hand, his cheek. I could see the skin harden, become hazy as ice crystals formed, fracturing fragile cell walls.

Some of the liquid circled the area beneath me, splashing the soles of my shoes.

I began to hyperventilate.

"I think he's going to cry," the baseball cap said. He and his friend snickered.

But I wasn't quite ready to shed tears. The hyperventilation was to saturate my blood with whatever oxygen was left at this height, to lower the blood's acid content so it wouldn't trigger respiratory centers as rapidly.

I sucked a deep breath and held it.

I kept my eyes on the floor, concentrated on keeping myself calm so as not to burn through my oxygen. I watched the liquid swirl and bubble and smoke, watched it pool around the plastic that had been under the chair. I listened to it boil.

"It's like school, man, when they froze the grapes," one of the men said. I guessed it was the baseball cap, the one who still seemed to remember something from science class.

"This is wild," the other said. Out of the corner of my eye, I saw a toe hook under Wei-jan Fang's hand. The forearm had stiffened and lifted like a board off the ground. "Cool," the blond said, and they both laughed.

Come on, come on. I felt the beginning of a burn in my lungs.

"Hold the doc's hand in it," the blond guy suggested. "He bit you. Freeze his hand."

Come on, I prayed. *Come on.* I felt my heart pounding, felt my lungs begin to ache. I counted seconds.

"Yeah," the baseball cap agreed. "See how much surgery he can do then."

Damn it, I thought. My hand will be frozen to the bone. Dorothy will be dead. I will be dead. And we'd had a chance. We'd had a damn chance.

A figure bent into my field of view. A hand grabbed my left arm and pulled it straight, pulled it down toward the floor. With a heave, my hand was thrust into the layer of liquid. For a second, it was just cold. Then, suddenly, it felt as though a blowtorch had been swept across my palm. I wanted to scream, but did not. I kept the air trapped in my lungs.

The blond guy took out his cell phone. "I'm calling Kwong," he said.

Suddenly, the hand on mine relaxed. Then it fell away. Then it hit the floor, followed by knees and torso. Finally, the body splashed into the film of liquid coursing over the concrete. The cap rolled off the head.

The blond guy yelped, "Hey," and I saw him begin to weave. He kept himself upright for a moment—like a marionette twisting on its strings—then he toppled. His cell phone and a gun clattered to the floor.

Despite the hyperventilation, the time had been too long, and I was dizzy from lack of oxygen. I tried to stand, but the pain in my left knee was too great. I grabbed it with my hands and forced myself upright, let out a short yell.

I staggered to my feet. My lungs were searing now, and I stumbled to the outside door, crashed into it. I managed to get my fingers around the handle: it wouldn't turn. I scrabbled at it.

And then, without warning, I had it open.

I fell to the concrete dock outside and sucked deep of the sweetest air I'd ever tasted.

115

THERE IS "NITROGEN ALL OVER the air," as my genius, now-dead captor had noted. Seventy-eight percent of the air, to be precise. Though nitrogen is ubiquitous, it also happens to be extremely dangerous. It's the cause of more laboratory fatalities than any other substance found. In large part the deaths are the result of complacency, of poor compliance to safety standards. No one really pays attention because no one thinks a little nitrogen is going to kill you.

I'd been lucky that safety standards at Tetra were lax, that they hadn't decided to store their LN_2 in a big tank outside the building. Perhaps they were making the transition. More likely, they just didn't care.

In the lungs, nitrogen becomes greedy: the gas forces oxygen out of the blood and into the lung, effectively reversing normal gas transfer. The brain can become oxygen-starved in a matter of seconds. And oxygen-starved brains are not conscious brains.

Much of the liquid boiled to a gas when the tanks were punctured. That gas gradually filled the room from the bottom up, first extinguishing Wei-jan Fang's fire, then the lives of my captors. God bless the basic laws of chemistry and biology.

My two friends in the loading bay should have studied a little harder in school.

I looked at the palm of my left hand, the one that had been thrust into freezing liquid. The skin was inflamed, but there were no blisters; the frostbite had not been that deep. Still, the skin stung. Second-degree burn probably.

I held my breath and took a hasty look back into the room. The three bodies lay motionless on the cement floor. The last of the liquid nitrogen was spilling from the tanks.

By now, all the broken and bruised nerves—in my face, in my knee, my hand, my wrists—had decided to assert themselves. It was as if they knew I was out of the woods, and wanted to let me know there were some biological troubles that needed tending. And—damn me—I admit I did think of stumbling across the lot and leaving all this behind.

It would be so easy.

I hyperventilated again, and walked into the loading bay. The bodies looked grotesque, frozen flesh extending a few centimeters off the floor; warm, supple flesh above. It was as if a small sliver of them had been cast in wax, the rest living tissue. I took the blond man's gun and cell, took the small black pouch from inside Fang's jacket, and limped for the door.

116

I WAS IN THE BASEMENT hallway now, making my way toward the service elevator, trying to figure out the damned user interface on the blond guy's cell. Finally, I got it. Last dialed call: Kwong.

The last thing the tattooed bastard probably heard was his friend hitting the floor. From my left, from up the hall, I heard the sound of a door being punched open.

Immediately I turned. I rounded a corner, dragged myself between beige concrete walls, along a scuffed concrete floor until I reached a set of double doors. I pushed the crash bar and opened the door.

A continuation of the hallway, leading to an intersection. I kept moving. To my left, a short distance away, was the main set of elevators.

I hit the call button. Once inside, I punched the button for the sixth floor. To find Dorothy and Tim, I would work my way down from the top. The elevator lurched skyward, then stopped. Ground floor.

"Shit," I breathed. I aimed the gun at the black split between the two doors as they opened.

When the man standing on the other side of them saw me, his mouth opened and he fell back a few steps. I pictured what he saw—a man he loathed, face pulpy, rivulets of blood streaking across hands that unsteadily gripped a pistol pointed straight at his brain. I didn't fault him for his panic.

"Get in here, Dan," I told him.

Dan Missoula didn't move. And, thank God, he didn't try to shake my hand.

"Move!" I reached out, and pulled him by the collar into the elevator. Grabbing the fabric caused pain to jolt through my frostbitten left hand. I smacked the button to the fifth floor. Change of plans.

"I don't . . . I don't know what's going on," Missoula said. "I didn't see anything. Please don't . . ."

"It's after midnight. Why are you here?"

"I figured something was going on with you and Alex. I figured the spill they talked about was a fake—"

"What spill?"

"There was a chemical spill late this afternoon. The HAZMAT guys came, but—"

"There was no spill," I interrupted. "They needed to clear out the building. Did Alex call you?"

"No," Missoula said, too loud. "No. I—"

"Where's Dorothy Zhang?"

"Who?"

I shoved him against the wall. He hit it hard. Strength was coming back into my muscles; the adrenaline load I carried helped. So did my anger.

"Where's Dorothy Zhang?"

"I don't know who you're talking about," Missoula whined. He was shaking now, and I'd be lying if I said I didn't take some pleasure in it.

The elevator stopped on floor five. "Get out." He didn't move. "Get out!" I shouted, and pushed him through the door.

My hand on Missoula's collar, the gun in the small of his back, I shoved him down the hall. The lab where the transfections took place was to our right, Dan and Alex's office to the left. "Is she in there?"

"Who?" His voice cracked with fear.

"Alex, you idiot."

"I don't—I thought you were working with her on something."

"You were wrong."

Missoula's keycard hung around his neck on a lanyard. I tore it off, held it next to the lab door. The lock clicked. "Open it," I said.

It should be known I mostly believed Dan Missoula. Earlier that day, he'd seen Alex and me confabbing about secret stuff, and he was obviously suspicious we were up to something. Hell, the guy was suspicious of me from the first moment I walked into Tetra. When the "spill" occurred and Tetra was cleaned out, he must have become even more wary. As it was, though, I couldn't take a chance that he was telling the truth.

A bank of fluorescents blazed at the far end of the lab, casting the big room in a dim, cold light. We moved past the cell culture room, where a UV light filled the small space with thick purple haze that filtered out to the lab through a large window. We moved past the benches topped with bottles of reagents: phosphate buffered saline, potassium hydroxide, hydrochloric acid. There were no humans here, but there was movement: orbital shakers gyrating like dancers, hot water bath shakers sloshing back and forth. Somewhere, I heard the whine of a centrifuge.

To our left was a cold room, about ten by ten. A digital

readout set next to its door showed 4 degrees Celsius, about 40 degrees Fahrenheit.

I rifled through Missoula's pockets, removing a cell phone and a BlackBerry. Then I opened the door to the cold room. Felt like a February day in Atlanta.

"No," Missoula protested. His skin had gone gray.

"Yes," I replied, shoving him inside the small room, amongst the stainless-steel racks full of ELISA kits, reagents, and cell media, the other things that needed to be kept cold but not frozen. "If you're telling me the truth, I'm sorry. If you're not telling me the truth, I'll be back. And I'll be pissed off."

The door closed with a heavy thunk.

On the door's outside handle, a pin dangled from a short chain. I dropped the pin through its hole, locking the mechanism. Not wanting to come back and find a hypothermic scientist, I hit a button on the temperature control, raising the environment to 22 degrees Celsius, a comfortable 70 degrees Fahrenheit. Dan Missoula would survive. The antibodies and ELISA kits would not.

Missoula's phone and BlackBerry went into a waste can.

I scanned the hallway, half expecting to see Michael Kwong bearing down on me with guns blazing, knives flashing. But the hallway was empty.

I limped from the lab and used Missoula's keycard to enter his office suite. A light shone from one of the offices. Alex's. I heard nothing.

Gun drawn, I stepped to the open office door. Her fingers froze over her laptop's keyboard, and she stared at me, a look of total surprise and dismay on her face.

And, with that look, I knew what the deal was. I knew it was not to buy time, then to tackle Uncle Tony and his gang or Dustin Alberts and his. I was not to be brought in as a partner in Alex's little scheme; I was to be sacrificed. That part of the plan—from its very inception with Murph—had never been changed.

For a moment, neither of us moved. Then Alex's eyes cut quickly to the screen. Her fingers began to tap on the keyboard.

"Don't," I told her.

"This isn't what you think," she said. "I'm trying to help you, Nate."

"You tried to help me a few times already today. Stand up."

Her fingers began to work. I jumped to the desk and slammed the laptop shut. Alex yanked back her hands and let out a little cry.

"What are you doing?" she said. "I was getting documents together for—"

"Shut up, Alex."

Her mind was scrambling for a way out of this. "—to help your story—"

"Shut up."

"—but maybe we should just go to the police. I have more than enough to take to the police, Nate."

I let her go on, since the verbal spray wasn't going to stop no matter how many times I told her to can it.

"We'll do this now," she bargained. "They were *threatening* me, Nate. They said that if I didn't help, they'd do the same thing to me as they did to Paul. But now we have the upper hand. We do. Think about it. I'll talk to Dustin and I'm sure he'll cut you in. You'll be a very rich—"

"You knew Kwong was coming for the boy. At the motel. You *knew*."

"I did," she whined. "That's why I tried to get you to help us before—"

"Where's Dorothy?" I asked.

"I . . . I don't know," she stammered. "Nate—"

And to my astonishment, I slapped her. Hard. My palm blazed with pain.

Her hand went to her face. And from the expression in her eyes, I had no doubt this woman would have loved nothing more than to see me sliced apart on a sheet of plastic.

"The animal facility," she answered.

"Where is it?"

"Basement. Left side of the loading dock."

"Stand up. Open the door." Alex did, and I followed her into the hallway. "Into the labs. Use your keycard."

She crossed the hall to the lab door, swiped the card. With the gun at her back, I moved her toward the cold room.

"Stop here," I said. "Hands on the wall."

She complied. I rifled through her pockets, removed her cell, took her keycard, dropped them both on the lab bench.

"Don't be stupid, Nate," she spat. Man, this woman could change tactics faster than a special-ops team. "What are you going to do to me?" she demanded.

I looked at the cold room, saw Dan Missoula's pasty face pressed against the small window, blurred behind the thick glass. "I thought you two might want to sing some Harvard fight songs."

117

FROM THE FIFTH FLOOR, THE moon splashed the landscape below me in monochrome. I could see the fountain where Tim had collected his wishes. Around it, the three silver buildings glinted coldly, the signage across their façades the only dash of color in a dark world.

I fingered the pistol in my hand and realized how ludicrous this was. A gun? Nate McCormick toting a gun? And what was I going to do with it? Shoot it out with a bunch of psychopaths?

I thought of the oath I had taken, first to do no harm.

I thought of Murph, believing his gun would protect him.

I thought of situations spinning out of control, of the weapon being wrested from me, of bullets flying—into me, into Dorothy, into Tim. Get real for once, Dr. McCormick.

I tossed the gun into the trash.

There was a telephone on the lab bench. I picked it up. Could not punch the keys.

Do it, I told myself. *Call the cops.*

And then what? The sirens wail. Kwong and Uncle Tony and whoever else keep Dorothy and Tim as their bargaining chips. And me? I sit on the outside with the SWAT team praying they can get inside before knives cut into Dorothy's flesh.

I placed the phone back in its cradle.

They would expect me to run. They would expect me to call the police. They would not expect me to limp around Tetra on a fool's mission to find Dorothy and Tim. Which is exactly what I was going to do. Truly, a fool's mission.

I removed Fang's black pouch from my jacket, unzipped it. There was a syringe with the needle still attached. I drew up a few more cc's of potassium chloride, enough to kill a horse. This was all very grim stuff, and I tried not to think about endpoints or implications, about the fact that I was preparing this for my own suicide.

I recapped the needle and slid the syringe into my pocket, pushed the pouch, needles, and empty vial into the trash.

As I moved toward the door, I heard the sound of footfalls—heavy slaps, as though someone were running.

Quickly, I ducked into the cell culture room and pressed myself against the door. The familiar odor of cell media—organic, sweet—filled my nostrils; the microbicidal UV light suffused the room. I shut my eyes against it.

There was a beep and a click, and I heard the door to the lab swing open.

Though I could not see him, I knew it was Kwong. I willed deafness on Dan Missoula and Alex Rodriguez. If they heard the door, if they knew someone besides myself was there, if they began to pound on the walls of the cold room . . .

The door closed. Silence. Then I heard the faint scrape of the door across the hall—the door to Dan and Alex's office suite—as it opened.

I pushed out of the cell culture room and crawled

across the lab, listening, my heart hammering. I heard a door close, then the sound of footfalls fading.

The ring of a phone split the silence.

Disoriented by the sound, I reached into my jacket pocket, but found no phone. I forced myself to calm down and concentrate. The sound was faint, not as loud as I'd thought. A musical trill. Not a lab phone.

I scrambled toward the lab bench and retrieved Alex's cell. Caller ID said, simply, "MK." Michael Kwong.

I hit Talk.

"Where you now?" the accented voice asked.

"I'm on the sixth floor, you prick," I lied. "Waiting for you."

118

IN THE CORRIDOR, I ADVANCED, hugging the wall as I moved. "Advanced." I liked that. Made me seem tougher. God knows I needed as much toughness as I could get.

To the stairs.

I paused, stiffened my left leg, let it fall to the first step. On impact, pain shot, but didn't cripple. Not thinking, I relaxed the injured knee, let it take the full weight of my body as I tried to work my way over the stairs.

Again, pain shot. This time it was crippling

The leg buckled. My arms flailed toward the railing, tangling themselves around the tubular steel. I heard myself cry out, tried to bite off the sound as it broke from my lips. The echo of my voice off the concrete walls seemed to go on forever.

I listened, heard only my breathing.

For an instant, I considered limping back to the elevators, but dismissed the idea when I imagined Kwong working his way floor by floor from above. Tensing against the pain, I managed to get my legs under me. I gripped the railing on either side of the stairwell, held myself like a pendulum frozen midway through its arc. The palm of my frostbitten left hand stung. My left eye watered. My ruined cheek throbbed.

"One," I said. "Two, three."

I tipped my weight forward and stopped myself, afraid now.

"Okay. Four, five."

I kept my body stiff as I swung my legs forward and dropped myself two steps below. There was pain, but it was tolerable. I slid my hands down the rails, swung my legs a second time. Each clunk of my feet on the concrete steps sounded like a cannon shot.

Five flights like that. *Clunk, clunk, clunk.*

I could almost feel Michael Kwong's breath on my neck.

Exhausted, I pushed into the basement corridor.

Affixed to the wall opposite the stairwell was a sign directing me to the animal facility. Ahead, I saw a set of locked doors decorated with red-lettered warning signs. A black card-access box jutted from the wall. I swiped

Missoula's card and pushed through. A blast of air hit me from both sides as I entered into an antechamber. Another set of doors here, another black pad.

I inched the door open.

The odor of cedar and food, bodies and feces hung in the air. A stainless-steel washbasin with foot pedals for water was to my right. Next to it sat a cart with gowns, gloves, booties, masks. Everything you'd need to protect yourself from contamination by the rats, mice, and rabbits that lived there. Or, more importantly, to protect the rats, mice, and rabbits from contamination by you.

Slowly now, I moved along a polished concrete floor, over small brass drains set into it. The walls here were pink, not the beige of the outside corridors, and interrupted every few feet by green- and red-lettered signs exhorting clean practices, posters detailing the proper treatment of animals. Inset into a metal door on my right was a tiny window. Through it, dimly lit, I could see hundreds of stacked cages housing hundreds of mouse colonies. Against the woodchip bedding of the cages, thousands of small forms stirred, as if the room itself were alive. An identical door on my left led to the rats; the next, to the rabbits.

Ten paces down the hall was a windowless door, not as solid as the others. I stepped toward it.

Behind me, I heard a blast of air, quickly followed by the sound of metal scraping.

I wheeled around.

"She scream very much, Dr. McCormick."

119

"SHE DON'T LIKE THIS AT all," Michael Kwong said. He breathed heavily. Sweat matted the front of his shirt to his chest. In his right hand was a large pistol, raised to my chest. In his left, he held a crumpled white cloth.

"Where's Dorothy?" I said. "Where is Tim?"

Kwong took a few steps forward. "She beg for you to help."

"Where are they?"

In answer, he tossed the cloth. It traced a low arc and landed in front of me. I stooped to pick it up; it was soaked with blood.

The white cotton fell open in my hands. Inside, I saw a fingertip severed at the first knuckle, the nail painted with chipped pink polish.

"She have nine more, Dr. McCormick," Michael Kwong said. "And the boy have ten."

"Walk."

I stepped forward, moving down the hall with a pistol stuck in the small of my back. When we reached the windowless door, Kwong said to me, "Open."

I took hold of the knob and pushed.

Tony was speaking into a phone. He sat on a functional

chair at a functional Formica table surrounded by more functional chairs. A microscope attached to a video monitor sat in the corner of the room. Dark green slide-storage cabinets were pushed against one wall. The walls—the same pink as in the corridors—were adorned with cheaply framed prints of animals—mostly reproductions of antique drawings of mice, dogs, birds. A desk and chair abutted one wall.

Tony hung up the phone.

Dorothy was not here. But, goddamn it, Tim Kim was.

Tim stared at me with a "holy shit" look on his pale face. Arrayed on a blue cloth in front of him was an assortment of two dozen or so medical instruments: tweezers, hemostats, clamps, DeBakey forceps. There were also a few bone shears and rongeurs, thick tools that looked like wire cutters. Whatever they'd used to cut off Dorothy's finger probably came from this set.

In his hand, Tim held a seven-inch pair of sharp-tipped forceps and was midway through picking up the corner of the cloth when I'd entered. He let the cloth drop.

In times of stress, it's easier, I suppose, to fiddle around with an orthopedic surgery tray than to concentrate on *The Hobbit.*

"You have made the situation more complicated than it needed to be, Dr. McCormick," Tony said. His eyes flickered over the bloodied cloth in my hand. "You have forced us to resort to measures we regret."

"Your niece," I said. "Your own niece."

"She has made sacrifices," Tony replied. "We all have."

In that moment, I wanted nothing more than to destroy. Cleanse the world of these men. I wanted to take the bone shears and remove parts of them, cause as much pain as I knew how.

Instead, I set the cloth and the finger onto the table, then returned my hands to my sides. Tony reached out and, pinching an edge of the cloth, slid the bundle toward him.

I'd be damned, though, if I was going to let them control everything.

While Tony was distracted with his niece's digit, I slipped my hands into my pockets, got the fingers of my right hand around Wei-jan Fang's syringe.

Kwong jabbed the barrel of his gun into my spine, causing me to stumble forward. "Hand out," he said.

Slowly, I removed my hands from my pockets, the syringe tucked into the cuff of my right sleeve. I kept my wrist bent to prevent it from sliding out.

Tim's eyes were wide, fixed on the severed finger.

"No more of this," I said.

Tony regarded the finger. "There will be no more, Dr. McCormick, if you do as we wish." He stood. "And what we wish is for you to make your telephone calls," he said. "We wish you to sign some documents." *Sign some documents.* Innocent, like closing on a house, or putting your John Hancock on a 401(k) form for work.

I looked at the finger on the table, at its ragged, glistening end, its wrinkled white flesh. By that time, Tim had turned his gaze from the finger to his great-uncle. His jaw was set now, his eyes narrow. It was the same furious look I'd seen when we were in the pet store.

Tony swept the finger into his hand, and placed it in the pocket of his suit coat. "We would like for my niece to be able to continue her journalism career," Tony said. We both knew, of course, he was lying.

"What documents?" I asked.

"Your authorization for wire transfers. For your *money,* Dr. McCormick." Tony smiled.

This money, I knew, would not go into my account to help me buy that place in Santa Barbara. The money would go into my account to establish my complicity in this mess. The conspiracy was not to be only Wei-jan Fang and Paul Murphy, but Fang, Murphy, and McCormick. And after I'd become a *de jure* conspirator, I knew they couldn't take a chance on me saying anything else ever again. The money would sit untouched in its account as beetles chewed through my flesh in some shallow grave.

"You won't hurt Brooke," I bargained weakly.

"There is no reason for us to harm anyone if you comply with our wishes."

"What about the boy?"

"If you comply, Dr. McCormick, the boy will be fine."

On that point, I was unsure whether to trust him. Kids don't forget things like this. Kids grow up. Vengeful boys become vengeful men. They become dangerous.

The furious look on Tim's face hadn't changed. *Play along with them,* I wanted to say. *For once, damn it, play along.*

"Dorothy?" I croaked.

"A boy needs a mother," Tony said matter-of-factly.

Despite his game face, I got the sense he was not thrilled about what he'd had to do to his niece. Dorothy was tainted, sure, but she was family. She had betrayed him with Murph—which perhaps could be forgiven—but then she had betrayed him again with me. And she would, given the chance, do it again. He knew that, which is why I was sure things would not end well for her. How bad they would end was up for grabs.

I focused on Uncle Tony: family man, businessman, maker of difficult decisions, killer. He probably wasn't a sociopath, but he lived with one fucked-up value system.

Tony said something to Kwong in Chinese. Kwong rounded behind me to the side of the table opposite Tim. He leaned toward the collection of medical instruments and removed from it a pair of bone shears.

"You won't need those," I said.

"Just in case," Tony answered, as Kwong took his position behind me. The tattooed man shoved me toward the door. I could hear him breathing.

A feeling of unreality hit me. Murph's eyeless face, blood sheeting from his mouth like a bib, loomed in front of me. His dying wife, frothing from the gash in her neck. The slit throats of the children. The finger with pink nail polish.

How had Dorothy felt as metal passed through flesh and bone?

What would the blades feel like as they pressed through mine?

As I limped forward I allowed the syringe to fall into my palm, squeezed the needle's cap between thumb and forefinger, and twisted it off. A cowardly way out, I know, but preferable to having my ears sliced off, my fingers cut off.

Two weeks before, the major concerns in my life had been getting a paycheck and figuring out the twists and turns of a relationship with Brooke. Now, my major concern was whether I'd be able to kill myself in time.

I thought, too, about other changes in me.

As I crossed the threshold of the door, I glanced back into the room. Tim wasn't watching me, but kept his small hard eyes trained on his uncle. I shifted my gaze to the older man.

"I'm going to kill you," I said.

"Hardly fitting talk for a physician," Tony replied.

Don't I know it.

But the opportunity to end anyone's life but my own was not in the cards. The needle pressed against the skin of my palm as I stepped into the hallway. I'd need only a few seconds. To find the vein, to pierce it with the needle.

The thoughts I thought were unbelievable to me.

Kwong had released my collar, but was still poking the gun into my back. We passed a door with a small window in it. I caught a glimpse of what I thought was a human form slumped in the corner.

The animal rooms were behind us now, but I was certain I could hear the rabbits, the mice and rats, screaming. It was probably just the blood in my ears, but the thought that something—even the rats—cared about my fate was comforting.

Totally, absolutely, unbelievable.

Then something happened. Something equally unbelievable. A man's scream, guttural and primal. It echoed from within the conference room down the hallway.

My first thought was that Tony had answered whatever questions he had about the boy and decided to kill him, to juice himself with a scream before he broke Tim's neck.

Kwong's gun shifted from my back.

My second thought was, *A chance.*

120

I AM NOT FAST WITH a pistol. I cannot punch or kick faster than many men. But I am quick with a needle. If I'd learned nothing else during residency, I'd learned to hit a blood vessel quickly. Very quickly. And very accurately.

I wheeled, rolling into Kwong's body so that we were face-to-face. The bone shears clattered to the floor. The uncapped needle was in my hand. For a microsecond, I eyed the external jugular on his left side, then my left hand flew to his neck and grabbed it, stabilizing the flesh. The gun fired to my side and I felt his hand kick up along my torso. I felt Kwong drawing back the gun to put it in my gut, his left hand coming up to break my hold on his neck.

The needle was already in motion.

He mistook what I was doing, thinking I wanted to strangle him. When he knocked my left hand away, he relaxed for a split second. My right slid along his neck, along the jugular laid out big and round like a rope.

Through the tail of the dragon, through the epidermis and dermis, through the four layers of the vein. By the time the needle had punctured the vessel wall into the lumen, I was already unloading its contents.

The velocity of blood in the external jugular vein is about twenty centimeters per second. The blood travels to the lungs, then to the heart, a distance of perhaps sixty centimeters. Velocity slows in the lung. Give it five seconds before Kwong's cardiac muscle saw more potassium than it ever had before.

In his surprise, Kwong had not maintained his balance when I pushed my body into him. We fell and thudded to the ground.

I used both my hands to grab his arm. But he was strong—so fucking strong—and he forced the gun toward my body. All my weight was on the arm now. The syringe, still lodged in his neck, bobbed like the needle on a Geiger counter.

His free hand clawed at my face. His fingers were in my eye sockets, his hand on my broken cheek, grinding the jagged edges of bone against one another. I yelped.

The fingers continued to press. I began to see colored snow on a dark background, began to feel the globes of my eyes deform.

And then he began to relax, slowly at first, then faster. His hands dropped from my face. His breath, which had been labored and regular, snagged in his throat as his heart began tumbling into an arrhythmic spiral.

Faster breaths now; realization and horror sparked in his eyes. His face contorted. He gave one last heave of his arm, one last desperate play to gouge out my eyes. Then he went slack.

Hardly fitting for a physician, I thought. I did not wait to hear his last breath. I rolled off the dead man and, quickly as my broken body would let me, limped to the conference room door. I was not ready to see what was inside. I was not ready to see Tim Kim's head lolling to the side, his neck broken.

Then I heard the sounds. A series of grunts, scraping. A crash.

I swung into the room, prepared to use the last of my strength to launch myself at Uncle Tony.

Just then, a small body crashed into my legs.

I pulled Tim back into the hallway. His eyes were wild and he clutched on to my pants. "I didn't—"

I pushed him against the wall.

"I didn't mean—"

"Stay here!" I shouted.

I stepped back into the conference room.

Tony was there, pawing madly around the Formica table seeking something. Whatever he was searching for, he couldn't see it. He couldn't see it because he had no eyes.

Blood and clear liquid—the vitreous humor that fills the globes of the eyes—trailed down his face and stained his white shirt, as if he'd been weeping crimson. The medical instruments had been pulled to the floor, except for one: the long, sharp forceps with which Tim had been playing. The bloodied instrument lay on the table, its two halves sprung wide by a boy who'd used his wits.

"Stop," I said to Tony.

He didn't, and continued to pat the table in front of him.

"Damn it, stop!" I shouted.

The beating of his hands slowed, then ceased. His arms were extended over the table like those of a blackjack dealer.

"There's a chair behind you," I said. "Sit."

Tony's arms fluttered behind him; they found the chair. He sat.

Tim stood in the doorway now, looking at his great-uncle, then looking at me. He seemed frightened out of his mind. "I'm sorry . . ."

"It's okay," I said to him. "You did just fine, kiddo. Just fine."

Tony barked something in Chinese, so loud his voice cracked. Tim looked as if he'd been slapped.

"Shut up," I said. "Kwong's dead. Is there anyone else here?"

Tony let out a long, low moan. I picked up the bloodied forceps and put them to Tony's throat; the metal dimpled the skin. Tony continued moaning.

"I will shove these through your neck if you move," I said. The metal burned on the frostbitten skin of my left hand, but I held tight.

I leaned over him, running my hands into the pockets of his jacket: wallet, PDA, Dorothy's fingertip. In the pants pockets were a set of keys and a cell phone. I threw it all onto the table. Without moving the forceps from his neck, I sat in a chair.

"Tim, go into the hall," I said. I turned back to the man whose moan had turned to a whimper. "Anyone else here?" I pushed the forceps into his neck, felt the metal punch through the first layers of skin.

"No one else. No one else. Not yet. They are coming."

"Where is Dorothy?"

"Down the hall."

I regarded Tony, his eyeless Oedipal face, his blood-stained shirt. Normally, the look of agony on anyone, on any human being, stirred my sympathies. It's why you become a doctor, right? To end human suffering. But the sight of this man's suffering did not arouse sympathy.

Whatever reasons Tony had for doing what he did, I had no pity for him. Blinded as he was, as painful as it might be, his pain couldn't compare to what he had caused.

"Why did the Murphy kids have to die?" I asked him.

"They were . . . not supposed to be there," he groaned.

"But you killed them anyway."

"B-business."

"Why did you assault Brooke Michaels?"

My hand tensed on the metal, pressed it harder into his neck. He winced. "Business."

I'd like to say that I didn't think about what I did next—that it was some uncontrollable urge, some fit of temporary insanity—but I did think. Having thought about it, I'd like to say it was for a good reason—to get more information, to save someone's life—but it was not. I brought my right hand to his face, placed my thumb next to the eyeless socket.

"Well, Garheng." I bent down to his ear, spoke softly. "*This* is not business."

I plunged my thumb inside. Tony screamed and lashed out with his arms, but my left hand drove the forceps deeper into the flesh of his neck, and somewhere in his pain-addled brain he realized he would die if he kept this up. So he dropped his arms, and I released pressure on the metal. But I continued to grind my thumb into the warm hole in his skull. Three seconds passed, seven. I felt the collapsed rind of his eye's sclera; I felt the wetness of blood. The man continued screaming, gasped for breath, screamed again. Ten seconds. Twelve.

I stopped. I slid my thumb out of his eye socket, slid the forceps out of his neck. I wanted to puke.

Tim stood at my elbow, silent and staring.

Shame and disgust filled me.

I wiped my hand on my pants, tossed the forceps to the floor, and turned to Tim. I reached for his hand.

He paused for a second, looked at the blood on me, looked at his great-uncle, then shrank away. He stopped in the doorway, gripped the jamb, and watched.

"Tim . . ." I said, trying to be consoling, unable to tell if he was horrified by what I'd done or by what he'd done. He stayed rigid and mute.

I dialed 911 and gave the dispatcher the situation. An ambulance would be sent, she said.

"Two ambulances," I told her.

After that, I dialed Information. I had them patch me through to the San Francisco Police Department. The operator was reluctant at first, but words like "emergency," "kidnap," and "die" seemed to do the trick. She put me through to Jack Tang's cell phone.

Tang answered, his voice dull and sleepy. The moment I heard it, I started talking. The words tumbled out, wild and out of control.

"Hold on, Doctor. You're safe?"

"Yeah. I guess you could say that."

"Give me twenty minutes. Wait there."

121

I DID NOT WAIT FOR Jack Tang.

I picked up the fingertip, wrapped it in its cloth. I ripped the cord from the conference room's telephone and pocketed Tony's cell.

In the hallway, I moved a rolling cabinet in front of the conference room door, hoping a blind man would be unable to exit without making a racket.

Then Tim and I went to find his mother. As we drew closer to Kwong, I saw Tim staring at the body.

"Don't look," I said.

I grabbed the boy's hand—I didn't give him the chance to shirk away from me—and pulled him toward the room in which I'd seen the slumped body. I peered through the small window set in the door. Dorothy was there, hunched in a corner.

She didn't look up.

I knocked, and still she didn't move. Frantic, I fumbled at the lock and threw open the door.

"Dorothy!" I shouted.

Her head jerked up. I felt relief lift me like a song.

Her hands had been tied behind her back, and her ankles bound with a cable tie.

"Mommy!" Tim yelled, and rocketed over to his mother. The kid's arms went around Dorothy's neck and squeezed so hard I worried she might black out. She toppled sideways, and I saw she clutched a white, bloodstained cloth in her left hand.

The room had been used for procedures on the animals—stainless-steel table, biohazard waste can, sharps disposal, cabinet filled with sutures and other odds and ends. On the table lay a pair of the heavy bone shears. Blood congealed on the cutting edges, on the shiny surface of the table.

Dorothy laughed, a light, lovely sound intermingled with crying. And when she did, Tim began to blubber, full-throated sobs that seemed to choke him. I realized it was the first time I'd seen the boy cry.

I gave them a moment, then took hold of the bone shears.

"Tim, stand back." The boy wouldn't.

"Tim, let Dr. McCormick . . ." She couldn't get the words out through her crying.

I maneuvered the boy far enough away that I could get the shears between Dorothy's hands and feet. Her shoulder was already wet, covered in tears. I set the ties between the blades and cut. There was a groan, and her limbs unfolded. They moved stiffly and slowly at first. Arms, then legs, wrapped around the boy, engulfing him. A flurry of kisses covered the boy's head. He giggled and bawled. They both bawled.

Tim twisted himself into her arms, his feet slipping on the concrete as he tried to push himself into her. "Ouch, Timothy. Mommy's hand hurts. Be careful."

Dorothy pulled her son close with her left arm, the bloody cloth still gripped in her hand. Her eyes met mine. "We're safe?" she asked.

I nodded, dropped the shears on the table.

"Your face . . ."

"Yeah, well . . ."

She reached her right hand out to me. I took it, and she drew me down to her.

"Thank you," she whispered. Her face pulled close to mine, and I expected a peck on the cheek. But she pivoted her head at the last minute and our lips met. I felt her unfamiliar contours, the uneven roll on the left side.

She pulled away, embarrassed.

I drew her up to me again and kissed her lightly on the mouth.

"Beauty and the Beast," she said.

"Come on, don't be cruel. I don't look that bad." I smiled. "Let me see that hand."

She took her left arm from around her son and raised it. Carefully, I unfolded the cloth, revealing a ragged, glistening red stump above the first knuckle of her pinky finger. Thick wet blood coated the hand.

"How bad's the pain?" I asked.

"I'll never play the clarinet again," she said, and forced a smile. I realized she refused to complain in front of her son.

From my pocket, I retrieved the cloth with the fingertip inside. I unwrapped it.

"Ugh," Dorothy said, "I don't need to see that."

I redid the little bundle, then sat there, looking at my feet. Now was perhaps not the time, but I could not ignore something so massive.

"Paul—" I said, turning to face her.

Dorothy glanced up from her boy, pulled him closer with one arm. The smile on her face faded.

"I know," she said, inclining her head toward Tim, as if to say *Not appropriate now.*

I ignored her gesture. I needed her to understand what had happened. "No. He betrayed us. Me *and* you."

"I know, Nate. You think they didn't tell me? You think they didn't blame me for everything?" Behind the brave face, there was real pain. She turned back to her son, nuzzled her face in his hair. He laughed. "Mommy wasn't thinking straight. Mommy got confused about what was important." She kissed the boy's cheek.

I forced myself to stand. My body hurt now, tremendously so. As I turned to leave the room—to leave Dorothy with the one thing she cared about—she said to me, "Both of us. I know."

In a supply closet off the hallway, I rummaged for saline in which to place Dorothy's severed finger.

When I returned from the supply closet, I saw the cabinet in front of the conference room door had been moved. The door was open. From inside, I heard the soft lilt of Chinese.

Dorothy was sitting in a chair next to her uncle, stroking his hair, speaking softly to him. She glanced at me when I entered the room.

Tim sat in a conference chair, immobile as a statue. The tears and snot had dried, leaving chalky streaks under the eyes and nostrils. He stared intensely at his mother and great-uncle.

I set the cup with saline and Dorothy's finger inside on the table.

"How did this happen?" Dorothy asked me.

"We need to pack his wounds," I said, ignoring the

question. Truth was, we didn't really need to pack Uncle Tony's wounds, since the bleeding had stopped. But I couldn't just sit around staring at a man who reminded me I was a torturer.

"I'll find some gauze," I said. *And get away from this man.*

I turned, exited the room. I stopped.

Hunched over Michael Kwong's body—shoes off, hands pawing, eyes wild—was Alex Rodriguez.

122

SHE GOT HOLD OF KWONG'S goddamned gun and grunted as she swung it toward my chest.

I heard Dorothy call from inside the room. "Nate, what's going on?"

I was too stunned to speak.

Alex pushed herself to her feet. "At least he let me out of the damned cold room before he died." She cut her eyes to Kwong. "You did this?"

I didn't answer her. Instead, I said, "Alex, this is over."

"Inside," she said. I backed into the room. Alex followed.

Dorothy was now turned toward us, her hand on her uncle's arm. The two women's eyes met, and Dorothy's face hardened. In that moment, I saw that she truly did know everything. Everything.

"You bitch," Dorothy said.

"Oh, honey. Don't say that. I'm just doing what I have to do."

I watched this woman, who found opportunities and seized them, who did what she had to do, who was, if nothing else, a survivor. It was the moment of her greatest opportunity: her chance finally to free Tetra from its shackles and its burdens, her chance to save herself from a long jail sentence. The quick PhD mind had assessed the situation and found a way out. A beautiful, elegant way out.

"They're not going to believe you," I said. I kept my voice even and steady.

"Of course they'll believe me. Who's going to tell them differently?"

"Where's Dan?" I asked, searching for anything to say to draw this out.

"He's waiting for the police because"—the tip of her tongue touched her lip—"I can't imagine that you didn't call them."

Though Alex played it cool, I could tell she was worried. The ambulance was coming, the police were coming. She was concocting her story, working out the flow of events that left this facility heaped with bodies.

"Well, we don't have much time, then. Stand," she said to Dorothy.

"What are you going to do, Alex?" I asked.

"Stand up!" she yelled.

Dorothy did.

"You ruined everything," Alex said. "All of you. All of *them*. Move to the corner." Alex flicked the gun toward Dorothy's left. Dorothy shuffled to my side. Tony moaned quietly in his chair.

"They got too greedy," she said. "They wanted too much and they were *so stupid* about things and now I have to deal with the mess."

"Alex—" I said.

"Shut! Up!"

Without warning, she lowered the nose of the gun, shifted it to the right, and pulled the trigger. The bullet tore into the blind man's gut. A yell ripped from his lungs and he fell out of the chair and began to thrash on the floor. Alex stepped forward, lowered the barrel. Fired again. This time the bullet smashed into Tony's chest. The body quivered, then fell limp.

Dorothy let out a tiny moan. Tim stared, frozen.

"What are you doing?" I screamed, dreading what would happen next.

For a moment, Alex did not move. Her eyes were wide, as if she had trouble comprehending what she'd just done.

Next to me, I could hear Dorothy murmuring, "No, no, no."

"Alex!" I shouted.

"Start with the hardest first," she whispered, and swung the gun toward Tim. Uncle Tony, I guessed, didn't even count. When he saw what was happening, Tim screeched, dropped from his chair, and began crawling fast along the back wall of the room.

"No," I said. "*Think* about this."

Tim had pushed himself into the corner between the wall and the stand holding the microscope's video setup. The stand shifted as he pushed himself hard into it.

"I have to do it," she said, moving to get clear sight lines to the crouching boy.

"Mommy," Tim wailed.

"Alex," I said, inching toward her. "They're coming. It's *over.*"

Suddenly, Alex swung the gun at me, and I froze. "You stay there or I will shoot you right now. God help me, I will shoot you."

I met her gaze. From the corner of my eye, I saw the kid cowering. "Then do it," I said.

The beautiful face held still for a second, then seemed to fracture. She swung her head and the weapon back toward the boy. I heard a tortured "ahh" escape from Dorothy's lungs.

"I have to do this," Alex said faintly, and I got the sense she was talking more to herself than to us. She stiffened her arm.

Suddenly, there was a blur to my right—Dorothy darting across the room. She launched herself at Alex, her arm sweeping toward the weapon.

I reached to grab her, but momentum carried Dorothy into the other woman.

Their bodies collided.

Then, a shot.

123

BRIGHT ARTERIAL BLOOD SQUIRTED FROM the jagged tear in the left side of Alex's neck, spattering her clothes and the floor. Darker venous blood oozed. Frantically, she pushed herself into a half-sitting position and slapped her hand to her neck. The blood pulsed through the fingers, gliding down her chest and bisecting the V made by her unbuttoned shirt.

Panicked, she started scrabbling at the floor around her. I stepped forward, kicked the gun away.

Dorothy was in the corner, cradling her son.

I knelt in front of Alex. As I opened my mouth to speak, a low voice rumbled from the corner of the room. "Let her bleed." Dorothy.

Let her bleed. The easiest thing to do. From the differing hues of blood, from the volume, I knew the bullet had torn through carotid and jugular. This woman—an architect of so much misery—was bleeding to death before my eyes.

Alex sagged against the wall. Her movements were slower now, as she lost more and more blood volume. "My . . . my . . ." she sputtered. Her hand slid around her wound as she tried to apply pressure. But her strength ebbed, and her arm fell to her side. She raised it again.

"I know," I said.

"Let her bleed." Wedged in the corner, Dorothy pulled her son firmly to her breast, as if she wanted to take him into her. There was something wild about her look: the clenched jaw, the scowl that stretched the tumors in odd directions. For the first time since I met her, she truly looked ugly. "She—" Dorothy glanced toward the inert body of her uncle, wrapped her fingers around her son's head, *"she did this."*

Yes, I thought, she did. And she deserved to burn in the same circle of hell as Paul Murphy.

But not today.

I brought my hand to the gash in Alex Rodriguez's neck and pressed my fingers into the thumping artery.

124

FINALLY, THE PARAMEDICS CAME, BOTH fresh-faced white guys who looked like ex-military: all buzz cuts, stocky builds, and precise movements. Dan Missoula was behind them, and bumped into their rear guard when they stopped to assess the scene. Even for hard-bitten medics, the view must have been a doozy: a bloody, eyeless man on the floor in front of them, a woman slumped against the wall to their left, dumping blood over her blouse, me, the floor. The boy in the corner clutching a woman whose face looked monstrous.

After the initial shock, the paramedics got down to

business with clipped questions. I answered. The man on the floor is dead, I said. The woman here has lost a lot of volume. The woman in the corner has a severed finger. The child is unhurt.

Dan Missoula had disappeared.

While one of the paramedics cleared Dorothy and Tim from the room, the other—Robinson, his nametag said—took my place at Alex's side. He ripped open a package of gauze and pressed it hard to her neck.

"There's some left," he said.

I looked at him, not comprehending.

"For you to clean up," he told me.

The gauze was sopping with blood by the time I dropped it on the floor.

The other half of the team came back into the room and began preparing fluids to dump into Alex's veins. I took the plastic cup with Dorothy's finger and left.

More first responders—mostly police—collected in the hallway. I told one of the uniformed cops about the bodies in the loading dock and about the hazardous-materials situation over there. This set off a flurry of radioed calls, and I could feel the chaos rise. Since no one seemed to be in charge, the whole thing threatened to devolve into a total cluster fuck, for a little while, at least. I couldn't really deal with that, so I cut the officer off mid-sentence with a "Thank you" and turned to walk down the hall, through the double doors, through the blast of air in the foyer, through the second set of doors, and out of the animal facility.

Dorothy pressed against the wall in the blank corridor. Tim leaned against her. Her right hand rested on his shoulder; her left was pulled against her belly, the blood-spattered cloth balled in her hand.

I handed her the cup with her finger. "Keep it with you until you get to the hospital."

She took it.

"You two should go upstairs," I said. "Wait for the other ambulance."

Dorothy raised her eyes to me. "Will she live?"

"Probably," I said.

Dorothy nodded slowly; I couldn't tell if she was pleased about this news or not.

I looked down at Tim. I wanted to touch him—tousle the hair, cup his cheek—but blood still covered my hands. He stared forward blankly.

"You did a great job. You protected your mom and me."

Tim said nothing.

For some reason, I felt I needed to get through to the boy, to hear the voice of the person who loved *The Hobbit.* I needed to know that he hadn't been bent and warped as I had. *Violence is searing, kid. The unbendable bends. The unscorchable burns. Ask Uncle Nate. Do not let it touch you, Tim. Wrap yourself in the knowledge that you did right. Know that you had no other choice. Forget this and go back to dwarves and dragons. Go back to being eight, to your mother, to your budding interest in path-o-gens.*

Do not follow me, Timothy Kim, into self-doubt and recrimination. Do not follow me into bitterness.

"It's over, Tim," I said. "You can—"

"Nate," Dorothy said. She tried to smile at me, but couldn't manage it. I waited for the comforting phrase, the explanation. Instead, she said, "Come on, Timothy. Mommy has to go for a ride in an ambulance. I need you to ride along."

Tim peeled himself silently from his mother, and began

to walk down the empty corridor. He did not move like an eight-year-old. Dorothy hesitated, stuck to the wall, a crestfallen look on her face.

"Tim," I said, shuffling along until I caught up with him. I touched the top of his head to stop him. "You're going to be okay. Look at me." He did. "What's going on up here?" I mussed his hair, dropped my hand from his head.

He shrugged.

"Well, I'll tell you what should be going on. You should be thinking you're the bravest, smartest kid in the world."

He was silent.

"You should be thinking you're braver and smarter than Bilbo even," I said, struggling to connect. "I don't think he could've done what you did today."

"Thorin," he said.

"What?"

"I want to be Thorin."

"Kiddo, you're just as brave as Thorin."

Tim sighed, a small whispery thing that seemed very age appropriate. His eyes had lost their steel. "Are you going to see us again, Uncle Nate?"

Upon hearing that sentence, I nearly lost it. "Of course," I said, trying to keep my voice from cracking. "Uncle Nate cares about you very, very much."

Dorothy was now at my side, her good hand lightly touching my hip.

"Let's go, Timothy," she said.

The boy reached up and took his mother's hand.

I listened to the swish of their feet on the concrete. It was over, I felt, without being over. There would be more cutting, more splitting of flesh. Razor blades would yield to scalpels, blood-drenched bedrooms and living rooms would become brightly lit operating suites. The hand with the knife would be that of a surgeon, not of a butcher. The flesh to be removed was corrupted, not virgin. Still, it was not over.

The scars etched in Dorothy Zhang's face would endure, and there would be new scars on new faces. That bitch Beauty would continue her siren song, spurring the pack in its rabid pursuit of the perfect skin, the perfect contours.

Before reaching the elevators, Dorothy stopped and looked back at me. She smiled.

This time it was I who tried to smile, but could not manage it.

Alone now, despite the crescendo of activity at Tetra, I found myself standing in the doorway to the conference room. Alex had been whisked away, and the room was quiet. I stared, unable to move my gaze from Tony on the floor. His arms were splayed wide, his fingers contracted like claws.

A voice came from behind me. "What happened?"

Tony's mouth gaped, the lips retracted over the teeth. Where his eyes had been were now clotted, mangled holes. The previously white shirt was a sheet of dark crimson.

I fixed on his face and became faint. I leaned against the doorjamb, slid down to the floor, my knee erupting in pain as I did so.

"You want to tell me what happened?" the man asked. I finally recognized the voice of Jack Tang. "You want to get to the hospital?"

What had I become? I wondered. A killer? A torturer?

Events had twisted me so that I could hardly recognize my two hands—lined in crimson—lying like dead things in my lap.

Tang was saying something to me, but I couldn't make out the words.

Tony seemed to be staring at the ceiling. He seemed to be screaming.

No, I wasn't to blame. Events had done this, I told myself. Others had done this. Michael Kwong, Uncle Tony. Alex Rodriguez and, worst of all, Paul Murphy. They had taken someone who wanted to do something for the world—who became a goddamned doctor so he could throw his hat in with the good guys—and they had warped him into an ugly thing. The blood was on their hands, not yours. You, good citizen, just wanted some justice. You, good doctor, just wanted to stop people from getting sick, to protect them from their pain.

You did the best job you could.

"Nate." Tang stood directly in front of me, and I could not ignore him. "We need to get you to the hospital."

I looked up at him, then back at my hands, my eyes fixing on the lattice of scars on the left, the ring of blood at the wrist. And crimson covering everything like paint.

"We want to get you out of here before the local detectives come," Tang said. "You'll be here for a week answering questions."

I tried to hide my hands in my lap.

"Come on, Nate. You okay?"

"I'm okay," I said.

Both of us knew that was not true.

125

ALL'S WELL THAT ENDS WELL. This didn't really, so it wasn't really, get it?

It had been a week since I'd driven a needle into Michael Kwong and a thumb into Uncle Tony. Seven days in which to lick my wounds, physical and spiritual. I spent the first forty-eight hours post-Tetra in the hospital, where the plastic surgeons wired the left side of my face back together. My knee was healing, my hand, my wrists. All in all, my body was on the mend. But my soul . . . well, let's just say the course of treatment I chose for spiritual healing wasn't the most effective.

It was eleven o'clock in the morning, and I sipped coffee in a shop a few blocks from the bare-bones weekly rental that I'd picked up. Brooke was out of the hospital by that time, but said she wasn't quite ready to see me yet, much less have me skulk around her home. Couldn't blame her, really. I knew too well what I'd done to her. So did she.

I tried to focus on the page from an alternative weekly paper I'd been perusing, my brain twirling from the surfeit of painkillers I'd downed two hours before. Therefore, the coffee: to counteract the OxyContin. So, things were not ending well for me. And they weren't ending well for a few dozen others who'd been shot full of Beautiful Essence and were unlucky enough to be Wei-jan Fang's half-percent.

In the Bay Area, there were thirty-three cases of what the medical profession was now calling "iatrogenic aggressive-form dermatofibrosarcoma protuberans–fibrosarcoma," or "IADFSP-FS." Quite a mouthful, but don't trust doctors to be wordsmiths. The *New York Post* caught wind of the story, as had every other news outlet in the world. The *Post* was the least medically accurate, perhaps, but by far the most colorful: "Exploding Faces in San Francisco" was their headline. I detected a bit of *schadenfreude* in that first article. Not so three days later when the *Post* proclaimed "Cosmetic Exploding Face Case Found in Queens." Wei-jan Fang and Tony, it seemed, had opened a whole box of Pandoras; in addition to San Francisco and New York, cases had turned up in LA, Vancouver, Seattle, Hong Kong, Shanghai, Sydney. There were at most sixty people in the other cities, but the worry was that Beautiful Essence would continue to circulate on the black market. "The results are just too good," one health official from CDC was quoted as saying.

Though the highest concentration of cases was in the San Francisco area, public health had, thankfully, gotten a head start here. With the help of the media and files found at Fang's home, the thirty-three cases—twenty-eight women and five men—had been identified within days. Ravi got his time in the spotlight and, all my expectations to the contrary, looked professional and composed on TV. Still, if you looked hard enough, you could almost see his head expanding in front of the cameras.

Unfortunately for the afflicted, this flavor of fibrosarcoma had a higher rate of metastasis than its cousins.

About fifty percent was the guess. So, in addition to being locally aggressive and destructive, it tended to migrate to other parts of the body, set up shop there. Eyes would be lost, faces mauled by surgery, bodies wracked by chemotherapy. People would die. But if I'm counting blessings—and boy, was I counting blessings—I guess I should have been happy that it wasn't invariably fatal. I guess I should have been happy we found it as early as we did.

I guess I should have been happy, too, that some justice had been served. Dustin Alberts was in jail, cooling his heels with Jonathan Bly and a few of Uncle Tony's associates. There were still bad guys to be found, though, and law enforcement in half a dozen states and as many countries were keeping themselves busy with the search. The California Department of Health was on the hunt, too, for the mole who'd tipped off Uncle Tony and his clan about the Mings and the poor bastard from Kaiser and whatever else. Despite Ravi's confidence—"We'll smoke the fucker out"—I figured the mole was safely back in his or her cubicle, counting down the days until the weekend, the years until the pension.

Renegade bad guys and renegade cancer didn't stop the march of business, and Tetra's board was busy dismantling the company, hocking its assets and intellectual property at fire-sale prices. Last word was that nobody had bid on Regenetine yet, but I assumed the vultures were circling, waiting for the price-drop deeper into the toilet. Despite the governmental scrutiny that would invariably follow Regenetine wherever she went, economics would ensure that she someday found her way into a syringe, into a face. The results were, indeed, too good; the market too big.

I closed the alternative newspaper, the only periodical I

bothered to read these days. I'd been through the articles—the newest bands, the hottest bars, the five-thousand-word feature about the Native American lesbian poet whose free-verse rants had gotten her onto MTV—more times than I could count. I avoided other news outlets. "Dr. Nathaniel McCormick" had been splashed over the more mainstream papers. The words and phrases they used next to my name—"courageous," "hotshot investigator," "respected physician"—seemed to describe someone else. A respected physician wouldn't be pulling a pill crusher from his jacket in a coffee shop, would he? A respected physician wouldn't grind two OxyContin to dust under the table, then drop the powder into a cup of water, then shoot it down, would he?

I sat, waiting for the drug to file down the edges in my brain. These were the dangerous times, the times when I could think too much. About Brooke, about Dorothy. About the bastard who got me involved in all this in the first place.

I should have pressed my thumbs into Paul Murphy's eye sockets when I had the chance. I should have punished him when I was able to. As if losing his eyes, ears, and tongue wasn't enough.

God, what have I become?

I slumped in the chair, trying to quiet my thoughts while the narcotic wormed its way into my blood.

That day, like the three preceding it, would be spent like this: morning with coffee and OxyContin, then to Dorothy's mother's house to greet Tim when he got home from school. A half hour of homework, some reading, then Tim, his grandmother, and I would go to meet Daniel Zhang at UCSF to visit Dorothy.

Her finger had been reattached, and she'd had the first of many reconstructive surgeries on her face. Reconstructive surgery was it for now, since—another blessing to count—the doctors hadn't found any evidence of distant cancer spread. For whatever reason, though, Dorothy did not want anyone sitting vigil with her all day. Our visits were relegated to the late afternoon, which was fine with me. The narcotics in my system would be largely flushed out by then and the drive across the city would be reasonably safe.

At the Zhang house, I sat down on the green fabric couch in the living room, listened while Tim and his grandmother conversed in the kitchen in a language I couldn't understand. Dumplings had been offered to me, but I didn't think my stomach—having just survived a battle with too much coffee—could handle them now. A grandfather clock ticked in the corner. Pictures of Dorothy and Daniel, their late father, dozens of extended family members, hung against the wall next to the window, their frames as close as tiles. Years of Chinese cooking had given the room a thick odor.

After Tim finished his dumplings, he settled on the couch next to me, and I opened *The Hobbit.* We'd made good progress through the book, and the day before, Tim had started yammering about getting started on *The Lord of the Rings* trilogy. Though I'd protested the heft of that undertaking—"Tim, you know how long those books are?"—I have to admit the prospect of reading to this kid offered one of the few bright spots in my life. It gave me something to do, some reason for being. The rest of my life was waiting: waiting until my bruised and broken tissue knitted, waiting until Dorothy finished her surgeries, waiting until Brooke gave me the green light to see her, waiting until something happened to make me feel like me again.

I began to read the book, doing my best to assign different voices to each of the characters. The task was daunting, however, and I always ended up hoarse after our sessions.

We'd arrived at the big climax, where Smaug, the dragon, gets a bellyful of black arrow. I was really getting into it, and hadn't noticed that Tim—who usually sat rapt next to me—was staring into his lap.

"You okay?" I asked in Nate McCormick voice.

"Why'd they have to kill him?"

"Who? Smaug? Well, because he—" And I realized then that the boy wasn't talking about the dragon at all. "Kill who, Tim?"

"I don't know."

Though the boy had been doing an amazing job of readjusting to normal kid-dom—back in school already, grooving on science and reading, tolerating math and social studies—there was still a bevy of demons floating around in his tiny head. I'd spent a good amount of time talking about Uncle Paul, about Uncle Tony, about how sometimes good people do bad things and vice versa.

"I did really bad things," the kid said, rehashing the conversation from the previous day. "I hurt Uncle Tony." He looked up at me. "So, am I a good person?"

"Like I said before, you're good. You did the right thing. You had to protect me and your mom."

"But maybe Uncle Tony had to do what he did. Maybe Uncle Paul, too."

Good people do bad things. Bad people do good things. So who's bad and who's good? And what does it matter, anyway? In the end, I figure it's all just gray on the moral ruler. Best you can hope for is, when the final judgment comes down, you're a little farther toward the bright end of the stick.

This, however, is not how I wanted things to be.

"Come on, kiddo," I said. "Let's round up Grandma and go see your mom."

Daniel, Grandma Zhang, Tim, and I stayed with Dorothy for an hour. The surgeons had already removed her tumors, and were realigning what was left of her face, now covered by bandages so that not much more than one eye peeped out. The conversation was light, revolving around Tim's studies, Daniel's work schedule, and Dorothy's recovery. There were a few "mommy-mummy" jokes tossed about. Before I knew it, it was time to leave.

As we filed out of the private room, however, Dorothy called my name. I stopped in the doorway and let the family file past me. "He's doing okay, isn't he? Tim, I mean." Her voice was muffled and indistinct from the bandages and the surgeries near her lip.

"He's doing great. We're flying through *The Hobbit*."

"And you?"

"I need to work on my dwarf voices. Other than that, I'm fantastic."

"Sure you are."

"This is healing nicely," I said, and picked at the bandage on the left side of my face.

"That's not what I mean. You look worse than I do."

"That's because the bandage only covers *half* my face." The joke fell flat. "What can I say? It's hard. I'm still trying to wrap my head around what happened. What I did and didn't do. Trying to figure out why Paul did what he did."

"What's to wrap your head around? You did your best. Paul became a rotten guy. End of story."

"Right. End of story." I touched her bandage. "You're in here. Brooke was in the ICU. Paul really did us a favor, didn't he? Oh, and let's not forget that I did things that make me sick to think about. I did awful things, Dorothy."

She pushed herself up on the pillows. "Things aren't that complicated, Nate. Try to see the situation clearly." This from a woman who could only see out of one eye. "You're an imperfect guy who fought an imperfect fight against an imperfect world and who still wants everything to be perfect."

"That's an oversimplification."

"Is it?"

"I should get out of here. Got to drive back to—"

"Nate," she interrupted, "listen to me. There's no perfection out there. Not in the world, not in a face, not in a relationship, not in the resolution of what we just went through."

"I know nothing's perfect."

"But you still can't handle things when they're not. I don't mean to be harsh, but you're like a child. You want everything to be so tidy and clear-cut. Learn to live with the mess, okay? It's like you either run away from the mess or you insist on getting in way over your head, trying to clean it up."

"Thanks for the psych consult." I looked into the hallway, to where Grandma, Tim, and Daniel were waiting.

Daniel was speaking with a doctor he'd cornered. I turned back to Dorothy, back to that one clear eye staring out at me from the gauze. "I really should go."

"Running away?"

I smiled. "Of course."

"Well, Nathaniel McCormick, I am not running away. I'm diving headfirst into the mess." She sighed. "Think about it. Think about who I'm falling for."

"Dorothy—"

"Yes. I'm falling for you, as if you didn't know. So, there it is. I'm falling for a man who has to work things out with his ex- or current girlfriend. Who has to deal with what happened and with what he's going to do next. Who has to come to some peace with Paul. Maybe that guy will figure all this out, maybe he won't. Maybe he'll just run, or decide he doesn't want anything to do with an out-of-work reporter who looks like the Bride of Frankenstein. Maybe I'll be left sitting at my mom's with Tim, telling him that Uncle Nate decided to go back to Atlanta, telling myself you're a jerk for not calling me. It's messy. But, guess what, McCormick? The mess is what life is all about."

I took her in for a second, this person who was a jumble of bandages in front of me. "Messy, messy, messy," I said.

"Learn to live with it."

"I don't want to live with it."

"God, you really are like an eight-year-old. Not even eight. Six."

I pulled a chair next to her bed. I felt a tremendous closeness to her then. And though I wasn't sure the feeling would last beyond this moment, I wasn't sure it would fade, either. "I would kiss you now, if I could."

"Well, nothing's perfect," she said. "Not even moments like this."

I pulled her hand to my mouth and touched my lips to the skin.

That night, I sat on the bed in my rented room. In addition to the bed, there was a chair and a small table. A guy who just got out of rehab lived next to me. This is what three hundred bucks a week gets you.

I cradled the cell phone in my hand. I was sober now, weaned temporarily off the narcotics. My head was clear.

An imperfect guy fighting an imperfect fight against an imperfect world. All this to make things perfect. The equation just don't add up, now, do it?

I dialed the number, listened to the ring cut the silence four times. Then, her voice.

"Nate?"

And though my mouth hung open, ready to utter the next sentence, I had no idea what it should be.

"Nate, is that you?"

I pressed the phone to my ear so hard it hurt.

ABOUT THE AUTHOR

JOSHUA SPANOGLE is a graduate of the Stanford University School of Medicine and Yale University. He has also served as a researcher at the University of Pennsylvania's Center for Bioethics. His bestselling debut medical thriller, *Isolation Ward,* is available in paperback from Dell, and he is at work on his next thriller, which Delacorte will publish in 2009.